Ashes

and

Light

Karen L. McKee

ASHES

AND

LIGHT

This book is a work of fiction. Names, characters, places and incidents are the product of the author's imagination or are used fictitiously. Any resemblance to actual events, locales, or persons, living or dead, is coincidental.

Twisted Root Publishing Edition
Copyright © 2010 Karen L. McKee
All rights reserved.

Twisted Root Publishing
86-9012 Walnut Grove Drive
Langley,
B.C. V1M2K5
Canada

Visit our website at www.twistedrootpublishing.com

Printed in the United States of America

First edition: October 2010

Dedicated to Mom and Dad
who've waited so darn long.

Acknowledgements

Special thanks to Kris Rusch and Dean Smith for their friendship and years of guidance and support. What would I have done without you?

Thanks to Adrian Phoenix, Marcelle Dube, Terry Hayman, Brenda Cooper, Matt Buchman, Richard Clements, Peter Orillian, Rebecca Shelley and Louisa Swann and the rest of the OWN gang for their encouragement, support and (many) readings. Your feedback made this book possible.

Finally, thanks to my Afghani advisor who volunteered her time to provide a woman's perspective on life in Afghanistan.

Prologue

August 2001, Bamiyan, Central Afghanistan

The night ran thick with screams, just like so many other nights.

Michael Bellis willed himself motionless as he peered out into the half-lit carnage. Behind him, Yaqub quietly crouched in the collapsed mud house, working his healing wonders as he methodically triaged the injured.

Yaqub had the almost supernatural talent to ignore the madness, the sounds, the gunfire, and work calmly over his patients. Michael vibrated with the need to move, to protect the Hazzara villagers, even though he and Yaqub were woefully unprepared for the large force of Taliban soldiers that had taken the town.

Another rocket seared the night. It slammed into a stately, mud-daub tower and exploded in hellish flame no one could have survived. The concussion ran up his legs as mud brick and dust rained down.

One of the women shrieked—her voice ululating like the cries in the streets and the buildings around them.

"Silence!" he ordered.

Fire glared off the rugged cliffs and the yawning alcoves where the Taliban had destroyed the giant, awe-inspiring Buddha figures.

Panicked quiet filled the little group behind him. The women and children huddled together, masking the vocal woman's sobs with desperate hands.

To comfort them would be the right thing to do, but right now all his attention was on survival——theirs and his. They would live or die together depending on the women's obedience. At least that was part of Afghan culture——along with the pride and stubbornness that had kept

Yaqub and the others fighting the Russians and now the Taliban.

He leaned back to his observations post, automatically inventoried the changes the explosion had caused to the ruined townscape. The knowledge would help their retreat from this shelter that would surely soon be discovered.

"We need to move," he whispered back.

Yaqub crawled forward just in time to see another woman dart towards their meager safety from across the ruined street. A sniper bullet spun her around and dropped her.

"The devil lives here, and his name is Hashemi," Yaqub muttered through his black beard. He was clothed, as Michael was, and as every other Afghani male, in the baggy trousers and long tunic and the black-and-white striped turban the Taliban required. "Praise Allah, Khadija is safe in London. These devils kill the women or they rape them and leave them for dead. We have to get them out."

He lifted his hairy chin at the cluster of bombed out structures across the street where more woman huddled hidden.

"Not easy." Michael muttered. In Afghanistan nothing came easy. In fact, all of Central Asia was a bomb waiting to explode into the flank of the West and the Taliban were looking to ignite it.

"When did Allah ever provide easy tasks?"

Michael grinned through his matching beard, then yanked Yaqub down as a jeep whined past bristling with Hashemi's armed men. The vehicle bumped over the woman's body, but didn't pause.

Michael held Yaqub's gaze.

"You know you're my brother in all but blood, and I would do anything for you, but to try to save the women trapped in those ruins is suicide. If we don't leave now, we won't be leaving at all."

"Then take them." Yaqub motioned to the frightened children and their mothers they'd managed to rescue. "I'll get the others."

"Like hell. You're too valuable."

"Then I'll just have to live, won't I?" Yaqub half-stood. "I'll see you in Kaabul, if not sooner."

Michael yanked him down.

"Damn you, Yaqub, I'm not kidding. A doctor's worth a damn-sight more than an agent. We came to bring messages. Not run a rescue mission." That was the trouble with Yaqub. He might be calm in the face of crisis, but he was no agent.

Except when he was providing medical care, he always ran head-long to do the right thing, leaving Michael feeling slow, stodgy and a trifle dishonorable when he proposed a more cautious approach. But caution had helped him live this long in a landscape where nothing lived out its natural lifespan.

Michael looked out at the flame-lit street, assessing each door, window, and slab of darkness in the ruins. Where the hell was that sniper?

"I swore a Hippocratic Oath to preserve life."

Michael glanced back at his friend and knew that look. Knew that tone of voice, too, and knew he was defeated.

Again.

Yaqub's expression was the same stubborn, passionate look Yaqub's father got when he'd decided on a mission. Or when he treated one of Hashemi's victims. The determined look meant nothing would dare to block his purpose. A typical Afghan expression when you discussed the fate of Afghanistan. There was nothing these people were *more* passionate about.

Getting in Yaqub's way when he was like this was like trying to stop one of Afghanistan's earthquakes. You only got crushed.

"Damn you, Yaqub.... What is it about all you Siddiqui?"

A palm tree's explosion illuminated the last mud tower of the city.

"*Khpel amal da lari mal*," Yaqub said. What you do, will come back to you. His dark gaze was determined. Then he grinned, knowing he'd played the trump card between them. Michael owed Yaqub and his father so much.

There might be a way. There might. Yaqub with his beard and turban could probably pass for Taliban. He might have a chance to talk his and the women's way free even if he was spotted.

"Look, I'll go for the others," Michael said. "You take these women. There shouldn't be any problem once you get to the hills."

Yaqub caught his arm. "You sure?"

"*Inshallah*, I'll live to drink your father's tea and beat you at chess again. Now go."

Yaqub grinned and turned to the women, speaking in swift Pashto of the plan. He led the small group out the rear of the ruin and into darkness. Michael sent a prayer after them and stepped beyond the shattered wall, rifle ready.

He eased sideways through shadows.

Farther east the last tower in Bamiyan laid a shadow across the street. If he could cross there and find his way to the women, he might—just might—be able to lead them to safety.

Well-honed skills settled over him and the night reduced to him gliding silent as a shadow over fallen brick and mortar. He glided across the street and ducked into an empty doorway as one of the patrols passed.

Yaqub's need to help the women was understandable. The damned Taliban hunted Shi'ite female flesh. In their warped belief, they'd been "married" by the Imams in the *madrasas* of Pakistan. It gave them permission to rape any woman they found. Many of the victims in this honor-bound country took their own lives out of shame.

In Afghanistan the chasm that now separated the Sunni and Shi'ite branches of Islam was as bad as the schism between Islam and the West.

He slunk through another shadow and stopped. Ahead, the low walls held only half a roof and he ducked under to find five women cowering in fear.

"You must be very silent and very brave. Understand?" he whispered in Pashto.

The grandmother of the group—all of thirty-five by his estimate—nodded and clutched the hand of her daughter's daughter. The girl could be no more than eleven by the look of her, but she'd been found by the Taliban. The poor child whimpered into the woman's shoulder.

Michael had them clasp hands and led them out of the shelter down through the maze of ruins and across the street. He started to breathe. Miraculously, they were going to do it. They were going to get free.

But then came the scream. Sheer terror, it lifted into the night, going octaves higher than a human voice should, until Michael wanted to cover his ears. Gun fire. More shouting and screams. Screams to the heavens. Pleading.

And then there were Yaqub's shouts.

Chapter 1

May 2002, KAABUL, Afghanistan

The accident between the old man and the military convoy unfolded much like the many pleats of Khadija's blue *burka*. One thing leads to another, they say. In this case, the covering and incident only showed that Khadija no longer belonged.

First there were the boys kicking a soccer ball at the side of the rubble-strewn street. Even half-muffled by the *burka* their shouts raised a brief, painful memory of Yaqub playing with his friends when she was so much younger.

Then there was the man with no legs. The baker's son, Omar, who sat on a pram-wheeled cart beside the display of the huge rounds of flatbread. He harangued female customers with lewd comments so Khadija made a point of crossing the street when she passed by.

Then there were Khadija's shoes.

They were boots really—Marks and Spencer boots she had bought against the cold and rain while she was in medical school in London. They were the problem—just like everything she'd brought back with her and everything she'd become. If she'd never gone to London, would Yaqub still be alive?

The accident happened like this.

The shouts of the two boys filled the gritty Kaabul air and Khadija wished she was young again and running after Yaqub. Though at twenty-four she wasn't old, in her country she would never again be able to join the boys kicking the soccer ball as she had done on the side streets near Victoria Station. And now there was no Yaqub to play with, anyway.

She'd come home to this place that was a strange land. Like a nightmare really. Her city and yet not. No longer filled with gardens, no longer filled with picnicking families and laughter and well-dressed woman like her mother had been. No longer with Yaqub and his laughter.

Around her, shattered buildings lined the sewer-sided streets, and were inhabited by stick-thin men and blue-clad ghosts. That was all that was left of Kaabul. All that was left of the place her father had said the ancients called the Light City of the Angel King.

She raised her chin, wishing for the wind that lofted the kites above the rocky slopes of Kohi Asamayi—Asamayi Hill. Once Yaqub had sent his fierce red kite into the clear sky, but now the sky was masked with dust off the mountains and the smoke of cooking fires polluted the fading blue. Only the wind still blew—perhaps it could lift her away as well. The *burka* made her light—less than nothing.

That had been her mistake—looking away—because the bread-maker's son spotted her shiny boots, so different from the clack, clack, clacking plastic sandals on most women. When she'd raised her gaze, Omar rolled up to her and grabbed her shoe.

"Khadija Siddiqui, you must sit with me awhile," he said, shocking her.

It was *Haram*—religiously forbidden—for a woman to speak to a man not of her family. And he—Afghani decorum said he should not speak to, or touch, a proper Islamic woman. But that was the problem, wasn't it?

The street rumbled as yet another of the omnipresent foreign military convoys returned to its compound just south of Kohi Asamayi. She looked down at Omar's grinning face and broken yellow teeth. The foul scent of his unwashed body and diesel found its way through the *burka* and she wished she was home. She wished she was with Yaqub who always made her feel safe. She should be home, not out wandering the dying city, but marketing had demanded it. She closed her eyes against the fear.

"Come, sweet one. Let me see your face. You can go naked like you did in London, now that the *kofr*—the infidels—are here. You come to my room. I know of British ways." He worked his pelvis back and forth lewdly so his cart rattled. "I have money."

She jerked back in revulsion, and his cart rolled into the street. Its left wheel caught in a hole in the pavement, sent Omar sprawling, swearing, right into the path of an old, bearded man.

Who tripped and fell, directly in front of the military convoy's first huge, green-yellow troop carrier.

Grinding brakes and Khadija saw the too-bright eyes of the female soldier driving, but the carrier was too big, too heavy, and moving too fast, while the old man was far too slow.

Khadija dropped her marketing bag and leapt; in emergency rooms you learned to respond.

Grabbing the old man's arm, she tore him from the pavement, hauled them both out of the way in time to look up at the fair faces of the soldiers that reminded her too much of a pale-faced doctor in London, and even more of the graveyard her city had become.

She shivered and turned back to the old man. Brown-grey beard worn long like the Taliban had preferred. Pale turban over shaken, black eyes.

"*As-salaam 'alaykum*." Peace be with you. "Are you all right?" she asked in her best medical voice, still steadying him.

His gaze changed from fear to disgust.

He spat. Right at the ornate grill that covered her eyes. Warm spittle sprayed her face.

"Worst of whores," he swore and jerked away. "Harlot! You do not speak to me!" His voice rose and Khadija realized the blue ghosts were whispering in the street.

Omar laughed as he hauled himself back on his cart.

"You see? I know what you are." He thrust his hips again and she grabbed her fallen market bag and fled.

Down the road towards the narrow streets of Kohi Asamayi. The skull cap of the *burka* was too tight. She couldn't breathe, couldn't breathe.

How could she ever think she could have saved Yaqub? She'd saved the old man and still she'd done wrong. Everything she did was wrong. All of her choices—going to medical school—allowing her father to send her to the west when the Taliban came to power. It was all one mistake after another.

Except coming home after Yaqub died. She had to help her father.

Catcalls and yells in the street behind her. She glanced behind and down the length of Darulaman Road to the ruins of the old king's palace and the fenced encampment of foreign soldiers who had come to "free" her country. Their flapping flags—red-white, red-white-blue—were an abomination given the state the country was in.

Closer, the stick men and blue ghosts called her the worst kind of whore, and the *burka* couldn't hide who she was.

Omar knew the abomination that was Mohammed Siddiqui's daughter.

Chapter 2

Half-running up the broken street, Khadija reached the last small house with its back pressed against the steep slope of the hill. She slammed inside, away from the sewer stench, into the comforting familiar shadows, the scents of bread and spices and tea and the faint scent of the English-leather soap she had brought back from London for her father.

She slumped against the heavy wood door. *Allah, thank you for this refuge from the world of foreigners and men.* She raised her eyes to heaven and realized she was almost hyperventilating. Forcibly she slowed her breath.

She should not be so shaken. *Inshallah,* she'd dealt with worse in London. A guilty flush warmed her face.

She'd done worse as well.

But today she'd been trying to help the old man. She'd saved him from death, and yet she'd still done evil. It was like everything she did in her life turned back on her and made things worse, made her less than nothing and soiled. She needed to sort through this confusion and find some way to redeem herself in the world.

"Khadija? Is that you, *Pishogay?*" The slight tremor was a new addition to Papa's voice that worried her. She realized she'd heard another voice as well.

Male.

All the relief drained out of her. Even here there was no stable ground for her feet.

A shadow filled the space beside the window—that was the place Papa would not allow anyone to sit. He said it had been Yaqub's favorite spot in the evenings. It was the place Papa still faced when he took his tea.

Home would never be wholly safe again, either.

She'd come running when her father sent her word of Yaqub's death. After 9/11 the *Amrikaayi* had ended the Taliban's hold on her country.

But instead of new life, she'd found a country inhabited by the ghost of her brother, and *kofr*—the infidels—flooding in. They said they were there to help, but they were too much like the Russians. They didn't build schools or houses for the poor—or at least not enough to make a difference. They only brought soldiers.

She'd seen the pictures of how the West helped. Iraq. And Afghanistan sat right in the midst of the oil-rich East. Oil. Pipelines from Uzbekistan. That, opium, and weapons sales were why they were here. She'd come home thinking to escape her dishonor and had found a country being stripped of its honor day by day.

That was why her hands shook. It was not just Omar or the old man— it was everything she was and everything bad Afghanistan might be forced to become.

"Khadija?"

She relaxed her fists, threw a shawl around her shoulders against the coolness of coming evening and gathered her shopping bags. "Yes, Papa. I'm coming."

"Could you make tea? We have a visitor. He will stay for dinner, I think."

Khadija hurried into the tiny kitchen at the back of the house. It gave onto the small, walled garden that would have been what attracted her father when he moved from the blasted concrete that was all that remained of their family home in Mikrorayon. She dipped water from the plastic bucket into a kettle, set it on the kerosene burner, and began dinner preparations.

Aubergine—bruised now—would make a flavorful *qorma* eaten with the yoghurt and garlic and mint. With lentils and tomatoes and rice *chalau* it made a fine beginning. But she had no meat. The market had held nothing that looked fit to eat. There was their last chicken, but they kept the hen for the eggs that seemed all that tempted her father to eat these days.

Yaqub's death had stolen his appetite. They had been close as only a father and son could be, and had worked closely together—two doctors in a country where doctors were a scarce commodity. Her hands still shook as she set rice to soak.

But no meat would dishonor her father. There was nothing for it; the hen would have to die.

She made the tea, tenderly filling the white and blue porcelain teapot that had once been her mother's treasured possession. She pulled her shawl over her head and carried the tray of tea and embarrassingly mismatched juice glasses through the curtain into the courtyard.

"Your tea, Papa," she said to the man she honored above all others. She stopped.

She had expected one of the neighbors who often stopped by to take a meal with the honored doctor. Tradition said a person's responsibility to help a neighbor was even greater than the duty to help a relative. It was *sawat*—something that earned you a place in Paradise. And so everyone who lived on Kohi Asamayi thought a doctor had the money to feed their neighbors. In truth, her father did much of his work pro bono, but honor said he would never turn people away—from care or a meal.

Mohammed Siddiqui turned his face towards her voice, a beam of late sunlight through the branches of the spindly pomegranate tree caught in the constant tears running from his half-blind eyes and incised deep lines on his face. He was so much older than she remembered. Too much time had passed.

He knelt beside the sad, silly circle of marigold plants at the back of the barren garden. The mangy leaves had managed to grow under his care—a futile attempt to bring life and color to a house that had only loss pulsing at its core. Beside him was a stranger, the man's hand guiding her father's to a newly opened orange flower with a gentleness she rarely saw—at least not among the war-hardened men of Kaabul.

"Khadija! Look! The marigolds are in bloom." Pleasure filled her papa's face—something Khadija knew he had little of—and it made her smile—and feel guilty.

"Wonderful. You'll have a lovely garden, then."

She'd seen the blooms a few days ago and had meant to show her Papa who, when he had his sight, had always been an avid gardener. But life had intervened—all the demands of keeping house in a country torn by war. The simple act of showing the flowers had slipped her mind.

And so she had failed him again.

Khadija set the tray on the ground, pulled her scarf farther forward to hide her hair, then shivered as she spread an oilcloth tarp for them to sit on. She should feel gratitude to this stranger who had been kind to her father, and yet—it should have been her task, her gift to him.

She was further dismayed to find the stranger supporting Papa's arm to lead him through the debris-littered garden. His familiarity said he'd done it many times before. *Who was he?*

The man was broad shouldered and tall—far taller than her father who was tall by the standards of *Kaabulay*. His hair was dark, thick as any Afghan's, but the sun caught places where it gleamed red-gold as copper, as if his head caught flame.

His shaven face—a bad sign—held the hawkish nose and thin aesthetic look of many a Pashtun man, but there was something about him. The way he walked—not with the swagger of the usual *Kaabulay* male—but with a confidence and weight that said he was somehow connected to the earth. Even the way the dark brown *karakul* cap sat on his head and the long shirt and waistcoat and baggy trousers of his *salwar kameez* flowed over his long legs suggested he was a man to be feared. A man who took what he wanted.

And that he was not from here.

His eyes caught her and she knew. Pale eyes like a rain-soaked London sky. They seemed to catch some part of her. The palest blue she had ever seen—as if they had been robbed of color. Somehow they carried the same look of the children she saw in the orphan camps when she and her father provided medical assistance.

Hungry, haunted eyes, sharp as a scalpel's edge, even though this man wore more meat on his frame than most Afghanis.

His gaze roamed up her to the shawl pulled over her hair, then came to rest on her face so she felt naked before him.

Khadija lowered her gaze, but his regard shook her. It was like he knew everything about her, everything hidden under her clothes, and he should not look at her like that.

To hide her tremor, she bent to aid her father, gently curling his gnarled fingers around his tea glass as the tall man folded himself onto the blanket with the ease of any Afghani.

"Khadija, I forget myself."

Papa caught her hand. His face turned towards her, the deep lines around his eyes like scars of age in the angled afternoon sun. His dark eyes swam opaque in his semi-blindness. It had come on so suddenly, his letters had said, and the lines—they almost made his face strange to her—a mask of age and pain he never used to carry. The incessant tears—she swore they were not a medical condition.

The wind caught in his mostly grey hair. He had cut it off as soon as the Taliban were ousted. But Papa was a devout man, even if he was shorn. He caught the strange man's hand as well, as if his body would bind them together. She stiffened at Papa's lovely smile.

"Let me present my old friend, Michael Bellis. He is the son of the son of the son of the son of my great-great-great-grandsire's cousin who left Kaabul for *Amrikaa* during the time of the Great Game."

He referred to the time when the *kofr* Russians and the English vied for supremacy over Central Asia. Afghanistan had been one of the prizes—one that had cost many foreign lives and was immortalized in the works of those like the *Inglisi*, Kipling.

Amrikaayi. A chill found Khadija. Someone to protect her father from. She glanced back at those hungry eyes and found their cutting gaze. There was so much in them—what? Pain? Longing? Waiting? For what? Still, the man showed proper manners and did not speak to her directly.

When had a Westerner ever waited—they always took. She looked away. Always Afghanistan was the pawn in someone else's plans.

Her Papa smiled happily and squeezed both their hands before releasing them.

"How good it is to have family here. So many have been killed in this long, sad, war, and yet it brings family back to us as well."

He slurped tea from his glass while Khadija tried to sort what he said. Family?

"This lovely creature is my daughter, Khadija—or as I call her—*Pishogay*—little cat, for as a child she was always under foot and always putting her paw into things she should not. She has just returned from medical school in England, though I wish she had stayed to finish her residency."

He smiled proudly at her, reaching for her hand again. Khadija looked away, glad he could not see the guilt she felt under the stranger's assessing gaze.

"I came home because you needed me here. Besides, I had no talent for the work."

"Khadija, you topped your class!"

"I had no—no bedside manner."

"You could have learned. You should have stayed."

He pushed too hard, but a clutch of sadness crossed her father's face reminding her she could never be her brother. He had been the light of both their lives—full of light and grace and brilliance and devotion to his studies and his faith. She could never compare to that.

And now she disappointed her father once more. Coming home before her residency was complete. Coming home in the hopes she would not dishonor him more.

It was a sore point between them after he had risked so much to send her out of the country.

"I was not meant to be a doctor, Papa. I'm sorry, I'm not… Yaqub." To speak his name still hurt her heart.

She caught a slight movement from the foreigner, a stricken look on his face.

"You knew Yaqub?" She turned to him, resenting that this man could presume to think he shared their pain. Yaqub would not consort with such a man—her brother had believed as she did, that Afghanistan must be free of foreigners like the Russian invaders.

But Michael Bellis nodded. There was a glimpse of pain again and then it was replaced by cold. Those cold, hungry eyes saw everything, but there was no way he could know her brother as she did, as her father did.

His suggestion somehow sullied Yaqub's name.

"You are *Amrikaayi*. How could you know my brother?"

Something passed between her father and Michael Bellis even through her father's sightless eyes. Khadija frowned.

"From the States, yes," he said in almost perfect Pashto. There was only a slight rapidity to the speech, not quite the long A's of the Kaabulay. More like a speaker from Herat. There was not a lot of traffic between Kaabul and the far west of Afghanistan. He sighed.

"I've spent many years in Afghanistan and Iran, have I not, old friend?" A soft, familiar smile at her father, who nodded.

A chill ran up Khadija's back. She looked away from those eyes that could devour the world and the full lips that seemed to mock her from across the blanket. This was worse than the debacle with the old man because she did not have her *burka* as a shield and she had this strange feeling that this *kofr saw* her and all her flaws.

The wind seemed to hiss over the garden walls, bringing dust off the flanks of Kohi Asamayi to dim the new pomegranate leaves. The voices of men called to each other and the laughter of children came from the street that ran the side of the house. She should just leave, as any proper Muslim woman would. This courtyard was a man's place, now.

"There were few things that would bring *Amrikaayi* to this country before 9/11," she said coldly.

Michael Bellis only shrugged, his face becoming a practiced mask.

"My father's company had interests in Western Afghanistan. When he died I took over the business. I've spent my life traveling between Herat and Mashhad."

"Then you did not know my brother well." Khadija chanced a triumphant glance. Yaqub had spent his life in Kaabul.

Those blue eyes held on her face as if daring further questions. She met his gaze, and a specter of warmth seemed to cross it, seemed to bleed into her. Her breath caught in her chest. Who—what—was this man who was so gentle with her father? *Kofr*—infidel—enemy of Islam. Or friend? She lifted her chin. No, she would not trust a man whose motives were so uncertain.

"Your eyes and your attitude betray you aren't Afghani. An Afghani man would never speak to an unrelated woman."

The skin around his eyes crinkled in laughter. "And a true Afghani woman would not answer."

All the blood ran from her head. She had forgotten herself once more and shamed her father. Her sins must show in her face and this *kofr* was laughing at her. Laughing!

Her father's laughter broke her sense of horror.

"*Pishogay*, you goad our guest. Didn't I tell you, Michael? Khadija, Michael is family. He has brought medical supplies and word of the outside to Kaabul all these years. How else would I have managed to provide care at the clinic?"

She knew what that meant. She glared at Michael Bellis. This man had brought secret supplies, had operated secretly under the Taliban. Had placed her father and brother in danger by his very presence. And now Yaqub was dead.

She eased to standing.

"Papa, it's time I prepare dinner." She looked at Michael Bellis—the smuggler of medical supplies—and other things, she was sure.

"You will stay for dinner, I suppose?" she asked in cold English.

Another flash of amusement across his face. Then it grew still, cold. Cold as the wind that blew over the garden wall and carried the scent of the last snows off the distant Hindu Kush. It chased away the tannin tea-scent and the scent of the marigolds.

"I think—perhaps not." He sighed, his voice carrying a tinge of—what?—regret?

"But Michael, you've not visited in a long time. Please, stay for the meal. Khadija is a proper cook, even if she lived abroad."

"I'm sorry, old friend." The *Amrikaayi* caught her Papa's hand again with that gentle familiarity that snagged somewhere in Khadija's chest. "I have meetings to keep or my business will surely fail. You know businessmen—they don't like to be kept waiting."

He stood with a lithe movement that spoke of years of action and caught Papa's arm as he rose to say goodbye. The two men embraced, warm Afghani-style. Then Michael Bellis turned to Khadija.

"It has been a pleasure." He held out his hand in a gesture so Western it took her breath away.

Stricken, Khadija looked at the proffered hand, then at his gaze. To not shake his hand would be rude and that would upset her father.

Michael Bellis smirked and held his hand steady as if this was a test. Well, she would not fail it. She hauled her hand inside her sleeve and lightly caught his fingers for a single shake, keeping the fabric between their flesh. Bellis's brows rose and he turned to her Papa.

"You have a proper daughter, old friend."

There was laughter and taunting and perhaps admiration. He stepped past Khadija towards the kitchen door and she hurriedly caught her father's arm to follow.

"You see him out, *Pishogay*. I would like to stay and smell the flowers a little longer."

Dismissed, she followed Michael Bellis into the haunted house. At the door he grabbed a *petu*—a traditional shawl—off a peg and swung it around his shoulders against the cool so that standing in the gloom he could almost have been any Kaabulay she saw on the streets.

Except for the eyes.

"Thank you for coming," she said, keeping her gaze lowered. "You are most welcome in this house."

He snorted and fingered her *burka* where it hung by the door. "These aren't required in Kaabul anymore."

"They are—for women of faith." And that was what she wanted to be.

He stood so close—close enough she could feel the heat of his body in the cool dimness and smell the male-animal scent of his skin. His tall presence made it difficult to breathe.

That infuriating smile again as he opened the door; he squinted against the glare of sunlight on dust as he checked carefully in both directions as if he expected English traffic. When he stepped out, he turned back to her, and their gazes locked again.

There was something more about those eyes. Something dangerous and almost beckoning.

"He's a good man, your father. Compassionate."

"He is a man of Islam. And he still has capacity to trust."

His face was so still, yet conveyed so much. Want. Need. Loss. A hint of kindness. She could not look away. In another world she might have touched him, offered comfort.

"And you do not." He shook his head. "Don't let his friendship with me lessen your opinion of him."

Then he was gone, striding down the street with a long fluid movement, her breath stolen by that last hungry gaze.

Chapter 3

Michael had been a fool to come here. He brought too much danger with him and the memories of family the house evoked were almost too difficult to bear. What must the old man feel? And yet he had been gracious.

Michael rubbed his hand over his eyes. He knew tonight the nightmares would come, just as they did each time some reminder came of what had happened to this family. He glanced over his shoulder at the battered door the woman had shut so solidly behind him.

It was like the clouds blocked the sun and she did not even know it—the haunted loveliness she carried.

He shook his head and eyed the weathered clay that covered the brick buildings. So battered and yet these streets only hid the life that ran like a vein of precious lapis, deep in this country.

On the hillside, a man in a gold-threaded Kandahari cap fed fodder to a goat tethered next to a mine crater. There was nowhere in Kaabul that had escaped the violence, and yet nowhere that small bits of beauty did not shine through. Like in Khadija's green-brown eyes.

Fool.

Mohammed Siddiqui and his daughter didn't need an agent of death in their midst. Michael rubbed his stubbled chin. Guilt had brought him to make sure the old man was cared for, to somehow make things right—as if that was possible.

All he'd done was manage to rile a daughter who carried her faith like a weapon.

It wouldn't happen again. He would leave them in peace with their loss.

"Work your way towards wisdom with no personal covering." He muttered the Rumi saying against attachment and covetous nature, and looked into the sun hanging low in the sky.

It was a ball of flame that caught on the mountain tops and impaled battered Kaabul like an interrogator's light. Michael inhaled the clean scent of the distant snows overlaid with the aftertaste of kerosene, charcoal, and wood smoke.

Once this city had been the subject of tales of wonder. Now poor mud-brick houses clung to the sides of the mountains. Most of the bricks had been dried in the streets in front of the construction. Most would fall in one of the frequent earthquakes that plagued this part of the world, along with the man-made destruction he so desperately wanted to prevent.

He strode the maze of streets, pulling his last cigarette out of the cloth bag he wore across his chest. The smoke was a godsend, spiked mildly with hashish that curled into his lungs to steady him. It wasn't that he smoked all the time, but when in Kaabul, do as the Kaabulay, they said. He inhaled a draught of the heavily laced Turkish tobacco and smiled.

Hashish be damned. The tobacco alone ought to take at least a couple of years off this life. The hashish—well, it was no good for any agent, but at least it numbed pain.

At the corner of Darulaman Road he nodded to three old men, white turbans wound loosely around their heads and necks, grey shawls around their shoulders as they smoked and talked companionably in a pool of late sunlight. Beyond lay the foreign military encampment.

He studied the men's faces and the way they looked at him. Safe. Not watchers.

From the base of Kohi Asamayi he followed a careful, circuitous route along the winding watercourse of the almost-dry Kaabul River. He'd visited this place when he'd accompanied his father as a small child on business trips.

He'd been part of his father's disguise, he supposed. More successful than Michael's current one, probably. Then, his father had had a small boy playing on a green river bank and climbing poplar trees as people strolled.

Now, after the hardships of the guerrilla war against the Russians, the disastrous fighting amongst the warlords and the depredations of the Taliban, the once-green lawns were sprawling banks of filth and plastic bags; the trees had been torn down for firewood. A gutted place, suited to what he'd become.

His fists clenched at the memory and the stench of the raw sewage that ran in the river. He'd reported the situation in Kaabul, but no one had listened. At least no one had cared. But things were better now, thanks to his efforts and the work of others like him. The Kaabulay, the people of Afghanistan—they were the ones he served—not his damned government. To hell with the embassy's Simon Cox and his accusations that Michael had gone native.

He bartered for another pack of cigarettes and casually scanned the street. To the northwest waited Chicken Street with its small red-light district and stores that stocked Western goods. Farther north along Bibi Mahro Road stood the well-guarded American Embassy.

Those streets were magnets for those looking for information to report to his enemies. The leaders of the Taliban would be pleased to get news of an old adversary. They were also the people who could tell him of the man he sought—Hashemi. The man he hoped to get news of at his meeting.

He ducked across the crowded street, between ancient automobiles, huge-wheeled horse carts, and trucks painted in psychedelic colors and mythic patterns. At a loudspeaker wailing Hindi music, he stopped. Turbaned men crouched along the roadway. Almost all wore leather belts with knives and ammunition slung over their *salwar kameez*.

Anyone could be a watcher. Anyone could be the enemy.

He crossed the river to the knotted streets of the Char Chata Bazaar and the old city, checking behind him. No one followed, it seemed.

Still, his visit to Mohammed Siddiqui was too easily marked and provided too easy a way to pick up his trail. He'd been a fool to take the chance, even if he needed to take counsel with his old friend. And to plead forgiveness.

In a corner of the main, sunlit square a group of old men drank tea and played a rousing game he had come to think of as speed backgammon. Their laughter and shouts filled the air. One of the spectators, an old Kaabulay, was Michael's contact.

Farid Jan had survived decades of war only to find that virtually his entire family had not. Now he ran the occasional errand for businessmen and reporters, acting as a guide into places that the Westerners might otherwise not see. A collector of information, once he had had a thriving business getting Michael and those like him in and out of questionable places around the country.

"*As-salaam 'alaykum.*"

Old Farid stood as he gave the traditional Muslim greeting, his brown *salwar kameez* falling beyond his knees, his untrimmed beard now saturated with grey that had come from too many hair-raising adventures.

The two men embraced. Farid was thin, his body still taut with the steel that came from years of war and a land where only the wily survived. His black eyes crinkled as he gave Michael the backslap of old comrades.

"I had not known you had returned to Kaabul," Farid said for anyone listening. He motioned to the low line of crumbling concrete that formed a loose seating area around the players. "Come, join us in tea. The evening is fine. See how the light shines on Kohi Asamayi."

Michael took the opportunity to study the scene. The old man still was a savant of subterfuge—like many Afghanis. The slight slope of the old city placed Asamayi's T.V. tower and military observation post in silhouette against the sky, and his gesture gave Michael the chance to see if anyone followed.

The Kaabul street flowed around him—all the tribes of Afghanistan trying to get their business done before the last call to prayer. *Karakul*-hatted Tajiks wandered among the more common Pashtuns with their dark turbans or *pawkul* caps. A few Mongol-featured Hazzara who had escaped the Taliban's deadly purges filtered through the edges of the crowds. The air stank of rotted fruit, coriander, garlic, and cardamom, and Michael smiled at the scents of vibrant life.

Farid lifted his bearded chin and hissed. "The *chai channa*."

Michael, feigning laughter, followed Farid's gaze past the dried-fruit seller with his burlap sacks of dried apricots and raisins and nuts, to the tea shop back the way he had come. A Pashtun in a faded, gold-threaded kandahari cap spoke with the animated gestures of the men of Helmund Province.

Michael's internal alarms jangled. He'd last seen the man on a hillside with a goat. The man glanced in Michael's direction and away.

"Perhaps I will sit a while, old friend," Michael said.

Sitting would make him an easy target, but a man with something to hide would not sit and watch a board game.

The game's Coke bottle caps clacked quietly, quickly, their audience studying the moves and the strategy, their voices rising and falling as first one player, then the other, showed dominance. The sun sank behind the mountains and sprayed the sky with long beams of amber light, like the flecks in Khadija's eyes.

Damn it, the woman was no traditional Afghani beauty. She was too angular, with her square jaw and wide set eyes, and yet those eyes still held in his head—clear and dark and haunted with green and gold—like the hillsides of Afghanistan where flowers bloomed in the spring.

Like Yaqub, and yet unalike. There was no overt passion to her like her brother had. Instead there was strength buried deep. The strength to obey a father's wishes and be exiled far away, and strength to come home again when her father did not wish it. She'd known Mohammed had needed her.

But her eyes held hidden wounds, too. He'd recognized them and they drew him, like to like. Too bad those eyes of hers did not also show Yaqub's friendship. Probably safer for her. Much safer.

He lit another cigarette and inhaled, but it just wasn't the same without the hashish. He ground it under his heel and glanced at Farid.

"Hashemi. Is there news?"

Farid's head-waggle of equivocation was enough answer. Michael swore under his breath. He'd sought Hashemi since Bamiyan, to no avail. Hashemi was an evil spirit—a djinn.

The man in the kandahari cap still waited and Michael curled his fists. Damnation, he needed news.

As if reading his need, Farid leaned in to Michael, a large smile on his face.

"You need to be away, my friend. Abdul Isabek waits. He has news of Hashemi—the Taliban—they increase the reward on your head. Let me lead you to the meet."

This was unusual. Farid usually just passed along the location of the messenger. Michael studied his friend.

"Just tell me where. You don't need trouble, Farid."

Farid waggled his head, equivocating again, which didn't quite make sense.

"*Aacha*. It is nothing. Time for an old man's blood to move again. Besides, my daughter's daughter hounds me for the funds to go to school before she marries. She's all I have left and mostly an obedient girl, unlike these whores who show their faces."

He lifted his chin at a passing group of women who had set aside their *burka* and wore only their long *jalabiyya* and scarves.

"But I will not see her locked away like those butcher Taliban did." He grabbed Michael's arm. "Come. I will only charge you double." He grinned.

Michael following on the old man's flapping sandals through the stench of raw sewage and swirl of people in the narrow streets. Gradually the shops lessened and became homes. Children screamed laughter at a tethered rat they poked with a stick. The animal shrieked and tried to leap away, only to be jerked back by the kite string that held it.

Then the buildings became bombed-out ruins. Likely no one knew who had destroyed them, but the people still brought life here among the craters and debris. Someone had planted a small garden plot amid the fallen brick.

Yelling came from somewhere ahead and Farid lengthened his stride. In the evening light they came to the bombed-out remains of a mud-brick home. A sheet of rusted metal hung across what had once been a courtyard entry and a single black shoe lay amid the rubble—strange in a land of many one-legged men. A tingle ran up Michael's back.

"Every craftsman searches for what's not there to practice his craft," Michael whispered the Rumi saying to no one at all.

Farid glanced at him as he ducked beyond the metal. Michael followed. Some would say he was a fool for entering this unknown place, but he knew Farid and he knew his own prowess. Besides, he needed the information Abdul Isabek had for more than his job.

There was Afghan revenge to be had and then the bitter self-hatred might ease.

The doorway gave onto the old garden of the house. The house itself, and a rear portion of the courtyard wall, had collapsed from the concussion of the bomb explosion that had left a deep crater in the centre of the garden. Some enterprising soul had enlarged the crater to create a cock-fighting pit lit with a circle of flickering torches already set against the gathering darkness.

A crowd of shouting men rimmed the pit. Not a good place. Certainly not a place you could easily watch your back.

Michael's senses shifted to high gear, tracking the flow of men, the currents of conversation as he studied the faces. At least Farid was there, would help to watch his back.

Sweat, poultry, and unwashed clothing tingled his nose—and blood. Farid led him behind the crowd to a space beside a barrel-chested, fair-skinned man who wore a bearskin hat with the cockiness of any Uzbek.

Abdul Isabek grunted as Michael and Farid pushed in beside him and stared into the pit.

A large black rooster took the attack to a red cock that had already lost most of its comb; the black cock's spurs had been replaced by curved steel gaffs that sliced lethally at the red bird. The red cock fluttered into battle, its own spurs slashing at its larger adversary in a last desperate attempt to save its life.

The press of men screamed and waved wads of Afghani bills. The black bird's spurs impaled the smaller bird's neck. The red bird slashed at the large cock's belly. The crowd's screams increased.

Abdul Isabek leaned close to Michael.

"Something happens in the north. We get word from Wakhan. Taliban. In China." It was spoken in accented Tajik.

Michael slapped the man on the back and held out bills as if they were agreeing on their wagers, but his mind assessed the information.

Not Hashemi, then. Wakhan, the narrow panhandle of Afghanistan that led to the Chinese border. It had provided Marco Polo with a route to China in 1272. It had been handed to Afghanistan by the British in the late nineteenth century to form a buffer between Russia and the English sub-continent—much to displeasure of the King of Afghanistan. It still acted as a remote route to China, and anything to do with the Chinese was important.

In the pit, blood pulsed from the spitted red bird. It struggled to free itself as the black cock pecked out its eyes.

The men's shouts rose as the red bird collapsed. It was now or never. There would be mayhem as the men exchanged their winnings.

"What word?" Michael asked.

"From Kashgar. The Uigher. An attack. The *Amrikaayi*...," Abdul Isabek began, then his face went stiff, eyes wide. He sagged against Michael. A knife handle grew from a bloom of blood on his back.

The crowd seethed around them, screaming at the birds. No one had noticed the knife work. Michael scanned the nearest men seeking the danger. Across the pit he spotted the man in the gold-threaded kandahari cap.

He was too far away to have wielded the blade. There was someone else. A trap.

Michael pulled Abdul Isabek close, but already his eyes filmed. There was too much noise and too much danger. Michael turned to Farid.

Gone. Michael caught a glimpse of him exchanging money with a Tajik.

Men pressed around him. The owner of the black cock collected his tattered bird and two new combatants were brought to the pit.

Just get out. Divert attention and get out.

Michael tumbled Khan's body into the fighting pit even as he shifted back through the crowd, aware of the knives, the danger. The ring of spectators went silent.

His knife filled his hand. Just get to the corrugated metal that formed the wall behind him.

A roar went up. Every man freed their weapon. Oaths, epithets filled the circle and Michael prayed for a fight. A fight would make it more difficult for the enemy to find him.

The man in the kandahari cap fought towards Michael, but was caught in the crush of shifting men. Farid yelled at him from beside the Tajik.

Friend or enemy? Decide later. Get out and get the information to others who could use it.

Michael made it to the wall, rusted steel at his back. He awaited the attack, the flash of steel.

Nothing. Only loose wire tethered the sheeting to the remains of the wall. It leaned against the crumbling masonry. Michael slipped between metal and wall, out into the narrow alley that ran behind the house.

The pungent odor of opium and sweat met him. The air was cool after the press of men. His pulse hammered with adrenaline.

Something. A shift of dark air. The hiss of cloth.

He spun as an attacker's knife slashed. The blade flashed in the glow of the cock-fight's torches through holes in the sheet metal fence. The knife sliced his side. Breath slammed out of his chest as the sweet rush of pain lit his brain.

Metal on meat. When knives entered the equation, flesh always lost.

The man slashed again. Michael leapt back, almost slipping in the slick of fresh sewage.

Damnation! The whole thing had been a setup. Kill Abdul Isabek and this was the logical escape route. The man had waited here like the answer to a prayer Michael hadn't known he asked.

He ignored the flooding shock from the wound. Stepped, twisted, slammed his instep into the other man's knee. Tissue and bone cracked. The man screamed, but lashed again with the knife. Met Michael's blade in a cry of metal.

He danced back and the other man's bloody blade caught in the loose fold of Michael's *petu*. He threw the shawl into the other man's face, following it with his knife. The blade slammed into the man's throat.

Bone crunched and the attacker's breath turned to a gurgle. The sound of fighting from the cockpit increased to a roar. The shawl fell away and Michael caught the man, pressed him up against the brick wall where a stray beam of torchlight found his features through the gloom.

Hawk-nosed Pashtun. Breath carried traces of the tea and lentils he had eaten as his last meal. Dark hair caught in a black-and-white turban. Mustache and full, ratty beard. Young. Too young. Probably one of the devout recruited from the Pakistani *madrassa* to fight *jihad* against the West.

"Damn you," Michael growled, and shook the corpse. "Why couldn't you be stronger? Faster? Why not help me die?"

Michael knew he should be leaving; the warmth of blood down his side said he needed medical attention, and he had to get his precious information to Simon Cox at the embassy. Anything that brought China into the Afghan equation was a problem Afghanistan and her allies didn't need.

He looked at the empty eyes. Sighed.

"Be free, my friend. Free of presence, free of dangerous fear, hope, and mountainous wanting."

Pain hitched his side as he leaned closer. Let there be some clue this time. Something that would make the decision easier, the death he knew he deserved, endurable.

"Pray, soul of fallen warrior, what waits beyond?"

No answer.

He dumped the body in the sewage, reclaimed his filthy *petu* to tie against the blood, and loped into the darkness. He'd acted like a damned neophyte.

No more.

Chapter 4

The single marigold filled his nostrils with a scent of earth and green growth and hope as Mohammed heard Khadija return from seeing Michael away. The tea cups and pot clattered together in a most unusual way; Khadija was generally much more careful with those precious remnants of her mother.

"They don't smell as sweet as I recall. Perhaps vision influences the other senses." He held the blossom up. "What do you think?"

"I think—I'd be no judge, Papa," she said with the saddest of tones.

Her swift step left him for the house and he heard angry clatter in the kitchen. He stood.

What was the matter on such a pleasant day? It had been wonderful to sit in the peaceful garden as Khadija tidied their house and then went out to shop. It gave him time to contemplate the possible husbands he had identified for her. Not that he was certain any of the young men would be a match for his *Pishogay*.

She was so full of strength and life and not afraid to speak her mind—something he had fostered in her, though he demanded obedience. And then had come the visit of Michael. The young man had been much in his mind.

He'd rarely visited since Yaqub's death.

The choking feeling filled his chest again and Mohammed ducked his head to inhale the scent of the flower.

Yaqub, dead. Why, Allah, when he only did your bidding? He raised his face towards the sun's fading warmth. Faint light was all that remained of his sight.

Praise Allah, that had been left to him. And he was alive. He reminded himself of that every day, though some days it was a curse.

He should have died and Yaqub lived. A father should not see his children die. Now there was only Khadija and his work to live for.

The sun was setting: he could tell by the brighter haze when he looked westward. The wind cooled and dust from the hillside peppered his skin.

It had been good to hear Michael's voice again. Their debates of faith and the things they fought for kept Mohammed's mind sharp, though he had the sense that Michael had something more to say. Something important Khadija's return had interrupted.

Touching the rough bark of the pomegranate tree, he began the slow walk towards the pots clanking in the kitchen, careful of where he placed his feet.

His *Pishogay*—always he remembered her laughter from her childhood. But she did not laugh so much these days. She worked hard, marketing, cooking, helping at the clinic. Usually she kept the garden clear of debris, but she had been so busy lately that stones and broken concrete from the hillside caught his feet.

From the kitchen came the scent of kerosene and onions cooking and the sharp clack, clack, clack of her knife through vegetables.

He brushed through the thick curtain.

"*Pishogay*? Is something wrong?"

She was silent a moment, then: "I have aubergine and lentils for dinner, Papa. It won't take long to prepare."

He frowned even though he heard her attempt to smile. He tried to respect his daughter's feelings, to understand and give her the privacy each person deserved, but now the air seemed to vibrate around her.

"You're angry. Why?"

A movement of air that said she tried to push past him to go about her business. The slosh of water as she filled a pot for rice, told him where she was. He caught her arm.

"You will tell me. I'm your father."

She *would* obey him. She would until such time as she left his home for the home of her husband and then he would be alone. A small grief caught in his chest.

"I just—how can you bring that man into our home?"

Her voice was sharper than he had heard it before. He frowned.

"He's an old friend—family. I told you."

"He's a foreigner. They bring nothing but trouble."

"He helped us during the hard times. He made sure we had medical supplies to treat our people."

"Because he wanted something."

"Nothing. He asks nothing. He's a good man."

"I—I don't like him. He frightens me." The way her voice broke said it was true.

"*Pishogay*—daughter," he said softly, reaching to comfort her and was surprised. She was shaking. "There's nothing to fear. He takes my friendship and my guidance, only."

"Guidance," she sniffed. "Papa, it isn't safe to have a Westerner here." She pulled away.

Her response made his shoulders stiffen. This he would not stand for!

"You doubt my judgment? In my own house?"

The air shifted at her sigh and suddenly she was his daughter again. Her fingers clasped his.

"Never, Papa. Never at all. It's just—I've been in the West and here. I've seen. I've felt. I've learned in the markets, while you've been hidden away here. The Kaabulay are no longer so happy about Westerners. His presence makes me fear for you."

Mohammed embraced her, feeling helpless at the strange tone in her voice. If he could see her face, it would tell him so much. His sweet little *Pishogay*, who had played hide-and-seek with him among the swaying blooms in the garden, her face so open and easy to read. Now her voice held an edge he could not understand.

What had his little girl learned in the West? It could not be worse than what he had learned of Afghanistan over the years. The test was what you did with that learning.

"He doesn't deserve your anger or your fear."

Her fingers tightened as if she would say something more, but instead she pulled away to stir her onions.

"I have the meal to prepare. Let me take you to the other room, Papa."

Before he could stop her, she caught his arm and led him to the sitting room where he knelt on the worn *kilim* carpet. Around him, he knew, hung the treasured faces of his family—photos of Shafiqa, Khadija's mother, and of the family on holiday in the cool heights of Charikar, which Khadija had taken from hiding upon her return. During the Taliban's reign they destroyed all representations of living things.

His fingers traced the rough pattern in the *kilim*.

"Sit with me, *Pishogay*. We need to talk."

"I've cooking to do. It won't take long."

And she was gone back to the kitchen and her coriander and lentils leaving him to his darkness and the textured carpet. How small his world had become.

Michael had been a pleasant diversion. A quick mind, but a man whose voice betrayed a need he would never admit.

Over the years of their friendship Mohammed had taught Michael the words of the Quran, and of the Prophet. The way Michael had embraced the words of the Sufis, he had seemed like a lost mystic, hungry for understanding. A strange quality in a man of action.

Khadija returned from the kitchen, bringing with her the scents of curried lentils and rice and tomatoes.

"The sun sets."

"Do I smell aubergine?" he asked.

"I told you. I found some in the market. They were small, but firm. I've made them with chilies, the way Mama used to."

"*Aacha*. Good."

With her help, he regained his feet and turned to face Mecca. It was like the magnetic pole to the compass in his soul.

Khadija brought him water for cleansing, the gentle motion of washing a balm that readied him. When they were finished, he bowed in the direction of the holy city, and knelt to intone the holiest of words.

Praise be to Allah, Lord of Worlds,
The Infinitely Good, the All-Merciful,
Thee we worship, and in Thee we seek help.
Owner of the Day of Judgment
Show us your straight path,
not the path of those who earn your wrath
nor those who go astray.

A sweet light filled him; pain faded as he surrendered.

He repeated the prayer four times, and then settled on the carpet to meditate on faith. Khadija returned to the kitchen.

Beauty was the meaning of the words. Compassionate beauty and love and giving. That was what his faith taught. It was what he held to. The beauty of his wife's face, and his love for her, as symbols of the grace of Allah. All the little things in life as symbols of the greater things above. As above, so below.

He picked up the marigold blossom he'd brought into the house and held its sweetness to his nose. His simple garden, his paradise.

Khadija brought the platter of food and set it before him, placing his hand in the rice so he could form a ball, helping him with the bread so he could use it to scoop the lentil and aubergine.

The rich blend of spices had him smacking his lips. "You cook as well as your mother. Michael should have stayed to taste your food."

There was a hesitation and then: "He likely would not like Afghani food. Too spicy, the *Inglisi* say."

He put down his bread.

"Michael is one of us. He has lived in Afghanistan many years. He works for it."

"He works for the *Amrikaayi*, Papa. It's in his face. He's probably a spy. How else would he be able to bring in medical supplies? I'll bet he brought in weapons, too—that were used to kill our people."

"You judge harshly when you do not know the man."

"I…I don't like the way he looked at me. If you had seen—no proper man would look at me that way. Besides, if he's an agent, he's too dangerous to have here."

Her words—there was something in her voice that tightened his chest. Not the voice of his daughter, his *Pishogay*.

"Khadija? Has something happened…? What haven't you told me?"

Silence. Not even the sound of movement or breath, as if she'd disappeared from the room, just as Yaqub had. Fear formed in his belly.

"Khadija?"

"Nothing has happened, Papa. It just wasn't easy among the *Inglisi*."

Her voice was so soft he had to lean forward to hear her. So soft he wanted to hold her, help her, but she sat on the far side of the carpet. Too far for him to reach. He heard her inhale.

"Everywhere there were pictures of half-clad women. The men had no respect, just as the old Colonial powers had no respect for our ways. It was worse after the towers fell. They hate us."

Her voice spoke of pain and confusion—the kind that could turn into hate. The thought churned the food in his belly. He'd lived through too much hate under the Taliban. If Khadija had been the brunt of it, it would take a long healing. Longer even than Michael's…. If ever.

"Michael is different. He seeks learning. I teach him. He understands Afghani ways."

"His actions towards me say he does not understand Afghani honor!" The words hung like a bright flame in the room. He had to calm her, but when he reached for her hand, it eluded him.

"Remember the lessons, *Pishogay*. Honor and family and hospitality are the heart of Afghanis, and compassion is the heart of Islam." He said it softly. "It shows our love of Allah and his Messenger."

He heard her scramble as she stood. Her voice seemed to come from very far away, carried on a wind of anger.

"I already lost my brother. I won't place at risk the only other person I love."

Chapter 5

The morning dawned cool. Khadija woke under a blanket on the hard floor and resented once more the comforts of London that had made sleep in Kaabul more difficult.

She'd laid awake a long time regretting the pain she had caused her papa.

He had just been trying to help. She should never have said what she did, but placing them both at risk for the *Amrikaayi*—she wouldn't do it.

Besides, her father's lessons were not the true word of Allah—they were Sufi—Shi'ite. And the West sought to undermine her faith. She needed to reject Western ways.

And that was a problem, because the Western ways seemed to be inside her and everyone but her father seemed to know it. Omar on the road. The *Amrikaayi's* knowing gaze. She wanted to tell her father of the incident on the road, but had been afraid that if she did, all her sordid past would come out.

In the next room Papa stirred. He had given her so much. He had even given up his dream of the pilgrimage Hajj to Holy Mecca in order to finance her escape and schooling in London. She would not shame him with the story. She would find a way to redeem herself in Allah's eyes.

Pulling on her shawl against the cold air, she went to her father.

"I'm sorry, Papa—for what I said last night. It's just—I was tired. And it was a shock to see an *Amrikaayi* in our home."

She opened the window onto the garden and inhaled the fresh air from the mountains. Sunrise made the bulk of Kohi Asamayi glow gold around the edges. She helped Papa to his feet and he touched her face with the gentleness she had craved so badly all those years in London.

"You worry me, *Pishogay*. Sometimes I think I was wrong to send you so far from me, but to stay here you would have had nothing." He motioned around him and sighed. "Sometimes I wonder at all my choices."

"Don't. You're everything important. I'm here. I'm well. The day looks fine in the garden. I see four fruit budding on the pomegranate."

She kissed his cheek, feeling the bristle of his old man's growth of beard.

"Michael counted five yesterday."

She stiffened in spite of herself. It made no sense that her father's friendship should make her jealous, that the mention of Michael's name should bring that warmth to her skin. She did not have to be friends. She could tolerate him to please her papa. She looked back at the tree.

"Perhaps he was right. I think I see five." She hoped she kept the tightness she felt out of her voice.

The morning prayer was a comfort, but failed to stop the way her mind whirled with condemnation and confusion.

Show me the path again, she prayed. Let me not go astray.

It caught like a sob in her throat and vibrated through her. Please, Allah. Let me be cleansed deeper than skin.

In the peace of prayer, it might be possible. But life was another matter.

After a breakfast of cardamom tea and bread, they left the house for Papa's small clinic in the bazaar.

Three days a week, all through the Russian occupation, the wars among the Mujehaddin, and then the Taliban, Mohammed Siddiqui had kept his medical clinic open.

At first he had done it alone, but then Yaqub had returned from his training in London and joined his father while their mother worked in the Ministry of Health. Even when Shafiqa had been killed in a guerrilla attack against the Russians, Mohammad would not close the clinic. He hid his mourning in making sure others lived.

Those years had been hard and Khadija had worked hard to try to make her father smile.

"Papa?"

He had sat on his favorite Persian carpet, a cup of tea she had made him near his hand, but his gaze was lost in the shadows of the room—as if he looked beyond into the Hades of the ancient myths, seeking his beloved.

"Papa?" She held out her report card—all A's again. She had worked so hard to do it for him, to make him proud so perhaps it would be like it had been before, when they had fun together and his eyes would dance with pleasure.

"Papa, look! All A's! I did it!"

He waved her away with a flick of his fingers and Yaqub caught her hand. Yaqub, so tall and brilliant and handsome as an Afghani prince. All her friends said so.

"Come, little sister. Papa needs peace right now. Show me your A's."

She looked up at him as he led her into the little kitchen, as tears filled her eyes.

"Aah, Khadija," he said wiping her tears away with the pads of his thumbs. "I know you got the A's for him, but Papa hurts right now. Hurts so very badly. He forgets us now, but he'll remember and he'll love you more than ever for being strong. Can you be strong?"

She nodded. She could always be strong. For Papa. For Yaqub, she had been.

After her father finally recovered, it had been the Taliban's turn to wreak havoc, and to make her father proud, she had studied with forbidden books at home.

He had rewarded her by sending her away—to London. Still, she'd been strong—until word came of Yaqub's death. Then she'd fallen.

Asamayi Road rumbled like the bowels of hell from foreign military convoys and stank from the diesel of the lumbering cargo trucks. Khadija and her father waded through the stench and debris until they crossed the river to the decrepit main square of the meager bazaar in the old city. As a child she'd thought it was wonderful here. Now she saw it as it really was.

By one wall, a small pipe filled an ancient fountain with grimy water. Brick-colored sparrows drank from puddles on the pavement. The fountain water joined effluent flowing to the river.

The bazaar was filled with a cacophony of sound—the frantic voices of people trying to prove they were alive and everything was normal. Vendors ratcheted up awnings, or clattered back metal shutters. They displayed burlap bags of purple-tinged salt from Badakhshan, saffron from Pakistan, cardamom from India, chilies and coriander and cumin and the other heating spices. Ropes of cheap necklaces and nets full of soccer balls bounced in the breeze. Tawdry carts of women's underwear and bras pushed through the crowd. The kite makers—closed down under the Taliban—again sat amid their paper and string and glue. That was the only thing familiar from her childhood.

Certainly a group of foreign aid workers laughing and sharing candy with children was new.

Khadija shouldered past them, resenting their presence, resenting the pretense of normal. Just get to the clinic. Papa liked to be there early, to have a cup of tea and check—once more—that he knew how to find everything in his space. He used his other senses as his medical tools now, just as he used Khadija.

A gloved hand stopped her.

"Khadija?"

She jerked to a stop, apologized to her father, and turned. Another faceless blue *burka*, but the voice was familiar.

"Mirri? How did you know?"

"Simple. I saw your father—and your shoes. It could only be Khadija."

Khadija turned to her father.

"You remember Mirri from when we lived in Mikrorayon? She was my dear friend. I told you we found each other a month ago. I took tea at her house."

"You should come for tea again, Khadija-*khor*." She named Khadija sister, and it warmed her heart.

Once they had always called each other sisters, but the years and a continent had intervened. Perhaps they could be sisters again. Certainly their meetings in the market had been the one small pleasure in Khadija's life since her return to Kaabul.

"I'm sorry, it's just—I can't often leave Papa alone."

"*Pishogay*." Her father patted her hand. "You should go. You need more people in your life than your old father who is perfectly able to care for himself."

Perhaps she should accept her father's offer. She turned back to Mirri, but Mirri stopped her.

"I have things to do now, but let me come to the clinic later and we can plan a time for you to come to my home. Will that suit?"

"More than suit, Mirri-*khor*. Perhaps we can even sneak tea when you come."

She saw her father's smile as she hugged her friend. It would be good to have a friend. A true friend. A woman friend.

A straggling queue of patients had already formed along the narrow side street outside the clinic. Mohammed unlocked the worn wooden door that still held the Taliban's warning bullet holes. They'd shot the doors when there were rumors Papa and Yaqub treated women.

Papa would not have the holes fixed. He said they were righteous holes—because they *had* treated the women—as compassionately as they treated every patient.

The simple, two-room clinic held two cupboards—one locked for drugs and valuable medical instruments and the other open with bandages and tongue depressors and other lesser goods—and a small, locked fridge that was chained to the wall.

A table set against the other wall served as both desk and examining table. The second, curtained-off, room in the back had a stool and a door that allowed access into a lane where a community well gave ready access to clean water. Totally primitive compared to an English hospital, yet it helped people more dramatically than any Western hospital.

Khadija unlocked the cupboard and set out equipment while her father fumbled into his medical coat. The stethoscope he placed around his neck seemed to straighten his back and remove years from his face. His hands shifted his treasured blood pressure cuff, the boxes of bandages, the tongue depressors she'd positioned, until he was satisfied.

One more thing she couldn't do properly, it seemed.

An old, lame Kaabulay in a tattered grey *salwar kameez* was their first patient of the day. His wife shoved him inside.

"*As-salaam 'alaykum,*" her father said. "What is the problem?"

"My leg. My foot. I cut it on a stone. My wife nags me and it will not heal."

The old man's voice grated in the room. He glared back at the door where his wife waited in her *burka* and Khadija almost grinned.

The old man's feet were covered in the worn, black boots of a shepherd, the legs of his loose-fitting trousers tucked into the tops.

"Sit here." Mohammed motioned to the table. Khadija went to his side. A faint odor came from the old man—something too sweet—and the scent of poppy.

Sometimes the old men chewed the tar because it helped with pain. She caught her Papa's hand and placed it on the old man's knee, then stepped back as the patient toed off his boot.

The gag-sweet scent of rot filled the room. Though the flesh gleamed pasty white with ragged yellow toe nails, at the heel a deep wound festered purple-black. Long trails of red ran from the wound up the lower leg and down the arch of the foot.

Khadija coughed and held her *chador* to her nose.

"The smell," she apologized.

"Tell me what you see."

The patient frowned as she hesitated. As a woman, she should leave the room. The patient could describe the wound as well as she.

But her Papa commanded.

With gloved hands she turned the heel, describing what she saw. She released the man's leg and stepped back, not liking the sense of defilement on her hands.

"How long ago did this happen?" her papa asked.

"A moon at least."

"A month. Khadija, ampicillin, please."

She unlocked the fridge and placed an unwrapped needle and the ampoule in her Papa's hands just as rumble rocked the room.

Explosion. Close. Too close. The clinic shook. Medical instruments rattled.

Dust rained from the ceiling and a medical tome struck her father's shoulder as it fell from the cupboard shelf. Papa dropped the needle. The old man shouted for his wife. Khadija ran to the door.

Screams came from the main bazaar. Dust and cordite ran up the street on the heels of terrified people. The line of patients—others from the bazaar—crowded up to her, past her, trying for the clinic's safety.

"Stop!"

The people ignored her.

"Stop!"

Papa's voice boomed and the frantic crowd subsided. She urged them back to the street, to a sea of frightened faces surrounding the door.

Papa fumbled to the door and gripped her arm, his blind eyes turned towards the distant screaming.

"The bazaar?"

"Yes."

He turned back to the people.

"You're safe here. Now let me do my work. Khadija, go help."

"Papa?"

"The hospitals take time to respond." He fumbled for another needle and filled it with the antibiotic. "You've been trained. You're more skilled than anyone else these people have. Now take bandages and go!"

Chapter 6

Khadija hesitated. Her medical skills—were Western. To use them meant she might have to touch men.

"Go!"

Her father clasped the old man's roped arm and eased the needle in.

People were injured. All her training kicked in. She grabbed packs of sterile bandages, needles, the last of their morphine, and threw them in a bag. She left the clinic at a run.

People still flooded uphill from the bazaar. She fought through them. Blood covered faces. Blood on their clothes. The iron-scent of blood everywhere. Screams.

She should run. Turn with the crowd and retreat. Let the military, the hospitals help these people. Or her father. He would find someone else to be his eyes, would treat the walking wounded as best he could.

But she kept pushing forward. Papa had ordered her to the bazaar. Allah had given her skills she must use. Obedience and faith. The cloud of dust stopped her.

Dust in her eyes and cordite burning her nose. Dust golden in streamers of new sunlight overhead. Below shadows and blood and bodies. The stink of bowels and raw sewage worse than anything she'd ever scented in England. The stench of spices from shattered storefronts. The cart of bras and underwear was embedded in the front of the kite maker's shop, its owner crushed under its weight.

Worse than she'd seen in London. This was a battleground.

She swallowed back fear and began her assessment. Clinical.

The fountain had been the epicenter of the blast. The wall of the pool had been destroyed, bodies there were almost unrecognizable. Blackened limbs and faces. The severed head of a donkey suggested perhaps the animal had carried the bomb into the crowd. A tattered red kite sank into the growing pool of water. A child's empty shoe sat next to it.

Cowardice. Bloody cowardice. Who would do such a thing?

A *burka*-clad woman moaned in the dirt. Khadija went to her aid. Blood stained the garment's pleats purple. A tearful little girl—what? five?—in a blood-stained scarf sat holding the woman's hand.

"What's your name, little one? You're very brave. Shall we be brave together?"

Khadija glanced at the girl as she tried to pull up the woman's *burka*. Hands under the blue fabric fought to stop her.

"Miriam," whispered the child.

She slid closer to Khadija, a small hand catching in the fold of Khadija's covering.

"Don't be a fool," Khadija barked at the woman, then smiled at the child. "Be brave like Miriam if you want to be here another day. Let me tend to this."

The hands stilled. Khadija pulled up the blue cloth and checked the woman's breathing, but the lattice work grill of her *burka* made sight difficult. She closed her eyes. She must do this. Her father said the Prophet only commanded that his own women be covered—not all women.

"Allah, forgive me."

She swept up the front of her *burka* and wore it like a cape draped from the crown of her head. Air and unfriendly gazes shivered across her skin as she examined her patient.

Something had torn into the woman's flesh, tearing through the *burka*, *chador* and *salwar kameez* to leave a gaping wound in her thigh. Tatters of cloth were embedded in the flesh. Blood flowed, but not with the pulse of arterial damage. Khadija slapped a thick dressing on the wound, then turned to Miriam.

"You must be very brave and very strong. I need you to hold this bandage here and press down. It will help your mother. Understand?"

The child nodded and Khadija moved on.

Don't think. Just do. Remember emergency triage.

It seemed so long ago that there had been an accident involving one of London's famed double-decker buses and an emergency room too full of victims.

Find those you can help. Those who can be saved. She went from woman to woman, doing what she could, but they were often not the ones who needed her most.

Blood seeped from the chest of a young man sprawled amid the dead near the fountain. His face was blackened, his body twisted as if he had been tossed aside by the explosion.

"*Amniat. Amniat. Amniat.*" His voice was weak as he pleaded for peace.

Khadija closed her eyes. She could not leave him like that, even though she should not touch him.

She was not a doctor!

But Allah had set her here. She was all the help there was.

In the distance she heard sirens. Perhaps he would live until they arrived.

"*Amniat.*" The soft pleading.

She knelt beside him, feeling naked, feeling she disobeyed everything she believed in—God's laws. Allah knew what he did. She did not have a calling for medicine as her brother had, but....

Check the airway. Fine.

Check the man's breathing. Liquid burbled in his lungs. Gently she shifted his hand away from his chest. Blood bubbled in the wound.

His lungs, then. She scanned his twisted body. Along with probable broken pelvis and left leg there was a good possibility of spinal cord injury. This was one for a hospital, not the middle of a bazaar in the midst of a city that was no more than rubble. That made her angry and she found strength out of that.

The sirens screamed closer.

The moans of the wounded were the groans of the earth.

"Khadija?" A frightened voice.

She looked up at the blue-clad form.

"Mirri? What are you doing here?"

The *burka* nodded. "I—I was still in the market. I—heard the explosion."

Mirri looked around and a shiver ran through the pleats that covered her.

"There are so many hurt. I never knew...."

Khadija checked the injured man's pulse, the devastation of his face.

"Someone sent a donkey loaded with a bomb. Now run to my father's clinic and get all the bandages you can. Bring whoever you can who can help."

Khadija pulled the vial of morphine from her bag and filled a needle, then plunged it into the man's arm.

"The donkey...yes." Still Mirri hadn't moved.

"Did you hear what I said? Our people are dying. Now go!"

Mirri went.

Khadija placed a thick bandage over the man's wound and placed his hands over them.

"Hold this." She tore open her last medicated bandage and tied it over his eyes. "Allah, let them be healed."

She wasn't hopeful, but Allah would do as he would, *Inshallah*. She touched his one good hand.

"There will be help soon. Stay still."

He nodded blindly and his lips moved.

"*Amniat, shúker*." Peace, thank you.

She went on and on, from man to man. Swift medical assessment. Do what she could with the training that had cost her father his dreams and turned her into a hollow thing. Some time in there Mirri returned and began to help her, handing bandages as asked, using gloved hands to hold an arm still as Khadija wrapped it, or to help pull cloth from a man's wounds. Occasionally Mirri would run back to the clinic for more from Khadija's father's meager stock.

Praise be to Allah, Lord of Worlds,

She slapped a dressing on a wounded belly.

The Infinitely Good, the All-Merciful,

She injected morphine into an arm.

Thee we worship, and in Thee we seek help.

Turn to the next victim and conduct the ABCs of emergency medicine.

Owner of the Day of Judgment

Show us your straight path,

not the path of those who earn your wrath

nor those who go astray.

She closed the eyes of a man who did not make it, felt grief fill her chest as she knelt amid the carnage.

The military and the ambulances arrived; police and medics flooded the area. Khadija kept working, going from one injured person to the next. *Praise be to Allah, Lord of Worlds*.

Suddenly there were only bodies and blood, and the growing pool of water from the broken fountain. *Show us your straight path*.

The stench of burst entrails and of cordite surrounded her as she stood, swayed. The dust coated everything. Her lips, her mouth tasted like dust and death and her body felt leaden under the weight of the hard sunlight on her back.

This was Kaabul. The Light City of the Angel King, no more. This was what the foreigners brought.

not the path of those who earn your wrath

nor those who go astray.

A slow anger filled her belly, like the sun heated the pavement and the shattered remains. A woman's sobbing filled the air. Where? Who?

A red-headed aid worker stood in the entrance to a side street. She wore bloodied jeans and a t-shirt, her head covered in a plain blue scarf.

"We only wanted to help," the woman sobbed in a Manchester accent thickened by tears. "We only wanted to help."

"Whore," Mirri hissed. "They deserved it, bringing their *kofr* ways to this place."

Khadija pulled her *burka* down over her face and glanced at her friend. Her *burka* was covered with blood, but there was nothing for it. She glanced back at the spreading pool of water. The bodies were mostly dressed in Western jeans and t-shirts. The donkey had had direction, then, even if the devastation had gone much farther.

The anger coalesced in her belly. At the foreigners who drew the bombs? At the bomb makers? She wasn't sure. Eventually the westerners Would learn they were not wanted in her country.

"I swear, the *kofr*—they distill a poison in our country."

"You believe this?" Mirri's voice was soft.

Khadija nodded. Every moment she looked at the destruction she believed it more. The whole world was infected with a poison. It could not come from Islam, because that was Allah's word. Mirri gripped Khadija's arm.

"Khadija-*khor*, we need you. We need your passion and your strength. Look at how you help your people. We need all Afghans of our belief to help in our cause."

This again. Khadija was too tired to argue.

"I told you, I can't."

"But you believe. You know we must get the foreigners to leave. We must bring back Islam—Islamic Law."

"I still can't help you. I'm here for my father. I'm all he's got. How would he live without me?"

"But the cause…."

"…will go on without me. Please, Mirri-*khor*. You're my oldest, dearest friend. Don't make this more difficult."

The blue *burka* sighed, the gleam of Mirri's eyes disappearing beyond the grill in the cloth.

"I'm sorry, Khadija-*khor*. I'd just thought we would be *Mujehaddin* together."

Mirri's embrace showed her warmth, though the faint scent of cheap Russian soap caught in Khadija's nose.

"We all fight for God's word—just in different ways," Khadija whispered, as they pulled apart. She would make sure *Amrikaayi* did not come to her house again.

"Then we will have tea together, instead." Mirri's voice carried her smile. "Come to the apartment. Perhaps tomorrow? Mizra will be waiting,

I'm sure."

Even through her fatigue Khadija felt herself flush and was thankful for the *burka*. Her friend had been playing matchmaker between her brother and Khadija, determined to make sure the two were suited before beginning negotiations with Khadija's father. So far Khadija had left Mirri to her fun, though her mild older brother was not the man of Khadija's dreams.

"First we'll have tea at the clinic. After all your help, that's the least I can do."

She dragged Mirri through the crowds, focused on the tea she would brew. It would be good, and with it would come clear water to wash the blood from her hands.

The clinic's queue had lengthened with many bloodied faces and broken limbs, but the door to the clinic was closed when they arrived. Khadija pushed inside, Mirri behind. The main room of the clinic was empty, but low voices came from the back room. Usually that was where women were treated.

Papa knew better than to treat a woman alone. Such actions would make the clinic a target for bombs.

"Papa? What are you doing?"

She pushed the curtain aside and stopped. Behind her, Mirri hissed. Not a woman.

Michael Bellis stood there, fatigue on his face, the knee-length shirt of his *salwar kameez* removed to expose a broad chest of hard muscle patterned with scars. The drawstring trousers slung low on his hips, showed the lean striations of his abdomen. Blood from a wound on his side stained his clothing.

She yanked her gaze to the floor, but the sight of his body was burned on her brain more strongly than any of the bodies she'd seen in London, more than the bodies in the bazaar.

"Were you caught in the explosion?"

"This wound is deeper than our friend thought. Thread a needle. It seems Michael cannot."

Her father flicked his hand at her. Thankfully, the *burka* covered her hesitation and embarrassment.

"Let me wash my hands." She retreated to the other room, her heart racing worse than it had the whole time in the bazaar.

What was it about this man—this Michael Bellis? She had seen a man's body before—much to her shame. She fumbled water into a basin and washed her hands, slopping liquid all over the desk with her shaking.

"Who is he?" Mirri hissed.

"*Amrikaayi.*" Khadija spat the word as she hurried to do as her father bid.

Mirri flipped back her *burka*, exposing her black eyes and the fine lips that had always as a child been turned up in mischief. Now they turned down as she grabbed Khadija's shoulders.

"How—how can your father do this after Yaqub?"

Khadija shook her head, still trapped by Michael Bellis's image.

"Papa—he—he says this man is a friend."

"Devil, more like." Mirri's black gaze burned. "You don't know, do you? Your father hasn't told you?"

A warning sounded in Khadija's gut. Something her father did not want her to know?

Mirri leaned closer. She stroked Khadija's face through the blue cloth.

"You are a good Afghani woman. Like Malalai who raised the flag against the British. But you, your father, should not be with this *Amrikaayi*."

Khadija barely heard. Something her Papa had not told her. Something about Yaqub? She turned back to the curtain. She had thought since her return her Papa shared everything—how Yaqub had been accidentally killed bringing aid to the Hazzara people.

"What has my father not told me?"

Mirri shook her head.

"That's for a father to say. I will go. Thank you for the offer of tea. You'll come to my house? My brothers would like to see you again."

Mirri slipped on her *burka* like she closed a door, but Khadija stopped her. Mirri's association with those who fought to free her country sometimes got her information.

"Tell me."

The blue cloth hid Mirri's face, but not the venom of her voice.

"Your brother. It was the foreigners—the *Amrikaayi*—who killed him."

Chapter 7

"Khadija! I need the needle!" Mohammed yelled as Michael shifted like a great restless beast. "Have patience, my friend. This is a lesson for you. She does her best."

Michael's dry chuckle filled the room.

"You don't know your daughter, my friend. The look in her eyes says she'd prefer to see me bleeding on the floor. I'm sorry I came. I wouldn't have, except I couldn't get the damn cut to stop bleeding."

Michael's description of Khadija was mortifying.

"Forgive my daughter. You're like a…son to me."

"You honor me, but I don't…want to cause problems."

Mohammed heard the hesitation and turned towards the curtain. Michael was an astute reader of people and there was worrying silence from the other room.

"My *Pishogay*…. She carries wounds I did not see. May Allah heal my internal blindness."

"May he heal your eyes as well."

"I thought you did not believe."

"I don't. But peace and compassion—those I understand even if they're beyond me. I've brought enough mayhem into the world, but you— you did not deserve your blindness."

Footsteps and a movement of air and Khadija's cool hand fell on Mohammed's wrist. She placed a needle in his hand.

"As you asked, Father." Her voice was stiff, brittle enough to crack. She guided his hands to Michael's side.

"Wouldn't it be easier if you did it?"

Michael's casual question hung in the room, but the slow heat of

Khadija's anger radiated from her.

"That's from a knife." Cold, cold voice of his daughter. Far beyond clinical.

"It's no problem, Michael. I've done this many times, as you know. It's just my sewing is not quite so neat as it was." Mohammed chuckled to lighten the mood.

He pinched the firm flesh together and felt for the correct spot to insert the needle. It slid in smoothly, Michael's flesh barely flinching. He tied off the suture and went on to the next.

Khadija stood just behind him, her presence like a pulsing heat, heard the stir of her robes.

"There's a long line of people who've been badly injured and you interrupt the only medical care they've got? Why don't you go to your embassy? Why don't you go to your military? My father's a doctor—to the Afghani people."

"Khadija!"

Michael flinched under the needle, but Khadija stopped her vitriolic attack.

"This man is a patient. We treat all who come here."

"If you don't give your life for your freedom, you will be ashamed of your country," she spat.

Another father might have struck her. He was a proud Afghan who defended his country. He always had been. He did not need to explain himself to an irrational woman. He swallowed his anger and focused on the flesh he mended.

"This is not the time."

His vehemence seemed to stop her argument. He completed another suture, inserted the next. The next. The next. The next. He felt the wound. It drained slightly from the bottom.

"You'll live," he said patting Michael's arm. Mohammed taped a bandage in place and handed a few extra to his friend. "Just change the dressings regularly and you should heal."

"Good. I need to travel."

"As usual." He smiled but heard the rustle of clothing, then Michael pressed money into his hands.

"No! We are family," he said, offended.

"Father, I've used all our supplies in the bazaar. We could use the money to replace them."

It was more than the *burka* that made her voice almost unrecognizable. Cold as dead flesh—worse than at the house. Was this truly his daughter?

"An Afghani does not take money from family."

"Mohammed, consider it a gift—or a loan if you must. A peace offering, perhaps. And now I have to go. *Allāhu akbar.*" God is great. Michael stuffed the bills into Mohammed's unwilling hand.

"*As-salaam 'alaykum,*" Peace be upon you, Mohammed answered.

There was a stir in the air, the scent of the well in the alley, and then Michael was gone. The room seemed empty without him. It had always been like that. The *Amrikaayi* had filled his life like a force of Allah's nature, ever since Yaqub brought him home so many years ago.

He turned to Khadija, releasing the money.

"We *do not* take payment from a friend. God will forgive you if you forget him, but not if you forget your neighbor."

Khadija's *burka* swept the floor as she bent for the money.

"Our neighbors stand in line at the door. He's not my friend. He's not yours either—but you knew that, didn't you?"

Her voice held ill-concealed venom. Mohammed stopped wishing he could see his daughter, her lovely face, for she would be a beauty. But not at this moment.

He remembered a small child running a park, her pretty pink scarf coming loose from her hair as she chased after her much older brother and his gang of Pashtun friends. Beyond them was another group of children—Hazzara—kept apart by the societal codes of the city.

"Khadija!" his wife called and stood up from their place on the blanket by the river. The child ran on, her chubby, young-girl legs pumping to keep up. Such a heart, she had, such determination not to be left behind.

"Khadija!" Again Shafiqa called, her musical voice lilting on the breeze amid the laughter of the crowds who were out on this holiday day.

Still Khadija didn't hear. She plunged on too close to the river where the boys were climbing down the treacherous rocks to the rushing water's edge. It was easy to slip on those rocks and the river was a high force in those days—like the heart of all Afghans.

Mohammed was on his feet in an instant, running for his daughter, grabbing her up in his arms and swinging her around as if in play before bringing her back to Shafiqa.

"I just wanted to show them the flower I found, Papa. Such a pretty flower. It smells nice." She held a small blossom up for him to sniff.

He took a whiff and shook his head. "Those are Yaqub's friends, Pishogay. They wish to play boy games, not smell flowers."

She sat in his arms, but her eyes—so like her mother's—telegraphed her desire to be free, to be with her brother. She looked at her father but waved her arms wide.

"But aren't they my friends, too? Aren't we all friends?"

He'd hugged her then. For all the love his child had for others. For all the helpless love he felt for her. To love so much....

What had happened to make her like this? Her compassion—it had been that quality that had made him sure she would be a good doctor.

"*Pishogay*, please." He caught her arm and tried to pull her to him, to recover his child, but she yanked free, leaving him alone, anchorless.

"Honor me in this," he said, looking where he thought she was. "You've been filled with love—like your mother."

"My *mother* died at the Russians hands."

Her voice came from near the door when he hadn't heard her move. "Why should I love foreigners?"

"Because love is the greatest of Allah's faces. Because it gives compassion, caring—all good things. You know this. It's what our faith tells us."

"How did Yaqub die, Father?"

The question sent him stumbling to the wall, seeking the stool in the room. He sank down. There were no words to tell her; there was no way he would return to that terrible day when the news had come and the guilt he still felt.

"What does it matter, how he died? He's dead." His voice cracked and the tightness in his chest increased. Silence filled the room.

"Islam also teaches *jihad*, Father. Against those who harm our faith and kill our people. And tradition demands revenge." Her voice was quiet, with none of the hesitation he'd heard earlier.

"You speak of war and that is not what Afghanistan needs. Another war. Where do you get these ideas?"

"I hear things, Papa. What else could Islam teach after all they've done—the colonial powers destroyed our ways of life, made us feel like we were less than them. And as for revenge—the *Amrikaayi* and the West—that's the only reason they're here. That and oil."

"Allah, save us all," he whispered through bile. How—where—had she learned these things? "Allah said the greatest *jihad* was the taming of the self. That is my belief. It is what I practice and it is what I taught you and Yaqub. It is what I've begun to teach Michael. What you do, will come back to you."

He reached for her again, but she was no where he could reach her.

"Then you fail Allah, Father. And me. And Yaqub. Most of all Yaqub. With your faith and your secrets."

He felt the air stir in the swirl of her *burka*, the sweep of the curtain.

"Khadija, please! Let me help you. Let us fix things."

But the slam of the clinic door said she was gone—chasing something other than Yaqub.

Chapter 8

Khadija rushed uphill past the clamor of Jadayi Maywand Street and the crumbling carpet bazaar with its scent of old wool and sour dye, up into the narrow twisted ways of the old city. It was how she felt—twisted, shadowed, unable to see what waited ahead, what was left behind.

What had she done, leavin her father...? It wasn't like her. She'd come home to help him and here she left him alone with patients to deal with.

But fury at her father had sent her crashing through the crowd outside the clinic. And anger at herself. She shouldn't have said what she said—not to her Papa. She shoved through shoals of blue ghosts and old men towards the upper market, avoiding the major thoroughfares where there was too much chance of running into one of the invaders' patrols.

Too much chance of seeing the hungry white faces of her enemy. She thought of Michael Bellis's eyes—ripped her thoughts away.

Get away. Just get away and clear her head. She was so furious she could scream at everyone.

Except Yaqub.

Yaqub, beloved, her defender and confidant. Yaqub dead at the hands of *Amrikaayi*. How had it happened?

She'd wanted to press her father, but suspected he'd lie if he hadn't told her by now. It was betrayal.

She searched for Mirri's blue-clad form. The woman—she had to be somewhere near. Somewhere she could tell Khadija the truth. But none of the blue-clad forms in the street moved in the right way or wore the silly pink sandals that Mirri-*khor* affected.

The road she followed ended in a locked door in a pitted wall, the ancient, battered, city wall looming above her from the slopes of Kohi Sherdarwaza She sagged against the brick and stone, fighting for breath.

Somewhere near, the wail of Hindi music had started again, but it came from so far away—down a distant tunnel.

How could her Papa be such a fool? She stopped herself.

She should honor her Papa. It was not him she was angered by. No. Papa was a good man. A man of faith, even if his loss of sight blinded him in more than his eyes. Perhaps it was just that with no sight, there was no chance for him to do his duty.

Or perhaps he would not do his duty because he feared for her safety. Thus he allowed the *Amrikaayi* into his house; he had no way to safely stop it.

She closed her eyes, encased in the safety of the *burka*, and wiped sweat off her face. She reeked of blood and the metallic scent of her anger. Nothing was safe and that saddened her.

Once she had thought so. Her father had held her in his arms, hugged her so hard she thought her ribs would break. Yaqub had done the same and then led her into the night to the distant cousin who would smuggle her out of Afghanistan and on to London.

It had been terrifying, posing as a too-young wife on the long drive through the night southeastward through the mountains, through the destroyed streets and gardens of the Jalalabad that she had visited as a child with her mama. Then up into the rugged mountains towards the Khyber Pass. The stark peaks had frightened her. Bodies at the side of the road had frightened her more.

She had awaited her visa in Peshawar and then flown to the safety of London, stripped of everything but her innocence—all before she turned sixteen.

It took the West to steal the innocence.

The sick feeling frothed in her stomach as she recalled the handsome face of Doctor James Hartness, the supervising physician at London's Grace Hospital.

"Khadija! Come. Sit with me awhile. I could use a break from these files."

James Hartness smiled over his half-glasses, his red-blond hair falling across his forehead in an unkempt way that made Khadija just want to push it back. She stepped into the office, scenting a slight sweetness in the air, and glanced around. No one here. The leather couch along the wall lay empty, waiting, inviting.

She seated herself in the armchair in front of his cherry-wood desk and nervously smoothed her skirt and white coat across her lap. His gaze still sent a flush up her shoulders and neck that she knew he wouldn't mistake.

James sat back in his chair and glanced at the open office door.

"You afraid to be alone with me?" he asked softly with a half-wink of

his too-blue eye.

Her body loosened at the way he looked at her. It evoked thoughts of being together, of their torrid three-month-old affair. Her body ached for his touch and the couch loomed like another presence in the office.

She shook her head and gripped the arms of the chair. Things had gone farther than she'd ever intended. She'd fallen too easily.

After avoiding all the randy young men in medical school, it had seemed James Hartness really saw her, really wanted to hear what she had to say. At first she'd been flattered at his attention, this man who was a doctor like her father; at how he had asked her to assist him on so many cases in the E.R.

She had been stupid—like a child—to let things progress farther. But then Yaqub had died and James had been a comforting shoulder to cry on. He was so understanding, so gentle when he kissed her, when he laid her down that first time.

It was love, wasn't it? He had told her he loved her that first time on the couch.

Then why had things changed?

"I wanted to talk to you." She kept her voice professionally level. "You've given Dr. Miller the Johnson case."

Amy Johnson was a five-year-old girl who had presented with low-grade fever that had continued for five days. Tests had been unable to confirm what was wrong, but while in the emergency room, the fever had spiked to 104 degrees. The child had been hospitalized.

James went to the door, closed it, then came back and leaned on the edge of his desk. His long legs stretched out in front of him, new Italian loafers gleamed on his feet. She expected the touch of his hand on her cheek, the offer of his palm to pull her into his body.

Instead he crossed his arms.

"Just what did you expect, Dr. Siddiqui? The right to follow cases is reserved for interns deserving of reward."

Her tongue felt stuck to the roof of her mouth. Finally she managed: "You said I was to follow the Johnson child."

He pursed his lips—those lips that had tasted the innocence of her body.

"You must be mistaken. Dr. Miller has shown herself to be a most capable doctor. That tracheotomy on Tuesday was almost a work of art. The case is hers." *He glanced back at the files on his desk.* "Is there anything else I can assist with? Otherwise I need to get back to these."

She looked at him not understanding, and yet, and yet—the sweetness in the office—a sweetness she recognized as Tanya Miller's perfume.

It made her gag, but the arms of the chair held her in place. She had to get out of here—was going to be sick. At Dr. James Hartness. At her honorless self.

Mostly at herself. She had stood, then retched all over James Hartness's gleaming shoes.

At least she had done that.

She had done it to herself—had lost her honor and her father should beat her for it. That was what Afghani fathers—or brothers—did to daughters who dishonored their family. Honor was everything. Family was everything. Yaqub.

She pushed herself from the wall and began to retrace her steps down the hill.

Just find Mirri and find the truth. She was no innocent—she could stand it.

She turned onto Jadayi Maywand and followed the traffic, paralleling the river. Once the city had been full of gardens. Even under the Russians, she could remember that. Could remember her papa stopping to exclaim over some lovely bloom, and point out its magnificence to her mother. Mama had always been the practical one.

Now the streets were ruined, the gardens lost in fallen bricks and weeds except for Bag Nawab, which had somehow escaped the devastation. On fine days she had taken her papa there to enjoy the green.

When he had been her papa.

She almost stumbled at the thought. He was supposed to be a man. Supposed to be Afghani and Afghanis did not let the death of a son go unavenged. Vendetta ran deep here—deep as the earth and as violent as the quakes that shook Kaabul.

But how was a blind man supposed to wreak revenge? It must eat him from the inside—her papa caught in his honor and unable to do anything. No wonder he would not admit the truth.

She held her head a little higher, scanning the blasted blocks of Mikrorayon ahead of her. The Russian-style concrete apartments had once been the face of the successful Kaabuli middle-class; now they were the symbol of the end of Russian rule in Afghanistan.

What had been an estate of green grass was now, due to drought and war, a sere landscape of blowing dust and concrete debris that crunched underfoot. Many of the buildings were no longer livable; the bombs had collapsed the floors, like naan stacked on a bread-maker's display.

Khadija threaded between the shell-craters and heaped garbage, breathing through her mouth to avoid the stench rising in the sun's heat. Tattered plastic bags made ragged hedges around the bases of the buildings. Building doorways gaped like hungry mouths, the wood long ago taken for heat.

Once she had been proud to say she lived in block 182. Once her parents had sat out front of the block on fine days, watching their son and daughter play with their friends.

But block 182 didn't exist anymore—was nothing more than rubble that children climbed. They didn't have the burden of memories of how the place had been before. They would grow up in a new Afghanistan. She would see to it.

Miraculously, while the Mujehaddin bombs had destroyed her parent's building, block 181 where Mirri and her brothers lived still stood relatively unscathed. True, one end of the building sagged precariously, but the apartment the Shahabuddin family shared still stood.

She climbed the four floors to Mirri's apartment. It had belonged to General Shahabuddin until the Taliban came. Then he had disappeared. Their mother had died in a rocket blast outside the building—the same blast that destroyed block 182.

At the corrugated metal that served the apartment for a door, she knocked and bobbed on her heels. She didn't like the darkness, the graffiti on the walls, the smell of human and animal waste. It was like a cave, a grave to be buried in.

"Mirri?" she called.

The metal shifted and an eye peered out, tilted, narrow, too high off the ground. The corrugated metal shifted further revealing Mirri's brother, Ratbil. He leaned on makeshift crutches made of long metal poles. Allah only knew where he had found such valuable metal.

"Khaditha?" His mouth was twisted from a hair lip. He peered past her into the hall. "Alone? Mirri thaid you only go out with your father."

"Is she here? I need to speak with her—with you and Mizra." She could speak to Mizra and Ratbil because they were like family, she had known them so long. But she could only enter if Mirri was home.

He nodded, hopped back to allow her entry, his swift turn of his body hiding the twisted foot and lower leg that happened in the same firefight that had taken their mother. He waited as she swept back the heavy folds of the filthy *burka*, letting it drape from her crown. The air was cool on her skin, moving through the empty window that provided the only light.

"You honor us with your visit," Ratbil said with a bow of his head and for a moment she thought he mocked her, but his narrow-set gaze was serious.

"Mirri! Mizra! We have a guest!" He ushered her into the main room of the apartment where a tattered Persian carpet covered part of the floor. Pots clattered from the small kitchen separated by a curtain; a shadow parted from the second, smaller, room and the younger Shahabuddin brother entered.

Mizra ran his fingers through a mat of dark hair. He had obviously been sleeping, but his sleepy gaze sharpened when he saw Khadija. He averted his eyes from her.

"An apparition surely," he said in his mellow voice. "Brother, has a *houri* come from Allah's pleasure gardens?"

Khadija pulled her *burka* close around her as if it was a *chador*. Mizra made her nervous with the ardor she saw in his gaze, though he took care never to take liberty with her. She knew he hoped to court her, but would await the customary process of a woman of the house obtaining approvals from Khadija's father. Of course, he would not want her if he knew she was dishonored.

He lolled on the carpet, his body half turned from her, so he would not sully her with his gaze. Ratbil lurched to a seat.

The two were so unalike. Ratbil thin, his face filled with the slow-boiled anger that came after his sudden infirmity. Mizra, on the other hand, was almost handsome, indolent, with piercing black eyes like his brother and a lithe, hard body that did not tend to Mirri's warm plumpness.

Khadija fought to relax on the carpet, though every part of her strained with her decision.

"No apparition. Just a friend who needs information."

Something passed between the two brothers. The kitchen curtain pushed aside and Mirri entered, carrying a tray of tea. The scent of her kerosene stove, and the chicken caged in the corner of the room, entered with her.

"Nothing in Kaabul ith free. Information comes at a price."

Khadija nodded as she accepted the tea.

"I'll pay. Mirri told me something today. I want to know more. How did my brother die? Who was responsible?"

The way Ratbil's gaze jerked to his sister told Khadija this was important. She'd done well to come here.

"You should not have thpoken. That was Siddiqui family busineth—not ours."

"She should know. Yaqub...."

Khadija caught Mirri's hand as her friend settled beside her. Mirri's warm hands gave her strength to push against Ratbil's will.

"Yaqub was my brother. My father has held the truth from me. I need to know. It's my right."

"Why think we know the truth? Why come to uth?"

"Perhaps because she knows we're her friends, *neh*?" Mizra's deep voice was soft in the room, but his gaze locked on her briefly.

Though he was the younger brother, the fact he was whole and healthy allowed him liberties within the family. Still, Ratbil's face twisted at the interruption. So, all was not peaceful in this remnant of a family. That was another product of the West—family infighting.

If war had not destroyed their country, if the West had interceded when the Russians came, then the Shahabuddin family would likely still have their father as patriarch over his sons.

"You are my friends—more." Khadija looked gratitude in Mizra's direction as she sipped her tannin-rich tea, but he would not meet her gaze. "Mirri is family to me. My father—I honor him, but he's old and blind and afraid for me. I realize now, he lives in shame that he cannot avenge his son. I cannot let him live that way."

Ratbil's narrow-set eyes seemed caught on her face. There was a force there that Khadija had not noticed before, as if he weighed each of her words before devouring them.

Mizra, on the other hand, cupped his chin in his hand, his sideways gaze one of furtive longing.

"You're a woman, Khadija. A lovely woman." A flush crept up Mizra's neck as he spoke. "Go home to your father. Go home and wait 'til you are wed, *neh*? Your husband can perform what needs to be done. A good husband will."

He looked at his bother.

"A daughter cannot take a father's role."

Those words raised Khadija's hackles. She would not be denied.

"My sister-friend told me it was *Amrikaayi* who killed my brother. I want to know who."

The flicker of looks that passed between the brothers, told her they knew something more. Khadija released Mirri's hand and fought the chill that ran down her back. Another sip of tea for heat. Finally Ratbil shrugged.

"We know rumors, *neh*? Your brother died in a battle between Afghani and *kofr*. It was a sad thing. We mourned for him—for the Yaqub we knew as children together."

Mizra's warm gaze finally looked at her, but it wasn't enough to bring feeling to her limbs. Hearing the words in this room made Yaqub's loss somehow more final and certainly more unjust.

"I remember as a child how tall he seemed. We all looked up to him, *neh*?" Mizra shook his head. "A waste. Truly a waste. Would that he had stayed in Kaabul and focused on our faith."

"Where did he die, then?" She almost choked on the words.

The two brothers looked at each other again and Mirri caught Khadija's hand.

"Bamiyan, we heard. Fighting among the filthy Hazzara."

Khadija frowned. The Hazzara people had been decimated under the Taliban. Many Sunni towns and cities had been purged of the Asiaticfeatured Shi'ites.

"But Yaqub had no links to Bamiyan."

Mizra sat up. "You see? Our words only confuse you, *neh*? We should have said nothing." He held out his tea cup for Mirri to refill.

"No!" She would not be protected. She would not be put off. She would not wait for a husband to do what needed to be done.

She ached with a need to take action. She knew by Mizra's frown that her voice was too loud, that she was wrong to interrupt him.

"I need to know. I need more information." She glanced at Mirri. "You...you know things. I know this. You can find out more—get me a name—something."

Ratbil's frown deepened. "I thaid information is valuable, Khadija."

"I don't care. I'll do what's necessary. Mirri has asked me to help you. It tells me you work for Afghans—not for the *Amrikaayi* and their allies. Let me help."

"And what could a woman do?"

"Pass messages. At the clinic we often give the patients medicine. It would be possible to pass other things without notice—things that will help our country regain its glory and stand against invaders. In return you find out who killed my brother."

"It will not be easy. We may only be able to find out an Army unit."

She just looked at him. Finally he nodded.

The tang of the cooling tea was the taste of triumph. Then Mizra smiled.

"*Inshallah*, you will be family one day. I will help you."

She needed to show them she was strong in her faith, in her honor. Strong enough she didn't need to wait for marriage and a husband. She sipped the tea again and found it cold—as her fingers—as the cold anger that filled her. She set the cup down.

"When I know, *I* will exact the Siddiqui revenge."

Chapter 9

July 25, 2002, Kashgar, Xinjiang Uigher Autonomous Zone, Western China

The woman called Ping returned to the room again, clad in the bright blue kimono and tawdry high heels she had favored since she took Michael as a lover a month ago. It had taken that long to gain her confidence—more actually, because it had taken overlong for him to realize there was no other way to get the information he needed. He didn't like to use her, but it was a necessary evil.

She teetered like a child as she crossed to where he dressed beside the pink satin bed and its clutter of stuffed animals. He found himself wishing it was another woman he had met—one with long dark hair and the clear brown-green eyes of a gazelle.

A foolish, wasted thought.

Ping touched his face and plunked down on the bed. "You did not sleep well last night. You spoke strange words in your sleep. What is Yaqub? You say, say again, again."

Michael pulled away, not wanting to leap into the chasm the question opened. There were screams in the blackness there—his own? The women? Yaqub? He shuddered and turned back to Ping.

She was Hui, one of the Muslim Chinese who had immigrated from around Xian to Kashgar near the border between China and Afghanistan. The Chinese government had encouraged the emigration and the Hui had come, hoping for economic opportunity. Ping had come because of her training and her job.

Her long hair fell around her blocky, small-breasted body. There was no question that her hair was her best feature. Still, her sense of adventure seemed to have found her many lovers here in western China.

"Micha," she said, running her finger down his chest past the pink scar of the knife wound. Her fingers casually cupped his genitals in the baggy fabric of his trousers. He knew she'd taken him to her bed as an experiment. To see what a foreigner had. Enough apparently, judging by her screams when they were in bed.

"You no go, now. We have fun, yes?" She spoke in halting Uigher as she tugged at the waist of his *salwar kameez*, pulling them even lower on his hips.

Michael caught her hands and pulled her close to his chest. Yes, the dream had troubled him last night. His lips found hers and she opened to him, pressed against him, the kimono parting.

He held her away.

Damn, he didn't like this, though she was a skilled lover. But Ping was a technician at a Chinese nuclear facility deep in the desert.

Before he left Kaabul, he had passed along his meager information to the American embassy via a foreign aid worker. He hadn't waited for the orders to come here.

Given he was one of the few agents who spoke both Uigher and Mandarin, he'd come north and across the border as quickly as he could. In Kashgar he'd cooled his heels, feigning he was a rich Afghani fur trader as he tried to find his way into the Uigher community.

Instead it was only bitterness he found running like a thick current through the Kashgar market. The Uigher's anger simmered at the Chinese government's ban on the call to prayer at the mosque, at the bulldozing of Uigher towns to "modernize" the province, at the immigration of Chinese while the Uigher had no work. Most of all they were angry they had no country of their own.

The anger flowed around the massive concrete housing blocks that had been built to house the hordes of Chinese immigrants. The population growth had stretched the resources of the oasis town to the limit and threatened to overwhelm the Uigher culture. He'd watched and listened and assessed for six weeks before, in desperation, he made his move on Ping.

Michael stroked the woman's hair. "You give me so many gifts, my piece of happiness."

In truth she had given him a way into the Muslim discontent in China. Michael had heard rumors of Ping's affair with a local Uigher leader and had watched and waited, finally seducing her away.

In Michael's skilled hands she had told him things—the things her Uigher lover had wanted to know—like the plans of the nuclear facility. Like how she hated the enemies of Islam. Like her part in the grand design.

Such a little thing to bomb the reactor—in bed she had boasted of her part to Michael.

She looked up at him, and a tremor of—fear?—seemed to cross her features.

"You are my first like you. So big. So hairy." She smiled and ran her fingers through the light hair on his chest. "You stay with me, yes?"

He stood and grabbed his shirt.

"I can't, Ping. You know that. The furs come with the Sunday market. After today I'll have a full load."

He hauled his knee-length Tajik coat off a chair, but Ping tugged it from him, her full mouth in a pretty pout.

"You stay. You leave–leave all the time. I want you stay here for love. Furs—they wait until next market."

Michael gently took the heavy wool coat from her, uncurling and kissing each finger one by one.

"The best furs are there now—early in the month after curing through the spring."

Her small eyes pooled with tears. "Please stay. Please?"

He might normally. What red-blooded man would turn down her desire? But he had no time; he had contacts to meet in the market and then the return to Afghanistan.

She wrapped her arms around him and held on with a fierce strength that surprised him. She was a stoic, a soldier, a product of the Chinese system who had fallen only to the need of a woman to feel beautiful and desired.

"Ping." He grabbed her shoulders and held her away again. Tears ran down her face, but she would not meet his eyes. A sob ripped through her.

Unlike her. He grabbed her chin and turned her face to him.

"What's going on?"

"You stay here," she said more firmly, the tears drying on her cheeks.

"We both knew I would leave today."

She turned to a drawer in the small dresser in one corner and glanced towards the small apartment's door. It was the telltale move.

She turned back to him with a pistol. Chinese Tokarev, by the look of the narrow stock. Good aim.

"It's Albemit, isn't it?" He named her Uigher lover who had never fully left the picture. "He comes?"

Ping's eyes went wide at his switch to Mandarin. Confirmed.

"Bastard. You use me."

"I thought we both enjoyed ourselves."

"They know who you are. They know you American. Now they come."

He shook his head. Too many women seemed to look at him with hate these days. The thought brought a grin that increased Ping's glower. Her hand wavered.

Clearly, she wasn't used to weapons, but in some ways that made her more dangerous. The Tokarev could drop a grizzly bear easily and the damned weapon had no safety.

"You don't want to do this, Ping." Use her name to calm her. Keep it familiar. "Do you want China at war?"

"You think I care about China? My people second class. We live in ghettos. But that end soon. Soon we have our own place."

Michael tensed. Soon? The one thing he hadn't gotten from her was the timeline.

He leapt before she could react. He had her pressed against the wall, his arm at her throat, the weapon knocked aside.

"How soon? When's it going to happen?"

She spit in his face as a sound came from the hallway.

"Shit." The side of his hand slammed the base of her neck and she collapsed to the floor. She'd wake with a stiff neck and some explaining to do to her lover.

How much time did he have? *Soon.*

He collected her gun—narrow in his palm—pulled on his shirt and opened the apartment door a crack. Uigher voices in the hallway, but beyond—where the hall turned towards the elevators.

He slid into the hall and headed in the opposite direction for the stairwell and sprinted up the stairs, for once thankful for the thick concrete that masked his steps. Get to the roof. Ping's apartment building was one of three towers crammed close together west of town. He needed to get to a phone.

Then he needed to bug out.

As he reached the top floor, he heard a shout. They'd found Ping. He heard her voice yelling in her defense. Footsteps clattered up the stairs.

He slid out the roof door into a maze of flapping laundry and fought his way to the edge.

As he'd remembered. The next building was a bare fifteen feet away.

He paced to the far side of the roof, clearing the laundry lines into a slumped pile in the center of the roof. He took a breath, swore that he was getting too old for this, and sprinted towards the edge.

The door opened as he reached it. He heard a yell as he launched himself across the chasm between the buildings. Then there was a shot and he waited for the end.

Chapter 10

July 25, 2002, Kaabul, Afghanistan

Khadija had news beyond the plague of dreams that had come since she learned of Yaqub. She scrubbed the top of the clinic's desk-table with disinfectant, fighting her nervous fatigue and glanced at the back room. Papa drank his tea there. At least *he* had his rest.

The dreams had disturbed her sleep for the past two months. Last night had been the same.

Tall, dark-eyed, and teasing—Yaqub stood on a mountain and flew a kite for her—fast and light, made of red and green paper like the flag. Another kite—one black as an Imam's turban—joined his—battling, looping, smashing into her brother's kite, the glass-laden string of the attacker sawing against her brother's string as Yaqub's kite tried to escape.

Not to be. His string parted. The bright paper lifted on the breeze, then tumbled through the sky as the kite chasers raced down the mountainside and into the brown buildings of Kaabul below.

She should run after them, find the precious kite for her brother and return it to him. He would hug her when she did and she would be happy in his strong, safe arms. But the kite had already disappeared.

She turned back to her brother, to console him, but Yaqub no longer waited. Instead Michael Bellis looked at her with those pale, hungry eyes.

She shivered at the memory.

Always Michael Bellis was there. Sometimes he held a gun to Yaqub's head. Sometimes he tried to save him. Sometimes her hate chilled her and sometime she felt heat flood her limbs. It left her confused and guilty and exhausted. But worse was what the dreams and her knowledge did to her relationship with her father.

Her need for revenge was a wall between them. She could not tell her father—this man of peace—of her dreams nor what she intended. He would be furious if he knew of the use she made of the clinic for Ratbil's messages. He would say she betrayed him and his principles, and in a way she knew he would be right.

But for Yaqub it was the right thing.

A movement at the clinic door brought her head up and an intake of breath. Mizra stood at the side of the door looking at her, when he should not. He looked away to the street, then stepped inside.

"Khadija," he said, low-voiced.

"You shouldn't be here," she whispered with a glance at the curtain to the back room and a swift tug of the *burka* to bring the garment down over her face. "It isn't proper."

"There was—there is an urgent matter." He stood close to her, a brief smile on his face. "Besides, Mirri says your father softens to me. She speaks with him each time she comes."

Khadija closed her eyes. How well she knew it. It was becoming embarrassing that after Mirri's formal approach her father still held off on a decision. At least with marriage she would be a proper woman again, even though she could not imagine a life with Mizra—living under Ratbil's watchful eye.

"What's happened?" He leaned in close so she could smell the mint of his midday meal.

"Our apartment was broken into. Police we think. Or military. The neighbors say there were *kofr* with them. We think they watch us. I chanced coming because any man may seek a doctor for his ailing brother."

"Khadija? Is someone there?" Papa stirred in the other room. She heard his halting footsteps and Mizra stepped away.

"It's Mizra, father. Ratbil is ill. I'll give him some medicine and send him on his way."

She went to the locked cupboard and drew out her key. Inside were the packages of antibiotics, anti-inflammatories, and pain killers her Papa prescribed.

"Here you go. It's a shame Ratbil's poor leg causes problems. Please tell him to get well." She pulled out a package of painkillers and leaned in close. "Papa goes on a journey north. His old friend Rabbani has asked him to assess the state of medical care in Badakhshan. It seems the President does not always trust his military allies."

She placed a few pills in Mizra's hand.

"There. You see he takes one every four hours."

The curtain pulled back and Papa stood there, hand out.

"Young man? You speak to my daughter?"

Guilt flooded color up Mizra's neck. He was a good man, a proper Afghani trying to do things the traditional way. She would be lucky to marry such a man.

"Sir. Doctor Siddiqui." There was a tremor in Mizra's voice as he caught her papa's hand. "I don't even have a gift for you. I'm sorry if I cause affront. It was not to see your lovely daughter that I came. Truly, *neh*?"

He glanced back at Khadija.

"Khadija, leave us. We men must talk awhile."

Papa motioned her to the door and she stepped into the street. Would her father agree to Mizra's marriage request? That thought made her mouth go dry as the clay dust under her feet. She would obey, of course.

Mizra shared her beliefs. He was honest. He cared for her.

Her wedding would be a happy affair for her father. He would know she had a life ahead of her. There would be grandchildren. A grandson named Yaqub. The thought left her sad.

Mizra stepped backward through the door, bowing all the way.

"Thank you, Sir. Thank you. You give me hope."

It was done then. A hollow feeling filled Khadija's stomach. Mizra saw her and hurried to where she stood, a broad smile on his face.

"It is good, Khadija. He spoke to me—asked me how my family does. How Ratbil does and who will marry my sister. We even spoke of his friend, my good father."

She looked back at the door.

"That's all?"

Mizra almost caught her hand, then stopped himself.

"It's enough. He speaks to me as an equal. Someone worthy. It won't be long." He grinned. "Not long at all—but I forget myself." He checked the street.

"Your father. You must go north with him, no matter what he says."

"Me?"

"I told you—we are watched. We can't go and there is a message to be passed—urgent beyond anything. Beyond even my life." He leaned towards her and she saw a strange light in his gaze.

He must have seen her hesitation. His hand grabbed her arm.

"As my future wife I swear it to you: If you wish to avenge your brother, you will go!"

Chapter 11

July 25, 2002, Kashgar, Xinjiang Uigher Autonomous Zone, Western China

Air. Only air under Michael and far below the narrow slice of Chinese real estate that would smash his body if he fell. The bullet whizzed past. It slammed into the wall ahead.

More shots as his hands caught the rough edge of the roof. Concrete exploded around him. Shards punctured his face. His feet scrambled for purchase, up, up over the edge, to cover. Dust in his nose. An old sock by his face. Bullets parted the air over his head. Allah be praised the Chinese didn't allow target ranges.

He crawled through laundry lines towards the door at the center of the roof, reached up for the knob, and bullets exploded the wood around his hand. He rolled inside.

The door slammed behind him—meager safety. If he didn't beat them downstairs he'd be trapped.

He took each flight of stairs in huge leaps, sliding down the banisters for support. When he reached the bottom, he pushed open the rear exit.

Voices, coming fast.

He ran, ducking into the brush along the edge of Dong Hu Lake. Keeping to cover, he made his way down to the murky water, then crept along the mud-caked lakeshore. When he reached the far side of the lake he climbed up the embankment and down to the gurgling Tuman River.

The narrow watercourse, the chief source of the town's water, was low as it looped around the edge of the hill that held ancient Kashgar. Once the oasis town had been the main staging ground for the Silk Road caravans traversing the treacherous Karakoram mountains, or traveled eastward around the edge of the Taklamakan desert.

Though the camel caravans had long since passed, the markets of Kashgar were still the most impressive in Central Asia. Each Sunday, tribes and traders of Kyrgyz, Kazak, Mongol, Uigher, Tajik, Pakistani, and even Afghani origins came out of the mountains and across the borders to trade.

It was the place to make contacts. It was the place he could connect with the Pakistani trader he'd arranged to travel with back to Afghanistan. It was the place he could pass his information to the local contact. But first he needed a phone and the town was the only place to find one.

The river bent towards the market grounds and Michael dared to wade across, past scarved women spreading laundry to dry.

He ducked up into the mud-daub houses and made his way towards the huge old Qiniwak hotel. Once it had been the British Consulate and had played host to many of the players in the Great Game of Central Asia. Now it was a lovely, old dowager clad in white and ringing with the voices of the Pakistani owners.

He stopped in the shadows of a side street and watched the curving driveway. A couple of Uigher lounged beside a rack of bicycles, wearing their ubiquitous flat caps and tweed sports jackets with the labels still on the sleeves.

A couple of backpackers came out of the hotel and approached them but were shushed away. Watchers, then—not bicycle renters.

Michael eased back onto the side street. No phone there, then, and it was likely the government telecommunications building would be watched as well. He'd have been better off losing himself in the market.

He looped back into the old town, making his way to the central square that housed the Id Kah mosque. The bread-maker's shop clattered as the large rounds of flat bread were tossed out the window to cooling racks. Old men sat talking at the front of the mosque. The street was jammed with bicycles and carts laden with steaming goats' heads. Normal.

He turned onto Jiefang Bei Lu Road and down around the hill and back across the river. Dust from braying donkeys, horses, camels, and sheep filled the air. The huge fields southeast of the main market stank of raw wool from the seething sheep herded together for shearing and barter. Men yelled at impromptu horse and camel races. Blue-tarped tea stalls were filled with tribesmen in long, oiled coats and fur hats. He could lose himself among them.

Relief flooded through him when he entred the narrow aisles of the wooden shops where the tarp roofs kept the light dim. His pale eyes—what marked him apart—were not so evident there. But relief was a traitor in this situation. Only vigilance would save him. He scanned the masses of people cruising the stalls of dried fruit and nuts and clothing.

Usually Tom Pierce, the ersatz leader of the UNESCO team and the controller of the few US agents in this part of the world, spent time in the market waiting for contacts. Michael had stayed away from him because Pierce's work for the government was well known.

Now Pierce could get the information out while Michael drew the heat.

He hurried past the barber stalls and knife sharpeners and entered the next aisle. Ahead stood a blond man a foot taller than the dark crowd around him. He wore a clean golf shirt and jeans among the many suit jackets and long oiled coats. Pierce's blond hair and his height were what killed any hope he might have had of field work, though Michael had gotten to know him in field training.

Michael inched through the crowd. Pierce examined fur hats displayed in one of the stalls. He tried on a luxurious lynx as Michael came up beside him.

"You look like a Minnesota pimp," he said softly in Mandarin.

Pierce didn't even interrupt his Uigher banter with the shop owner. He took off the hat and examined its interior for workmanship. "Bellis. Heard you were here. Hadn't expected contact."

Michael scanned the crowd.

The tribespeople crowded the spice and vegetable stalls. Here, in the fur aisle, the people were sparser. Fewer ears to hear and eyes to note their conversation. He picked up a mink hat, his fingers sliding through the lush fur and over the slight, rolled brim. It would grace some elder tribesman one day.

"There's trouble," he said, switching to Afghani. Pierce had served in Afghanistan in his younger days. Michael prayed he was still fluent. "The Uigher are linking with Islamic Jihad. They're planning an accident at the Xinjiang Nuclear Facility. I'm not sure what, but it'll be big. Probably contaminate most of the oil fields. They've planned it so the U.S. will be blamed. I'm not sure how."

Pierce set the hat down and shook his head.

"Not good. We've got an agent missing. I've got men looking, but so far nothing."

Michael considered. "If he was found at the accident...."

"That's what I'm thinking. Shit. What's the timeline?"

"All I know is soon."

"I'll get the word out."

Michael looked around. Standing in one place like this made him uneasy.

"Do it fast, buddy. They're on to me, so I'm bugging out."

He set the mink hat down, smiled at the proprietor, and slid back into the crowd. He had to find the Pakistani trader.

The man had planned to leave the next day. Perhaps he could be persuaded to leave earlier. Alternatively, he could meet the trader on the road west towards Tashkurgen.

He left the fur bazaar and headed towards the carpet makers. The Pakistani made his money buying cheap Uigher carpets and trading them in Afghanistan. Sometimes he managed to find traditional Uigher *kilim*. Those beauties he sold for high profit in Islamabad's bazaars.

At least Pierce would do his job. The American government would warn the Chinese and together they'd hopefully stop the incident. A nice patch of Sino-American relations to follow. Relief flooded through him. The Uigher would have to wait a little longer for a homeland. Poor bastards.

A woman screamed behind him.

Michael turned in time to catch a flicker of blond hair at the end of the fur-seller's aisle. Pierce's face turned towards him. Blood burst from the American's lips. It spilled down his golf shirt. Pierce collapsed to the ground.

Tribesmen scattered, leaving Pierce in the dust. Only Michael remained to get the warning out.

Chapter 12

August, 2002, Wakhan Corridor, Afghanistan, near the Chinese border

Something woke Michael from warm dreams of a woman—the first good sleep he had had in weeks—into the cold and blackness that only came in this part of the world. Instantly awake, he set the dream aside.

Something he heard—there was nothing to see in the complete darkness of his room.

Even in Tibet and Nepal, there was electricity to push back the night, but here there was nothing except the occasional Jeep or generator—or firelight. No phones, either—much to his frustration.

No way to get the warning out.

Outside Kashgar he'd been forced to take refuge against the cold in one of the hay stacks that abounded in the rich oasis. They were looking for him. He'd heard their Jeeps go by.

He'd stolen a man's long, oiled-wool coat from inside a courtyard and left cash behind even though the coat was far too small for him. He'd stolen blankets as well. The trip into the mountains was no place to go unprepared.

In the morning he'd managed to wave down the Pakistani trader in his battered Jeep. Together they had traveled westward, up over Yuli Pass into the mountain village of Buzai Gumbad, and finally to the circle of mud-brick buildings called Qala Panj where they had stopped tonight. It had taken thirteen days to cross the roof of the world and all he could think was "Soon."

The lack of a date for the "accident" beat at him like a new pulse.

He inhaled the darkness, trying to understand what had woken him. The snug room in the caravanserai reeked of the musty carpets he slept on, and the tang of the bundles of furs that had been part of his disguise in western China.

The Pakistani had said he brought the goods in hopes that Michael would turn up. The man hadn't lied well. The furs would fetch him high prices in Islamabad and to hell with Michael.

There—the sudden snort of a horse outside. That was what had woken him. He pulled the cover off his watch and checked the time. Two a.m. Too early for the animal's natural rousing.

Too early for the Shah of Qala Panj's men to be readying the horses for the latest Japanese expedition to the peak of Pik Karla Marksa, just across the Tajik border.

Michael rolled, fully-clothed, out of his blanket, and pulled on the knee-length wool coat he'd traded his stolen one for once they'd crossed into Afghanistan.

He stood listening, feeling the still air around him. Cold. The small hairs on the back of his neck stood on end—always a bad sign. Danger. Something different in the building that passed as a way station for man and animal and cargo. But he and the Pakistani trader were the only guests of the place.

The muffled sound of voices came from beyond the mud walls. He hauled on his calf-high, felted boots as the voices came nearer and then stopped beyond the wooden door.

There was no reason for someone to be here—at least no one who meant him well. He went to the window that had made him choose this room and parted the shutter to peer out into the night.

The last light of the setting moon glowed on the rocky landscape of scree that lifted up the mountainsides of this, the narrowest part of the Wakhan Corridor. Afghanistan, here, was a bare twelve kilometers wide—a single valley that lifted to the Tajik and Pakistani peaks to the north and south.

Closer in, poor tufted grass fed a loose herd of horses and Bactrian camels that grazed around the low houses at the edge of the river that became the ancient Amu Darya.

Aside from the foraging horses, nothing moved but the wind in the grass. Good. Whoever it was hadn't scouted the fact his room had an escape route. Their mistake, he grinned. He slipped the shutter open farther, careful not to extend it to the point where the ancient hinges squeaked. He slid outside.

The clouds blew around the peaks of the Wakhan Mountains just over the Tajikistan border. To get his bearings, Michael's gaze settled on Pik Karla Marksa. The stars around its peak glittered like bits of glass held aloft on the chill wind. The first snows had fallen two days ago. Winter came early in these parts.

Voices carried through the clear air, but the wind stripped the words away. He hunkered down, loping from the building to the stone wall that surrounded the caravanserai.

He slid over the wall and headed southwest, away from the village, to duck down behind a cairn made of the enormous curled horns of Oxus sheep that still held on in these mountains. He waited. Patience had always been his virtue; a survival trait honed amid the Mujehaddin.

A crash and loud voices came from inside the caravanserai. Men burst out of the enclosure, searching the night. Their voices came clear, bits of Afghani brought to him on the chill breeze. *Amrikaayi.* Catch him.

Michael breathed in the darkness and swore. They spoke Dari with the accent of the Pashto of the south. Their dark jackets only half-covered the over-long *salwar kameez* the Taliban had decreed men should wear. There had been rumors that extremists held a stronghold in this area. He had even heard hints of Hashemi and had thought he might search for the man once this mission was over.

He turned into the night, waited for a cloud to block the last of the moonlight, then stayed low and glided across the landscape westward towards the graveyard. Thank God he'd made this trip before and knew the area.

The cloud shifted; the swift winds of the peaks betrayed him with a shaft of moonlight that caught him before he could reach cover.

A shout from the caravanserai and then a shot. Michael threw himself down, rolled and heard the ping, ping, ping of bullets impacting on gravel where he'd been. He rolled again. Again, at more rifle reports.

He scrambled up and ran.

The cloud shifted and darkness set in. He dove into the vacant doorway of a grave house. The Wakhan people built domed, mud-brick houses over each gravesite, the open doors and windows he supposed were for the spirit to come and go, for the Wakhani Islam seemed intertwined with vestiges of older beliefs.

Well, he would be a spirit this night and be gone.

He crouched, his hand going to the Tokarev tucked in the back of his *salwar kameez*. The pistol was the only thing he'd brought out of China, and far better quality than any weapon he'd find in Afghanistan. Here most guns were made in Pakistani weapon shops.

The wind whistled through the windows, carrying the scent of fresh horse dung and the sour stench of camel.

A crunch of stone brought him to full alert. Slowly, he raised himself to the window. The long valley was a funnel to his gaze. In the distant east there was only darkness. Closer in came the rush of the river, the squeal of a horse. The villagers wisely had decided to stay inside to avoid what happened here. Either they, or the Pakistani trader, had betrayed him.

His money was on the Pakistani.

The local Wakhi people were friends to the West, and Ismailis besides—a Muslim sect frowned on by the Taliban.

A shadow moved where there should be no shadow. It slipped along the rough mud-brick wall of a nearby burial house, into the doorway, then back out. He was good, this pursuer. Only a slight click of stone gave the man away.

Michael could slip out the door and escape the next time the man entered a grave house. The problem was where to go. The only road ran beside the Amu Darya River—once called the mighty Oxus. There was virtually no cover other than boulders, and the narrowness of the valley made it almost impossible to move without being seen

He had no choice. His enemy knew he was here, but if he took out this man there'd be less chance of being spotted as he headed west towards Khandud. Perhaps he could get help from the Wakhi governor there.

Crouched by the door, he waited for the man to check the next grave house. The man entered and Michael crossed the loose gravel silent as a ghost.

The man stepped outside and the blow from Michael's hand crushed his enemy's throat. The man went down without a sound. Let him smother in peace.

He hauled the body into the grave house, then sprinted across the road to the river where terraced fields were separated by low mulberry bushes. Moving from bush to bush he approached the hill that held a shrine to Ali.

The small building stood on a low hill of loose shale and stone. Keep going or climb it? It could give him cover and the advantage of height, but with the morning light he'd be trapped.

Keep going, then. Head down, he began a ground-eating lope parallel to the river, his chest heaving to take in enough oxygen at this altitude.

From behind came a shout and the grumble of a Jeep engine. They'd found the dead man. The location of the body told them he was headed west.

He ran. Cover was impossible. Just put as much distance as possible between himself and the vehicle. He darted closer to the river. Here it was a narrow, rushing, rock-torn maelstrom, but if worst came to worst he'd take his chances in the water.

Headlights cut the darkness and Michael hunkered down behind a mulberry bush. The vehicle drove past him, one hundred yards, two hundred yards farther down the road. If they kept going he might stand a chance.

The vehicle stopped. Damnation.

Doors opened and the backwash of headlights illuminated four men holding Kalashnikovs—the weapon of choice in this part of the world. They turned back towards Qala Panj, fanning out between the river and the road. There was no way they would miss him.

Michael looked over his shoulder. There'd be others left back at the village. No safety there.

After finding the body, the men were cautious, weapons ready. It would be hard to catch them by surprise.

Michael grabbed a fistful of river pebbles and stayed low. Now the men were silhouetted by the Jeep's taillights. He sent one pebble sailing over their heads and off to the men's right.

It cracked against the rocky ground.

The men turned, weapons up.

Michael sent another pebble farther into the night. Again the small clack. The men's heads tracked it. One of them motioned to the others to wait and stepped into the darkness.

This was Michael's chance. Their attention was turned to the valley floor. He might—just might—be able to slide by in the river if he was quick about it.

He sent one more pebble into the darkness, heard it fall, and then waded into the shallows, tucking his pistol in his belt.

Cold, so cold, the water born of glaciers that formed the headwaters of the Pamir and Wakhan Rivers. He inhaled, inhaled again when all his breath was stolen by the shock of the frigid water. Immersion for any time would be deadly.

"Don't move," said a familiar voice in Dari.

Michael froze. Idiot. While he'd watched the men from the Jeep, someone had stalked him. His damned death wish had finally betrayed him.

"Raise your hands."

Michael obeyed and turned to face the Pakistani. The man's AK-47 gleamed dully in the starlight.

"You don't want to do this, Hamid." Michael spoke softly. "This has nothing to do with you."

"You steal secrets, American dog."

"Not your secrets, Hamid." Use the man's name. Remind him they were friends and travel companions.

"You think because I'm Pakistani my goals are different than theirs? Why do you think I travel this way? I know more than carpets." The four Afghanis stepped out of the darkness. The Jeep's engine whined as it reversed back down the road.

Michael kept his gaze on the Pakistani. Yes, the Pakistani ISI had financed the Taliban for years, but what did they know? How far were they involved in this thing? Far enough, it seemed. Another part of his message.

His brain beat with *soon*.

Michael shrugged and eased back into the river. He'd lost all feeling in his feet. He had to either take the plunge or forget his attempted escape.

"So when's it going to happen? What are *your* goals, Hamid? What are they worth?"

The Pakistani chuckled.

"You could not pay me enough. I want what all Islam wants—the end of the evil empire—your United States. The end of the decadent West. We will do it, too-" He grinned. "-with the unknowing help of those heathen Chinese." He raised his rifle. "Come out of there."

Michael threw himself backward.

The frigid water slammed into him. Breath exploded from his body. The current dragged him away. He heard—no—felt the hail of bullets striking the water. He dove under the surface.

Pain. No breath. No feeling. He fought against the natural panic and stayed submerged, slammed against boulders, was torn away. How long could he stay here? How long did he dare?

His feet were two lumps of stone, his hands not far behind.

Breathe. To breathe!

He surfaced, gasped for air. Sweet and cold in his lungs. He went under again and fought towards shore. The cold stole his strength. Would steal his life, if he didn't get free soon. Light shone upstream. Eastward the night still held out against the first grey of dawn.

Just get to shore and cover or they'd have him. But where the hell was shelter in this tube of a valley?

He'd find a way.

Just find a way.

Soon. The message he carried was too important.

Soon. It was a mantra as he floundered his way into shallower water and his numb legs gave out.

Soon. He managed to get to his knees, managed to stand, managed to stagger out of the river.

The wind bit through his sodden clothing. Keep moving or he'd freeze. He tracked along the river, prepared to dive back in. His limbs didn't work. Too slow. His feet were leaden, painful. He stumbled over a larger stone.

Just move. Move!

Clothes will dry. Get to Khandud and the governor. Get word out.

The roar of the Jeep engine sent him staggering faster. He searched the landscape for some place to hide. Some place to wait for sun and warmth. Some place safe. How long had it been since he was truly warm, truly safe?

An image of marigolds.

Only low rocks and darkness across the Wakhan Valley. Even the neat lines of cultivated mulberry bushes had ended.

A shout, and gravel clattered under the Jeep as it sped towards him.

Breath burned in his throat as he ran, as he turned, as he hauled out his sodden gun and aimed. His first shot shattered the windshield and the Jeep careened to a stop. The doors opened and men fell out, took cover.

Michael's next shot slammed into one man's leg. He screamed. The others scrambled to the rear of the Jeep and Michael knew his moments were few. He aimed for the vehicle's gas tank, praying for luck.

A hail of bullets struck around him. Rock shattered. Shards peppered him. Something struck him in the side. It threw him backwards—hard.

His head cracked against stone.

Slow. Everything so slow. Cold. Numb. He rolled over. His gun—where?

He pushed to his knees, but the earth fell upward to meet him.

No! He belly crawled.

Get the warning out.

The first boot caught him in his wounded side and the pain curled him on himself. He couldn't breathe, couldn't think as the next blow found him.

And the next.

Chapter 13

August 2002, Feyzabad, Badakhshan, northeastern Afghanistan

Aisha, the heavily pregnant second wife of the hospital administrator, leaned on Khadija's arm as they walked down the narrow road between the ramshackle, mud-daub buildings that made up Feyzabad. The wind off the mountains carried the clean scent of the swift-running river, but lifted omnipresent dust that teared Khadija's eyes even under her *burka*. It was even worse than Kaabul.

Feyzabad sat in the northern Hindu Kush mountains in a broad river valley that caught and held the smoke of the cooking fires like a pall tarnishing the vivid blue sky. The mountains were jagged brown walls imprisoning the green, terraced wheat fields. Those steep mountain slopes held the rest of the world at bay.

Getting here had involved a long circuitous route north from Kaabul to Kondoz and Taloqan and then eastward over barely passable gravel roads to arrive in Feyzabad in darkness last night. The city had little electricity—but they had been made comfortable in the home of Aisha's husband, Ahmad Mali Khan, and his first wife Fatima and two grown daughters.

Even after a night's rest, every muscle in Khadija's body still ached, and her head throbbed from hitting the Jeep roof once too often on the bone-wrenching trip. Aisha's chattering voice and her weight on Khadija's arm just made it all worse.

The only thing that had made the week-long Jeep trip endurable had been the knowledge she carried a message precious to her cause. And then she'd been expected to become a part of Ahmad Mali Khan's household.

They were an odd assortment—old Fatima defeated by the second marriage of her husband; Zahra, the youngest girl, convinced the West would bring all manner of good to Afghanistan; and Hamidah, the eldest daughter, engaged to a Kaabulay, but plagued by a terrible wound on her cheek.

Apparently a local sand fly caused it; such wounds were common in the area. Hamidah was lucky because her father was a doctor. For many it went untreated and left horrible scars.

And then there was Aisha, who had lain in the women's quarters, her dark hair fanned on her pillows like a princess. She was secure in the knowledge she was pregnant with a son. In the night she had woken Khadija, surprising her with words assigned to show that she worked for the *jihad*.

The morning carried the familiar scents of tea and baking naan. Khadija'd thought to spend today acting as her father's eyes, but he was to attend a meeting. There was no need for her. It gave her the chance to complete her mission.

The sense of purpose filled her as if the Prophet himself had placed words in her mouth. When she spoke the message, she'd have done her part. She would learn who killed Yaqub and avenge him. That act would return honor to her and bring Allah's words closer to the world. So many things born from six small words.

She squeezed Aisha's gloved hand.

The other woman was so big with child her breath labored just from walking.

"Thank you for your arm."

"It's nothing, Aisha-*khor*. We're sisters in Islam, are we not?"

Aisha hesitated.

"You surprised Zahra last night. All week she's preached about the wonders you'd bring—an Afghani woman—a doctor trained in the West."

Surprised Aisha, too, it sounded like. Khadija shrugged. She held no wonders.

At the corner, men queued in lines waiting for work, while she who could have more work than she wanted, would prefer to turn from it. Her choice still chafed her, but she had done the right thing. Escaped from London to home.

Run away, more like.

Once she'd thought medicine was her calling. Before Hartness. Before Yaqub. His death had stolen her certainty.

"I'm not a doctor. I haven't finished my training."

"But you know things, correct? You work for your father?"

"I work for him, yes."

Aisha's fingers linked with Khadija's gloved hand. "And you've brought a message. Then let's be soldiers of Islam together and do this thing."

Khadija's nerves jangling as they cut through the bazaar. Mirri had said something similar in Kaabul.

But here the spice sellers set out small bags of orange and ochre and red and yellow all tingeing the air with the scent of heat. A line of turbaned men crouched behind purple-hued salt blocks, and pieces of lapis—indigo, light blue, and green. Both salt and lapis had been mined for centuries in Badakhshan.

"My mother left me a necklace of the darkest lapis," she said to the shopkeeper, an old bearded Tajik. He was dressed in tattered Western trousers and shirt, with a Tajik vest overtop.

"The neeli." He named the most precious of the three colors of lapis and placed his hand proudly on a small display of the deep blue.

"We mined it seven thousand years ago. Egypt used it in King Tut's golden mask."

"How do you know?"

"I helped a Western man who studied stone. He told me."

"*Kofr* lies," Aisha hissed.

Khadija considered. Afghanistan had been at the heart of the caravan trade for millennia. Yaqub and her father had taught her that.

"It could be true."

Aisha's eyes flashed through the *chador* lattice.

"Believe nothing of what a *kofr* says. They are the *galamjam* of these days. No better than carpet thieves. They take everything."

"But sometimes they know more of our history. So much has been destroyed."

"History is not as important as Islam."

"History brought me here, Aisha." Khadija felt the other woman's anger as Aisha dragged Khadija from the lapis display. "My mother's great-grandmother was a Tajik princess. Her father was a great mystic and a poet. Rabbani hopes my father's marriage to that bloodline will aid in the meetings here. That history let me bring the precious thing I carry."

"It is a history of unbelievers," Aisha said. "It should be destroyed. The devout have no room for pretty stories or poetry. There are only Allah's and the Prophet's words. They sustain us."

Khadija's logical side thought of her father's penchant for Sufi philosophy, of her mother's family. They had been Shi'ite. Why should that history be rejected? It was Afghani. But she was not here to argue family pride.

They passed the two ragged buildings that served as hotels to the few foreign press, and avoided the new town that housed aid agencies such as *Médicins sans Frontières*. Aisha led the way down to the bridge that crossed over the Kokcha River where old men used sheepskins in an ancient practice that netted gold dust from the water.

Not far along a dirt road outside of town, they came to a stone-fenced holding with a low, crumbling, mud house.

Aisha knocked boldly on the faded wooden door and they waited. The scent of sheep and dung lay sweet on Khadija's tongue, but the wind was too cold, the sunlight too bright reflected off stone.

All her small Kaabul errands were nothing compared to what she did now. She *had* become a soldier of the *jihad*. She would kill those who killed her brother.

"This is no place for women. Leave!" A man peered down from the roof of the house, brandishing a rifle. He was dressed as a shepherd, with a shepherd's small, crowned hat.

"We have business," Aisha said. "We are the sheepskins of Allah."

The door pulled open a crack.

"We find the gold of his words. We reject the *kofr* ways the West would impose." A man's voice came from the dark interior.

The door pulled farther open, exposing a thin, bearded man wearing a long *salwar kameez* and a black turban. His eyes were almost black, and seemed to glitter coldly with inner light. His gaze flickered disapprovingly from Aisha to Khadija.

"This is the one? A woman?"

Aisha pulled Khadija inside. "I told you it was so."

The man scanned Khadija up and down, as if he could see her through the *burka*.

"Give it to me."

"There is nothing to give except words."

He frowned and cast an angry look at Aisha as if to say the kind of fool she was.

"This was too precious for paper." Khadija stepped forward and whispered to the man, fighting back a tight bubble of elation.

She could laugh at how easy this had been. She could finish helping her father and then—then she could resume her life in Kaabul. Mizra would finish his courtship and she would be married and her life would have honor again. Mirri would truly be her sister and Khadija would be worthy of Allah's love.

The man considered her. "You are a doctor? You trained in the West?"

The question surprised her and her elation crumbled like dust.

"I—I trained in London, but did not...."

"You come." He didn't allow her to finish and fear tightened her stomach.

Was she to be punished for her time in the West? Killed? Surely Mirri would not send her on such a mission. But soldiers of Islam could be sacrificed.

The man in the black turban waited by a door that opened into the house's courtyard. Heart pounding, she followed.

He led her from the safety of Aisha's company out the rear of the house and across the stone enclosure, then up slope towards a copse of aspen, cedar, and pistachio that grew at the edge of the valley. A small trail led through the trees and Khadija shivered as the mud-brick house disappeared from view.

All bird call stopped. The landscape filled with foreboding. She wanted to ask where she was being taken, but she was a soldier. Then why was she so afraid?

The slope steepened as the narrow defile wound into the mountains. The only sound was the scrabble of her footfall. The man moved silent as the wind. The trees ended and the loose stones tripped Khadija. They were on the mountainside now and she would not be able to manage much more of this, dressed as she was.

The trail led up amongst the scree, through a maze of huge boulders, and then Khadija teetered on the ragged lip of a hole that tunneled deep into the mountain. The damp breath of the earth blew in her face and she tasted fear.

Her companion leapt down worn stones to the tunnel floor, and beckoned her to follow.

"Stay close." He ducked beneath the low ceiling and led her into the mountain.

Like a thick curtain, darkness stole everything but the sound of her breathing and their footsteps. The over-sweet scent of old urine and bat guano made her queasy. The wind sighed against the tunnel entrance and she stole a glance at the receding disc of light just before she stumbled around a corner and into total darkness.

She froze.

Seconds ticked by—warped into forever. Did the tunnel keep turning? Was she in an open chamber? Was there a pit before her?

She reached, but her fingertips found nothing. She was afraid to move. Where was her escort? Her breath came in sharp little gasps and the scent of bat guano choked her. Panic twisted in her throat.

It wasn't the dark. It was not knowing her next step was safe.

"Please," she said in a whisper too loud, too distorted by echoes and distance and time. "Please. I'm afraid."

To move. To live. To listen to her father.

A low epithet and the sound of stone crunching, and then a hand closed on her arm. He jerked her forward.

"I said stay close!"

As usual she was a fool.

She stumbled after and light blinded her as they turned another corner. The scent of smoke and something copper hung strong on the air. Another corner and Khadija found herself in a room piled high with boxes.

Some were marked with Chinese figures. Others held Cyrillic letters. Three men sat smoking Turkish cigarettes and talking quietly. Trails of cigarette smoke and kerosene vapor coalesced in the space near the ceiling. A fourth man, an Arab by his darker skin and aquiline features, sat apart reading the Quran.

When he saw Khadija, he stood. "You bring a woman here?"

Her escort paused—why did he, an Afghan, act subservient to this Arab? This was his country!

"She's a doctor. She brought the information. I thought she could deal with your other problem—unless you've completed your work...?"

The Arab's full black beard couldn't disguise lips pressed in a line as hard as his eyes. He was taller, straighter than the Afghani, and wore his black turban like a crown.

"I will—though he does not know it—yet."

"Why not kill him and be done with it. He knows too much."

"And we must learn his secrets if we are to cleanse our world of infection." The Arab turned back to Khadija and his gaze lashed her, even through the shelter of her *chador*. "Where did you train?"

"London."

He spat.

"Then why are you here?" he asked in perfect, Oxford-accented English reminiscent of Dr. James Hartness's clipped tones. "Those who train in the West are subverted by the wealth. Few return home."

Memories of the couch, of James Hartness's hands, sent a shiver through Khadija. But she had done Allah's will and brought the message.

"My father needed me. He's blind," she answered in Dari, hoping her trepidations didn't show. A flicker showed in his gaze.

"In English," he demanded.

Uncertain, she repeated her answer. He interrogated her about London Hospital.

"So. You did train there. Why do you work with us, then? The *kofr* say we treat our women ill."

She was glad the *burka* hid how she colored as she lifted her chin. This man would read the truth and would not condone her past.

"Islam treats women with honor. I know Islam and the Word. I saw the *kofr*'s evil in London even as they killed my brother here."

"So you help us for revenge?"

"I'm a soldier of the faith!"

Doubt filled his face. Then he shrugged.

"I am Abdullah Hashemi. You will obey me in all things. When you leave, you will speak to no one of this place, your message, or me. Do you understand?"

She nodded, suspecting he would kill her if she disobeyed. Then he turned towards a farther tunnel and crooked his fingers for her to follow. Leading her with a kerosene lantern, he took her farther into the mountain. The tunnel sloped down; the lantern created strange shadows across rough stone walls. The weight of the earth made it hard to breathe.

Finally Hashemi stopped and Khadija shivered behind him. The lantern illuminated a small, low-roofed chamber carved from the mountain. Yellow-brown walls and floor were splattered with rust-colored streaks. The stench of burned flesh, vomit, and blood overpowered the stink of bat guano.

All, it seemed, had come from the man sprawled on the floor.

Chapter 14

"Who is he?" Khadija asked as she stepped into the cell, for cell it was. Cold and lonely with the ceiling pressing down. Hard to breathe the stink. If the earth quaked would the roof hold?

The man lay, half-twisted on the floor, dressed only in the bloody remains of a brown *salwar kameez*. Lantern shadows danced crazily across him as he lay, face towards the wall, his skin pasty white, bloody hands bound behind him. She had never seen anyone like this in the emergency room in London. A prisoner.

"A *kofr* agent. He meddled in our affairs. We need to know who helps him. When we rid Afghanistan of his kind we'll bring a holy Islamic state."

Khadija shivered at the cold hatred in the man's voice. Against one wall sat an old car battery with two long, raw, wires. Beside it stood a blood-stained wooden bench. To be trapped here. To die here. Would Hashemi let her leave?

The lantern hissed and spit as she knelt beside the man. The left side of the man's *salwar kameez* was caked with blood in a crazy piebald pattern. Thankful for the gloves propriety demanded when in public, she gently rolled him towards her and he groaned.

Alive and responsive, then. She grabbed hold of her medical training to steady herself.

The sight of his face almost made her let him go. Made her stand. Run.

Covered in yellow dirt, bruised and blackened around one eye, still the fine features and hawk nose, the smirk of lips could only belong to one person.

Her hands recoiled from Michael Bellis.

Did Hashemi know how this man confused her? Was this a test to see if she would kill him? Or to trap her?

The weight of earth was too much and a cold wind seemed to gutter the lantern. She stood, fighting for calm when all her inner alarms jangled.

"He's a *kofr*, a man. Our Afghani brother is right—let him die." What would her papa say if he knew? She turned towards the tunnel, but Hashemi shocked her by grabbing her arm.

"I need this man's information more than I need your devotion to Islam. If you're a soldier, you'll do what's necessary. Has not the Prophet said there is no good or evil, but by Allah's provenance?"

Her father had once said something similar, but did Hashemi know that she knew this man? To touch him was more dishonor—she had dreamed of Michael Bellis.

In person and in her dreams he had been proud, like a lion the way he moved, like a mountain the way he made you look at him. She remembered the way light caught his hair, turning it copper like the sides of these barren mountains. Even now she felt the man's powerful life force.

But to treat him would bring an intimacy she dared not feel. Had not Allah said that women carried nine parts of desire within them, while men carried only one. It was women who tempted and were corrupt at the heart.

"Are you a doctor or a child? Allah said even the enemy is to be treated in justice and kindness. Not to provide it is to disobey God and be admitted to fire, to suffer his punishment!"

The harsh words cut through her fear. All her training had made her a doctor, but her desire to regain honor had stripped that away.

"I can't."

Hashemi's fingers dug into her arm. "You say you're a soldier of Islam. Then do as ordered. If not, there are many dangers in this world." He shrugged. "Who can say what will happen—especially to the old and infirm."

Khadija went cold at the words. Papa was a blameless old man, but Hashemi's hard eyes said it was more than a threat. She was glad of the *burka*, for it hid her fear.

She looked at Michael Bellis.

To treat him she would move her hands so. She would do this first and that second, following the ABCs of trauma work just as she had done in the market. Her teachers had taught her well. It was more natural than honor.

She shuddered.

"Bring me water. I must be able to see what I work with. And any medical equipment you have."

Abdullah nodded at a small backpack that stood at the entrance to the room.

"The medical supplies. I'll have one of the men bring you water."

He left her, the lantern swaying from a hook in the rock. Wild shadows danced over the walls, so the world was unsteady under her feet.

She grabbed the pack and went to Michael Bellis, then pulled the front of her *burka* back over her head so she could work. An old set of scissors in the medical bag allowed her to saw through the rope that held his arms.

He slumped onto his back and a long sigh escaped him. She checked his airway and breathing. His breath came even, but its stentorian rattle was counterpoint to the hissing lantern.

She checked pupil contraction and pulse. Slow—very slow, but steady. That could be due to blood loss, or to the overall good conditioning of the man. But his body radiated heat and sweat beaded his forehead.

She dug in the medical kit and found a rusted stethoscope, then eased apart the shreds of his shirt. The brown *salwar kameez* stuck to his chest in many places—on his left side where a crude bandage was caked with dried blood, and over numerous burns that wept serous fluid. She tried to ease the fabric away from his skin, but finally used the scissors to cut away the tattered cloth.

The broad expanse of his chest lay before her again. She remembered the look of him in her father's clinic, the way his skin gleamed, and the way he looked at her with those hungry eyes.

Now his skin was ruddy with fever and the livid burn marks dotted his torso. The fingers of his right hand were blackened at the tips. She glanced at the battery and shivered at the pain he must have endured.

The torture was for a purpose, though. This man was a spy. He might be her father's friend, but he was *Amrikaayi*—one of the *kofr* who had killed her brother.

By the look of him, it was not his first injury, but then she'd seen that at her father's clinic. She touched the puckered ridge that ran a patchwork across his left shoulder. A larger scar trailed into the top of his low-slung trousers. It took effort to pull her gaze away and listen to his heart and lungs. This close, even through the stench of his clothes, he smelled of forge-heated metal. His slow thump of heart showed the honed strength she'd seen in him.

She easily peeled away the bandage on his side; the cheap medical tape was not like what she'd used in London. The stench of rotting flesh caught in her throat.

A bullet wound—she'd seen enough of them—had ripped through his well-developed latissimus dorsi, not far from where the scar of her father's stitching gleamed pale pink on his skin. The entry wound had almost fully closed with new flesh, but around the wound the skin was red-blue. Livid red stripes trailed across his side.

Khadija swore as all her medical instincts kicked in. If the infection had made it into the chest cavity, there wasn't much she could do.

Where was the water? She needed to get this wound cleaned.

She dug in the bag to inventory her supplies. An old scalpel complete with a few drops of dried blood. She wondered if it had ever been used to help someone.

A few antiseptic bandages of various sizes, still in sealed wrappers. Tensor bandages. A small tube of antiseptic cream long past its expiry date.

She fought back frustration. This was a medical bag? How could they run a war like this?

Footsteps came from the tunnel and she pulled her *burka* over her face. She was met by an Afghani carrying a bucket of water still murky with river sediment.

"I need hot water. Water that has boiled."

The man ignored her and she almost grabbed his arm.

"I can't do my job with this. I need hot water and clean cloths." She saw the refusal in the man's face. "You want to anger Hashemi? He wants this man saved."

The Afghan dropped the bucket and left her with a mounting anger. She didn't dare try to clean the wound with this. At best, this would do to wash the filth from her patient and possibly bring his temperature down. She hauled the bucket closer.

A strip from the hem of Michael Bellis's ruined *salwar kameez* became a cleaning rag. She dabbed carefully at his face and chest, but a fist shot up and caught her arm like pliers.

Pale blue eyes glared at her, and then the shock of recognition filled his gaze.

"You?" His hoarse voice was barely a rumble in his chest, but the grip on her wrist made her hand numb. The heat of him flooded into her body.

"Let go," she hissed. "I'm trying to help."

Why was she whispering? She tried to twist free.

"Save me, so they can kill me?" There was his wry humor. "I didn't think you were inclined to sadism."

"You know nothing of me."

"Aah." He went to move and pain flickered in his face. Then his nose wrinkled and for a moment she saw a small boy—the boy that had grown into this man before her. He would have been a wild child—running the streets of a city and causing his mother constant consternation. But that wildness meant he had found ways to deal with pain.

He looked down at his body. "How bad?"

"Bad."

He closed his eyes and swore. "I need to get out of here."

As if the needs of a *kofr* mattered. Khadija focused on her work, but felt the weight of his gaze, knew she was too aware of his hard body under her hands had too much knowledge of the hidden parts beneath his clothes. No innocent, she. She pulled away, but if anything that was worse. She needed something to distract her.

"You're the enemy of the Afghan people," she said as she rummaged through the pack once more.

He snorted and winced.

"Be with those who mix with God as honey blends with milk…" he murmured.

Khadija glanced at him, momentarily disconcerted. It was something her father would say.

"Rumi was an Afghan, though his life took him elsewhere."

"As am I," he whispered. Then he went still. "They come."

His eyes closed, his body suddenly limp beside her in a convincing show of unconsciousness. Khadija turned towards the tunnel. Tell them he was awake? She was no conspirator with this man.

The same Afghani carried a steaming bowl into the cavern. He set the water down at the entrance and left without a glance in her direction.

She dipped water to wash the wound, then washed the scalpel and turned back to her patient. There was nothing for it. She had to work with what she had.

Michael Bellis's gaze met hers as he caught her wrist again—so tight her fingers turned white. There was distrust—and so many questions in his eyes and—and a plea?

She yanked loose. "It's my help or slow death. Your choice."

That grin again, as his gaze bore into her.

"I think—you would prefer my death."

His voice broke as he tried to sit up and she resented the fact he'd read her mind.

A death for a death. It would be easy to plunge the scalpel to its hilt and finish the job. She could imagine the blood spray. Its warmth on her face and hands and the way that pale gaze would fade to emptiness.

"I've been ordered to save you."

Was that regret in his eyes? Certainly it matched the regret she felt.

"Then do what you have to."

His fists ground into the earth. His hands were broad, the fingers long and fine—not a soldier's hands. More like the hands of an artist. They were so large compared to hers, the flesh toughened by years of labor.

In Afghanistan?

Had he helped prop up the puppet-king, Daoud—only to remove Western aid so the Russians could put in their man? He was old enough. It was the type of thing *Amrikaayi* would do. That was when the worst of the trouble had begun—at least that's what her father said. And that led to where Afghanistan was today. Her anger gave her resolve.

"The wound's badly infected. I'm going to drain it." Her scalpel slashed the livid entry wound, but found no satisfaction as Michael Bellis jerked. Only his fingers scrabbled in the dry cave earth. Viscous yellow-green fluid gushed out as Khadija excised the exit wound. The stench teared her eyes, but Michael only mouthed Rumi.

"I died a mineral and became vegetable; from vegetable I died and became animal. I died an animal and became man. Then why fear death? Next time I will bring forth wings like angels; after that, who can say what I'll become."

His voice was less than a whisper, yet she found comfort in the ancient prayer. In death, Yaqub would become an angel. Would it be so for her?

Michael Bellis's eyes were closed, his recitation stopped and his breath came in shallow gasps. Even his poetry had escaped him, it seemed.

"I'll clean the wound as best I can," she said. "I don't have the equipment to do it properly." His hungry eyes flicked open, but all his strength seemed to have otherwise fled.

She poured the stale-dated disinfectant into the still-steaming water, and found an unopened syringe. This was going to hurt like a demon, but he deserved it. She used the syringe to flood the wound with water.

Michael Bellis gave a strangled cry that ended as quickly as it had begun. His back arched. His fist came up, then slammed into the earth. His eyes caught hers, then closed, leaving Khadija shaking.

Those damnable hungry eyes. They had looked at her as if he expected her—no, wanted her—to—to help him die. But worse was the trust she had seen. Even though they were enemies and always would be, for some reason he trusted her. Didn't he know only Hashemi's order made her help him? Didn't he realize it was only so he could reveal his secrets?

That was the reason.

Wasn't it?

Chapter 15

Had it been a dream? A different dream—one without the screaming. A different kind of nightmare, more like.

The stone lay rough under Michael's cheek. Pain throbbed in his body. Each breath caught his side, but: *I welcome difficulty as a friend. I joke with torment and prepare myself to know the sweetness that follows grief.*

Usually the recitations gave him strength, but now the thoughts tremored, just as his body did. Just let him die.

No. He could not—yet. There was the message. Soon. His arms were no longer bound and that gave him a chance. He had to get his warning out.

He kept his eyes closed, though the darkness of the cell—cave—grave—told him no one was present. No sound but his breathing, the trickle of stone fall nearby. How long had he been here? He'd tried to keep track of the days, but in the darkness it was impossible. Only the coming of Hashemi told of the passage of time, and that could be any time at all.

It was like his enemy floated somewhere outside of time, an apparition that brought questions and torment. So far it had not broken Michael, but with each day and his weakening body, he wondered if he had the strength to hold on. And in the West the clocks ticked, the calendar of days marched past, and....

Soon. Urgency filled him.

Antiseptic scent and the feel of cool air on his chest made him think of a woman. Had she been here? In his dream, gentle hands had pulled him back from the dark places he walked since the rough Jeep ride from the Wakhan.

They had brought him—somewhere. On the transfer from the vehicle he thought he smelled the scents of sheep, cooking fires, and cedar, and had heard the rushing of wind and running water. But there were many rivers in Badakhshan—five rivers fed the Amu Darya in these parts. He could be anywhere in one of the strongholds of the Hashemi's *jihad*.

Had she *truly* been here?

He inhaled. Antiseptic, yes, but something more. Something—feminine. A light, reviving scent he remembered, like fresh coriander and citrus.

His mind sorted the scent, reveled in some purpose, and landed on a recollection. Shampoo. He had last smelled it at Mohammed's clinic. It was a Western shampoo she must have brought from London.

Khadija. That was the face in his dreams. Those wide, green-flecked eyes and that striking face with its strong jaw and full lips. Those eyes so filled with strength and distrust. Yet she'd treated him with the quiet competence of a skilled physician. Odd—she'd denied such skill to her father. How the hell had she come here?

A slight sound and a glimmer of light filled the tunnel. Michael feigned unconsciousness. It was too damn easy.

Red light glowed through his eyelids. Footsteps paused. They came closer and Michael tensed. Overpower whoever this was, he'd be free. He had surprise on his side.

The footsteps stopped beside him and he heard the whisper of cloth as the person moved. Michael rolled to his knees and opened his eyes. Hashemi! Kill him!

Michael lunged upward.

Ignore the pain, but dammit, his body didn't move. His fist was too slow. Pain as he grabbed for Hashemi. More pain as Hashemi's knee found Michael's face.

His legs—disobeyed as if they belonged to another. His feet were leaden lumps. The cave—tilted.

Michael toppled sideways and a booted foot found his gut. More pain. Bile in his mouth. The world slipping, slipping away. No! He had to be aware. It was the only way to be sure he did not tell them things. The world steadied—a world where Hashemi stood over him, a gun held casually in his hand.

"I see you feel ready to continue our conversations. That is bloody good, Michael. I'm glad."

He called down the tunnel, and an Afghani Michael had come to know as Farhad arrived. Michael knew what was to come and his mouth went dry. His gaze locked on Hashemi. Remember the Arab's face. Track him forever and kill him for all he has done.

Too weak to fight, Michael could only twist in Farhad's hands as he was dragged to the blood-encrusted bench and trussed on his back. His arms were tied below the slats, his legs bound to the wood, his chest and abdomen exposed even as he glared useless defiance.

Forget the agony in his side, the reopening of the small oozing wounds on his chest. Focus on Hashemi.

The Arab stood over him.

"Michael," he said softly, reasonably, his Oxford English so strange in the room. "How long it was I wanted to meet you. Ever since the night I heard your name."

He smiled. "We know you *Amrikaayi* work with The Doctor. We know you undermine the righteous force of Islam, but we *will* cleanse this country of you. You know I bring pain. This is your chance to escape it. Tell us what we want to know and release will follow."

Michael clamped his mouth shut against temptation to speak the real name of the man who had led the Afghani resistance to the Taliban. Hold to anger. Don't converse. One word could lead to another. One name to another until all his secrets lay spilled on the floor along with his blood.

Anything he said would only increase the river of blood across Afghanistan. He thought of the men and women lost to the Russians and Taliban. What difference had their deaths made, had his efforts made, if he told?

Maybe if he hadn't come, if America hadn't interfered with the tribal factions, the country would have reached equilibrium by now. Maybe, though he doubted it. Maybe Hashemi was right—he, Michael, the *Amrikaayi*, all the interfering foreigners—were the source of the problem.

He looked up at Hashemi and the release the Arab promised.

To be free of the burdens this life entailed. Mohammed Siddiqui would say the only way to be free was to surrender to the burdens, to show Allah you accepted and still found the strength to live compassionately and with love. That was living as Allah and the Prophet lived. That was when love would find you. Michael had been in-country too long. He knew too much. After all the things he had done, there was no love in this world for him. There was only this mission and emptiness. Michael strained against his bonds.

Soon.

Hashemi shook his head.

"Listen to logic, Michael. You *will* tell me. It is only a matter of time and the only question is what remains behind when I'm done. I can wound you and maim you and heal you so I can wound you again. I can ask these questions forever. It can be a hard process, or an easy one. It's your choice. Your blood makes no difference—to me."

Michael knew the truth of the words. That was why Khadija had come—to heal him so he could be tortured again. He had not thought Mohammed's daughter held that capacity for evil.

Stay focused on his task. Stay focused on emptiness.

The Arab shrugged.

"Aah well. To work then." He nodded and Farhad, hands hidden inside thick rubber gloves, dragged the long coils of battery wire to Michael.

His body cringed on its own as Farhad sparked the wires over his body. His mind screamed his protest, but he held his mouth closed, held himself still.

A stone I died.... Let death come, and peace.

No—he had to get the message out!

"Tell me the name of The Doctor!"

The wires touched down and Michael lost his words—himself—in a landscape of pain.

Chapter 16

Mohammed Siddiqui held lightly to Khadija's arm as she led him along the echoing corridors of Feyzabad's Hospital. The stink of human waste filled his nose.

Ahmad Mali Khan had left them to take a phone call. With the echoes it was as if they were alone in the world. Would that it were so. Then perhaps he would know how to heal this chasm that separated him from his daughter.

Even Khadija's arm seemed so far away.

"Khadija? What do you see?" He felt her stiffen slightly, her pace quicken.

"Not London Hospital." Disgust in her voice, then silence again. It was as if she could barely stand to speak with him.

"Tell me. You are my eyes."

A sigh, then: "The wards are clean, but the walls are cracked. The tile lifts everywhere. There are cockroaches in the kitchens. Flies get into the patient's trays. The equipment at the nursing stations is broken. There is nothing on the supply shelves but what we brought with us, and—you smell it—the ammonia is enough to choke on."

He squeezed her wrist. "Not what you see in a proper British hospital."

No sign she'd heard. Just their quiet footfall. Her voice had brought her close for one precious moment, but her silence set her as far away as when she was in London. Farther, even.

At least then, their letters had spoken of their affection, had told him of her life. Now Khadija had become a foreign creature—as if a stranger had come home to him. He had missed something in her letters and the realization made him feel so helpless. A father should not be helpless.

"I fear this trip has been difficult for you." He heard the rustle of her *burka*, felt the slight hesitation in her step and each hesitation broke his heart anew.

"I'm fine." Such brittleness in her voice.

"Your voice shakes as if you're tired. The trip was long."

"The trip was fine."

"Then... what is it? *Pishogay*, we used to talk about everything. Now we barely speak."

"I was a child then. Now I'm a woman. I focus on my duties and your question. This place is a mess. They must lose more people to sepsis than to injury or illness. It's like we've stepped back a hundred years. And my name is Khadija, father. I'm no longer *Pishogay*."

It was the final rejection and left him empty.

He had always called her *Pishogay*. It was their joke, a name given of a father's special affection. When she pulled her arm from him, he was too alone in the darkness. He wanted to reach for her, but was afraid he would find her gone.

"The foreigners—they put money into battles and forget hospitals or helping our people earn a living. They don't care about the people."

The fatigue and finality in her voice said these words had been bitten back for many days, but he could not tell her how she was wrong. He could not chance another barrier. Only gentleness would show her the error of her ways.

"The foreigners funded this journey."

Even spoken softly, he regretted how his words seemed to hang like a challenge. He knew Khadija would treat it like a vendetta. She'd become so strident in her views.

"It's their money that funds the supplies we brought. It's their money that sends the foreign doctors here."

"As usual, you side with them. How can you, after Yaqub, father?"

He caught a bit of *burqa* fabric before the wave of strangeness swept her totally away.

"*Pishogay*—Khadija—you must listen! Please listen. You used to be able to hear the other side of things."

He found her hand and felt the tension in her thumb, her palm. She wanted to pull away, wanted to abandon him. He would not lose her!

"The foreigners can do things we can't. Think of the women, Khadija. Many have ailments like Ahmad Mali Khan's daughter. Many die in childbirth because there are only male doctors. The foreigners don't hold with that. Surely you want the women to get help."

"So you'd have foreign men touch our women?"

There was ice in her question. Since when had she become so strident about Islam?

"What have you become, father? The Law says that women are to be with their fathers and their husbands. They are not for other men. That...is sin!"

Her voice held such loathing and so much pain. He wanted to pull her to him, take her in his arms, stroke the fear out of his child, but he knew this time he could not. Her hand was too rigid. Her breath was too quick. She was ready to run, ready to pull away and never come back.

He could not chance that.

"I... I feel like the barest breeze, the puff of my breath, could send you from me," he said. He bowed his head. "Let's speak of this no more."

Chapter 17

The pale sunlight through a warped hospital window placed lines on her father's face Khadija hadn't seen before. Were those scars around his eyes? Certainly there were shadows under them and a slope of sorrow to his lips.

She wished she could help him understand that his ways were old. He failed to see what was happening to their country. To allow foreign doctors to touch Afghani women—what was Papa thinking?

Finally he grasped her arm lightly and started down the barren hallway towards the operating theater. He seemed to have lost weight on this journey. She would need to make sure he ate more. She had to care for him, protect him, and for that she would deal with Michael Bellis.

It had been two days since she had been there and she had said nothing to her papa. He would not approve of her actions. She kept telling herself it didn't matter, nor did it matter that the *Amrikaayi* was her father's friend. What mattered was saving her people from a dishonorable fate.

Michael Bellis held information Hashemi needed to cleanse Afghanistan. So the *Amrikaayi* had to live and that required antibiotics. His life would be traded for the information she needed.

A full course of ampecillin would probably do it. Or some of the chloramphenicol her father had brought north for the hospital. It had been unloaded their first day here.

In the operating room she described more disaster, but her father only identified ways to make the place functional. He would settle for Afghanistan being a backwater of the world, a second-class place.

Damnation, why were tears so close to the surface? Because she had been forced to accept the leavings of Dr. James Hartness? Given fewer and fewer chances to do her work until she had finally complained and then he had said her competence was in question. In her shame, she'd believed him.

Well, she would see her father never knew. When she had redeemed herself she would be released from her past. She would be whole again. Perhaps then things would be better between them.

"Khadija?"

Her father's hand fell on her shoulder, but she couldn't let him know how upset she was. She pulled away.

"Aah. There you are." The cultured voice of Ahmad Mali Khan rescued her. "Mohammed, I've come to take you to tea and discuss our key needs. We must spread the resources as far as possible." He glance slid to Khadija in dismissal. "My Aisha is at reception. She enjoyed your chatter so much the other day, she hopes you might walk together this afternoon."

"Father?"

His shoulders slumped a little more. A horrible grief radiated across on his face and she had to look away.

"We are done, I think. You go. Do your woman things."

Ahmad Mali Khan gripped his wrist and the two men left.

She listened to her father's voice down the hall, knowing she had hurt him. A part of her ached at the knowledge, but she had to finish this. Satisfy her family's revenge.

"The friend of my enemy is my enemy, as well," she whispered. And yet—and yet—how could the gentle old man ever be her enemy?

Someday he might know the truth and appreciate her for her strength of faith and how she had redeemed herself.

Now that faith demanded antibiotic.

Surely one vial of chloramphenicol would not be missed. She hurried back through the hospital corridors. She had never stolen anything in her life. Under Islamic Law she could lose a hand for this, but it was for Allah, just as Hashemi had said.

She stopped around the corner from the nursing station where the pharmaceuticals were stored and took a deep breath.

Show me your straight path,
not the path of those who earn your wrath
nor those who go astray.

The nurse—a young Afghani woman with her hair hidden under a scarf, but her face still woefully exposed—looked up at Khadija. "May I help you?"

"Mohammed Siddiqui asks that I check how you have stored the supplies. Unlock the door." She went straight to the supply room entrance.

The young woman stood. "We've stored everything as it should be. We know our business."

"We'll see, won't we?"

The nurse fumbled with keys. She unlocked the door and went to lead

Khadija inside.

"I don't need your help." Khadija pushed past and eased the door shut behind her.

Shelves held neat boxes of bandages, syringes, medical tubing, stethoscope, blood pressure monitors, and jars of pills. The nurse was right. The hospital might be falling apart, but they did know their business. The pills should be locked in a proper pharmacy, but that was beyond this dismal place.

Her gaze reached a box that held medicated dressings. Michael could use those. She checked over her shoulder, but the nurse had returned to her desk, though the stiffness of her shoulders showed she wasn't happy with Khadija's invasion.

Half the dressings slid under her *burka* into her pockets. Then she slid the box to the back of the stacked supplies, hoping her theft wouldn't be discovered.

A small, ancient fridge gurgled and chugged in the back corner of the room. She yanked it open because the nurse would expect to hear the sound. Inside, the shelves were still almost bare, even with the supplies her father had brought. The vials of ampicillin were tempting, but she had no way to refrigerate them if she took them. No, better to find the chloramphenicol as she'd planned.

Voices at the nursing station: she glanced over her shoulder and caught the flash of one of the hospital security men through the small window. She froze.

If she was caught, she didn't think she could lie her way free. She'd never been good at fabrications and with the dressings in her pockets there was no way to hide her intent. Just find what she needed and get out.

The precious antibiotic sat on the lone shelf above the fridge. She fumbled one of the small glass bottles free, then patted the box closed. She dared not take more. There were too many others in need. She shoved the ampoule into the pocket with the bandages.

She should leave now.

Needles.

She had a few syringes in the medical supplies at the cave, but the sharps were not there. She needed to make sure she had sterile supplies to make use of the chloramphenicol.

She stuck her hand in one of the boxes and pulled out a handful of capped syringes, then pushed them into her pocket as well. She was trembling, damn it, and her legs felt weak. Just get this over with. She ran a practiced eye over the boxes, straightening a corner here and there. Not bad. The nurse who had arranged things had an orderly mind.

She let herself out the door and nodded at the nurse who was still in conversation with the guard. The way her face stiffened, Khadija knew she'd made an enemy of the woman. Let her not check the supplies.

"I'll advise my father you've done well. It will be reported to the administrator and to the government."

She strode down the hallway, feeling their hostile gazes on her back until she turned the corner. Then she almost ran to reception and Aisha.

"Let's go. I've got what's needed." She grabbed Aisha's arm and glanced at the nurse behind the counter—a man. At least that was more proper.

Cool air waited outside, but charcoal smoke quickly soured Khadija's throat. The poplar along the rushing river were still deeply green, but closer to the base of the mountains the aspens had a lovely, but telling, tinge of gold.

"Fall comes early here."

"That is the way of the mountains." Aisha shrugged. "We should hurry. You'll not be able to stay as long with our leader as you did before. My family will expect us for the evening meal."

They crossed the bridge where the old men still collected the gold of the mountains, and followed the road to the isolated farm house. The door opened before they reached it and the same Afghani stood there, in his dark turban.

"Come."

Khadija followed him up the trail to the cavern. He left her at the entrance.

"You know the way. Hashemi waits."

Khadija faced the darkness nervously. How the men lived buried in the ground, she didn't know. One of the frequent earthquakes could crush them or trap them. But each did what they must, she supposed. She took a deep breath and stumbled into the darkness, her hand trailing the stone wall beside her.

The darkness went on too long, her fear bubbling inside her like a pot almost to boil. In the darkness she might have taken a wrong turn. Fear clogged her breath. Tears rose in her eyes. She was lost in the cavern. Lost and no one would find her.

Allah, she was strong! She swiped at her tears. This was the emotional weakness that had led to her shame. She was not like this. Allah had a purpose for her.

Suddenly there was light. Hope.

She fought back tears of relief as she stumbled into the room where all the crates had been stored. Most of them were gone. Abdullah Hashemi looked up from his reading, his features shadowed in the lantern light.

Nodding, he lit a second lantern and led her into the second tunnel.

She knew they were at the cell even without the light. The air filled with the stench of burned flesh and copper like English pence.

The lantern swung shadows around the room where Michael Bellis lay splayed over the wooden bench. New purple-blue bruising masked his handsome face. Worse, horrific, blackened circles pocked his stomach and nipples and the tops of his feet—cigarette burns like she'd seen on abused children in London. Charred flesh wept near the bandages on his chest. There was no sign of movement, barely the rise and fall of his chest.

She rounded on Hashemi.

"I left him beginning to heal."

"He was well enough to question."

"He was weak. His wound is infected—has infected his whole body, and you do this?"

She went to the mutilated man's side even as she wondered what she was doing. She worked for Hashemi. This was *why* she saved Michael Bellis. But there were medical oaths she had taken.

"If you want him dead, don't bother with a doctor. Just do this again. He'll not trouble you long."

At least the man's chest rose and fell, regular as sunrise.

"You dare to question me?"

Her anger turned to fear. Grabbing the medical bag, she knelt beside Michael Bellis.

"I'll need hot water."

"There's no one to get it."

She turned back to him and hated the arrogant carriage of his head, the haughty hook of his nose. He was no Afghani, no matter that he said he fought for her country.

"Sometimes one must do what one must—in the service of Islam—and if you want him to live."

She turned back to the Michael Bellis, hoping her little barb would get the result she wanted.

When Hashemi left she almost collapsed, then lifted back her *burka* and set to work. The man was still strong, *Inshallah*, even after what had been done to him.

She lifted his eyelids and the pupils reacted. Good. The stench was so strong she could almost taste the burned flesh, but she'd seen burn victims before.

The lantern's light swung shadows across the room and across Michael Bellis's face as if death was trying to get in.

She would not let it. Hashemi had brought her here because he needed a doctor, and a doctor she would be if it would earn her the knowledge she sought.

She focused on her patient. Blood had pooled into his wrists and hands. The bindings cut into the swelling so his fingers were blood-red sausages. She hoped they had gone numb.

Using the scalpel, she sawed through the rope. When his arms were free, he groaned and slipped. When his legs were loose he toppled to the floor. Khadija dropped the scalpel to roll him over.

An elbow slammed her to the floor.

Michael Bellis knelt above her, hand on her throat. Pale eyes held only hunger and a promise that froze her struggle.

His other hand produced the scalpel.

"I should kill you," he said.

Chapter 18

Michael knew he should just follow through on his threat. Khadija's hate was as clear as her fear. She only kept him alive so he could be tortured again until he told everything in his need to leap into the cleansing abyss of death.

He had been so close he could almost see what waited beyond.

A warm breeze and peace. There had to be peace there, because there sure as hell hadn't been any in this life.

And now she'd brought him back again.

Khadija squirmed in his hold and he watched her calculate her chances. Such darkness in this woman. A symbol of Yaqub's death; or Yaqub's revenge?

He glanced at the tunnel, but no one came. So far his pitiful plan had worked. Feigning near-death had not been hard, and it had gotten the result he wanted. He yanked the woman up and fought the slow spin of the cave. The wound in his side throbbed like a bitch, but there was no time for that.

When he released her, Khadija scooted backwards, her *burka* left in a tangle on the floor, her scarf yanked around her neck. A wave of soft, black hair fell around her shoulders that left her vulnerable, desirable. But even under the high collared, back wool of her *jalabiyya*, he could see the angry heave of her breast. Fury filled her heavy-lidded eyes.

They were so like Yaqub's. He'd teased his friend many times about his "bedroom eyes" and how the British girls must have swooned over him when he was in medical school. He swallowed back the painful memory. Time to move.

Had Hashemi really gone for water, or did he wait in another part of the cave?

His legs went weak and he slumped onto the bench as they studied each other. Strength come back to him, please, because whatever he did, by the look of her it wasn't going to be easy.

"How many?" he demanded.

"How many what?" She almost spit her answer and it could have made him smile in another setting.

"Men in the cave. How many?"

"I—I only saw Hashemi." The peaks of color in her cheeks were fading to white, her eyes huge and dark. "Please—let me go. My father needs me."

Michael smiled at the ploy.

"And does your father know who your friends are?"

"My father's blind." Her full lips hardened, telling what he already knew. Mohammed Siddiqui had no idea what his daughter did. He dared not think of how Yaqub would be shamed.

"So you know who you work for? What you do?"

"I work for my people. For Allah."

Michael winced at the words that had justified so much evil. It was hard enough to think, let alone argue such beliefs. She knew Hashemi and condoned his atrocities. This would be more difficult than he'd thought, but he needed to get out where there was light and hope and life.

Soon. He stood and fought his swaying.

"Get up."

She stayed where she was.

God, his head was so fuzzy. He needed air.

"Get. The. Fuck. Up."

"What are you going to do?"

"What do you think?" In one stride he crossed the room. Pain. Pain in his feet. The burns on their soles.

Didn't matter.

He hauled her up, ignored her fists on his chest. He trapped her blows between them as he inhaled the faint scent of citrus and warm woman. A sudden memory of marigolds and golden dust on the hills almost made him release her.

Almost.

She struggled until he brought up the scalpel. Then fear bloomed larger in her wide-set eyes.

"The way I see it," he grumbled, "I've got three choices. One, I take you with me and hope they treat you as a hostage they want alive. The second is I leave you behind so they can blame you for my escape. I can't imagine they'll be gentle. Or I can kill you myself, but I'm leaning towards option one. What d'you think?"

It was a stupid choice, he knew, but he wouldn't be the reason Mohammed Siddiqui lost another child.

"My father needs me now."

"You're not with him now. He'll manage, though he'll worry. But then, he'd worry if he knew what you did, wouldn't he?"

Suddenly he held a hell-cat. Somehow she got a hand loose. She clawed at his eyes. She kicked at him, punched the wounds she knew pocked his chest. She was stronger than he thought, or else he was weaker than he'd realized.

He grabbed her fists, twisted them behind her until she moaned, but she was still fighting mad.

"My father forgets his duty. He sells out to foreigners—like you. Bastard *Amrikaayi*."

She spat the words. She barely missed stomping his bare foot and he jerked up on her arms until she cried out.

"Darlin', you've got a thing or two to learn about manners."

He pulled her into him until the trim muscle of her buttocks was against his groin. He forced her to pick up the medical pack, then he slung it over his shoulder and pushed her ahead of him into the tunnel. The pack bumped against his injured side.

"My *burka*."

"You'll have to make do with a scarf."

"*Galamjam*," she swore. He leaned into her, inhaling the scent of her hair.

"Does your father know you've got such a mouth?"

She twisted in his hold. "Just how far do you think you'll get in the condition you're in?"

"As far as my own personal doctor can get me. Now shut up."

Her chin came up in frustrating defiance. "I won't treat you."

"I said, shut up."

The tunnel echoed. The air carried the scent of dampness from deep inside the hills and the scent of her fear. He clamped his hand over her mouth as they reached the main room. He peered around the corner. Empty, except for a large crate with Cyrillic lettering. He needed a weapon— something more than this bloody scalpel.

He dragged her forward and released her left arm.

"Open it."

Her lips set in a straight line—until he twisted her right arm up a little farther. She pushed the lid back.

Ammunition, boxes of it, but no rifles. He swore and scanned the room again. An ornately bound Quran—that was it. Well, the Word was the biggest weapon, wasn't it?—firing up a *jihad* that was sweeping the world.

He grabbed a *petu* from where it was discarded in the corner and found a treasure underneath. His boots, discarded for some reason. Perhaps they were too big for anyone here.

Still holding her arm, he stuffed his feet inside and forced Khadija to tie them. Ignore the pain. Ignore the fact it would be immeasurably worse taking the boots off once the wounds had oozed into the leather.

He pulled the *petu* over his shoulders to hide the tattered remains of his *salwar kameez*, then pushed Khadija towards the next tunnel. In the darkness she stumbled and her body temperature increased.

Afraid of the dark are you, little one? Good. As long as you're afraid, you'll be easier to control.

They pushed onto the sunlit mountainside where Michael hauled them around a boulder and leaned against the heated stone. The hillside seemed to tilt. The sudden light blinded. Only adrenaline kept him upright.

How long had he been here? The blue sky and dry hillside gave no clue. But they did to his location. Feyzabad—he remembered the way the mountains had slid away from the road when he was a prisoner in the Jeep. Feyzabad sat in a valley like that and Feyzabad explained how Khadija was here.

If he was right, there had to be a phone nearby. He could get the message out. He pushed Khadija ahead of him onto the trail.

"You're not going to get away. They'll see us."

"Not if I can help it."

A narrow defile led down the steep flank of mountain scree. Beyond that lay a copse of trees. Golden leaves. How much time had passed? Shit, the attack on the Chinese reactor could happen any day now.

Fear pushed him faster, until Khadija stumbled, slid on the loose rock, and almost pulled them both down. He slowed. At the copse of trees he stopped briefly. Golden leaves rattled overhead. He could smell the snow coming, even this far out of the Pamirs. Time had passed without him. *Soon.*

Beyond the wind in the trees came the comforting sounds of civilization. Jeep horn. Truck dieseling. The cries of men. The scent of salt and charcoal in the air.

He had been right about Feyzabad and right about the phone. In the city they would be loading salt and lapis at the old caravanserai. When he was last here five years ago, they had donkey-packed the goods over the mountains into Pakistan—a trip of two weeks from the border. Longer from here.

At the sound of voices he drew Khadija deeper into the trees and clamped his hand over her mouth. "Don't try anything."

He could feel her rebellion as the voices came closer. He should have left her trussed in the cave. Here, she was nothing but a threat—and she'd slow him down. But he dared not leave her here. She'd tell them his condition and which direction he headed.

A simple answer existed.

Kill her. A simple twist of his wrists would break her lovely neck. Her eyes locked on his as if reading his thoughts. Yaqub's eyes.

"Shit."

He looked at the sky. Mohammed Siddiqui had experienced enough loss. Killing his daughter was out of the question. There was no help for it, then—taking her with him was the only option.

The voices barred the direct route to town and there wasn't enough cover to wait for Hashemi and his cronies to pass so he marched her through the trees. When the voices came closer, he swore and pushed faster.

Brush tore at the baggy remains of his *salwar kameez*. There was no way he could trust her. His only hope was to get her away and then release her in Feyzabad. It wasn't that far.

Then she bit his hand. Her elbow found his side.

Breath whooshed from his lungs. His hand released her and she screamed.

He barely held onto her wrist as he fought back the pain. Eyes blinded, like a fool he dragged her after him through the trees. Just leave her behind. She was Mohammed Siddiqui's daughter.

"Help!" she screamed again and he yanked her to him, slammed his hand over her mouth once more.

"Do you think they won't blame you for my escape?"

Her eyes flashed fury. "Then shut up."

A shot parted the air near his head and exploded in an aspen trunk. Another hit the medical pack he carried, almost tearing it from his grasp. He'd already left one Siddiqui behind. Hew wasn't leaving another.

He dragged her through the trees, fighting the struggling woman, his weakness, and his anger. Dammit, they were forcing him eastward across the mountain slope, away from the city and safety. There were few good roads, little vehicle traffic, and little-to-no chance of communication eastward. He needed to go south or west to get the warning out.

The trees ended in an open slope and battered stone fences—at least down to the road and the river. Behind came his pursuers. They were closing on his position.

A sound of diesel and a cloud of dust spoke of a truck heading east from Feyzabad. It might not be where he wanted to go, but a ride would get them out of range of gunfire. He could come back to town after dark and release Siddiqui's daughter then.

He dragged her down slope, his body waiting for the shot, the wounding, the death…. The woman stumbled, unwilling, beside him. Pain hitched each stride, but he was fucking stronger than this. With his training he should be able to do this in a heartbeat.

Dust outraced the truck as it labored up from the river. A shout came from behind just as the truck crested the hill. It was one of the late model trucks with brightly painted wood slatting walling the cargo deck. There would be cover in the cab or in the cargo area.

Michael half-dragged the woman over a stone fence that lined the road and waved to the truck. The sound of the down shift was music to his ears. Upslope, two men cleared the trees—Hashemi and Farhad. Both carried AK-47s. A hail of bullets slammed into the stone wall. He and Khadija were sitting ducks, so the poor aim meant Hashemi still wanted his information.

The truck ground to a stop and Michael yanked open the passenger door. He passed the struggling woman up, but bullets slammed into the driver's door. The driver swore and stomped his foot on the gas. Khadija tumbled back into Michael's arms and the passenger door slammed shut.

"Wait!"

The driver didn't. The weight of the full load slowed the truck's getaway, but he wasn't going to let them on.

Michael dragged Khadija after the truck, fighting to keep it between them and Hashemi, but the damn vehicle was picking up speed.

Soon there'd be no shelter. Nothing but recapture.

The truck passed them and Hashemi yelled just as Michael spied an opening in the rear of the truck. Space between bales of cloth and dry goods.

Michael threw Khadija into the back of the truck, threw in the medical pack, and leapt in behind her. Pain shot through his side. Bullets exploded the wood around him. Close. Too close. He pressed further into the truck, shoving his prisoner before him as Hashemi and Farhad made the road. Bullets peppered Michael's hiding place, pinged on aluminum pots and pans like some horrific hail, and tore into crates and blankets.

Michael swore at the truck's sluggish acceleration. When the bullets stopped, Michael chanced a look back. Hashemi and Farhad loped towards town. They'd pursue soon enough, and the city would be aswarm with informants. Feyzabad no longer offered a way to get the message out.

He glanced at the woman at him. The alternative would not be easy.

Chapter 19

Panic woke Khadija. Where was she?

The stench of diesel, the roar of the engine, and the lurch as the truck shifted down all conspired to remind her. Abduction and anger. She twisted to glare at Michael Bellis.

His chin bobbed on his chest in exhausted slumber. The iron scent of his fever filled the small space where they crouched. It was hours since they leapt onto the truck, but the pursuit he had predicted—her prayed-for chance of escape—had not yet arrived.

She should have pushed him off; his injuries weakened him enough. Then she looked at her hands in resignation. They were small compared to Michael Bellis's fists.

Praise be to Allah, Lord of Worlds…

…Show me your straight path,

not the path of those who earn your wrath

She was kidding herself if she thought she could hurt him. She was a messenger. A woman who wanted revenge and so she pretended to be a soldier.

nor those who go astray.

It was a painful admission. At least she didn't help the enemy who slumbered beside her. The truck bucked through a pothole and he winced, his copper-tinged hair falling over his brow.

He'd dragged her into this danger. *He* was why they had shot at her. *Amrikaayi.*

He was also the one who had shoved her into the deepest corner between the bales of cloth and shielded her from bullets. She still felt the hard press of his chest, the warm strength of his arms around her, but damnation she wouldn't have even been in danger if he hadn't forced her here.

She would not feel grateful!

She swiped at her arms, her torso. The scent of him—man and fever—still filled her nostrils.

His slack body bumped against the bales of clothing. His face had the look of the boy he once must have been and she softened at his vulnerability. But when they'd first climbed aboard he'd pulled a new, loose-fitting, cotton *salwar kameez* from one of the bales and changed right in front of her.

The memory rekindled her anger. The way he'd looked at her…. Laughed at her, more like it. He was so unlike soulful Mizra. Michael Bellis was a man to be feared in too many ways.

"Allah, help me to earn my honor. Let me help my country revive like a phoenix from ashes."

She was kidding herself.

She was no soldier. What she really wanted was to curl up into a ball and have her father protect her—but he couldn't. He couldn't even avenge Yaqub.

A small moan escaped Michael Bellis and her first instinct was to help him. Or was it just that she wished to see his bare flesh?

She pressed her fists to her eyes, hated questioning herself. The man eroded her faith. Let him die of his wounds. Let her escape.

She peeked past him out the back of the truck. Dust had hidden the road behind, but now the truck labored slowly up a hill.

Green fields ran beside the road and down to a glittering slash of river. The moisture in the air only reinforced her thirst.

Cragged, brown slopes ran up and up—like layers on one of those hideous Western wedding cakes—to peaks higher than any she'd seen before. Poplar and aspen made a line of green-gold in the thin soil along the base of the barren slopes. The road stretched back, a long, uncoiling snake. In the distance a V-shaped cloud rose from a vehicle moving fast.

Khadija strained to see. She scrambled to her feet. If it was Hashemi and his friends she would be rescued. She just needed to get free.

And she needed a *chador*.

She hauled at the black edge of one caught in a bale stacked beside her. She would be decently covered when they found her. Finally the garment came free and with relief she swept the stolen cloth over her head and pulled the front closed around her. The truck engine sounded different now and the vehicle felt like it picked up speed. If she was going to escape, it had to be now.

Quietly, carefully, she stepped over Michael and clung to a steel stanchion that held the wooden siding in place. One more step and she'd be free. Just another step and she'd be returning to her father. A pothole almost sent her sprawling.

"What the hell are you doing?"

He was on his feet faster than she had thought a man could move; his fist tangled in her *chador*.

The truck's speed had increased. She had to go now.

She turned, but his fingers clamped on her arm. He wouldn't let go, but he couldn't hold her. She was strong enough and he was injured.

She leapt, and the road slammed into her.

Something heavy smacked into her back.

Scalding gravel. Pain in her hands, her side, her knees. When she quit rolling, she fought the pain until Michael Bellis yanked her to her feet. She jerked free and straightened her *chador*.

"What the fucking hell were you thinking?"

His fury was clear and his hands were fist. She thought he might hit her.

"What do you think? Ridding myself of you, *Amrikaayi*! Going back to my father."

"We're in the middle of fucking nowhere." He motioned around them.

"You might be, but my friends are coming." She turned down the road.

On one side, a steep slope led down to the river, and on the other, the slope became a mountainside. Whoever came was hidden by a jut of mountain, but in the quiet of the truck's departure came the faint sound of another motor.

Michael Bellis grabbed the back of her *chador* and hauled her towards the river.

"You don't need me," she said as she tried to pull free. "I'll only slow you down."

"Damn straight," he growled, but he never let go.

Chapter 20

Every f'ing step of the way the damned woman fought him. Over the lip of the road into the loose scree of the bank where the footing shifted until the bank became a river of its own, and took them with it.

Everything moved. Khadija lost her balance and pulled him down. They slid-slipped-tumbled down, down the twenty feet to the river's narrow bank. When they stopped all Michael could feel was the pain in his side. It stole his strength.

But she was already getting her feet under her.

Dammit, he was too slow. It took all his will to catch her ankle and he paid for it with her boot in his chest. His vision exploded. He held on, but barely managed to grab an arm.

A frigging hell-cat, to be sure—difficult to hold on to even if he was healthy. Now it was only the bloody *chador* trapping her arms that allowed him to restrain her.

"You've done this to yourself," he said, trapping her arms between them. "I was going to leave you in Baharak—the next town—but I can't leave you here. They'll know where I left the road and where to hunt me."

"I hope they shoot you. You're no better than an animal."

"And where is the dishonor in the noble falcon or the leopard of the mountains? *I died an animal and was born a man.*" He grinned.

"*Galamjam!*" Carpet trader.

It was such a quaint epithet his smile broadened, but the sound of the Jeep engine was closer. Along the river there was no cover—just the tumble of gravel down the slope to the water's edge. They had to reach cover.

Across the river, a green field rolled to the base of the mountains. Five horses grazed there and there were trees for cover on the far side of the field.

Somewhere southeast of here the Darya-ye Kowkcheh—one of Badakhshan's five rivers—joined the Kokcha on its route to find the Amu Darya. If he could find the Kowkcheh, he could follow it southwest towards safety. If he could make it to the Panjshir Valley and the leader who had taken over after the assassination of Massoud, the Lion of Panjshir, he would have communication.

He dragged her to the river and she swore at him again.

"Watch your mouth. You should be praising Allah. The water's low at the end of summer."

"Don't you dare use his name! You defile it as your kind defile Afghanistan." The Jeep was coming fast.

He chuckled as he pushed her into the torrent. The swift water quickly reached his thighs as he followed, the current making it hard to stand. Her *chador* flowed around her, billowing like a dark cloud, until unsteady footing sent her down, her head sucked under the surface.

Michael hauled her up as she spluttered and splashed him with her free hand as he half-carried her to shore.

"You okay?"

"As if you care."

The green grass filled the air with a sweetness he'd wondered if he'd ever smell again. Michael dragged his captive towards the trees. The five horses raised their heads as she protested. Dammit, they had to move faster. Just reach the trees. Just reach their cover and he might keep his life.

The Jeep came around the jut of mountain and he heard the engine rev, saw it fishtail to a stop as it came even with them.

"Come on!" He ran, fighting the woman every step of the way. He considered abandoning her, but knew they'd kill her or worse. Hashemi was ruthless and vindictive. Shouts came from two men with Kalashnikovs.

Just move. A few more yards and they'd be beyond the four-hundred-yard range of the weapons. Just a few more yards. A few more.

The woman stumbled and he half turned to support her.Instead of thanks, she plowed a hand into his injured side.

His lungs emptied. The sky went dark as his knees gave and she twisted free, hefted her *chador* and ran—back the way they had come.

"No!" He heaved himself up. These men were not here to help her. She was a tool to be discarded, no more.

The first bullets slammed the earth in front of Khadija.

"No! It's me!"

She kept running. The bloody woman was going to run right into their fire.

A bullet tore through the edge of her *chador*. Another exploded earth close to her right foot, but she still didn't stop. Michael chased her, swearing at her unerring belief these men would help her. Hashemi's men wouldn't miss forever—it was only because they were almost at the end of the weapon's range.

He tackled her, covering her with his body. Softness under him. Vulnerability even as she struggled and bullets pinned them down. They wanted him alive. They wanted his information.

Across the field, one of the armed men started down to the river. "Come on."

He grabbed her and rolled once, twice, keeping her close to his chest. Just get out of range. Then he sprang to his feet and dragged her with him. At least some of the fight seemed to have gone out of her.

Just reach the trees. Follow them southward around the jut of the next mountain—that should give onto the Baharak Valley and the juncture of the two rivers. Reach the Kowkchek. That had to be his focus. Don't care about the woman. Leave her here because she'd just slow him down and he had to move fast.

But he couldn't leave her for too many reasons and too many debts. Life was cheap or precious in this country.

The horses thundered across the field. The scree on the river slope had taken down their pursuer. He lay at the river edge. It gave them a chance.

The light changed, dappling the earth as Michael dragged them among the pale trunks of the aspens. The golden leaves applauded his efforts. Shadows dampened the sun's heat.

Michael propped himself, panting, against a tree and peered back the way they'd come. Hashemi himself was climbing down the slope from the road, his black turban dull in the sunlight. His man lay beside the river holding his leg.

"*Inshallah*, the man is hurt. It may give us a chance."

He turned back to Khadija. She stood quietly, shrouded in black. The cloth clung to the form of her face and shoulders and down over her *jalabiyya*. She swayed as if all fight had been stripped from her.

"We have to go. They'll be after us," he said gently.

For once she said nothing, but that only left him pondering what scheme she hatched. He caught her hand and hurried them along a path. Shepherds and their flocks had worn the trail into the base of the hills over the thousands of years this countryside had been inhabited.

Leaves scattered the ground. The air smelled of dust and the tang of fall. Just how long had he been a prisoner? The sunlight gradually dipped towards the western mountains behind them and shadows lengthened. Only the sound of their breathing and the twitter of the sparrows carried. It could almost lull one into thinking they were safe.

He knew better.

In Afghanistan danger could come from anywhere. Even your closest friends could betray you, if they thought doing so would benefit their family or clan.

But he had no family.

When his father died, that lack of family had made Michael perfect for this work. No ties meant there was no one who could be used against him.

They had come to him at Harvard, catching him as he sat studying beneath a tree on the spreading green lawn of the Old Yard between Matthews and Grays Hall. It was three months after his father had died in an accident in Afghanistan.

Michael considered his future. He could take an advanced degree in languages. He could take over his father's business. Neither option was particularly appealing. Neither would meet his need to somehow move—change—make a difference—except for the fact that the business would return him to Afghanistan. He still missed the country and its people.

He closed his eyes and turned his face to the sun. Maybe he shouldn't worry about it. Maybe he should just wait for the choice to come to him.

"Michael Bellis?"

He had looked up at the figure that draped shadow across his sun. The man stood so his face was hidden, and Michael had a sudden sense of unsteadiness in the earth. He nodded.

The man squatted in front of him, revealing a hard face under grey hair. "I'm Ron Hall. A prof of yours told me I'd probably find you here."

Michael studied the stranger, alarm bells going off. There was something lean and hard about the man. Something in his gaze that would not take no for an answer.

"I was a business associate of your father," Ron Hall continued. "My partners and I wondered if you might be interested in continuing your family's association with our firm."

Michael had gone with his father to business meetings many times—both in Afghanistan and America. But this man—he had an edge more like the Afghani Mujehaddin he'd seen in Iran after the Russian invasion. Men fighting for their country's freedom.

"What kind of association?" Michael asked cautiously. He had his suspicions. His father had always disappeared for short times on their business trips, had occasionally had business meetings and phone calls he would not allow Michael to attend.

"Come on, Michael. You're bored. It's written all over your face. Even your profs have noticed. What've you got ahead of you? More school? You can only bury yourself here so long. Besides, you've got other talents. My partners and I—we'd like you to keep up your father's import/export business. We'd like you to go back to Iran and Afghanistan—on our

behalf."

They'd talked to his professors.

Michael looked at the man's eyes. They were brittle blue—too much like his father's—always assessing. It had been that assessment that always made Michael feel like he could not measure up. In consequence he'd always excelled at school, in sports, with women.

"Who the hell are you?"

Ron Hall smiled. "Good question. Now why don't we take a walk and we can discuss who I am and who you might be."

That unsteady feeling again, but the mystery of Ron Hall raised a surge of adrenaline that made him feel suddenly alive, suddenly as if he knew his future.

He had stood.

A year later he had been in Afghanistan again. Then he met Mohammed Siddiqui and Yaqub. Michael grimaced and tightened his grip on Khadija. Over fifteen years the Siddiquis had become family.

The mountain slope turned back on itself, ending in a pile of scree and the broad valley that spread eastward towards Baharak. In the east, the sky was indigo fading to black. Only the peaks of the Hindu Kush were lit like the faces of ancient gods.

This country was like that—full of the works of God, as if the divine lay close to the surface here. Perhaps that was why so many of the world's religions had lain across this land at one time or another. Perhaps that was what had brought him back so many years before.

There you go, again, Bellis. Lying to yourself. You came for the adrenaline—to feel alive.

Smoke hung over distant Baharak and the smaller villages that sat along the blue ribbon that gleamed in the last of the daylight. The Varduj River. Nearer, a second thread of blue joined the Varduj.

The Kowkcheh. Follow it south and he might have a chance. The world might have a chance. He followed the course of the river with his eyes.

Now would be the time to leave Khadija—if he was going to. From here, she could make her way back to Feyzabad where Mohammed waited. The old man would be frantic about her.

He glanced back. The wind pressed the *chador* around her showing hints of the body he recalled from her father's house. She was slim, feminine even, with the green-brown eyes of a fawn—in the unguarded moments when one could see past the anger. And she was the enemy. He had no business taking the enemy with him.

Soon.

Had the events that would start the war occurred? Had the rhetoric before war begun? He was flying blind here.

To the east, only the first stars glittered over the distant peaks of Tajikistan. Beyond them lay China and the nuclear reactor.

"Has there been news?" he asked.

"News?" She almost spit the word.

"From China. Of war?"

"The only war is the one against Islam."

He rolled his eyes. "Who taught you that?" he muttered.

It was hopeless arguing against it. Eastward, though, the war was coming—he felt it in his blood like the precursor shock to a major earthquake. Any serious conflict between America and China could easily go nuclear.

Leave her, the logical part of him said. Your task is too important. But he knew he couldn't let her go.

Chapter 21

"We'll stop here," Michael Bellis said from out of the dark. His hand tightened on Khadija's wrist and she winced at his bruising hold. He'd brought them to a halt by an old stone fence close by a river. The scent of the water and green grass filled the night air.

Khadija sagged to the ground, the pain in her leg and her exhaustion almost more than she could bear. She wondered how Michael Bellis kept going.

She'd never walked for so long or so far, and certainly not when injured. Her feet were sweating in the Western boots she wore, but the rest of her was shivering. Shocky cold that made the darkness something to be feared.

She didn't like it in the darkness and that made it hard to breathe. Even in Feyzabad there were fires in the street and braziers cooking kebabs, the faces of the men illuminated in the ruddy light. In Kaabul during power outages there were candles in her father's house and the blue gleam of the propane stove as dinner was prepared.

The wind blew through the night-darkened fields they had traversed, carrying the scent of wood smoke and sheep and late melon ready for harvest. Overhead was the steady swoop of bat wings and the eerie cry they made. Her shivers deepened.

She rubbed the circulation back into her hand, trying to rid herself of the feel of him. His touch, the fact she was alone with him spelled disaster. If she only dared remove the *chador* she could decide what to do. With the dousing, the *chador*'s headband had tightened around her forehead. That made it hard to think. Or maybe it was the pain in her leg.

They had shot her.

Hashemi and Farhad had shot her.

It had probably been an accident, a stray shot when they were aiming at Michael Bellis. She kept telling herself they could not afford his escape.

She glanced up at him as he moved through the darkness seeking wood and old grass to make a fire. The way he moved—his *Amrikaayi* pride showed in everything he did regardless of the mess he'd made of her plans.

This was supposed to be a simple trip northward. Help her father and deliver a message and learn what she needed. So what if Mirri and Mizra and Ratbil had asked her to do more? So what if Hashemi had forced her to use her medical knowledge? Michael Bellis was the one who had turned everything on its head and brought her to…this.

He returned from beyond the stone wall carrying an armload of sticks and branches.

"The nights are cold here. There's not much fuel, but I think we can manage a small fire. The wall will shelter it and us."

She knew he was right, but turned away as he fumbled in the medical pack.

"Are there matches in here?"

She ignored him. The medical pack held what she needed to treat her leg. The pain was bad enough she didn't know if she could stand, and the last thing she needed was infection. She thought of the supplies still secreted in the pockets of her *jalabiyya* and wondered if the vial of antibiotic had survived her falls. By feel, it seemed intact, buried among the syringes and dressings.

A grunt came from him and a match flickered to life. The acrid scent caught in her nose. He held the flame to a bit of dried grass under a pile of tinder. The fire caught and soon the darkness receded to beyond the circle of boulders, revealing her captor in the warm glow.

Michael Bellis eased himself down against a boulder pushed near the fence. His craggy face was half-hidden in shadow, but she could see pain cross his features as he settled his side against the stone. When he caught her glance, the pain smoothed away.

"You did a good job of this dressing. One of mine wouldn't have lasted through today."

She didn't bother answering. She'd simply had training and been forced to use it on him.

"I was going to free you, but I don't dare, now. Hashemi's going to be out for blood. He'll blame you."

"So he'll take his anger out on someone else."

She turned back to Michael Bellis, hating him for the truth of his words. Hashemi—truth be told, he terrified her. He was the kind of man who would follow through on his threats to her father.

"Your father must have soldiers with him and he'll stay in a well-guarded home. He'll be safe."

Her gaze jerked back to him. How did he always know what she thought? She studied her captor through the lattice of her veil. He was everything she hated, and yet he seemed to know things. And he was strong. Very strong to do what he had done today.

"I heard Hashemi and Farhad talking about your father." Again he knew her thinking.

She had to admit there was something extraordinary about this man. He must be in pain and yet he acted like there was nothing wrong, had not even limped though the burn marks on the balls of his feet would have halted anyone else.

A sound startled her and she looked past him to the night.

"Horses. There's a group of them in the field. They're probably coming for water."

How dare he be so calm when he'd brought them into danger, had left her father alone, had destroyed her delicate, reconstructed honor. A woman alone with a foreign man—even Mizra wouldn't want her now.

"So what do we do now, oh Great *Amrikaayi* Leader? Sit in the middle of a field and await some great *Amrikaayi* general to rescue you? Perhaps a helicopter will swoop out of the sky?" She spat the words, pulled her *chador* closer around her and tried to curl her knees to her chest. The movement made her gasp.

"Are you alright?" He was at her side in a movement like the smooth flow of a leopard. She could smell his heat.

"I'm fine."

"I know the sound of pain, Khadija."

There was concern in those pale, hungry eyes and it made her angry. If he'd just left things alone, she wouldn't be hurt. She wouldn't be here.

Michael Bellis might be dead. She shuddered. The explosion in the Kaabul market had been enough. She didn't want anyone else dead.

"I can deal with it myself."

"Spoken like a true Afghan."

The sarcasm made her want to slap him. That was what she hated most about *this* man in particular. He made fun of her and her faith and her people at the same time his presence and strength made her feel—safe?

He didn't go away. Instead he crouched between her and the flame.

"You're blocking the heat."

He didn't move. "We're out here together. If you're hurt, we need to do something about it."

"You're hurt. You do nothing for that."

He shrugged. "I can manage. It's you we need to take care of."

He touched the edge of her *chador* and she jerked away. A gasp escaped her. She was dishonored enough. She would not make things worse.

"That's it. To hell with your propriety." He caught the edge of her *chador*. She fought to hold it in place, but he wouldn't be stopped. He forced her fists open and lifted the *chador* until she felt the full impact of his gaze on her.

She suddenly realized she was sobbing "No. No. No. No," like some small child. She swiped the tears away.

"It's not proper. It's bad enough they forced me to care for you. It's bad enough we're out here together. What will people say?"

His pity felt hot on her skin. She should not be crying. She was a soldier, wasn't she? A warrior. *A messenger.*

"I can care of myself," she ended, weakly.

His gaze was locked on her *jalabiyya*. A rough tear in the long coat allowed the paler color of her *salwar kameez* to show through—except it was wet red in the firelight. A black stain ran over the left side of the dark fabric.

"Allah, above." His voice was soft. He didn't wait for her response. His hands were already slipping open the row of buttons on the coat, flipping it open as she cringed back. He swore.

She numbly considered how the blood stained her *salwar kameez* from thigh to ankle. She realized what the moisture in her boot must be. Not sweat.

"I need to see your leg." His voice rumbled with anger.

"I can take care of myself." But her breath came in quick, sharp gasps and she knew she was in more shock than she'd realized. The night buzzed in her ears.

"Like hell. We've got a hard journey ahead and there's no way you'll make it like this. Now let me see."

She fought to slow her breathing.

She shook her head, though it was foolish.

Her fingers picked at the trouser fabric embedded in her flesh, but her hands were shaking. Then Michael Bellis's large hands eased them away. He caught her gaze, held it.

"The Chosen One came to bring intimacy and compassion." He gently turned her leg towards the firelight.

Pain and she wanted to cry, wanted to close her eyes, but she must watch what he did, make sure he did things correctly.

"You've got two choices. I tear the trouser, or you haul them down. Your choice."

Allah, the ignobility of having this man see her private flesh. But to tear the trouser meant she would be bared to him for as long as they traveled together. It would mean she would be too ashamed to escape.

"Look away."

He turned to the flame, leaving her to struggle one leg out of the trousers and then carefully cover herself with the *chador* and *salwar kameez*.

When she was ready he turned back and she felt herself color, wondering if he'd truly looked away. She flinched as he gently eased the tattered cloth from the gaping lips of the wound. Those, he pulled apart.

The world went dark. Then his hands left her skin.

"I think you got lucky. It wasn't a bullet that hit you, thank the Prophet. One must have shattered a rock. Shrapnel burst the skin, but I don't think it's left anything inside." He raised his brows in his infuriating manner. "Do you concur, Doctor?"

It took all her strength not to swear at him, not to tell him what she thought.

"I'm not a doctor yet."

"Aah, so you intend to go through with your training, then? Things have changed since we met in Kaabul."

She looked away, uncertain where her statement came from. It was so hard to think and she was so cold her shivers seemed to go on forever.

He pulled a worn plastic bag from the medical pack and left her for the river, returning with clear water running from a thousand tiny holes in the bag. The cold water washed away the worst of the dried blood and left her fighting for breath. Then he dug in the medical pack, frowning at the stale-dated antiseptic cream.

"Dammit, no antibiotics. No proper dressings either. How the hell do you run a *jihad* like this?" He grinned up at her. "Sorry. But just using a strip off my tunic isn't going to cut it for this."

Freezing, Khadija leaned her head back against the cold stone. Cold and death just like everything in Afghanistan. Cadavers and ruins and bleeding bodies and she was one of them.

Just let him do whatever he would and let her be a burden to slow him down enough so Hashemi would catch him. Then she could go home to Papa.

Her shaking hands pulled the dressings and the vial from her pocket before she could reconsider.

"Where the hell'd you get this?" His eyes glittered as he read the labels. "Standard U.S. Army issue."

She couldn't bear the question, his closeness. She closed her eyes as he tore open a package and then his hands were on her again. So intimate on her flesh, so close to her privates. Heat radiated from his hand up into her body.

"This is going to hurt."

He squeezed the lips of the wound together and sutured it in swift, certain stitches. When he was done she grudgingly had to admit she couldn't have done better.

"Just put a dressing on and I'll be fine," she said, fighting the pain and the way the darkness seemed to pulse in and out. She drowned in the darkness and in the feel of Michael Bellis's hands on her flesh.

Then everything went away.

Chapter 22

Rock grated against rock and Khadija's eyes flew open. The tickle of grass on her face. Above the stone fence was the watered blue sky that existed only before sunrise. The color of Michael Bellis's eyes.

She remembered where she was.

The sound of water over rocks was an incessant rush. Her nose and ears were cold. The *petu* thrown over her had a rime of frost but carried the scent of him.

She scrambled up—or tried to, as pain felled her into frosted grass. Her clothing was tangled around her, and she was weak, so weak. Everything from yesterday slammed into her and the pain was a sickness she could not withstand. She wanted to curl up and cry.

Michael Bellis had done this. Another sound and she huddled, seeking the strength of her anger. His hands had dishonored her again—no matter his gentleness and skill.

She glanced at the *petu* she'd thrown off.

And now he'd left her here—wherever *here* was.

Another crack of rock and she realized her problem was more immediate. She could not be found with her clothes half-off. She pulled her blood-caked trousers over her injured leg, fought to haul herself to her knees. All hells take Michael Bellis.

He had absconded like a thief in the night. Abandoning her like the world had abandoned Afghanistan when the Russians came. Fear and anger battled in her as the scent of horse brought her head up.

The steady pace of the hooves over rock told her it was not horses alone. Loose horses walked a few paces and stopped to graze, a few more paces, then more grass.

Using the fence as support, she sat up, her injured leg stretched before her. She was surprised the *jalabiyya* was buttoned to her chin. Hurriedly she covered her hair with her scarf. The *chador* she hauled over everything and sighed in relief as she pulled it tightly around her.

Inshallah, she would stand. Her fingers scrabbled and caught on the stone and she hauled herself up. Her breath caught at the pain, but finally she peered over the top of the wall.

The morning sun over the mountains placed long shadows on the glittering dewed grass. The glare half-blinded her, but through the haze of steam off the river, a ghost rider approached, leading a second horse.

She swallowed back a quaver of fear. He must be the herd's owner come to check them. *Inshallah*, he would help her.

"Help! Please help me!" She took an unsteady step away from the wall. "Please. I must get to Feyzabad. My father needs my help. Help me return to his house."

Her injured leg threatened to give, but she tottered forward. The rider stopped, silhouetted by sun.

"As good a story as any, I suppose."

Michael Bellis swung easily off his horse and Khadija's legs gave as she backpedaled. Not Michael Bellis. Not Michael Bellis of the gentle hands.

All the pain, and fear and confusion coalesced in her chest. She shouldn't think of this man in that way after what his kind had done. He was supposed to have left her. She wanted to go home. She wanted her father.

A sob rose unbidden and there he was at the head of the horses with that taunting grin on his face.

He laughed at her. By all the hells, he was laughing!

Laughing when she was furious and in pain and lost in the countryside with a man she dared not trust. She buried her face in her hands, thankful the *chador* covered the worst of her weeping.

Then he was kneeling in front of her.

"Khadija? What is it? Your leg?"

His voice was too soft, carried none of the sarcasm she expected from that damnable grin. He almost touched her, then stopped himself. The helplessness of his expression could have made her smile if she wasn't so—so—she didn't know what she was anymore.

Damn Michael Bellis and the way he confused her.

"I thought you left me to go home." She managed to keep the words steady. "But it was you."

Emotion ballooned to fill her chest again and she dug her fingernails into her palms. She tried to get up, but her damnable leg wouldn't work.

Ignoring his offer of assistance, she scrambled to stand, but each time her injured leg gave out.

Finally, he caught her elbow and she could have screamed her frustration as he lifted her up and tugged her *chador* into place while his lips wore that smirk she despised. Then he helped her back to the dead fire, leading the slow clop of the horses.

"Did you check your leg?"

"Did you check your wounds?" she retorted and knew she was being pissy.

"Actually, no. I was busy. I thought I'd ask you to take a look."

She turned to him, and the dammed grin was still there. Her hands closed to fists as she half-fell against the stone fence. She should refuse to be his doctor, but she recalled the touch of those gentle *galamjam* hands.

This morning he looked different. From somewhere he had found a finely felted wool vest and a *petu* he wore over his *salwar kameez*. A length of brown cloth had been wrapped around his head in a loose, Tajik-style turban. Over his shoulder hung an ancient-looking rifle, so he looked like any other Afghan she had seen in the north.

Except for the expectant blue eyes that were so unusual amongst her people.

"Been out stealing, have you?"

His steady gaze met hers.

"Actually, I paid rather more than I should have. Had to when I showed up looking like I did."

She hated herself for the way she remembered the muscles of his chest, as he left the horses grazing, stripped off the vest and shirt, then settled himself near the ashes of the fire.

Damn him for just assuming she'd help. But in the new sunlight his skin gleamed ruddy. The smooth expanse of chest read more like a roadmap of Afghanistan. The burn marks were weeping bomb craters rimmed in red. The blood-caked bandage on his side was like all the Afghan blood that had been spilled.

She sank down in front of him, and was forced to push her *chador* back from her face. She fought back awareness of his hungry gaze and focused on his injuries.

The livid color of his wounds was not normal—as if everything was going septic. Who knew what injury had been done to his ribcage and the chest cavity?

"You need a hospital."

Michael Bellis just glanced at the sky.

"Just check the wound and we'll leave."

"Then lift your arm."

She kept her voice professional and jerked the bandage loose, taking satisfaction in the quick intake of his breath. She would pay him back for her humiliation, but first there was the wound.

Its lips were bright pink, swollen, the skin around them red with broken capillaries. Red marks still ran down his side, though perhaps not so pronounced as before, but his skin was still hot and gave off the stench of rot. She grimaced.

"Not good?"

"There's infection. I think it should drain, but we've no equipment to do it properly and we don't dare leave it open in these conditions."

"Then just bandage it. We've been here too long."

She nodded, using one of the precious dressings to cover the wound, but her gaze kept slipping to his chest and abdomen. Michael started to pull on his shirt but she stopped him with a touch on his arm and motioned to the burns.

"You need those wounds cleaned and some of the chloramphenicol."

She was too forward. She was brazen. She was everything she'd come to hate in London.

He waited patiently as she cleaned his chest with river water and wiped the ancient antiseptic on the burns. When she retrieved the antibiotic, a slight question formed in his eyes.

"I stole it, all right? From the hospital."

"For me?"

There was that damned grin again. She stabbed the needle into his arm and was happy when he flinched. When she finished, he rubbed his bicep.

"I've had bullets hurt less going in."

Ignoring him, she went to discard the syringe, but he stopped her.

"Where we're going, that sort of thing is irreplaceable. We may need to reuse it."

She considered the syringe. All her training said you didn't reuse such a thing.

Just where was Michael Bellis taking her?

Chapter 23

Darkness no longer frightened Mohammed Siddiqui, but the question of his daughter's whereabouts did.

He had grown used to the darkness that had eaten all but a small, glowing porthole of his vision since the blindness was gifted upon him. He had found ways to cope through the use of his smell, his hearing, his sense of touch, and through his logic and the eyes of his son and daughter. Then Yaqub had been taken from him and still he had prevailed.

But with Khadija missing, the darkness suddenly seemed to smother whatever light he still had.

Hamidah, Ahmad Mali Kahn's eldest daughter, sat beside Mohammed in the Feyzabad police station, holding his hand as if she was Khadija. It had been three days since she went missing. Three days since Aisha came home with lies on her breath, telling her stories of Khadija.

Lies Ahmad Mali Khan had listened to.

Even the other women of the house had seemed to believe—Zahra almost too much, as if the disappearance of Mohammed's daughter was a battle cry of women's freedom. Only Hamidah had stayed silent. She had been there to help him through the three frightening days, though no one could quell the fears that kept him awake in the night.

Khadija, where are you? His fingers squeezed Hamidah's, seeking strength.

"Tell me again what you have found of my daughter?" He leaned forward in the chair Hamidah had pulled before the police commander's desk and heard the scrape of chair legs on rough floorboards.

The commander smelled of goat grease and naan and unwashed clothing—all overpowering the stench of Turkish tobacco that filled the police station. The man's wife should be disciplined for not caring properly for his things—but then, men did as they would, regardless of the woman's wants. Perhaps he preferred to live in filth.

"There's nothing to tell. The administrator's wife said she took your daughter for a walk. A man came to them and your daughter threw off her veil and went with him. These city women—they are not proper daughters of Islam. Allah forgive them, they do not know their place."

"My daughter is devout. She wears the burka." Mohammed tried to quiet the anger clenching his chest.

"*Aacha*. And we found such a thing on the road. It is evidence of her actions, I think. She rests in the arms of her latest lover. Who knows how many she has had?" The man clucked his tongue in false pity like a gossipy old woman.

"You have the *burka*? Is this true?" Mohammed spoke more to Hamidah than to the police officer. If he could hold the *burka* he would prove the lie. He knew the feel of the fabric from their long time together. He could even show the smooth place where his hand rested as she guided him. Hamidah's gloved hand squeezed his in answer.

"Then show it to me."

The scrape of the chair said the man shifted his position.

Mohammed had been shocked when Khadija arrived in Kaabul—not that she would wear a *burka* during the dangerous journey from Peshawar and over the Khyber Pass from Pakistan to Kaabul. The *burka* gave a slight advantage of safety. But then she had continued to wear the garment. It was one she had purchased in London, she said, made of finer cloth than most made in the factories of Pakistan or the sewing shops of Kaabul.

Hamidah lifted Mohammed's hand and placed it on soft cloth. He ran them down the fabric and a weight stole breath from his chest.

He pulled back the folds and ran his palm across the weave until his fingers found an almost smooth patch.

There was no breath, no air in the room. He jerked his hand away, spilling the fabric onto the floor.

"My daughter would not run off with a man. Someone has taken her. Someone has done this."

"There is no proof."

"Don't you listen? I know my daughter."

"Spoken like a father. But didn't you say she lived among the *kofr farangay*—the foreigners—for a time? How can a father know what is truly in his daughter's heart? A woman is like a piece of fruit, gleaming and good on the surface, but may be filled with rot in the core."

"My daughter is not."

"And you are a loving father who cannot believe the black truth."

Mohammed pushed himself up from his chair. "My daughter would not! Khadija would not!"

He felt himself sway under the weight of the smothering darkness. If she was lost to him....

But was she not already lost to him since she returned to Kaabul? The way they had argued about his old friend, Michael. She had seemed to hate the man, though they had barely met, and that was not the Khadija he had sent to England to study. That girl had been full of the questions that made a good scientist and doctor. That girl had been one who rejected dogma.

"Friend Siddiqui. I know you love your daughter. Every father does. But how can a father ever truly know his daughter's heart?"

All his doubts fell on his shoulders. Who knew the truth? This man had already made up his mind.

"Come, Hamidah. He will not help."

She caught his hand, placed it on her arm, just as Khadija had, but she was too short, her flesh too soft under the cloth. Allah, what have you done with my daughter? Please, keep her safe for me.

The cool air of the morning found his face when they stepped outside, but it did nothing to lift his sense of breathlessness. His legs wobbled under him and suddenly he was overcome with a sense of age and loss. Without Khadija he would be alone.

There would be no hope of his son-in-law going against tradition and moving into his home. There would be no grandchildren's laughter. None of Khadija's singing that had brought a smile to his face all the years of his life. There would be only silence to go along with the smothering darkness of his country.

Something had happened to his daughter in England.

What had happened to her now?

Chapter 24

Crack!

The recoil of the ancient rifle slammed into Michael's shoulder and sent shocks through his side so he almost dropped the weapon. He coolly set the pain aside and lowered the rifle.

On the sere hillside a cloud of partridge feathers shuddered on the breeze and then subsided. He grabbed his horse's reins and led it down to collect the carcass. The shells of the old Lee Enfield rifle were enough to almost blast the bird apart, but there was still enough flesh that he and Khadija would have meat to supplement the lentils and rice he had bought from the farmer who had sold him the horses.

He'd almost left her that night, but she'd been so vulnerable after he'd finished suturing her leg. Who was he kidding? No matter the fury in her green-brown gaze, there was something about her—when he'd lain bound to that bench in the cave delirium had convinced him there was something larger at work here.

Like when Rumi finally met the teacher he'd prayed for, Shams of Tabriz.

No, that had been a mystical union of spirits, of minds meeting at a glance in their love for Allah. There was no damned way he had prayed for feelings for this woman. Still, he'd worried about her the whole time he'd been gone.

And he'd paid top dollar for two horses and then the old man had been willing to part with the rifle—something that made Michael a damn sight happier, even if the weapon harkened back to the Second World War.

Even if it meant he was killing again. In these parts, even an ancient weapon made a man, a man. An unarmed man was only a victim-in-waiting. He swung up onto horseback and turned his brown gelding upslope, to the place Khadija waited.

Her chestnut mare cropped grass down-slope from her, while she rested in a hollow near the ridge of the mountain. She startled when his shadow fell on her, and her face didn't exactly light up at his presence, but at least she managed to hide her hate. An uneasy truce had developed between them over their week of travel. Or perhaps she was just worn down by her pain. In any event, she'd stopped wearing the *chador* pulled down tightly around her when they were alone.

"How is it?" he asked as he sank down beside her and began to pluck masses of feathers from the bird.

Not even the harsh light off the rocks could destroy the fine grain of her skin, but it also revealed the pain lines around her eyes. And the fear. It was a constant in her face and he wondered how she lived with it—how it had come to fill her. He hoped it wasn't solely his doing.

"I told you, I'm fine."

She looked at the sun and struggled to her feet where the wind off the peaks loosed strands of her hair from her kerchief. It softened the hard angle of her jaw in a most provocative way.

"Did you see the flowers?" He pointed to a small group of pink blooms struggling in the dust. He'd not seen their kind before.

Khadija gave him a considering look, her fear finally hidden, but it was as if she was blind to the flower's small beauty.

"We should keep moving. I know I slow you down."

"You need to rest."

"You said the old shepherd was a danger and that we're only south of Yskan, not to Ghowrayd Gharam like you wanted."

He closed his eyes. It was true, all of it. She'd not been able to travel the distances he knew they needed. They'd traveled less than forty miles, and in Yskan their luck had run out. Until then they had traveled the narrow road along the river, nary seeing another soul. It was nearing harvest and most people were busy with those labors, while the shepherds were still in the hills with the flocks.

But at Yskan an old shepherd had found them as they made camp east of the straggle of houses that made up the town. First they had smelled the scent of sheep, and then the weathered face had appeared at the edge of their firelight, wearing a tattered, flat-topped Tajik cap and mutton-scented clothing.

Khadija had hurriedly pulled on her *chador* before offering tea, but it was too late. The fact she sat without her covering, the fact that Michael's eyes were such an unusual color—that was enough to give the old man information to sell if he was so inclined.

They'd left the road after that, traveling the deep valleys the other side of the jutting mountain that edged the Kowkcheh River. It made water difficult, and they and the horses suffered, but it also made them harder to find.

Michael collected the horses and brought Khadija's to her. Walking still pained her, though her leg improved each day. The antibiotics seemed to deal with *that* infection, at least.

He aided her onto her horse, her bad leg hanging over the heavy, carpet-patterned saddle pad, sweat in little beads on her brow. She patted the neck of the little mare she had begun to call Anaargórrey—after the small pomegranate that was the same ruddy color as the horse's sun-faded coat.

Carefully, he lifted her foot to the stirrup and heard her swift intake of breath.

"You'll carry me safely today, yes?"

She stroked the mare's neck and the horse's ears twitched. Michael liked that about her—the way she opened her heart to the animal. Too many treated them as machines.

Mounted on his trusty brown gelding, he led off down the slope for the flatter ground in the valley bottom. Less chance of being seen and less chance of a stumble and fall. The horses were surefooted little beasts, but even they could falter in the rocky terrain.

The air became stifling, the landscape caught in a pause in the war between the Asian and Indian tectonic plates that had thrown up these mountains. Sweat ran down his neck from under his turban. Khadija seemed to sway in her saddle, as if the heat sapped her strength.

"You doing okay?"

Her gaze flashed green-gold. "Would you stop! I can go on as long as you."

Temperamental woman. He avoided her as his horse picked its way through the debris of ancient pebbled alluvial and dead scrub. He'd bought the little animals thinking of Khadija, but truly it was him that was thankful of the beast now.

His side didn't seem to be improving. He'd avoided Khadija's help, and had seen the striping peek out from under the bandage when he washed in the river two nights ago. But rest was a luxury he couldn't afford. Opening the wound to allow it to drain as Khadija had suggested would only make him more prone to infection.

Better to just have her administer the antibiotics daily and pray for the best. But then, no deity would help a man like him. He carried too much death within him.

The daylight faded as the sun fell below the scoured edges of the western mountains. It sent fingers of light skyward, pointing towards Allah.

Or perhaps Allah reached for them. Rumi would write of the gold beams as the power of lovers yearning for each other, man yearning for God. So Rumi had felt when he met his teacher—a man so holy and learned it was as if Rumi instantly attained awareness of his connection to something greater.

Michael eased the growing stiffness in his side. To find that connection—it was every man's desire. Until the man gave up hope. Perhaps that was why Rumi was not so favored in Afghanistan any more.

The base of the mountain they followed began to twist westward to the river and Michael reined in to study the landscape. The way the earthquakes had re-carved the glaciated landscape, there was only this path towards the river and the road. A mountain slope blocked their way southward.

"We could use the water," he said, laying his hand on their almost-empty water skin as Khadija came alongside. He studied the scoured slopes for the enemy. Nothing moved but the wind along the distorted mountain shoulders.

His horse sidled under him, restive at the river-scent. The animals had gone without drink since yesterday. Khadija soothed Anaargórrey, making a small song of her name. "Ana, Anaa. Anaargórrey."

The mare's large ears flipped back and forth. Michael's solid gelding stomped his feet.

"They have to drink some time. Just let me go first." He urged his horse into a jog towards the narrow pass between the two ragged slopes. Khadija's mare followed eagerly.

Late afternoon shadows hid the details of the slopes. Anyone could lie in wait amid the boulders and scree and he'd have no way of knowing.

His shoulders itched as he stopped the horse at the path to the roadway. There was no foliage except dried scrub grass along the river's high-water mark, no cover, just the narrow track that posed as a road and the river beyond.

He looked up at the sky, deepening towards evening and saw the wheeling form of a peregrine against the blue. Something was amid the stones that had caught the bird's eye.

He scanned the hillside. Nothing moved—not even the normal trickle of stone. Then why did he have this sense of watching? He'd learned over the years to listen to this sense. Had the old shepherd told someone?

He'd said he was returning back to the hills with his flock, but he'd been a garrulous fellow. Drawn to their fire and the chance for conversation, he'd told them.

If Hashemi's men had camped nearby, it was likely they'd heard news of a man and woman traveling south. Michael unslung the rifle from his shoulder.

It was Anaargórrey who decided enough with caution.

The mare drove her head down to loosen her reins, and then leapt in three great bounds to the river, ignoring Khadija's protesting yank. The mare waded in, plunged her nose deep, and sucked deep draughts of water. The sound carried loud in the air.

Against his better judgment, Michael urged his horse forward. The mountains threatened to the east. He placed himself between the slopes and the woman. They were sitting ducks, but they had to have water. Skin crawling, he dismounted to fill the water skin. One good shot would have him dead.

The full water skin slopped as he tied it to the saddle. He started to mount—more difficult as his side grew worse.

Crack!

Anaargórrey squealed.

His gelding jumped. The movement caught Michael before he could throw his leg over the saddle.

His foot slipped through the stirrup. The gelding tore the reins from Michael's grasp. He grabbed for the pommel, the gelding's mane. Anything to stop his fall, anything to stop from being dragged.

His fingers caught the saddle pad and he threw himself across the animal's back, grabbed for the reins to bring the animal's head around.

Another shot.

Anaargórrey screamed and went down on her haunches, throwing off her rider.

Khadija screamed as her mare toppled, slammed into the edge of the river. Her forelegs thrashed. Red spray filled the air as she fought to rise.

The bullet must have found her spine. The horse's screams filled the air. Khadija rolled to her knees by the mare's head. Pain and confusion filled her face.

Another bullet sprayed gravel. Michael hauled on the gelding's reins, turning his horse back. The river ran red with the mare's blood.

"To me!" he roared, startling Khadija to her feet. She limped towards him.

Another bullet hit the water where she had been.

Get her out of there, just get her before she was shot. They knew he wouldn't leave her. They knew if she was wounded it would slow him more.

He spurred the gelding, grabbed Khadija's waist, and hauled her in front of him even as he twisted the gelding's head around. Just go.

A bullet slammed past his head.

He leaned forward, the horse's mane streaming into his face, Khadija fighting in his arms. Down the road at a gallop, then cross the river. Clatter of hooves. Spray flashing gold. A scramble up the far bank, then ramming his mount right at the mountainside.

Up. Up. Just get them up and the breadth of the mountain between them and those who pursued.

The little horse lunged up the hill, great heart, carrying them both to safety as the day died around them. Khadija sobbed in his arms.

At the crest of the mountain spur he glanced back. The red mare still fought in the river shallows. Three men slipped-slid down the hillside to the road. A cloud of dust heralded the arrival of two Jeeps from farther north.

He looked southwestward. A pall of smoke caught the last sunlight. Ghowrayd Gharam. He had made it almost that far, but they would be watching that town now. Watching and waiting.

And there was still three quarters of the journey to go.

Chapter 25

They shot Anaargórrey.

The wind off the night-bound mountains blew cold, catching the dust from the horse's hooves and tearing Khadija's eyes. She shivered in her still sodden scarf and *jalabiyya*. Even the *petu* around her shoulders was not enough to warm her, but her *chador* had been such a sodden mess carried it across her lap in hopes it would dry. She tried to focus on the heat from the horse beneath her—not the man's arms around her.

They shot Anaargórrey.

Somehow it was worse than the wound in her leg. Anaargórrey was innocent. Her little pomegranate mare had nothing to do with the war waging between the West and Islam, but she had paid like so many in Afghanistan.

So many innocents. So many dead—like those in the market—like Yaqub. It made no sense when surely Allah had intended them all to live.

Anaargórrey had had such a soft eye, was so full of trust. Her coat had been such a rich red in the sunlight and her muzzle hairs had tickled against Khadija's palm.

She died because they wanted him.

Her breath hiccupped and Michael's arms tightened around her. His breath brushed her cheek and stirred the ends of her hair where they fought free of her head scarf. If she turned her head, she would see his lips.

She shivered and looked up at the stars.

They and the almost-full moon were the only light. The mountainside gleamed black and luminous grey, the largest stones silvered like the edges of bones. The footing was hard to see—full of the remains of glaciers and the broken stone from earthquakes, and yet Michael kept going, had given the gelding its head, so the wise animal picked its way across the slope.

Its passage sent pebbles down the hillside in a clatter that reminded her of gunfire. It seemed to echo off the mountainsides, or else it just caught in her ears. Just as the rifle shot that had killed Anaargórrey had seemed to echo forever.

It hurt to think of the little mare's struggle, and how she—Khadija— had just abandoned her to those men and death. So frightened, and Khadija had just left her to die.

Her breath hiccupped again. Please, not tears. The wetness in her eyes was caused by the dust—not grief. Not another sign of weakness.

Suddenly Michael's arms were too much, too strong, too safe. They stopped her from breathing. They stopped her from being what she needed to be. She should have run to Hashemi. She should have pulled Michael Bellis from his horse to demonstrate her devotion to revenge.

Owner of the Day of Judgment
Let me live your straight path,
not the path of those who earn your wrath
nor those who go astray.

Allah, she had shown she was nothing less than a traitor! She yanked free of Michael's arms, but he caught her again.

"Damn you! Let me go! I need to walk."

He released her as if burned and she threw her good leg over the horse's neck and slid down before Michael could rein in.

Pain shot through her, but she ignored it. She stumbled up the slope, needing to see where they were after the hours of riding. She needed to rid herself of this sick feeling. If she was true to her mission, she would never have been carried away, would have found a way to kill her captor, would have at least worn her *chador* at all times. The face of James Hartness flashed in her head. His body. Her shame.

She tripped, fell to her knees and scrambled up.

"Khadija." Footsteps behind her—man and horse. She scrambled ahead, slipping on patches of loose stone, almost running when the ground felt more solid. She had to get free of this man, free to find her honor again. As things were, Mirri and the others would never name her honorable. Hashemi would see to it. And he might do worse.

"Khadija?" Louder.

If she could get to the ridge she could see. Michael had said that a town lay not far away. If she could make it there she'd find a way back to her father, find a way to mend things with Hashemi.

"Khadija!"

A hand caught her shoulder and swung her around, just as her tears won free. Allah, don't let him see.

"I'm *mujāhid*—I give effort in the faith."

She gasped the name for warrior, but knew she was trying to convince herself as much as him.

"I am Malalai—I give everything for my country." She turned her face away, hoping the darkness would shield her, but he only stepped closer and caught her other shoulder.

"Khadija. I work for this country, too. And for faith. We're all seeking."

"Stop it!" She yanked loose. "Stop it with your gentle voice and your gentle hands and your questions and gentle understanding. I don't want to know you. I don't want to listen to you sleep across the fire. I don't want to listen to you quote Rumi and point out wild flowers on the slopes. I don't want to be near you. Your kind caused my brother's death."

He froze as if struck and she stumbled across the hillside, making for the black edge of the ridge across the night sky.

He caught her as she reached the top, as distant fires told her there was some form of settlement spread in a broader curve of the river. His hand pulled her around, so her weak leg gave.

She fell against him and her scarf slipped back, freeing her hair. It caught in the breeze, even as his arms went around her, his warmth found her, and he steadied her.

"Khadija, I'm so sorry. I know you shouldn't be here. What is it you *do* want?"

His voice was a low growl. In the darkness his pale eyes seemed lost in a sea of dark emotions she had never seen there before. He stood so close, her world narrowed to his fierceness, to his warm arms around her, the scent of him. To the curve of his lips. To the question he'd asked.

To kill him? To go back to Hashemi? To be with her father? To hold to her faith? Warmth and a home and honor.

Home and safety would be so much simpler, but they came without honor.

Still, the scent of him, the hold of those strong arms, they sent her honor away like the dust on the night wind.

Those pale eyes seemed to rest on her face as if they could wait for a hundred years, a thousand years. As if they had waited forever, and she was what they had waited for.

Her breath came too fast. She felt dizzy, caught in those eyes, falling into those eyes pale as an Afghan morning sky. She reached up. Stopped herself when his gaze flickered, but it solidified, held on her, still waiting, and suddenly the flat of her palm and her thumb were tracing the hard angles of his face, the edge of his mouth.

How long had she wanted to do this?

His lips found the edge of her hand, even as his eyes held hers, even as he waited. A man who had waited so long could wait a little longer, but she could not.

She stepped into him and the safety of his arms folded around her, drew her into his chest, so her head rested against the strength of his shoulder. He kissed her hair, ran his large palm over her head.

His breath was warm on her skin and suddenly she was crying full out, the sobs choking her.

"Khadija." Her name was almost like a hymn on his lips. "Why are you crying?"

The truth was there were too many things. Her father, her faith, her fear, her unwanted feelings for this man. She had tried to be a woman of Islam, a woman of the law, and yet here she stood in a *kofr* man's arms—Michael's arms, she corrected herself.

"They shot Anaargórrey." She managed to choke the words out, knowing they were inadequate—as much a failure as she.

Chapter 26

She trembled in Michael's arms, a frail leaf the wind would tear away. As if the earth shook and she was torn loose and left spinning in air.

The question was, was this real, or just some act she used to lull him. But lull him to what? She hadn't attempted to betray him since her mad run in the field.

He inhaled the scent of her hair and closed his eyes. Precious, yes. Mohammed and Yaqub had known it.

Yaqub's love for his sister had been deep. Michael had waited a long time to meet her after listening to Yaqub's many tales of his brilliant, passionate sister safe in England. And he—after meeting her he'd hoped this slim, strong woman would see him as something other than the enemy.

But he was a romantic fool, not too unlike Yaqub. It had gotten Yaqub killed. The Khadija of his dreams was just a woman he'd created. Like him, the real Khadija was willing to use another person in the interests of the Great Game.

Still, she was warm and in his arms, and her soft sobs drilled into his dead heart. Her normal stoic strength made this breakdown all the more tragic.

All for a horse.

He ran his palm over her head, his fingers catching in the smooth flow of her hair. Smooth, like her skin was smooth. Her lips were so close he could take them. In her vulnerability he might even own her body. Then, no Afghan man would want her. He lowered his head to inhale the sweet scent of her neck and knew he would never be free of the tenderness it evoked. Then he eased himself back.

"I'm so sorry," he said.

Her lips quivered, full and inviting.

He would be honorable regardless of what this woman was. Honor was his armor in an agent's dishonorable world. It was all he had.

And the Hui woman? You treated *her* so honorably? Hell, he barely remembered her name. Maybe he fooled himself. Maybe this was just a way to comfort himself on this journey. She was here, why not have her?

Because she was Mohammed's daughter, Yaqub's sister. Because she was Khadija and deserved better. *Because when he dreamed of her, the nightmares went away.* He turned her to the gelding.

"I want to be long past Ghowrayd Gharam by morning. We'll rest during the day," he said and let the wind come between them, then helped her mount.

At least his arms were around her as he urged the horse downhill towards the distant firelight. Khadija might be vulnerable, but she was also strong, just as this land was strong—even with the faults that ran so deep beneath the surface. Something fine and feminine and alive and beautiful as the Creator's names of beauty. The Koran spoke of Allah as being formed of both masculine and feminine, his essence as the female Beloved, and his worldly face of Creator and Sustainer as his masculine side. Surely that was why a man and woman came together, to unite as a form of embracing Allah.

At least she no longer sat so ramrod stiff against him. At least she'd left her hair loose so the long strands ran against his face like a memory of her palm.

#

Daylight, two days later, and Khadija looked around her as Michael stopped their horse in a narrow stone defile of the mountains.

They'd been riding through a maze of narrow, boulder-filled gorges south of Ghowrayd Gharam. The mountains had sharpened here; the side-hills were too steep for the trusty brown gelding. Now, in the nighttime, they rode in the narrow valleys between the mountains, sometimes venturing out to the silver-slicked river by the light of the moon. In the daylight they dry camped at the edges of dry glacial lakes.

"We'll make camp here." Michael helped her down off the horse and she was too aware of his hands at her waist.

While Michael took care of the horse, Khadija cleansed herself in a palmful of water and spread her shawl on the ground. Then she knelt, facing Mecca for her morning prayers.

Praise be to Allah, Lord of Worlds,
The Infinitely Good, the All-Merciful,
Thee we worship, and in Thee we seek help.
Owner of the Day of Judgment

Show us your straight path,
not the path of those who earn your wrath
nor those who go astray.
Allah help me reclaim my honor.

When she finished she found Michael looking at her.

"What?"

He looked away.

"What?"

"It's nothing. But sometimes I question every faith. Christ on a cross. How the Taliban treated people over the years. I saw friends hung bloody and dying from a tripod in a village square at the order of a Taliban Imam. And women, prostitutes some of them, but still good women, stoned by the same men who used them the night before. The Imams demanded the crowd applaud."

He went silent a moment, and glanced at the sky.

"Now I focus on saving the living."

He moved stiffly as he finished unsaddling, but often his gaze went up to the sky where the moon faded towards rebirth.

"What is it you watch for? What are you expecting?"

"It seems like we're caught in that moment of silence before an earthquake. When the birds sing again, the quake will begin."

"You've kept us hidden from Hashemi."

"Khadija, if he finds us again, I want you to run. Don't trust him. He comes from a form of Islam so harsh, the world will break under it because it has no tolerance for anything but itself. We've been lucky so far—he wants my information. But with each mile closer to the Panjshir Valley and Kaabul, Hashemi'll have to rethink his tactics. Dead, I might not provide information, but I also can't betray the Taliban's plans."

Plans? What did Michael know?

He left the horse to graze the desiccated grass. The animal had lost the glossy plumpness it'd had when they got it.

"Tea?" she asked, wanting him to talk further and hoping for some rations.

"There's no fuel to heat water." He scanned the sear landscape. Little grew here.

His lips quirked in a genuine smile that lit his face. "When we reach the Panjshir we'll have tea everyday."

The offered friendship made her pull back. Since that night on the ridge top she'd been careful to keep well away from him, except when they rode together. He seemed to study her even more than he had done in the past. In unguarded moments she thought she saw a look of open self-loathing that confused her.

He settled himself against a boulder.

"If it means anything, I didn't want it to be so hard."

She hauled her gaze back from a falcon high in the sky.

"I mean the travel. Leaving your father. Being alone with me." His pale gaze looked away. "If it's any comfort, your honor's safe."

She couldn't help how she startled. She pulled her *petu* over her head to hide her uncertainty.

"My honor was lost when you brought me with you and when I failed to wear the *chador*. Everyone will think we were lovers."

"Not even if I swear it didn't happen?"

"And who will listen to a *kofr*?" Bitterness soured her tongue.

"Khadija, I'm not *kofr*. I worship Allah—something beyond—in my own way."

"You don't pray."

"Many Muslims don't do the daily prayers, but they still follow the Word."

"Then they aren't Muslims." But she knew that wasn't quite true. Her father's second cousin had taken her in when she was in London and he was a good Muslim man, even though he didn't pray at all required times.

"All beings are of the same breath, Khadija."

Anger snapped her head up, the *petu* sliding back on her head.

"You sound like my father—always quoting Rumi. Well, I'm not Sufi. I'm Sunni and don't believe in Sufi lies."

"What I say isn't Sufi. It's the Quran."

That almost stopped her. She pushed herself to her feet.

"You twist my words. Why should I even listen to you?"

"Because we travel together. Because I want to keep you safe. Because I want us to understand each other. I'm not your enemy, nor the enemy of the Afghani people." He stood to face her. "I was born of Afghani-American parents."

"My father told me, remember? Your great-great-grandfather was an Afghani spy for your country." She shook her head. "A family tradition, this spying?"

"I'm not a spy."

"What are you then? You come to this country and run little plots that get innocent…animals…killed. How many have died for your plots, Michael Bellis? How many more will?"

He looked away.

"I…deserve that. I've deserved to die many times over, but sometimes one must…."

"… do what is necessary." She finished the old refrain and it made her furious. "Damn you Americans," she swore in English. "Damn the

Canadians and the British and the Russians and all your kind."

She stomped off after the gelding, stopping to run her hand down over the animal's soft neck, its shoulder. She leaned into it, burying her face in the rough mane and the safe, warm scent of living animal.

She heard him approach.

"Khadija."

She would not let *him* near her again.

"You and the Arabs. You fight wars in my country. You seduce our people one way or another so we no longer know our own minds. What is Afghani anymore? Taliban? The vision that the West has of a democratic Afghanistan? That is my father's vision. Why not something different? Why not an Islamic state that lives under the Law?"

"Where women are locked away?" he asked softly. She heard rock-fall above them on the slope. The horse's head went up and it snorted.

"Where women are safe." She faced him and the landscape lurched.

Lurched again as tectonic plates squabbled, and she fell against the gelding. Michael staggered and then the landscape stilled. Pebbles skipped down the slopes around them.

"Aah, but are they loved?"

The question made the landscape seem to lurch again. Michael's open look changed to wariness. Did he know what he asked?

"My father loves me." It came out stiff.

"Yes. He does."

There seemed more he would say, and oh, Allah, the open wound of his eyes.

Before she could stop herself she was on her toes pressing her lips to his, tasting vibrant life and hope. The world seemed to explode.

Horrified at what she'd done, she fell back before his arms came around her. She turned to run, but he grabbed her.

Then he threw her on the ground.

Chapter 27

The gelding squealed and cantered away as Michael yanked her down behind a massive boulder. Khadija fought against his too-tight arms, against his body on top of hers, his breath coming fast.

She was a fool. A bigger fool and sinner than she'd ever been in London. She'd been fascinated by the way a man and woman's body fit together, and by the feelings it raised. She'd been hungry for it, to learn, to experiment, only to be made a fool of. Then she'd been shocked at what she'd done and at James's betrayal.

And now she opened herself to such a thing again. She had no honor and deserved what he was going to do to her.

"No! Please, Michael, Stop! I...I shouldn't have done that." She pounded his back with her fists, scratched his face. He raised his head.

"You shouldn't have done a lot of things, but now's not the time." He held her down as he unslung his rifle.

She stiffened. "You'll kill me after, won't you?"

His gaze dropped to hers.

"What the hell are you talking about?"

A bullet pinged off the boulder. Another slammed into the earth to one side of their hiding place and she suddenly realized what was happening.

"I didn't pull you here for my health, woman. Or to take advantage. We'll save that for later." It was as if he read her thoughts again.

His grin cut her and she felt herself color. Another bullet slammed into the earth beside them.

"Shit." He rolled away to peer around the boulder.

"Stay here. The bastard's up along the ridge, but he's alone. I have to stop him before he calls reinforcements."

He was on his feet and moving like one of the snow leopards that lived in the high mountains, somehow bringing life to the dead landscape even as he blended to become part of it. She managed to follow his movements a few moments, but then he was gone, leaving her huddled behind the stone with the shreds of her dignity.

Another shot echoed off the valley walls. Was it Michael's rifle or the other one? Silence. This was her chance to leave. If she stayed with Michael, no good would come of it.

On her knees, she scanned the landscape. No one there.

If she could follow the valley until the eastern mountain ended, then she could make her way to the river and the road. It wasn't that far. Even someone as ill-equiped for the mountains as she was should be able to make it. Then she just had to avoid Hashemi and she'd find help and get back to her father and safety.

He must be frantic. How was he managing with no one to help him?

She picked out a shelter not too distant—a flattened slab of stone leaned against a boulder. Guilt bent her low as she half-ran, half-limped, across the open space. A rifle report sent her diving for cover, the bullet slamming into the ground where she had been.

Her hands shook. Her knees shook, but she had to keep moving. There. The next boulder. She wormed her way there. Ahead, the horse stood with its nostrils flared, ears twitching as it scanned the defile for what caused the danger.

Khadija aimed towards it. The animal must be beyond rifle range. She would be able to run, then, no matter what happened to Michael Bellis.

She glanced back,not knowing if she wanted him to live or die. "If you die, it's because you deserve it. I wish I'd told you that."

But she left him the horse. At least give him a chance to complete his mission, because she'd be on her way home soon enough. Past the animal she ran openly down the valley, sun in her face, wind at her back, but the sound of rifle shots stopped her. Ahead, the mountainside ended. Two long defiles ran eastward, but one angled northward, the other south. Michael Bellis would go south if he lived. That meant her path lay northward.

She jogged now, the terrain rough under her boots.

"*Allāhu akbar*," she intoned as she ran. God is greater than anything we can conceive of. "*Inshallah*, let me end this now. Let me be free of this madness."

Her thigh burned with effort. The sun rose higher. Behind came the echo of more rifle shots. She didn't stop this time.

She stopped just as the earth lurched again and went still. So many earthquakes in this unsteady land. The wind picked up dust and in the silence she heard it pattering against the stone.

Faith was not something that could be swept away like dust. Faith—
tawhīd—was something that swelled you with certainty. Once faith had
been a shield, a fortress that would help her avenge Yaqub's death. But
now—now she was like Kaabul's ancient walls—or—or the earth under her
feet.

The thought brought the memory of warm arms steadying her.

"Damnation. Michael Bellis, get out of my head!"

Gravel slid on the mountainside behind her. She spun, but the morning
had passed and the sun was from the west, blinding against the hillside.

Something moved there. Animal? Man? She squinted. There was
nothing that could mean her any good. She turned and ran.

Her feet slipped on the loose stone. She tripped on an outcropping of
rock. She went to her knees, scraping the heels of her hands and her knees
through the thick cloth of the *jalabiyya*. The sun beat at her back. Her blood
was loud in her ears. Her breath tore through her chest and her leg screamed
for relief, but she dared not stop.

A shout behind her and she stretched her stride. Ahead the defile
narrowed. The rush of water filled her ears. The river. She had made it. The
road beside it would bring safety. If she turned north she would find the last
town. They would help her to her father, give her life back to her. If only
Papa were safe.

The shout came again, but this time from in front. How could Michael
have moved so fast? She slowed, wondering if she'd erred again. So many
of her actions had turned back on her like a snake.

She was right to escape. Her father needed her and she would not
forget that again. She darted past the mountain spur towards the bright flow
of water and the road.

Right into the arms of Abdullah Hashemi.

Chapter 28

Khadija fought, but Hashemi held her firmly. His breath carried the sour scent of old tea and cigarettes.

"Whore! Have you enjoyed fornicating with the enemy? Has he paid you for your time?"

She fought harder, trying to twist away from the darkness of the words and the guilt they brought.

"I've done nothing to shame myself."

He snorted his disbelief, his grip tightening on her arms. His black gaze bit into her, cold as a cobra's. This man would kill her and feel justified doing so. Michael had warned her, she realized.

He shoved her towards three waiting men.

"You show yourself like a brazen. What man could not have you?"

The men's hands held her arms. The stench of garlic and naan clung to their clothing. Hashemi looked from Khadija back the way she had come. "Where is your lover, now?"

"He's not my lover! I escaped. I came because I wanted to get back… to you."

"A lover's quarrel, then? Is that what sent you scurrying to my arms?" He looked thoughtful a moment, the sunlight catching on the few grey threads in his beard. "Bring her. We might use her to flush him."

They marched southward along the hard-packed road to where two Jeeps sat beside the river. One of the men whistled what sounded like a falcon cry and from the slopes came an answer. Another came from farther down the river. And farther.

The number of men Hashemi had hunting told how badly he wanted Michael. The thought gave her pause. Not a spy? It was what she'd heard American medics in the refugee camps call a "bald-faced lie."

They made camp beside the river as the sunlight failed. Khadija they shoved to a spot close by the water.

"Leave this spot and I kill you," growled the armed man she recognized as the lookout from the house in Feyzabad. Two of the men ranged along the riverbed, seeking debris for a fire. Two more men appeared along the road from down river, the dust on their clothing and the fatigue in their faces, suggesting hours searching the mountains. One carried a brace of partridge along with the automatic weapon slung over his shoulder.

"Has anyone seen Babrak?" Hashemi scanned his men.

The others looked at each other and shrugged.

"He took the slope, just there," said one man, nodding at the mountain north of them. "I went father north and kept him in sight until he passed the first ridge."

Hashemi glanced in her direction. "Then we might assume good Babrak is no longer with us." He turned to her. "What do you say? Do I have the right of it? Shall Babrak's wife and children sing of his passing into Paradise?"

The look in his eyes sent chills up her spine. He hated her—possibly all women. Finally she nodded. "Your man shot at us. Michael—the *Amrikaayi*—he went after him. I heard many shots."

"And he left you in safety and yet you left him. Interesting."

"I told you. I escaped. I need to get back to my father." Khadija kept her eyes averted. Once, when he needed her, she had goaded this man to carry water for her. Now fear of him left her weak. She needed to be strong, to make Hashemi understand.

"He cares for me. I see it in his eyes. I lulled him into thinking I felt the same, and waited my chance to get free. That's when you found me. I was trying to get back to Feyzabad—and you." Why did bile sour her mouth as she spoke the words? She did want to get back to Feyzabad, and Hashemi's faith was a clean wind, wasn't it?

She must have hidden her confusion better than she thought because Hashimi considered her and nodded.

His men placed a kettle to boil and Hashemi settled beside the fire, his gaze still on her. The shadows lengthened about them, the sunlight abandoning the river valley to the wind that blew down from the snow fields of the Hindu Kush. Khadija shivered. In the silence the kettle boiled and one of the men brought Hashemi a cup of the steaming liquid.

They brought nothing to her.

The sky turned indigo and the men roasted the partridge whole in the coals of the fire. The smell of burning feathers changed to roasting meat and set Khadija's stomach rumbling. Another man brought rounds of bread from the Jeep and they dipping the bread in their tea, wrapping the seared meat in naan and eating. Their voices were harsh as the ridge of mountains caught against the sky.

What were they waiting for? What were they going to do to her? She realized she was shivering.

And still Hashemi watched her. Beyond, in the hills, Michael would continue southward. It was a relief to know he was gone.

An ache grew in Khadija's belly as she watched the men eat.

"Please. It's been a day since I had food." Hashemi nodded at one of the men who tossed a hunk of bread in her direction. It landed just out of reach.

"May…may I get it," she whispered and was instantly furious for at herself for being cowed. She was strong. She had completed medical school. Well—almost. She had traveled to a far country when she was barely more than a child. She had lived through that experience. Not well— but lived.

Ignoring the men, she retrieved the bread, stuffing it into her mouth, ignoring the grit of dust and gravel. Hashemi treated her like nothing—like less than nothing. She might be flawed, but she was worth more than that.

"You say the *Amrikaayi* wants you."

She nodded at Hashemi around the food. He stabbed the earth near his feet with the point of his knife, but his gaze never left her.

"I'd thought I'd have to kill him without knowing his secrets. He gets too close to the Panjshir and the Panjshiri have never been our friends, though things have changed some since the Lion's death." He peered at her from the tops of his eyes. "Perhaps you offer us another way."

Khadija stopped eating.

"You say he trusts you."

"He did until today." The bread suddenly rested heavy in her gut.

"What did he tell you of his work?"

Khadija frowned, trying to determine what Hashemi was getting at.

"His work? He's like his great-great-grandfather who worked for the *Amrikaayi*."

"He told you that?"

What could she say to keep him happy?

"He wanted to tell me more before I ran."

"Good. Very good, in fact. You must build on his trust."

But she was going home—back to Feyzabad and then Kaabul.

Hashemi stabbed a choice piece of bird flesh from the fire and devoured it as he walked. When he came back to her, his beard gleamed with grease.

"Everyone here is a tool of Islam, to be used to the cause."

She nodded, uncertain even though, according to faith, he was right.

He suddenly caught her wrist, twisting it so hard she groveled on her knees. He was framed by the stars, his face ruddy with firelight.

"You *will* be a soldier, Khadija Siddiqui. You'll learn Michael Bellis's secrets, whatever it takes. Your body is your weapon. Do you understand?"

"No! Not that! I want to go home." It escaped before she could stop it. Hashemi backhanded her.

She sagged to the ground. When he hauled her to her feet, his hand was raised again.

"You've fallen so far there's nothing further that can defile you. Only Allah can redeem you—if you do his work. You *will* do what is needed."

Shame flushed up her neck. She heard low laughter from the men.

"But promiscuity is not permitted." It came out a whisper.

His free hand formed a fist and she cringed away.

"Do you think suicide bombers were permitted in Islam? Times change. We use the weapons to hand and you are ours."

She couldn't do this. Not this. Not with Michael Bellis.

"Please..." she started, but his raised fist stopped her.

"You'll escape this night. You'll let the *Amrikaayi* find you and you will go with him. You'll gain his trust, become his lover. In Skazar we'll be waiting. By then you'll know his secrets. Do you understand?"

Not this. Anything but this. She wanted her father. She wanted Yaqub. She wanted home. But her father was in Feyzabad and her brother was in Paradise, a victim of the *kofr*.

Hashemi's grip demanded her answer. Her skin burned. "Do you understand?!"

She nodded.

"Good. As long as you obey, old men can be left in peace."

Chapter 29

Michael left the horse far down the defile back from the rushing river. He tied the gelding there, for fear the thirsty beast might try to reach the water. Water would come later for them both—if he was successful in rescuing Khadija.

Frankly, he was a fool to even try. He took a chance he couldn't afford. His path lay southward, in a race against time to get the message out, but something wouldn't let him leave her even if she'd run away.

She'd looked back and seen him and even then she'd run.

He was a damned fool. She was the enemy who had lulled him into trust while waiting for her chance. He should know better—had known better.

Once.

But he'd seen the way Hashemi dragged her to his camp. She hadn't been welcomed as a comrade of the *jihad*.

He shook his head as he finished his careful crawl to the ridge and peered down to the river. As he'd waited for darkness, he'd prayed that Hashemi was bold enough to camp nearby. Now, his prayers answered, he counted six men at the fire. Of course, that meant nothing. There were probably at least that many again, up in the hills. They waited for him, just as he watched for them.

The weight of his Enfield and the weapon of the man he'd killed rested comfortably against his back. The dead man had carried a copy of an Uzi manufactured in Pakistan, but the piece had been cared for by a man who lived by his weapon. It had the shine of new gun oil, and a sweet balance in the hands that the ancient Lee Enfield did not.

But neither weapon helped him a damn bit in rescuing Khadija. There were just too many of them for a frontal attack.

From where he crouched all he could hear was the wind and the rushing river, but the air carried the scent of their food, and the tea they drank. He could see the gleam off the hoods of the two vehicles—and how they treated Khadija.

There was no question she was a prisoner. The way she sat apart, the way the men denied her food, said her status was worse than that of "woman." And then there was Hashemi's lording behavior. He remembered it all too well.

When Khadija stood to face her captor, he knew she was in danger. When Hashemi struck her, Michael's hands tightened on the Uzi. One shot and Hashemi would be done—paid back for all the things he'd done. But if he did that, Hashemi's men would kill Khadija. So get her first.

"You're a fool, Bellis. You should be riding hard, not trying to rescue a woman who runs from you."

He grinned. When had he ever claimed wisdom? The wise man would have said "no" to Ron Hall all those years ago.

A less-wise man would have gotten out of the game years ago.

A man with a small light of wisdom would have left after things fell apart in Bamiyan.

He could almost laugh at his idiocy. But a man had to do what was right, and this was more than. It was *maktūb*—it was written—he was meant to do this or die trying. For Khadija, for her father. For his own salvation. That took precedence even over his mission. *Soon.*

God help him, if he was wrong. He closed his eyes. *Just a small wisdom? Please?*

A rattle of stones interrupted him. He scanned the spur of mountain below him. Yellow khaki soil stained grey, rock black in the remnants of the moonlight, boulders in their pools of shadows. Was that movement? The glow of a cigarette?

Michael sank lower to the ground, his body suddenly taut. The man hadn't seen him silhouetted against the night sky, thank God, but he could have.

Michael knew he was getting sloppy, and sloppiness was the surest way to get yourself dead. For the first time in a long time, he wasn't ready for that inevitability.

He lowered himself down the slope. The camp was guarded. The hillsides were guarded. That left only the river that ran swift and deep in this spot, compressed between the jut of the mountainsides.

He shuddered, remembering the cold of the Wakhan, but he had survived that and he would survive another dozen dousings as well, he supposed. Not much of a plan, but the only one he had.

He slipped back down the slope, gliding from shadow to shadow, back to the brown horse. The animal snorted at his arrival.

Michael ran a hand down the gelding's neck. "We'll get you water, old friend. A little farther and you can drink."

Mounted, he turned the horse up one of the defiles that headed north, back the way he had come, knowing that there were other breaks in the hills that gave onto the river. When he had traveled far enough, he tied the horse again and climbed the ridge to study the landscape.

Nothing moved. The peaks of the mountains across the Kowkcheh ranged back and back and back, the snow on their crests gleaming white in the thin moonlight. Once, many millions of years before, they had been islands in a primordial ocean, but the world had shifted under them. Below him, the dark cord of the river curved sharply westward.

Michael stopped. That made no sense. The Kowkcheh ran almost due north through its entire length, except for a single jog westward just south, of the town of Ferghamu. He sat back on his heels.

"You came farther than you thought, Bellis. You were fucking lost in the hills." He didn't understand how that could be, but perhaps leaving the valleys near the river had found him a more direct route southwest. That was all it could be. It gave him a chance. Maybe. Just maybe, he'd still get his warning out in time. If only he knew when the bloody "accident" would occur. An accident at that power plant would devastate huge tracts of oil and mineral-rich land and if not cripple, at least lame, the Chinese industrial complex. The usual American reassurances of innocence would not placate the Chinese after taking such a hit.

Soon.

He looked back at the river and the sere mountainsides that rose from its banks. Just get this done. This far from Hashemi's camp, there was a lower chance of sentries, but he still had to be careful.

He studied each shadow, each crevice in the rock, then retreated to the horse. He took the gelding for water, allowing the horse to dive its nose into the cold liquid, sucking up the water in desperate gulps. Michael drank beside it.

When he was done, he pulled the horse's head up.

"Not too much. You'll give yourself a belly ache."

He marked the way by how a jut of the mountainside looked from beside the water, and then led the horse back to where he'd been. He retied the animal, doffed his *petu*, vest, and turban, and returned to the road.

Now came the hard part. He started southward, upriver, following the watercourse until he knew if he went any further he'd probably be spotted by Hashemi's men.

He waded into the river. The cold shocked his breath away. His *salwar kameez* stuck to his legs. His boots filled with cold water. When the force of the river struck his chest, he turned upriver towards Hashemi's camp. He was counting on them not watching the river. After all, only a fool or a madman would subject himself to the frigid water for the sake of a woman who was his enemy. If Hashemi's men spotted him, he'd be a sitting duck: easy to pick off in the water, and still easier to pick off when he came to shore.

The river ran deep and strong, almost tearing his feet out from under him as he slipped, tripped on unseen rock, and kept wading against the current. How much easier the Wakhan dousing had been. He'd only had to let the water take him.

Already the cold sapped his strength. He could barely feel his feet. His hands he kept curled against his chest for warmth—not that it gave much when the water stripped away any body heat.

Twenty minutes later he didn't know if his plan had been such a good one after all. Ahead lay the glow of Hashemi's fire and the bulk of the two Jeeps, but the cold had left him without any feeling in his legs. He had to get out of the river before the hypothermia was severe. Already his breath came in ragged shudders. How the hell was he going to rescue Khadija when he damn well needed rescuing himself?

He'd been in enough Mujehaddin camps to know how things operated. Hashemi ran a tight operation, from what he'd seen. When the Taliban ruled, Hashemi had been an advisor to the Mullahs while at the same time leading the "cleansing raids" in the Shi'ite Hazzara villages. He'd still have to run tight operations to survive as a hunted man.

Michael scanned the area for sentries, but found none. Instead there were only the humps of bodies rolled in blankets. Not as it should be. More as if Hashemi had set a stage for viewing. A tempting stage and there could be only one audience in these hills—him.

His senses prickled. Were the sentries watching his approach even now? He sank down to his chin, his breath catching in his lungs. In the moonlit current his head probably looked like another stone—except it was a stone that shifted against the current.

In the camp a form—low to the ground—shifted slowly towards the river. Michael tensed. A scarfed head lifted and was caught in the moonlight. Then there was swift movement.

Khadija threw herself into the river.

The wind carried her soft splash. Then there were limbs flailing in the swift-moving current. A cry from the camp. Men leapt to their feet. A lantern suddenly bloomed, sending light glittered towards Michael as the water rushed Khadija towards him. If he didn't move, they'd see him.

He let the current tear his deadened legs from the bottom. The water slammed him into a boulder. Air burst from his lungs. The pain in his side denied him new breath. An eddy pulled him under.

He grabbed for the surface, for air, and something slammed into him. Something soft. Something struggling. Khadija. He grabbed for her and she fought him; her small fist found the side of his head with surprising force.

He wrapped one arm around her and burst into air. God, where were they? How far had the water taken them? Where were Hashemi's men? Khadija's face streamed water beside him. Her eyes were clamped shut. She clawed at his face.

"Stop it."

Her eyes flashed open and then the water slammed his shoulder into another boulder. His arm went numb and the water tore them apart.

She was darkness and a white face Michael fought towards. She floundered in the river, her heavy *jalabiyya* weighing her down. She'd drown if he didn't reach her.

Michael swam, but the river tore her lighter form away. He pulled his legs up to the surface, arrowing his body. It was dangerous if there were sentries watching. He would make a large target, but it was the only way to catch her.

The river tore them northward, northward. The stars overhead said he entered the great westward curve. It he didn't get her out soon, he'd be past the horse, past safety. With every minute he lost ground in his need to go south. He lost sight of her as the river pulled her under again.

Then she burst through the water, struggling shoreward, even as the river yanked her down. Her struggles were weakening. The cold sapped her strength. *Inshallah*, he *would* reach her in time. *Inshallah*, he *would* save her.

He reached her as the moon fell behind the mountainside and a greater darkness fell. Cold wool in his fingers. The feel of warmth as his arms closed around her and her arms came around his neck. She almost pulled him under in her panic to breathe.

"Just hold on. Hold on and I'll get us to shore." Where was safety? Were Hashemi's men tracking them? It didn't matter. Saving her did.

His knee slammed against hidden stone. His feet touched down on gravel. He staggered through the water, the current still threatening to tear his feet out from under him. To dry land. The horse.

His knees gave in the shallows and Khadija fell beside him, her black hair a sodden curtain over her face. Their breath sobbed in counterpoint to the rush of the river. Michael pulled her to him as he scanned the shore. Khadija shuddered in his arms as he marked the outcropping he'd picked out on the far side of the river. His plan had worked—almost too well.

Nothing was ever this easy.

Unless it was a trap.

Chapter 30

Michael had to get them to the horse and to safety, and somehow find warmth in this landscape that gave almost nothing for fire.

He managed to find his footing and hauled Khadija up. Her legs gave, so he lifted her into his arms, ignoring the knife-blade of pain in his side. He was surprised at how light she was even in her sodden coat. Then he clambered up the river bank and crossed the road.

The horse snorted as Michael set Khadija down in the lee of a rock. The wind was their enemy now. Each night since Feyzabad the temperature had dropped a little further. The autumn wind came swiftly in these mountains and said the wheat harvest should be well under way in the north.

The wind plastered his *salwar kameez* to his body, but it was Khadija who was most affected. Huge shudders wracked her so her teeth clacked together.

He had to get her out of the wet clothes, out of the worst of the cold, but there was no shelter anywhere near. All he could do was get them farther into the mountains and find a safe spot to light a fire.

"Khadija?" She peered up at him, abject misery on her face. "I'm going to take the horse for one more drink and them we have to go. We'll make a fire in the hills."

She nodded, her hair masking most of her face.

He wrapped their two dry *petu* around her shoulders, and pulled on his felted vest. Her eyes were dull as she huddled into the shawls. They wouldn't do much, but it was something.

When he returned with the horse, he helped her mount, then climbed on the animal behind her. She flinched as his arms came around her, but his arms would warm her and hopefully save them both from hypothermia.

As the horse picked its way southwest he grew more concerned. Her shudders deepened. By the time he judged they were deep enough into the maze of hills, her shivers were constant and she was limp in his arms.

He reined in and slid off the gelding, feeling his side like a piece of jagged glass impaled him. Things did not go well there, but he had no time to attend to it. He hauled Khadija off the horse and carried her around a jut of hillside to a hollow that provided a meager shelter beyond.

The ground was flat, and the wind avoided sending the worst of its cold fingers here. In a back corner were signs of fire. So shepherds had used this place before. That was not so good, but there was no help for it. Khadija needed warmth and he wasn't much better. He went back to the horse and claimed the medical pack and their supplies. The horse he set free to graze.

When he returned to the alcove, he carried as much fuel as he could find and started a small fire on the old fire pit. Its heat reflected back at them from the rock wall. In that hint of warmth he stripped off his shirt, pulled his damp vest back on, and went to Khadija.

"We have to get these wet things off you."

Her hands clutched the shawls around her. They were damp from her coat, but they were the driest things they had. He gently loosened her fingers and pulled the shawls away, laying them by the fire to heat, then began to unbutton her coat.

At first she fought him, a terrified look in her eyes.

"It's all right. It's all right. Khadija, Allah saved us from the river. Now he gives us warmth to live." He explained it to her as she was a fearful child.

Finally her hands collapsed to her sides and a look of resignation came over her face. His half-frozen fingers shook as they worked the buttons and pulled the coat off her shoulders. He laid it beside the fire, but knew it would be a long time before the thick wool would dry.

She shivered like a reed in wind, her hair, scarfless, tangled in damp threads around her shoulders. Her *salwar kameez* was plastered to her pale skin.

"You need to get out of those wet things," he said softly. He held up one of the *petu*, now warm from the fire. "You can wrap yourself in this while your clothes dry."

There was defeat he didn't understand in every line of her body. He supposed it was because she was back with him, when she had tried to escape.

He knelt beside her. "Here. I'll hold this up. You remove your wet clothes and wrap yourself in this. On my honor, I'll do nothing."

She did as she was bid, then huddled by the fire. He brought her *chador* to her and covered her with it up to her chin. He settled the other *petu* around his shoulders and watched the way her chin nodded towards her chest even as the shudders took her. The fire wasn't enough. He barely felt it himself.

"Sit close to me. I'm warmer than you are."

She didn't move, so he draped his *petu* around her shoulders, then sat, bare-chested. When the cold was too much, he pulled her to him, felt her resistance, but would not be denied.

"Let me have one of the shawls." Her eyes were dull as she obeyed. Her hair fell around her face, her almost limp body, as he pulled her against him and draped the single *petu* around them both.

She was soft against him. Her hair, as it dried, lifted and tickled his nose. Somehow it still smelled of herbs and wildflowers. Gradually her fatigue conquered her and she relaxed against him. His arms came up around her, brushing the *petu*-covered swell of her breast.

Michael leaned back against stone, settling Khadija against him. All it would take was a flick of his fingers to have the weight of her breasts in his palms, her body against his. It felt right to be like this. And his body knew what it would do next.

He pulled her *petu* closer around her chin and considered.

Something was not right, just as something had not been right at Hashemi's camp. To leap into the river had been downright foolhardy for her, even if this was one of the strongest women he had ever met. But the fact that no one had seemed to give chase was the real concern.

It was likely Hashemi had sent her. The question, then, was what did Khadija Siddiqui want?

#

He woke to full daylight—noon at least—and the scent of fire. His arms registered that Khadija was gone.

His eyes flickered open. Not gone. She knelt beside the fire pit, grey *petu* still around her shoulders as she nursed the small fire into smokeless flame. Her long fingers gently nudged bit of tinder into position, sticks and bits of grass to best catch the flame.

She was so precise in her movements, precise and yet filled with unknowing grace as she pushed a heavy lock of hair back behind a delicate ear. He would like…. He swallowed, feeling like a voyeur as she checked her *salwar kameez* top and his and the *jalabiyya*. She frowned at the coat. It obviously was still sodden.

But she pulled her top to her and in a quick motion had shrugged the *petu* from her shoulders, sitting half naked in the strand of sunlight that found their haven.

Her skin was pale as milk, smooth as calm water, and her long hair fell to a slim waist and beyond to the swell of her hips hidden in the bottoms of her *salwar kameez*. There were songs and psalms to be sung to her beauty, and she did not even realize it. He would tell her so. Sing the songs.

She was braless as she warmed herself by the fire, the shift of her torso allowed him a sweet glimpse of the fullness of her breast. Then she stretched her arms up over her head, arching her back. Muscles worked under that smooth skin. Her spine bent with the grace of a willow.

He shouldn't be watching. This was a private thing.

He closed his eyes and cleared his throat and heard the swift flurry of cloth before opening his eyes for the second time.

She looked at him as she smoothed her *salwar kameez* over her hips. By the look of her she'd managed to replace her bra as well. A strange look was in her eyes—resolve and something he couldn't identify—pain, perhaps. Or panic.

Then she was on her knees in front of him, and her lips were on his.

Chapter 31

Khadija sensed his initial surprise in the way his arms came up, the way his hands plucked at her shoulders, then relaxed to slide slowly, inexorably, down her back.

Oh, Allah, what she did.

His lips, hard on hers, became harder and insistent as his arms tightened and he half-lifted her onto his lap as if he would own her. As if he would do all the things she remembered. Warmth and wanting surged into her, and she hated her weakness. Hated that she did this for Hashemi.

She pulled back, her head full of his scent. Perhaps...perhaps it would require no more than this kiss and he would tell her everything. She rested her head against his chest, her own heart pounding in hate of what she did—just as she had hated him this morning when she woke warm in his arms and had fled for fear of what she was. Her choices and her feelings named her whore—not Hashemi.

"Thank you," she whispered. "I was a fool to run. Hashemi—he's an evil man."

His arms pulled her closer, and his lips graced her cheek, her neck. She stopped herself from stiffening.

"Why did you, then?"

His voice was soft and yet it rumbled with a power deep inside him, as if it came from the earth. She replaced her ear on his chest and heard the long slow beat of his heart. This man was more alive than she could ever be.

"I—was afraid. I wanted my father."

Best to stay as close to the truth as possible. She felt his chin on her head as he nodded. His lips on her hair. His hand ran up and down her spine like a parent comforting a child, a man gentling a timid beast. She relaxed into the warm safety his arms offered and hated herself.

"And yet you left him."

Not so safe, then. There was a cold question underneath his statement. If she was afraid of him, why had she come back? She remembered Hashemi's words. The question was whether she could she say them convincingly.

She pressed against him, feeling the way Michael Bellis's body responded, the answering heat that flooded her. She *was* a whore. Hashemi's whore, and she wanted to weep.

"They were going to kill me for helping you escape. I realized I was wrong to help men like them. I wished I'd stayed with you." Closer to the truth than she wished to admit.

Michael's fingers dug into her shoulders and he held her from him. He looked into her eyes and she found herself bound by the naked wanting in his gaze. She looked away lest triumph show on her face. Instead she raised her fingers to his lips, his cheek, and felt him tremble, lean into her touch.

He was hers. He would tell her what she needed to know.

Then he shoved her aside.

She tumbled to the ground. In one swift movement he stood, bare-chested save for his vest, looking southward and running his fingers through his wild hair. When he turned back to her, his gaze was hard.

"Either you're one hell of a liar, or I'm a fool."

She looked up at him, aware that her still-damp *salwar kameez* clung to her body, that her hair hung loose like a whore's.

His guarded look brought a pain to her chest. Worse than the aching need she'd seen every other time she'd met his gaze, this was the look of an honorable man who was used to betrayal—who saw it in her.

What would she have to do to learn what she must? She climbed to her feet. "Trust me or not. I'm here for you. Take me back to my father as you promised. I won't try to run again."

She turned back to the fire, making herself busy spreading the front of her *jalabiyya* to dry it.

"You should bring the kettle. We can have tea."

She heard Michael retreat and sagged against the stone. That had been the hardest thing she had ever done. She felt sick at her actions, worse because his arms, his warmth and caring, had meant more than James Hartness ever had. That said nothing good about her, for she used this man's caring just as Hashemi had said she must. Just as Hashemi used her. Honor was only a tool to be used.

It didn't fit the Quran's exhortations that all good Muslims must work for good. She knew her actions would lead to this man's death. She covered her face with her hands until Michael brought the kettle. Then he stood above her as she made tea, smoking something he had pulled from the roll behind his saddle.

Hashish. The smoke coiled away from his face, but his gaze was far away. After the tea, she spread her coat in the sunshine, knowing the dry wind and the sun would steal the last of the river water away. It would allow them to move on tonight.

When she was done, she looked for Michael. He had urged her to sleep, while he worked around the horse. She watched him check the animal's hooves and frown. When he was done, he settled on his heels beside her.

"He's got hooves like concrete, but one is still splitting from the rocky ground. We're going to have to take it easy for a few days."

She waited. She'd been around him enough to know when there was something else he would say. Finally he shook his head.

"Khadija, I've been a fool keeping you with me. At first I couldn't have my route exposed. But Hashemi knows where I am and he knows I've got to be heading for the Anjoman Pass—that's the only way I could be going. That's not the kind of place you take a woman. We've passed Ferghamu, but the lapis mines at Sar-el-Sang, the Blue Mountain, can't be far. There's a small town where traders stay. I'll leave you there. You can get a ride back to Feyzabad and your father."

He stood up.

The wind seemed to roar in her ears. It was all she had wanted and she could not accept it. "Thank you, Michael. *Inshallah*, I will see my father soon."

"*Inshallah*, we will see."

She waited, unable to sleep, as sunset threaded blood across the sky. Michael dozed against the far wall of the alcove, his dark lashes masking the pale eyes that were a window on his soul. He slept like a soldier, catching it where ever he could.

She was only a worthless tool to be used and discarded—just as Hashemi planned to discard Michael Bellis.

And that was not the Afghan way. The Afghan way was to take the discards of others and make something of use from them. In the ancient past they had taken the ruins of empires and made Afghanistan. These days old Russian tanks had become fence lines near Kaabul. Pieces of Russian engines had become well pumps. She had even heard that explosives from old bombs were used to mine the emeralds and rubies of the Panjshir Valley.

That was the Afghan way. It seemed more Michael Bellis's way as well. He could have cast her off. He could have left her bleeding. He could have left her with Hashemi or in the river where she would have died.

Perhaps what she saw in Michael's eyes was only pity. She could have read him wrongly. Or perhaps it was only animal lust, but that would make it easier to do her duty to Islam. Get the information Hashemi needed. Protect her father. For herself.

Praise be to Allah, Lord of Worlds.

She completed her prayer and asked for strength.

After sundown they rode in total darkness, the quarter moon hidden behind clouds, the bleak landscape gone. She rested against Michael, too aware of his arms—of their strength and of all the things she needed to know. She had to begin.

"When I was small, my brother and I used to play in the park along the Kaabul River. I still remember it: there was water in the river then and my father and mother would walk with us and laugh as I chased my brother around. He was always so much faster than me, it was easy for him to outrun me, and yet he let me catch him. I didn't realize he let me until I was much older." She shook her head. "I think I may have wanted to become a doctor because of Yaqub, even more than my father. I was still chasing my brother. He left for medical school when I was only fifteen and I missed him so much."

She stopped speaking and a void seemed to wait to be filled.

Allah Infinitely Good, the All-Merciful,
Thee I worship, and in Thee I seek help.

There was a difference in him—a stiffness in the way he sat. Would he answer? Would he speak at all? Instead he sighed.

"Your brother was a good man. You must miss him. I do."

"You knew Yaqub well?"

"Of course. As I know your father. We were—friends."

Friends. The word hung in the night, like the unfinished end to the sentence. Friends and yet your kind killed him. Friends and your kind betrayed him, just as my father does by not avenging his death. Anger blossomed in her chest and she forced herself to stay still, to be a silent cat listening for prey.

Allah, Owner of the Day of Judgment

"You started to tell me of yourself the other day. What is there to tell?"

"What indeed?" She could tell by his tone that the taunting smile was on his face. She stiffened and felt a slight rumble in his chest.

He laughed at her again. Was she that bad a spy that he could see through her words to her motivation?

Show me your straight path,
not the path of those who earn your wrath
nor those who go astray.

"Why were you in Feyzabad?" she asked.

"I wasn't—by choice. Hashemi and the others brought me."

"From where?"

Silence behind her, then: "Khadija, why this sudden interest in me? You've not asked one thing since we've traveled together."

She heard weariness in his voice.

"I know you better now. You rescued me." She half turned and looked back at him, trying to compose a wicked grin. "We slept together, didn't we? Surely that counts for something?"

Her stomach curdled at her brazen words.

Silence again. Perhaps it was his silences that evoked such loyalty in her father and such hate in Hashemi.

"You know how I live, Khadija—or at least you suspect it. Why else would you ask these questions? Yes, I'm a spy and no, I can't tell you more than that. That knowledge alone is enough to get us both killed."

His sharp, bitter words closed a door, and his arms were no longer warm around her. Instead they were a prison. He urged the gelding into a trot and farther into the maze of hills, following Michael's reading of the stars. When the animal slowed at the next hill, she tried again.

"Does my father know?"

"Your father knows many things. He taught me poetry and Islam. But he should be left out of any discussion of my life."

She opened her mouth to ask another question.

"I mean it, Khadija. My life leaves a man hollow and incapable of caring. There's only duty. My duty says I'll say nothing of anyone I know. Names are lives, and I've seen too much death to trade a name so easily, *Alhamaduli'Llāh*—Praise be to God."

"But you said Yaqub was your friend. Friends care for each other."

His whole body stiffened so the horse seemed to jar him in the saddle. The wind rose around them, until finally he said: "Yaqub's dead. You know nothing."

But his protest told her more than she wanted to know about her father. She thought of the scene in the clinic, of her father swiftly mending a wounded Michael Bellis when the foreign army medical services were only blocks away, when any Kaabul hospital would have opened all its resources to serve the foreigner.

But Michael Bellis had come to her father. She should have seen it then.

"Stop. Stop the horse."

Michael obeyed and she threw her leg over the horse's neck and slid to the ground, stumbled away and leaned against a stone. Her stomach heaved and she was sick.

The retching brought her to her knees, and then Michael's hands were on her, holding her *chador* and hair back from her face, rubbing her back, offering her water to cleanse her mouth when there was nothing left in her stomach to lose.

He helped her to her feet and steadied her as she accepted a sip of water. She felt him so near to her, too near her heart. Whether he told her anything more, she already knew too much.

Her father was more than a casual acquaintance to Michael Bellis. He was one of those enemies of Islam Hashemi sought. He was in league with the *kofr* who had killed her brother.

Chapter 32

Mohammed Siddiqui clutched the brown paper bundle on his lap as Ahmad Mali Khan shook his hand through the Jeep's side window. Through the pinprick of light he could just see the brown walls of Ahmad's courtyard. Beyond the walls would be the brown buildings of Feyzabad and beyond the town were the brown mountains and valleys. Everything colorless brown.

"Safe journey, old friend. I wish for you joy and safe meetings as you return home, *Inshallah*," Ahmad said.

An empty wish with Khadija gone, but he knew it was meant in good faith.

Mohammed sighed. "I will see Hamidah meets with her family to be, and that Zahra is enrolled in school. They will be waiting in my home for you."

Ahmad released Mohammed's hand and his fingers dug into the paper bundle, seeking the control he had lost these past few weeks. The package held the blue *burka*.

He could not, would not, believe this bundle was the only piece of Khadija, of his family, left to him. His daughter would not leave him like this. But perhaps she was no longer his daughter.

That sent a cold knowledge through him. He had lost sight of who she was and had become blind in more than his eyes. She had come back from England no longer his studious daughter who would burst into peals of laughter so easily—finding joy even in dry text books. Instead she was serious—and full of anger? Or was it fear?

It had seemed as though she even blamed him for Yaqub's death. In truth she might be right. Yaqub had wanted to return to England to work, but Mohammed had asked him to stay to aid their country.

Always a dutiful son, he had. And he died.

Mohammed huddled in his guilt as the Jeep engine roared and the driver urged the vehicle out the house gate and down the Feyzabad street to the gravel track that passed as a road. From the rear of the Jeep, beyond the cigarette-smoking soldiers who provided security in his war-torn country, came Zahra's excited whispers and Hamidah's calm voice, silencing her.

Why he'd agreed to take the girls to Kaabul, he could not say. Perhaps they would fill the emptiness in his house. Perhaps in this small way he could fool himself into believing everything was all right. But Hamidah's meeting with her betrothed was really just a way for Ahmad Mali Kahn to deal with his guilt that Mohammed's daughter had been lost while guesting at his home.

In truth, it was probably Aisha who urged this. It left Ahmad alone with his wives, and old Fatima alone with Aisha. Even blind he could see what happened and how Aisha ruled her husband. There were currents running deep in that household that could affect more than the medical care available in Feyzabad. He'd heard rumors of attacks on foreign medical workers, though Ahmad denied it. He hoped the flood of women's emotion would not be the final thing to drown his old friend.

"So what will you do when you return to Kaabul?" The driver asked as the Jeep bounced over the potholes and the wind through the open window carried the river scent and the dust of wheat fields in full harvest. The bleating of sheep reached him, the flocks coming lower as winter neared. So much life and he was not part of it.

"Report my findings. Arrange for more supplies to be sent." The road ran westward, the sun heating the Jeep from the back.

"*Aacha.*" The man hocked and spat out the window. "I'd not want to do this journey all the time. It's hard on the vehicle. Hard on the bones as well."

Was his daughter only bones? Where were they now? Had she been killed and left to rot away? Was she prisoner somewhere, waiting for ransom? If so, why hadn't they contacted him? There was nothing he wouldn't give for her.

But Khadija held for ransom made no sense. The whole thing made no sense. Why were the women on the road? Aisha had said they went for a walk, but Aisha had proven herself a woman who would rather lay about and let others walk for her—"her pregnancy," she said. Yet there had seemed to be something that drew Aisha and his daughter closer.

"Khadija," he whispered.

"Pardon, sir?"

"I just think of my daughter. Khadija." After her disappearance everyone was afraid to say her name. Except for the filthy gossip they thought he didn't hear in the house and the hospital.

Well, he knew Khadija. She would not harm their honor. Hadn't their worst fights been about Yaqub's death needing revenge, about honor and shame for the family? Khadija might have spent time in the West, but her Afghani pride ran as deep as the earth and as high as the sky.

No, she had not run off; something had happened to her after she wandered too far from him in Feyzabad. In Kaabul, she had begun wandering far, as well. Before they left for this trip she had often disappeared to visit her friend, Mirri, and the young man, Mizra, had made clear his intentions to marry Khadija. But the Mirri who had come to visit was not the bright-eyed girl he'd known before. This Mirri had concerned him for her open dislike of foreigners, though she admitted never meeting any. And Mizra – he might be the brother of a friend, but he was far too traditional to be a husband to Khadija.

Mirri's irrational thinking made no sense. It made less sense for Khadija to befriend such an illogical girl or even allow Mizra's attentions. But they were signs he should have seen. Thinking back, there had been so many.

Mohammed clutched the *burka* to his chest as the Jeep careened around a curve. He might not be able to get anyone to search for her in Feyzabad, but truly that was just where she had finally disappeared. He needed to understand her. In Kaabul, he would seek to understand her and what she had become involved in—he had the connections there to at least begin the search.

Kaabul, where she had begun to fade away.

Chapter 33

The village at the edge of the river had no name. Beyond it, the high mountains ranged back towards the Pakistani border. Perhaps, Michael considered, he should give up his mad dash for the Panjshir and go that unexpected way. It would, however, mean a further two-week delay over mountains and held the chance of arrest, or worse, at the border. And rumor said the bloody Pakistani border guard was in league with the Taliban.

Soon. Just leave the woman here and move on.

The town disappeared behind the mountain slopes as he guided the horse down a ravine. His chin brushed the top of Khadija's head. Something had changed with her since her dousing in the river—something that made her as changeable as the wind in the mountains, as uncertain as shifting ground. Everything she did was suspect.

He had respected her anger when he'd dragged her away from Feyzabad. He had hoped she might have stopped hating him after she'd first kissed him. It had felt like an honest kiss; he'd seen the confusion in her eyes. But now the staged little display of her body, the way she pressed herself against him—there was something awkward and untrue in it. He knew he could have her if he wanted. The question was, at what price?

Plus there were all her questions now, when previously she had only watched and waited for a chance to escape.

He inhaled the soft scent of her and wished, again, he didn't harbor these suspicions. Let her return to Mohammed and if they met again, it would be with all the etiquette of Afghani ways as a safe barrier between them.

The town came into view again and Michael reined in. The village was nothing more than a string of red-brown, mud-brick buildings strung along the road close by the river. Other structures clung, almost invisible, to the hillsides, but the village's flat roofs gleamed in the harsh sunlight. A small copse of stunted aspen shed golden leaves that the wind scattered around the hooves of a string of donkeys tethered in front of one building. The *chai channa*, most likely. Those places drew visitors and residents alike.

Beyond the donkeys, in the shade of one of the buildings, sat a Jeep bearing Afghan military markings. Michael felt a little stir of excitement in his gut.

The reins slipped through his fingers and the gelding dipped his nose, searching for grass amid the stone.

A military Jeep carried soldiers or dignitaries. Such vehicles usually had radios—usually with good range. He might not be able to reach Kaabul, but he might reach Feyzabad and send out a warning.

"*Allāhu akbar.*" God is great.

"What is it?" Khadija looked up at him, then followed his outstretched arm as he pointed.

"What do you see?"

"A ragged town. A few donkeys."

"A Jeep, Khadija. A government Jeep. We may be able to meet both our needs—you for escape, me for a radio."

"Radio?"

"Come on." He dismounted and pain shot into him. It took a moment to catch his breath. Then he helped Khadija down.

His side had gotten worse, dammit. Awareness of it ate like a worm inside and he had no time to deal with it. The antibiotics weren't helping. The hashish he'd traded for in Baharak eased the pain a little, but he knew it just masked the thing eating at his side and made his reactions slower as well. A dangerous combination.

"We'll leave the horse here, and check things out."

"But you said it was a military Jeep. The soldiers will help us."

"Maybe."

Years of caution stopped a headlong run into the village, even though things looked hopeful. Getting into the town would be no problem. It would be the getting out that could kill him—if things were not as they seemed. Still, if he could leave Khadija here, it would be a blessing. If he could get access to a radio, then Allah truly was great.

"I'll get you down to the road. You walk into town and ask for help. These are honorable people. They should get you back to Feyzabad. I'll take a less direct route and if all is okay, I'll meet you in the *chai channa*."

Her gaze met his as she pulled the *chador* over her head. There was fear there, but she nodded. The hint of her eyes beyond the lattice was an enticement he would not have thought possible. What was it about this woman and her contradictions?

He led her down the last of the defile, helping her through the slippery gravel, and out on to the road. She looked up at him.

"Thank you, Michael. My father will honor you for your care."

Michael studied the hints of her eyes through the veil and thought there might not be anything more seductive.

"Perhaps," he said and turned back to the mountain hating the suspicions that ruled his life. Perhaps the old man did not know what his daughter had become. Or perhaps Mohammed Siddiqui was no longer a friend. Hidden amid the boulders, he watched her start towards town. He should just carry on southward, but the chance of a radio was too much.

Soon. Getting the information out was the priority. Then others could take over the task of stopping the plot.

For all he knew, the war could already have started, though he had watched for the contrails that would write such a disaster on the sky. So far, all he had seen were the liners on the few commercial routes that dared cross near Afghani airspace.

He headed cross country, swiftly traversing the slope, boulder to outcropping to boulder, using the grey of his *petu* to help him blend with the landscape. When he emerged from the defile, he was even with the southern end of town and close by cover offered by the copse of aspen.

He crouched amid the trees. There was little movement in the town. Occasionally a man would come out of one of the buildings and head to the *chai channa*. A thin, brown dog got up from the shade of a building and repositioned itself in the sun.

The sound of voices brought Michael's head around. Behind him, the trail to the mines wound into the hills, and a string of donkeys laden with dusty burlap bags and carrying cinder-covered miners threaded down into town.

This was his chance. Michael stepped out of the trees and hailed the men. He came even with the lead donkey and its old-man rider.

"How was the *neeli*?"

The man glanced at him. "*Aacha*, it has been a good start to the season. Allah himself heated our fires so the earth released the jewel to our hands. *Neeli*—the best of indigo color. I had not thought the mines would give such gifts so early in the year. It will bring good money for dowry for my son's bride-to-be."

The garrulous miner patted the bags under him and laughed back at his companions. The five men had the look of sons, all with the same long nose and narrow-set eyes as the father.

Knowing sometimes the best hiding place was in plain view, Michael walked with them into the village. The men stopped their beasts outside the *chai channa* and stood discussing their profits—a bad habit when they had yet to sell their stone and the Pakistani traders were well known for driving hard bargains.

Michael slipped past them to the Jeep, the shadows of the building hiding how he scrutinized the vehicle. Typical army issue, but with only the bare bones of equipment: a medical kit clamped down in the back, many metal boxes of ammunition—some left open in plain view. Poor practice. Plain seats, with the springs showing through, a bare metal dash with a vacant bracket where the radio should be.

"Dammit, work with me."

He looked to the heavens and then back at the miners. They had quit their self-congratulations and were entering the *chai channa*. Best be with them if he wanted to be unremarked. At least his weeks in the hills had left his clothing as worn as theirs.

Five long strides brought him to the door, just after the miners. He caught its edge, but it yanked from his hands and a figure slammed into his chest.

Frightened eyes framed in black cloth met his. Then Khadija pushed him back into the street.

"Hashemi," was all she said.

#

He just stood there!

Khadija pushed him again, looked over her shoulder. Did anyone notice? *Inshallah*, they would not notice.

The door thumped closed behind them and Michael grabbed her by the arm and dragged her towards the shadows by the Jeep.

"What the hell are you talking about?"

"Hashemi's men are in there. I saw two I recognized from the camp. They didn't recognize me."

He shook his head. "There are government soldiers here. They're on opposite sides."

She looked up at him. Surely the force of her will could help him understand.

She couldn't chance him being caught, because she didn't dare trust his strength either. Not when her father's life depended on it. She'd seen the desire in Michael's eyes. Had felt the way he leaned into her palm.

This man had a price, just as every man did, and she was the price. Hashemi knew it and would use it if he caught them.

She might care nothing for the names Michael Bellis carried, but she would not give Hashemi her father. She needed time to sort things through—to understand what had led to Yaqub and her father being on opposite sides and why her father had betrayed Yaqub and their people.

Then—then she would decide how to deal with it.

"In Afghanistan who can say who is on what side? Sides change like sand shifts in the desert. You work amid my people and you do not know this?"

He shook his head, and she knew she'd gotten through. "Shit."

The *chai channa* door slammed open, spilling two soldiers and another man into the street. They turned towards the Jeep and Michael dragged her around a corner of the building. His hand clamped over her mouth as if he did not trust her. She could hardly breathe beneath his horse-scented palm. From the shadows around the Jeep came the soldier's voices.

"As we said, we have sixty boxes of shells. Russian Uzi. Best quality, down from Dušanbe. The generals there—they sell their souls until we hold all the weapons." Laughter from the three.

"And the fee?"

"All the gold in the earth, of course." More laughter.

"And I'm to bargain with *galamjam*? With men of no faith? What of Islam? These bullets will be guided by Allah himself."

"It doesn't pay for the risk we take. If our officers found us, we'd be shot." The speaker's voice was tight—he did not take the insult well.

"Then shoot your officers."

The two soldiers barked nervous laughter and Khadija shivered. She squirmed in Michael's arms. They had to get out of here.

The barter for the ammunition carried on, and Michael slowly half-dragged her along the rear of the building. They flitted to the edge of town, and he yanked her into the aspen grove where he shoved her to her knees.

"What game are you playing, Khadija?"

What was he talking about?

"Are you blaming me for Hashemi's men being here?" she demanded.

She'd saved them both—had saved Michael from being caught, and yet he questioned her.

"I suppose I'm responsible for the soldiers, too. And for the *jihad*. And for the Taliban and for the Russians and the British and all the other conquerors who have traipsed across my country."

She knew her voice was starting to rise, but this man was unreasonable beyond anything she knew. More so when he only grabbed her arm and dragged her back amid the boulders and along a snaking trail that led to the horse.

"I'd hoped to buy supplies, at least," he said as he half-threw her on the gelding and mounted up behind.

His body was hot with anger as he turned the horse around. She sat stiffly in front of him, wishing Anaargórrey still lived; if she did she'd kick the mare away and leave this damned *Amrikaayi* to his business.

But Anaargórrey was dead. She was stuck riding towards Skazar and into Hashemi's trap. She had to get something to tell him or Skazar would trap her as well. She had no doubt Hashemi would kill her if she failed to get information, just as surely as he would kill Michael Bellis.

If she could get some names, any names but her father's, she could at least control what Hashemi knew and direct him away from Papa. If Michael would only trust her.

She twisted in the saddle and saw only an unyielding set of his jaw.

"You've got no business treating me like this. I'm not your enemy. I warned you, didn't I?" He had to recognize that, at least.

He only grunted, his gaze on the narrow track between the mountain ridges. Then he glanced at her, his eyes like the brittle blue flakes of the palest Asmani lapis.

"This time," was all he said.

Chapter 34

Michael rolled on his side and stared at Khadija across the remains of the fire. It had heated their tea as dawn broke over the back of the mountains. Now, at dusk, the fire was only brittle ashes and she lay like a Middle-Eastern Cinderella, wrapped in her *chador* and *petu* against the coming night.

He dared not trust this woman. Everything told him that in all his years in Afghanistan, she was the most dangerous creature he had ever met.

More dangerous and less predictable than the quakes that regularly destroyed whole towns.

Khadija changed like the clouds changed the shadows on the faces of the hills. Who was he kidding—she was more dangerous because he felt something for her and feelings were something he'd trained out of himself a long time ago.

He sat up and winced at the wound. It was a constant throb like an extra heart. He reached for his pack and pulled out a hashish cigarette, lit it, and inhaled the acrid smoke.

He didn't like to blur his senses—not under these conditions—but the pain made it almost impossible to move and Allah knew he needed to keep moving. He stared across the fire.

Just looking at the soft curves of her form he felt his will soften. He shook his head. The funny thing was he'd known he would feel something for her just from listening to all of Yaqub's stories.

The brother had loved the sister very much, had described her beauty and her strength and intelligence and caring. What Yaqub hadn't described was the effect the woman would have on Michael—the way all her qualities coalesced into something that spoke of—precious life?—that sent a heat running deep into the cold empty places where Michael dwelt.

He inhaled another deep draft of hashish. Khadija tried to mine him like the old miner after lapis—using heat to loosen the semi-precious gem. The trouble was that fire *could* loosen his words. Better to keep his heart hard.

Another long pull of the smoke and he released it in a series of small concentric circles. The pain eased its clamp on his side. Or perhaps he just didn't care anymore. Soon he would face the tasks of saddling the horse and mounting, and then the long hours of riding. He wanted to be numb by then.

When he looked back at her, her green-brown eyes were open, considering him. He stood and took another drag, the cigarette sizzling as it burned to the roach. The sun had fallen westward beyond the mountains and dusk would come quickly. At least there were no contrails. No sign of the impending war. *But soon.*

"We need to get moving."

She sat up. "It's not nightfall for a few hours yet."

He shrugged.

"Won't caution serve us best?"

The folds of the *chador* framed her face. In the faded daylight her features were a picture of grace and symmetry, even with the little lines of worry between her brows.

"Caution slows us." He tamped the roach between his fingers and pocketed it, exhaling the last of the smoke and feeling the muzzy gentling of the fire in his side.

"This is about more than escape. But then, you know that."

He heard his own bitterness and turned away, but felt her nearness as she came to him but did not touch. Not like when she came from the river. There was none of that tempting. Another shift of the clouds of Khadija.

"I don't know what you're talking about."

He ignored the unspoken question and left to catch the horse while she packed their few possessions into the medical bag. The bandages were almost gone. The last of the antibiotic had long been used to treat both their wounds.

Not that it had done any good for him. He winced as he tightened the girth under the animal's belly.

She brought him the last of the partridge from their previous night's meal. Their supply of lentils and rice was perilously low, so they were dependent upon whatever he could shoot on the trail. Thank God for the Pakistani rifle. Most nights he had been able to find something. The landscape was actually full of life—if one knew how to see. He rubbed his eyes against a sudden double vision and caught himself against the horse.

"Michael? Are you all right?"

"Just the hashish, doll. Just the hashish."

"It's not good for you. You need to eat more, too." She held out the wing of meat she nibbled. "You can have mine, if you like. I'm not hungry."

He pushed her offering away.

In truth the pain had taken his appetite away, but thirst was becoming a problem. He could down half the water bag at one sitting if he wasn't careful, and it was becoming harder and harder to be prudent with their supply.

He didn't like what that meant. Sometimes he felt his fever thickening his thoughts. Even the hashish was better than that. They mounted and he looked at the egg-crate peaks of the mountains before him. They seemed to stretch forever. He had to get through them soon or he might not get there at all.

The ride took them almost due south into darkness. Night masked the stark landscape. Skazar could not be much further—a few days at most. It was a larger town and with a larger town it might be easier to gain the supplies he needed to make it through the mountains.

"You're avoiding my question, Michael. If this isn't just escape, what is it?" She shifted against him and he felt his body react—even through the muzzy hashish cloud. She still had that effect, no matter her allegiances.

He was too tired to spar with her. Too tired for far too much. In truth he'd been so tired for so many years it seemed like he had lived lifetimes.

"All right. As well as having information Hashemi wants, I have information he doesn't want me to share. That information's critical to the safety of the world. Something big is about to happen in China that could lead to a war. I just don't know when."

The hashish let him hear the absurdity of his words. He snorted laugher. His damned head ached. Lights seemed to dance in the darkness. Fireflies? He'd not seen them since he was a child in New Hampshire. He'd not thought they lived in Afghanistan. Did they? The idea made him chuckle.

"Happy now? You asked how I came to be Hashemi's prisoner—he caught me bringing a warning to the *Amrikaayi* you so hate. The *jihad* plots to blow up a nuclear reactor in the heart of China's major oil fields. It'll be seen as a major blow at the economic heart of China and Sino-American relations will be blown right out of the water. It's likely to start a war and I'm trying to stop it. Is that enough for you? Now will you quit with your damned questions?"

The light of the fireflies hurt his eyes. They buzzed around him, buzzed in his ears, filled his head. Buzzing and the crack of stone on stone as rocks rolled from the horse's hooves and the earth groaned under the burden of humanity. The wind in his ears carried the voices of all those who died. Yaqub and screaming.

He gripped the reins harder.

"You are the keeper of secrets and I can't hide. You are the beauty of the world but I am trapped on the ground. You are the direction of spirit, but I am caught only watching clouds."

Rumi again. Had he spoken it aloud? He wished they rode near the river. He'd like to douse his head to clear his mind.

"That's a heavy burden, Michael." Softly, so softly she spoke he could almost think it was his own thought. "I wish you'd shared it earlier."

"Sharing's not an option. People die."

"And so you choose not to live to keep them safe."

Her words chased the muzziness away. He tried to see her face. How long had they ridden? What had he said? He looked up at the sky. Clouds hid most of the stars. In the mountains there would be snow. The Anjoman Pass would be more difficult. The fireflies returned, almost blinding him. He swiped at them, but it made no difference.

"It's time to call a rest."

He reined in and slid off the saddle, but his legs were someplace else—gave under him. Khadija caught his arm. Where had she come from?

"Michael."

He jerked away and went to squat on his heels, but he swayed and almost fell. Had she seen? He looked up. The fireflies were gone. Now streaming colors filled the night. They hummed in the sky, hurt his head, until he covered his eyes.

When she touched his shoulder, he pushed her aside. "Leave me. I'm the one they want. I'm the one with too many secrets buried inside. Get out while you can."

"Michael?"

A soft touch on his brow. He yanked away. He needed none of her and her cloud-shadow ways.

"You're burning up."

"You think I don't know that? Your damned antibiotics did nothing. You can't heal me anymore than I can heal the faults in this land or the flaws in your people. You helped me die and I helped your country fail? How's that for a trade?"

The humor of the situation caught in his chest. Laughter boiled out of him. It was better than the anger, better than the bitterness. Better than the desire to die.

"I spent my whole fucking life trying to do something for this country, and all I've done is fail."

Gentle hands on his chest. Gentle hands pushed him back.

"No!" He lashed out, and his fist met something soft. He struggled to his feet. "You can't have my secrets, bitch. I paid for those secrets. So did others—far better than you." He turned away and plunged into the colors, the snowstorm of colors. Let them bury him.

"Michael!" The voice came from such a long distance. It was no friend, certainly. Easy to be sure of that, when you have no friends. More laughter ate his side.

A stone tripped him and he sprawled onto the gravel. The heels of his hands found jagged rock.

"Something else to get infected," he said with a chuckle.

Let the earth open and swallow him. It was all he could ask. All he deserved. He tried to get up, but his legs betrayed him. Why not them, too? Everything else had. Did. Would.

A strong hand rolled him over. Roselight showed a beautiful face with eyes the shades of night.

"Are you a *houri*?" He chuckled at the idea of Paradise.

"Shhh."

Hands on his vest, his shirt, hiking them up and: "Bloody hell, Michael. Why didn't you tell me?" Thickly accented English.

"Not my doctor, didn't you say?" The giggle welled up, and became a bark of pain as she tore something from his side.

"Oh my God. Stay here."

And then the rose-colored face was gone, the earth quaked and there was only darkness and the wind that came with falling.

Chapter 35

"*Allāhu akbar*—God is great," Khadija prayed as she stumbled over stones in the darkness. "Let him live. Let him live."

How had he managed to hide this from her for so long?

Because you trusted him to tell you. Because you were so consumed with your honor and your worries that you didn't even ask!

She grabbed the gelding's reins and dragged the horse and the medical pack tied to its saddle back to the man lying on the ground. He was still when she returned, but his lips moved when she touched him. His hand closed around her wrist.

"Kohendil?"

A Pashtun name.

"It's me, Khadija."

"Kohendil. You have to get word to Sirdar Khan. Their troops move from Helmund this way." The hardness of his voice frightened her.

"Shhh. Michael. Don't talk. Stay still." She did not want his names. She did not want to know.

In the dark she couldn't see what she dealt with, only smell the stench, feel the heat and the swelling in his side. She needed light. Somehow she found fuel in the darkness, stealing fodder from the gelding, anything else that might burn. She needed light!

The wind blew colder when she returned to where he should be. He wasn't. She shivered as she stared into the night. Where had he gone? The horse still grazed nearby.

"Michael!" The wind stripped his name away, leaving her alone in the dark. Please Allah, she had to help him. She wanted to run into the night to find him but knew she dared not lose the horse and their few supplies. In his condition, he could not have gone far. Stripping off her *chador*, she started in a spiral from the medical bag and nearly tripped over him. He had tried to crawl away.

"Michael," she said, on her knees beside him.

She rolled him over and his eyes flashed open. His fist caught on her cheek and sent her back onto her butt. Her vision blurred with stars.

She held his hands, trying to stop his thrashing, repeating his name over and over. Finally he collapsed.

He still breathed. At least he breathed but his body quaked with fever. She released him and found it was her who trembled when she couldn't afford to be afraid. She retrieved the fuel and the medical bag and set about making camp on the sere slope where he lay.

There was no shelter, but she could not move him. He simply weighed too much.

She shifted rocks to make a hearth and fought the wind to make fire, sheltering the flame with her body. Finally, it caught.

It was a welcome eye into the darkness, but what she saw of Michael was no comfort. His side was hideous. The flesh had healed over but the wound had festered, its edges now black. The stench of putrescence was overpowering. As she'd feared, the wound had healed from the outside, stopping the drain of infection.

"How could you let this happen?" No one answered as she heated a pan of water and seared the old scalpel in the flame. She turned back to him, holding the heated metal with the edge of the *petu* he had used to keep her warm after the river. The stench of burning wool caught in her nose.

The river dousing would have exacerbated his wound. The dressing would have been soaked through, the dampness a perfect breeding ground for bacteria.

"What kind of doctor are you? You had an injured man in your care and you don't check his progress? Not even after he helped you?"

"But he seemed fine, strong. So strong."

And that was it, wasn't it. She hadn't demanded to check his wounds because she'd been scared of that strength, scared and fascinated and angry at him for making her feel safe, when she was so weak and confused. She'd told herself to let him be—that she didn't need him—that she would not treat her enemy. But he wasn't her enemy.

"Michael, this's going to hurt like hell."

No response. Probably better that way. She looked warily at his hands, her cheek still throbbing from his last blow, but there was no way to tie him that wouldn't get in the way of her work. She lifted his arm across his body and began.

At the first incision, green ropes of liquid pulsed from the wound. She sat back, wanting desperately to find clean air to breathe. She didn't deserve it. He'd borne the pain for so long, the least she could do was bear the stench. She leaned in closer, gagging, as the firelight flickered over the oozing sore.

So much for the chloramphenicol. The wound was far worse than it had been at the cave and she had no antibiotics now.

She lanced the exit wound and allowed more of the filthy fluid to drain onto the ground, gathering more fuel as the fire flickered towards death.

With the scalpel she carved the blackened flesh away, seeking clear, red blood before she stopped. Then she allowed herself to sit back for a moment.

Let the blood carry the poisons away. Then she would take the next step.

Michael muttered again, his head thrashing back and forth as if he relived something he did not want to see. His mouth released a long string of names and towns he had memorized in verse. They were far too memorable, because she did not want them.

She clenched her fists over her ears, but his hands started tearing at the scabs on his chest. She grabbed his fists, held them, waiting, waiting as the names filling her head and then he went still.

His eyes flashed open as she readied the boiling water and a syringe. They locked on her face.

"Yaqub? Yaqub, is it you, my friend? How can it be?"

Khadija couldn't move, couldn't speak as his pale gaze roamed over her face. His skin was slicked with sweat that glittered in the firelight.

His hand flashed out and caught her wrist. "Yaqub, we should leave. There's nothing more we can do." He cocked his head as if listening.

"I know. The Hazzara women. But we can't get to them. We've got the others to get out. We have to leave now."

A low moan came from his belly and he lashed out. His voice rose in a scream. Then he shuddered.

"Noooo! Yaqub! No!" His body arched up off the soil.

"Allah, no. No." She gagged on the words. The world trembled around her. Not Yaqub. Not her Yaqub. Her legs gave so she sat down hard beside Michael.

He had said her brother was his friend—more than friend it seemed. Which said that Mirri's information had not been true. All that she had done. All the messages she had passed.

She wanted to be sick at what she had done in the name of honor and revenge.

She could barely see as she filled the syringe with boiling water. She had hated so much. All the time she had been working against the very things Yaqub had sought to do, to protect. How many people had she harmed by her error?

"You can't die, Michael. For Yaqub. For the man he was. I'm sorry. I'm so bloody sorry."

She wept as she stuffed the corner of his *petu* into his mouth and sprayed the stream of boiled water into the wound.

He screamed, then collapsed.

The gelding trotted a few strides, then stopped to graze again. Khadija inspected the wound, then went back to the fire. The water had cleaned out the worst of the poison, but there was one more thing she could do. She heated the scalpel again, holding the handle wrapped in her *petu* and praying the tempered steel would accept what she would do.

The woolen *petu* smoked and she had to change hands many times. The blade blackened first, then grew hotter until the steel began to glow. It was probably as hot as this small fire could get—what with the altitude and the poor fuel. She bowed her head, then lifted the scalpel to Michael.

"*Allāhu akbar*—God is great!" She said as she placed the heated metal against his tortured flesh.

Smoke! The stench of burning! But it was better than the rot that had been. Again, she reheated the scalpel, repeated her action, trying to cauterize the worst of the wound. Whether she had caught it in time, she didn't know.

When she was done, she dug into the medical pack for the last of the dressings and finished bandaging the wound. There was nothing for it. At Skazar the medicines would have to be replenished and *Inshallah*, she would begin to undo all the evil she had done.

At Skazar they would have to evade Hashemi.

Chapter 36

He woke in the night to wind on his face and warmth all around him. A shawl pulled close to his chin, smelled of raw wool, but it could not cover the scent of burned flesh and of the woman pressed against him.

Where was he?

Who was he?

The woman's arm lay over his bare chest, her softness, clad only in a thin, cotton *salwar kameez*, pressed close to him. Her *jalabiyya* lay across them both. Was he dead?

He blinked to clear the sense of strangeness. Overhead the stars shone lantern bright—too bright. Nearby a horse snorted and stomped. The woman next to him sighed as his arm came around her, as he pulled her close and kissed her hair.

Who was she—he knew he should remember.

Across the sky chased a brace of tiny arrows, red and white, and he was suddenly afraid.

"Michael?"

That was his name. His arm lifted her to him and her lips found his. Soft. Soft as milk and more quenching to drink. They tasted of peaches and Kandahari melons—all things he loved.

His mouth drank her in, his hands—they slid down her back, found the smooth round of her buttocks under the thin cotton and pulled her to him, tight against his body. Pulled up her top and found the smooth skin he dreamed of. His fingers traced the notches of her spine, ran up her sides and felt her shiver, traced the weight of her breast and heard her gasp.

"Michael."

The way she said it made him sure he was alive. If he could only remember her name.

He closed his eyes and slept.

#

The sun had traveled a great deal of the way towards noon when Michael rolled over. His side hurt like hell. But it was no longer like a weight rested on his heart.

He rubbed his head and found his upper arm caked in an ill-smelling substance. What had happened?

"You're awake." A figure stepped before him. Waist-long hair blew around a slender figure dressed only in *salwar kameez*. The sun cut through the thin fabric and outlined a female form. For a moment he did not recognize her.

"Khadija?" His voice was hoarse as if long unused. He coughed to clear his throat.

"Who else?" She sat on her heels beside him and caught his hand. The sun almost blinded him. So did the smile on her face.

"Who died?" he asked as he tried to sit up.

"Pardon?"

He glanced at her as he tried to understand his weakness.

"I asked who died. You never smile like that for the living—at least not that I've seen."

The smile faded as she released his hand, and he regretted his jab. His head filled with the scent and image of a woman beside him, a woman in his arms. Khadija caught her hair in her hands and began to twist its thick mass into a coil at the back of her head.

"Don't," he said, his voice catching as he looked at her, as he saw both *petu* and her *jalabiyya* draped across his body. "I'm sorry. You don't deserve that."

She was still in the wind, her hands still holding the ropes of her hair. Only her gaze moved across his face. He wanted to catch her hands and free that hair. There had been such joy on her face and he had ruined it. He'd give anything to see that smile again.

But she was the enemy. She finished twisting her hair in place, tempting him by leaving the lovely arch of her neck free to his gaze.

"How do you feel? You were very ill last night." Her voice had gone clinical.

He closed his eyes.

"Better. Whatever you did has done something."

He tried to lift his left arm above his head, but she stopped him with a shake of her head.

"Not too much. The wound is grave. You were a fool not to tend it."

The way she moved—she must know the reaction she caused in

him with every slight touch, each graceful motion. She had to know. The Englishmen must have been mad for her. A Western woman would have left obliterated hordes in her wake. Perhaps she had, as well. Perhaps that was how she tempted him.

"I had other things to tend to."

"You could have died." She had moved closer, was close enough he could scent her musk.

"Is that supposed to scare me? I died and was born a man. What would death lose me?"

"Rumi again." She shook her head.

Her liquid eyes were so large and clear—the green like the deep lakes of Band-i-Amir that let you see clear through to their heart. There was something different, something softer. Something that waited.

He broke the gaze.

She is the enemy, remember that. She wears the face of so many women in skillful masks. You can't trust her any more than a wise man trusts the earth under his feet in these unstable places. He looked down at the bandage on his side. One edge was crusted with a green fluid. "How bad is it?"

"The infection has increased. I'm surprised you're able to sit up. I lanced the wound again, and cauterized it as best I could. And kept you warm."

A memory of soft skin under his hands. She must have seen it in his face, for a sudden bloom of color spread up her neck and across her cheeks like a rose-colored dawn. A real memory, then.

His head throbbed just above his eyes. His side ached like a bitch and suddenly sitting took all his strength. The world swayed and Khadija was suddenly helping him settle on the ground.

"Rest while you can. I'm going to get water."

"Don't be a fool. You don't know the way. You might be seen."

Worse, she might be going to tell someone where he was. To bring them to him.

"I used all our water last night. You need to keep hydrated. I'm going and there's nothing you can say." He tried to sit again, but his strength failed him. She had already saddled the horse, so now she pulled on her *jalabiyya* and mounted.

"Just rest, stubborn man. You've labored long enough." There was a soft smile and then she wheeled the horse away and began a slow trot down the defile in the direction of the river.

Michael fell back and closed his eyes. He was so tired, weak, just now when he needed to be strong. The question was, how weak had he been last night? Fevered men said things. He'd seen it often enough—had even used it to gain information from wounded Taliban. One of the many things he wasn't proud of.

"You've labored long enough," Khadija had said.

"*Inshallah*, please not that," he whispered. Please not betrayal. Not by me. He looked down the defile where Khadija had supposedly gone for water. He didn't dare trust her.

It took everything he had, but he clambered to his feet with the help of a boulder. He stood shivering. He hadn't realized the wind had turned so cold. Khadija should have worn one of the shawls. He wrapped one *petu* around his shoulders and left the other on the ground with a rock holding it in place. She would need it if she was to carry on alone.

The medical pack he slid over his good shoulder.

He turned up slope, thinking to cross the ridge into the next valley, but when he tried to walk, his legs gave under him. Damn and damn and damn. He was not this weak. He could do this just as he'd done everything else.

He looked over his shoulder. Had he spoken the truth of Yaqub and how his best friend had died? She would truly hate him, then, and with the names she would betray him and so many others. It would be an apt revenge.

Slowly he hobbled back to camp. There, he collapsed on a rock and caught his breath. Cold had sunk into him again, had found the deep places inside, as he considered the long, fragile column of her neck.

It was not just the infection that drained his strength; it was the knowledge of what he must do to avert so many deaths.

Chapter 37

The wind ran cold into the neck of Khadija's *jalabiyya* and the water bag slopped against her leg. Water absorbed into her *jalabiyya* and ran down into her boot as she stared up at the rough red canyon walls and the blue sky above.

Was this the right way? She'd spoken with such confidence when she left Michael, but what if he was right? What if she couldn't find him again? Hadn't the return trip gone on too long?

She should have taken that last turn an hour ago. That had been the right one. But didn't that outcropping against the sky look like the one she had marked?

The darn shadows had shifted and everything looked different. The sky was a deeper blue as the afternoon faded away. The wind had gotten colder. She had to find camp soon, or night would fall and then there would be no way she could find her way back. She swallowed back the panicky feelings. Michael would think she'd deserted him.

No. She'd shown him she wouldn't leave him by helping him last night. Blood rushed to her face again. What had happened last night when she tried to keep him warm. He had been so fevered, and their coverings so meager, she'd only done the same thing he had done for her after the river dousing.

But it had caused something she hadn't foreseen, hadn't it? He'd pulled her to him with a gentle hunger that had raised something in her as well. She shivered at the memory of his hands, touching, easing, loving, even as her hands explored as well.

She stopped and considered where the canyon split into two.

"Don't be a fool. The need you see is your own." Michael might be a troubled man, and a troubling one—but it was her problem that he filled her mind so much. His touch….

"You won't feel his touch again, if you don't find him."

The wind took her words away, but not before Khadija realized she wanted that touch again. If had lit things in her she had not felt before. It was a hot ache deep inside, more true than anything James Hartness had evoked in an inexperienced girl.

When the soul lies in the grass, the world is too full to talk about—her father had said something like that. Knowing her father, it was probably Rumi again.

But that was how she felt, wasn't it? Too full of the knowledge of him whenever he was near. She shook her head. She should be full of piety and thoughts of Allah.

Praise be to Allah, Lord of Worlds,
The Infinitely Good, the All-Merciful,
Thee we worship, and in Thee we seek help

Which way to go? The left defile carried a few boulders she thought she remembered, but didn't that strange hooked crag mark the way back?

She should have marked the way with small cairns. That was what Yaqub or Michael would have done. That was the thing, wasn't it? Michael was much like her brother—brilliant, methodical, and capable of a burst of thought or speed that always kept her chasing to catch up.

The sun had fallen below the ridge, leaving deepening shadows in the valley. Neither trail looked right. Either of them could be. Keep moving or make camp, those were her choices. Make camp and admit Michael was right about her, or keep going and show him she knew her way in the world. She knew it shouldn't be so important to prove herself, but it was. She looked down at the gelding.

"So, my friend. Which way do you think? Your choice is as good as mine at this point. Better, probably."

The gelding's ears twitched back and forth at her voice. Just loosen the reins and let the horse take you home?

"You'll probably just lower your head and graze, won't you."

Another ear twitch.

She loosened the reins, holding to the end of the loop and the gelding stretched his neck down and forward, grabbed a bite of dried grass and began walking.

He took the defile with the hook-shaped crag and walked, stopping to grab a bite of grass every so often.

Around them, the day faded into darkness. Khadija huddled in the saddle, staring into the black. Would Michael have started a fire to welcome her? Would he be glad to see her?

The darkness was so thick she wondered that the horse could see. The animal picked its way along the defile, changing direction every now and again, so Khadija knew there was no way she would find her way back. Should she take back the reins and direct the horse?

Too late for that now. She had started this and she would finish it. Her father's life depended on it. She had to get Michael and his secrets to safety.

The gelding paused for another bite of grass and she lifted her gaze to the stars. A meteor shot across the sky, then another and another, and she remembered standing with Yaqub and her father outside their apartment in Mikrorayon, watching the meteor showers that always came this time of year. Both of them had taken such joy in showing them to her. "Signs of Allah's joy," her brother had said.

But her brother was dead and father could see them no longer.

The horse had paused long enough. It should keep moving them on. She gently set her heels to the animal's side and the gelding's head came up, just as something came out of the darkness and caught Khadija's arm.

The horse shied sideways, snorted. Khadija tumbled from the saddle, falling onto whoever had pulled her.

She scrambled away, but a hand grabbed her arm, shoved her down. She tried to roll away—once, twice. Something in the way.

Her breath rang harsh in her ears. Hashemi had found her! Hashemi would kill her for trying to run away!

She swung her fist and slugged her captor on the side of the head, but whoever it was did no more than grunt and slam her firmly to the ground. She was on her back, hands pressing her shoulders down, a weight on her middle as someone straddled her.

"What did you tell them? How many are coming?"

"Michael? Michael, it's me!"

Had the fever taken him again? Please Allah, no. His poor body cannot take much more.

"I know who it is. Do you take me for a fool? Hashemi must, if he thinks I believe your escape. Now answer me."

"You're crazy."

Hands encircled her neck and pressed. Strong fingers dug into her windpipe, making it painful to breathe.

"Hashemi set you free, sent you for information. How much did you get when I was ill? How much did I tell you?"

She heard the desperation in his voice. That and something else, something dying, hating himself. She coughed, trying to breathe.

"Nothing," she croaked and the hands eased a little. "You told me nothing I wouldn't guard with my life."

"Dammit, no!"

His hands left her suddenly and she sat up, feeling her shoulders, her neck as he paced away from her. He had probably held back, she knew. The strength of his hands could have crushed her windpipe.

She scrambled across the ground and caught his hands. He smelled of fever and of man.

"Please Michael. I understand. I understand so much. *Inshallah*, forgive me for what I've done, for everything. I didn't know. I didn't know."

He swung back to her, tears and fierce resolve filling his gaze. His hands caught her throat again, this time blocking her air, blocking her life.

Didn't she deserve it?

She wanted to help, to heal, to keep the memory of her brother alive in this man. Her fingers dug into his hands.

"Michael, no," she gasped.

His hands still squeezed. She heard her breath, his own sobbing as he pressed the life from her.

"Michael…."

It was all she could manage. There was no breath. Stars speckled her vision. She would die and she deserved it. He did what he must to safeguard the others, her father. He was stronger, could resist telling. There was no way she could have held up under the torture this man had seen. She went limp in his arms. Let it end.

Against the sky, the starlight caught on his hair, caught in those pale eyes and on his tears. She reached up to cup his cheek—and felt him freeze.

Suddenly his hands released her neck, arms were around her, crushed her to his chest.

"Khadija," he sobbed, his breath in her hair. Kisses on her forehead slid down to her lips, bit hungrily at hers. "Khadija."

Her name was like a prayer on his lips, his need an open wound in his eyes. She touched his face, trailed her fingers to his lips, and he closed his eyes and groaned.

"Oh my god, Khadija. What have I done? What have I done? I can't let you go."

"Then don't."

Her arms encircled his neck and she raised her face to his, welcomed his hard kisses, welcomed the weight of him as he lowered her to the ground, as his hands and his lips traced the shape of her face, the length of her neck.

He paused at the collar of her *jalabiyya* and she caught his hand, helped it to the buttons and sat up to slide the garment off. Spread wide, it was a blanket to their bodies.

She slid her hands up the hardness of his chest, felt other hardness pressed into her middle and knew the burn of anticipated pleasure, as his head lowered to the bruised skin exposed at the neck of her tunic.

His hands were in her hair, pulling it down, running his fingers through the length, running his fingers down her sides until she arched her back, arched her body into his and pressed him up. "Wait."

She sat up and pulled her blouse up over her head, then sat with eyes lowered, waiting to see if he would think her too forward.

He was silent in the night, then he caught her chin and tilted it back to press the lightest of kisses on her lips, on her throat.

"You gift me. Melt away the shame and modesty, Khadija. When in love, we become one. Love is the yearning of the soul for God."

His finger traced the line of her breastbone down between her breasts and farther down to her navel. Then his large palm caught her back and lifted her up from the ground to his lap, as her smaller hands stripped his shirt up over his head until finally the promise of skin against skin was fulfilled.

He touched her everywhere, and she reciprocated, exploring the scars and the strengths of his body, surprised at her own audacity as her fingers slipped loose the tied waist of his trousers.

Needful fingers found the clasp of her bra and it was loose with a flick. She shrugged it from her shoulders, welcoming the feel of his palms under her breasts, gasping at his thumbs found the nipples, as he lowered his head.

He laid her back on her coat, the wind sliding over the skin his tongue left damp. It had never been like this—this feeling, this wanting, this ache, this pleasure. What had happened in England—it was smoke stripped away in the wind.

He took her nipple in his mouth and she moaned, her arms coming around his head, her body lifting to his, wanting more. Only wanting more. *Inshallah*, let there be more!

The love of man and woman—only Allah could give a gift so fine and rich.

Michael's mouth teased her. His tongue and teeth raised small cries from her as his hands worked the small knot at her waist, slipped inside her trousers and found where the heat waited and built.

She opened her eyes and found him gazing down at her. His fingers stroked her, igniting small, broken gasps she could not control.

"The lovers will drink their wine night and day," he whispered as his fingers found the source of her moisture, stroked, spread, eased themselves deep, deep, so deep it shocked her and yet there was more she wanted. She arched up into his hand, saw a smile—a true smile—blossom on his lips.

"What?" she gasped, her body catching the sliding rhythm of his hand.

"I see your pleasure."

He leaned down to kiss her, lifting her hips to pull her trousers from her, then slipped free of his own.

She could not look away. She knew a man's anatomy, but this was different. This was no rutting English doctor—this was a man in his glory, the starlight glimmering on his skin. A man erect and full of need, proud and ready even though he was wounded.

He came to his knees beside her and laid himself along her length, kissing her.

Her mouth, her neck. Time on her breasts, suckling so she almost cried with pleasure.

His hand urged her legs apart with a gentle touch, his body slid down hers, tongue in her navel, tasting, mouth-tongue on the secret parts of her body, exploring her darkness, tasting her, knowing her. Teasing her, as his fingers spread her, as his hands slid beneath her, held her buttocks, fingers spreading her cheeks, caressing, as all the while his tongue and teeth and lips found places she did not know existed, brought her to places she's only dreamed did.

Higher. She floated above her body.

Higher. She was a speck of dust on the wind.

Higher, and she would scream if she could, if it would not shame her.

Higher, and the scream escaped. She was water pouring from a fountain. No control, just thrusts with her hips, her hands on his head, fingers buried in his hair as the waves of pleasure beat through her, as she lost herself and as he lifted himself from her and smiled once more.

Chapter 38

It was the most beautiful look in the world—Khadija, eyes wide and dazed with pleasure. She was natural, new, and his alone. No one had ever seen this look in Khadija's eyes, Michael knew.

It was to be treasured, this look. Treasured and built upon. To only bring this woman pleasure—that was what was written. He'd known it since he first saw her, since even before, when Yaqub had shown him a picture of his sister.

He lowered himself beside her, stroking her skin, seeing her breath stutter in her chest. Her skin was erotic silk. A simple touch of her side brought him to hardness, a caress of her taut nipples almost more than he could bear.

"Shall we finish this, love?" he stroked her hair back from her face as he lifted himself above her. His length lay heavy on her stomach, pulsing as he anticipated what would come.

She swallowed, and a sudden boldness filled her eyes. "A condom?"

He chuckled and kissed her fiercely again. "Spoken like a western woman. But unless you have one, I fear that's something we lack."

She met his gaze a moment and he read her hesitation, knew this interlude was probably over. Then she surprised him by reaching down and feather soft fingers ran the length of him. He thought he might explode. He closed his eyes and groaned, heard her small chuckle.

"At last I find power over you."

His eyes flashed open but there was only pleasure on her face, a joy that she could do this for him. Her small fist closed over him.

He kissed her as he kneed her legs apart. Her hands on him, made him drink deep of those rich lips, made him pull lower to take her nipple in his mouth, to bite down until she moaned.

In one swift move he raised himself above her, lifted her hips and ran himself over her. She wiggled in his grasp, opened herself like the petals of a flower.

Her eyes were huge, lashes fluttered as she waited, as he pressed himself further. Further, feeling her part before him, welcoming, soothing, sheathing him in her flesh and her eyes closed and her neck, her body arched, and "Oh" softly escaped her lips as the night disappeared.

He began to move. Slow, sensuous moves that would teach her a rhythm. He rested on his elbows, his mouth finding hers, finding her neck, trailing down to a damp nipple that jutted, tempting, into the air.

She moved with him, shifting herself to allow him entry, lifting her hips to bring him deeper and deeper until he was buried in her, lost in her, as her rhythm matched his.

Her hands came around his shoulders, trailed down his back and found his buttocks, pulling him into her, demanding he find his way deeper still.

He would oblige. He draped her knees on his shoulders and buried himself until the world might explode. He stopped and she ground against him, heard her breath ragged in his ears. Her little hands were on his hips, urging.

"*Houri*," he smiled into her ear, and began his thrusts again.

Different this time. No more of the gentle probing, she was his now. His and she wanted him. Wanted him in her, wanted to be impaled on him, wanted each thrust and movement of him inside.

He moved faster, his back arched, his skin slick with sweat and her juices, his ears full of her cries, his name, her fingers on his hips, pulling, pulling.

She was warm around him, tight around him, he was where he should be, slicked with her, with him and her eyes were closed, and he wanted those lips, those breasts, those eyes. They were his, his alone and he would have her and have her and protect her forever, and sweet God could this go on forever, as he slammed into her, as she slammed into him and he exploded inside her with a yell matched only by her scream.

When he could see, she looked up at him from veiled eyes. Still inside her, he felt the small shudders still pulsing through her. He smiled down at her and saw a light bloom in her gaze.

"Michael." Her hands came up to his face, trailed carefully down his chest. She pulled him down to her, ran her hands over his buttocks to keep him inside her.

Her walls throbbed and he hardened in response.

"What are you doing?" he growled in mock anger.

"Something I read about. All those medical books had to be good for something."

She smiled innocently up at him.

Too innocently.

He pulled himself free and laid back beside her, his hands stroking her body. He could not stop himself. What the hell was he doing—had he done?

He'd just allowed her to do what he'd vowed he would not—get power over him. He'd allowed her to touch his heart.

The damned thing was, at this moment, with her breast under his hand, with her leg draped over his and the open wanting in her eyes, he didn't care. For once he didn't care that he'd probably killed himself, and everyone else as well.

Tonight all that mattered was this woman and their bodies and the fact they might not live another day. He might still kill her, though he doubted he had the fortitude.

She ran her hand down his slick length, smiled at him and dipped her head down his body, engulfing him in the sweep of her hair—pleasure in itself, and the skilled doctor's fingers found him, her mouth found him and he was lost to the pleasure only two bodies can bring.

He stopped her before he came and lifted her up to his lap, ignoring the pain in his chest as she took him inside, as she rocked on him, his hands on her hips sliding up to her breasts, catching on her nipples, watching the joy on her face as she lost herself in pleasure under the stars and the wind caught her hair and spread it around her as if she was part of night itself until she came with a cry, and the pulsing of her body set off his own great shudder and they collapsed together onto her *jalabiyya*.

He chuckled and pulled her onto him, her breasts against his injured chest, the taut nipples a teasing pleasure. Her moist body against his belly, her head tucked under his chin.

"Are you laughing at me?"

He shook his head.

"I was just thinking this is probably not the purpose intended for your coat."

She was still a moment and then a soft laugh came from her—a sound that melted his heart. She should laugh more often.

"I think the blanket of night is enough," she said.

Her breathing gradually slowed and he knew that she slept. He managed to snag one of the *petu* and dragged it over their nakedness, then lay looking up at the stars, trying to see what else they had written, before falling into a deep, sweet sleep.

He woke to Khadija's shy smile as she tried to extricate herself gracefully from his embrace. Morning light filled the ravine with blue-grey shadows. The wind had paused as it often did between the inhale of day and the exhale of night.

She pulled the *petu* around her and scrambled to her feet, trying to gather her clothing, straighten the tangle of her hair, and not look at the naked desire her movement had created in his body.

He rolled onto his side and watched her as the *petu* slipped, revealing a shoulder, a half a breast, a length of thigh. It was better than any of the peep shows he had seen as a teenager, and more erotic.

She pulled a hand through her mat of hair and glanced in his direction. "You should wash and dress yourself."

"Why? I'm not ashamed. I'm a man. I'm alive."

He sat up, not bothering to cover his nakedness. If anything he felt better than he had for a long time, but that was a fool's sense, wasn't it? He was still left with the problem of a woman who knew his secrets, a woman he did not fully trust, but whom he cared about—too much.

He grabbed his *salwar kameez* and pulled it on, suddenly conscious of the ache in his side. When he stood she was fully dressed, the *jalabiyya* buttoned to her chin, a *petu* draped across her head, hiding the luxury of her hair. She collected fuel for a morning fire.

So it was to be like that. How quickly Khadija's clouds hid the woman he thought he might—love? No, it was only simple physical need and the bond that came from close quarters and too many perils.

Not surprising that she pulled back from him. It said she'd already gained his secrets. What reason was there for her to continue to pretend? It must pain her not to be able to cleanse herself of his touch. He sighed and scanned the sky.

Soon. Best keep your mind on the mission, Bellis.

"We should move on, regardless of the daylight."

She stopped. "I thought we'd rest another day. Give you a chance to rest."

He'd already slowed them down too much. They should have ridden last night. Two nights lost and time was ticking—he'd tested his side—in more than one way. It was time to go on to Skazar and the Anjoman Pass.

Skazar: the place she would betray him.

Chapter 39

The village of Skazar sat in a broad valley at a confluence of rivers, caught in the confines of the mountains. Southwestward the land rose in great ragged, red steps up towards the Anjoman Pass and the green Panjshir Valley beyond. Here earthquakes rocked the land from the inundation of the Indian tectonic plate by continental Asia. Crossing the pass was the last hurdle—one Michael had done in a Jeep in one day—back in the days when this route brought ammunition down from the former Soviet states. Then there was only a dirt track that followed a river for part of the way, and then a hard scrabble over the high pass. Who knew the condition of the pass these days.

The town of Skazar was typical of Afghan hill towns. Flat-roofed houses spread along the river and the road. Many of the houses were in ruins—homes only to horses now.

After five days and an increase in elevation, here the typical white-limbed poplar and mountain ash were almost bare, the ground littered with their golden leaves and the air was chilled with the approaching winter. Dust over the brown-gold fields told of the last of wheat under final harvest. A few horses loafed in pastures and a shepherd guarded a herd of goats just downslope from where Michael crouched.

Khadija and the gelding waited back in the fold of the red hills while he scouted the town.

The enemy had done its best to disguise the fact they waited, but his trained eyes had seen the sun bounce from metal that should not be in a courtyard—not even in the courtyard of the fat Mujehaddin leader of the town who had gotten rich on the lapis trade that funneled through Skazar to Pakistan.

The Jeeps were parked under his porch roof to hide them from more than casual glance.

Once the Mujehaddin in these parts had been deadly enemies of the Taliban. The Mujehaddin leader, Massoud, the Lion of the Panjshir, had been martyred by Taliban assassins as a signal to the world of the *jihad*'s might. Once Michael had supped at the Skazar leader's table, but time and profit made strange bedfellows these days.

Hashemi underestimated this time, though. Michael looked over his shoulder and his hands made fists. Do you know I know your plan, sweet Khadija? That I have not been lulled into walking into a trap?

He closed his eyes and leaned back for a moment, sun on his face. Last night, as if to wear him down, she had taken the initiative, removing his clothes, kneeling before him to minister to him until she pulled him down and shifted so she rode him to exhaustion and forgetfulness of the pain that ate at him.

At least the screaming no longer came into his dreams.

In some ways the sex was better than the hashish, but it sickened him more.

She had lain with him afterwards, cradling her small buttocks against his groin until he grew hard again and took her from behind.

Allah, she bewitches me.

But in the night he'd heard her crying.

Let her cry.

Having her in front of him on the horse was almost unbearable. He found his hands snuck under the folds of her *petu*, to cradle a breast as she leaned back against him. Dammit, his own body betrayed him.

This was the woman who had spat at him in Feyzabad. This was Hashemi's harlot, that was all. He grimaced, not truly believing.

She was Yaqub's sister and yet—he could not have been the first. She showed such bold willingness in her loving. Maybe she was Hashemi's mistress.

Michael's stomach twisted at the unfair thought. If only he could be sure his doubts were unfounded.

She was his. His smell was on her. Her smell was in him.

She was the enemy, no matter how she inflamed him.

Soon. So soon it must happen any day. That was what mattered.

He scrambled back through the rocks to the horse and the woman. His side throbbed. Damnation, just get supplies and get on through the mountains.

"Is it safe?" she asked.

She put her arms around him and looked up at him with those large, lustrous eyes. She'd placed her palm over his heart in a gesture of such intimacy his breath caught in his chest. Her skill as a courtesan could not be excelled by a professional. But then she was, wasn't she?

He wanted to pull back, but that would make her suspect his knowledge.

"The town looks clear. I figure we might be able to trade one of the rifles for a horse and some supplies."

He watched her face tighten.

Signs. Signs and clouds that shifted across her face like the landscape itself shifted. No one was as they seemed—at least not this *houri* with an angel's face. He tasted bitter almonds in his mouth as he helped her onto the horse.

"We'll ride to one of the houses on the outskirts and see what they can tell us before we chance town." Dammit, keep your feelings out of your voice. You're no novice at deceit.

He mounted behind her, ignoring the way her body fit so naturally to his as the gelding picked his way down the trail. He saw her scan the village buildings as they came out of a copse of trees. Her jaw stiffened and she looked away from Skazar and back towards the hills.

"What is it?" The question felt brutal.

"Nothing. It just feels strange to be with other people again. I'll miss being alone." Such casual lightness.

"We still have the mountains to pass." He nodded towards the heights. "Plenty of time for whatever you might have in mind."

His voice was rough to his ears.

"Is everything all right?"

She half-turned in the saddle, the wind catching at the edge of the shawl and freeing small wisps of her hair.

"Clear as crystal."

He looked back at the town, hating a world that could make them enemies. How could he ever have loved this land when it could do this to friends, to family, to lovers? It hurt to look at her, to have her so close and yet know she was someone he must push away. But here he would trap her. He would force her to be honest or he would leave her behind. Probably both.

Or kill her.

He'd thought long and hard to find the strength. If she lied he would find the coldness in his heart that had served him so well before, no matter what was between them.

He urged the horse towards a farm west of town and close by a river bed that was half-empty with the season. In spring it would flood, but now it would be easy to ford. At the front gate to the yard sat an old, bearded man in felted vest and black rubber boots. He smoked a pipe that gave off a lazy coil of sweet-scented opium. The people of the north often smoked the poppy to deal with arthritic pain, not realizing it was addictive.

"*As-salaam 'alaykum*—peace upon you," Michael began. The old man returned the greeting.

Michael dismounted and helped Khadija down.

"Sir, we've come a hard route from Feyzabad. We've lost a horse and would like to trade for another and supplies. We need to make it through the Anjoman Pass quickly. Could you help us?"

The old man waggled his head, than called over his shoulder. A younger version of him, in a traditional Afghan flat-crowned hat, came from an outbuilding, wiping his hands.

"*As-salaam 'alaykum*. I am Seyyed. You are welcome in my father's house."

Leaving his father to care for the gelding, Seyyed brought them inside, letting a young woman he introduced as his wife, take Khadija aside. There were four young boys, the oldest no more than a four, playing with carved wooden rifles. A fire in a corner hearth filled the room with warm smoke that escaped out a hole in the roof.

"It's a long time since we had guests," Seyyed said, motioning to a place of honor on a worn carpet near the fire. "The war keeps most people away. From Feyzabad most people take the road west to Taloqan. Please— you will take your evening meal with us." There was curiosity in his voice, but a traditional welcome just the same.

Michael gratefully accepted, but he could feel the man's gaze on his face, on his pale eyes. His father was just as curious and traditional when he joined them and Seyyed called his wife for tea.

Michael repeated his request to purchase a horse as they took their leisure over the tea. It was flavored with almonds and unusual to the taste. Beyond the men, he heard the women talking quietly.

Seyyed sipped his tea and looked at his father.

"We have but one horse we might part with, but we have not finished the harvest. Town might be best for supplies."

Michael considered and glanced across at Khadija, who sat against the wall with Seyyed's wife.

He'd thought that might be the case. What he needed—many hard rounds of naan because the dry, salted bread lasted many days, meat if he could get it, lentils or chick peas that traveled well—it would strip most households.

He nodded to Seyyed and drank back his tea.

"You are a good host and I would still accept your hospitality, but it seems I must go into town. I can purchase supplies and return for the horse."

Seyyed nodded as Michael pushed himself to his feet. He swayed at the stab of pain. Damnation, the wound was festering again. He knew it. The women's voices had gone quiet. When he got to the Panjshir he would have to try to drain the damned thing again.

He swung his *petu* around his shoulders and Seyyed stood to instruct him about the town. Soft fingers found his arm as he stepped to the door.

"Michael. Should you be going into town?"

He smiled at the stiffness in Khadija's voice. It told him what he needed to know.

Got you.

Chapter 40

She couldn't let him go to town. The thick walls of the household and the warmth of the hearth had made her feel safe, but now Michael's words peeled that safety away.

Khadija tried to think of something more to say, but somehow this time words escaped her. All morning as they'd neared Skazar the fear had built, and she had tried to think of a way to stop this disaster, a way to keep them safe. She'd thought when they'd come into the dimly lit farmhouse everything would be all right. But now....

She couldn't do what Hashemi demanded and betray Michael. She couldn't let him go and betray her father.

She just couldn't let him go.

But how could she tell him the truth—that she had lied and was more than a doctor for Hashemi? That she had carried messages for them, including the priority message to Feyzabad? That she had seduced him under orders to gain his secrets? That she *had* learned names—too many names to betray him with?

Worst of all, she had betrayed herself. She'd fallen to lust with a *kofr* man and had enjoyed it. She had no excuse of vulnerability as she had after Yaqub's death. No excuse of not knowing. She had knowingly gone to a man's bed when he was not her husband.

The word "whore" suited her this time.

That first morning she hadn't told because she was too shocked at her actions and too in love with the look in his eyes. But then his gaze had changed and she knew if she told Michael the truth he would hate her as much as she hated herself—there was too much of the Afghani in him.

He would leave her or kill her, knowing Hashemi could make her betray everyone she loved. But she had kept being with him, hadn't she, not because of Hashemi, but in hopes of seeing again that softness in his eyes.

She was a fool as well as a whore.

"Khadija? What is it? You're pale as a ghost." His gaze was as hard and brittle as the palest lapis. His lips—those lips that set fire to her body—were as hard as his eyes.

"You can't go into town, Michael. You can't leave me here."

It was a stupid girlish thing to say, but it was all she could think of. He looked at Seyyed then back to her, mockingly.

"My good wife hates to be parted from me. But dearest, after such a long journey, surely you would rather rest here."

"Michael, please. We can make do with less—if we get the horse and some lentils—that will be enough. You can hunt for meat. We'll be fine."

He looked at her with calculation in his eyes, then caught her shoulders. His fingers were anything but gentle.

"I don't understand, sweetness. Why's it so important that I not go into town? Would you prefer to go in my stead?"

"You're hurting me," she whispered, and tried to tug free.

It was useless. His hands demanded her obedience, her answer, and the horrible thing was his touch made her want him. She would beg him to stay with her, to not leave her, anything to keep him safe.

"And you know I can hurt you more."

His voice was soft and dangerous as a viper. Her gaze jerked to his hands as his fingers dug a little deeper. She knew there'd be bruises.

Never had he hurt her, until now. Her mouth went dry. Unless he suspected.

"Michael, when we came into town I saw something. It looked like it might have been the gleam of a vehicle. A Jeep like Hashemi has. He might be here, waiting."

She was talking too fast to be convincing, all her nerves jangling in her stammers.

He cocked his head.

"Really? You saw this? Where did you see the vehicle, my sweetness? Perhaps I should go there? Or perhaps you'd like to go in my stead, perhaps return to your lover?"

He spat the last word.

The room was silent, Seyyed and his family staring. An adulterous wife was worthy only of stoning. An adulterous wife in their midst was fascinating and worthy of gossip for a year of days.

"No." She managed to choke it out. "I'm not.... He's not.... That's—that's not what I want."

"Maybe you can take me to him and we can have tea before he tortures me again. You can be there this time and make sure I live as long as it takes. Would that make you happy, Khadija? Was it worth the price of your false modesty?"

He released his hold on her and it was worse than the power of his hands. There was such anger, such hurt, in his gaze as if he just discovered she was filth of the earth. He turned from her to Seyyed.

"My wife betrays me. I ask you to hold her here two days to allow me time to get through the pass. Then send her to her friends in town. Can you spare me food for one in exchange for this rifle?"

He held up the old rifle he'd traded for in Baharak.

Seyyed looked from one to the other of them and nodded. An honorable man would help a man dishonored by his wife. He caught her by the arm.

"No! Michael, no! You can't leave me here. I—I know too much. You spoke while you were sick. You named names. Please Michael. Don't leave me."

She clawed her way loose of Seyyed and caught Michael's hand, his beautiful, long-fingered hand.

His eyes were cold slate.

"What do you know?" He glanced at Seyyed. "Your family should not see this."

He yanked her out of the house and across the courtyard so the family would be less likely to hear—or perhaps so they would not see what he would do. A hard wind blew down the river valley and battled around the low homestead walls.

Michael grabbed her by the shoulders, backed her against the wall, and she knew she deserved anything he did. She was worth nothing.

"What do you know? Name me a name."

"No. You told me the names would mean people would die. I don't want people to die." She heard her voice—small and frightened. Just make him understand. Make him stay here. "Please, Michael. Hashemi wants you. And then he wants you dead."

"The names, Khadija!" He shook her so hard she felt like a rag doll in his grasp.

"No. You said they were never to be named."

"You little fool. I'm trying to save your life. Show me you know nothing of importance." He shook her again.

"Kohendil." The name spilled out. "Sadar Khan. Ammed Haghighi. Nazzar of Herat. Those are a few. Please, Michael, take me with you. Don't let Hashemi have me—he'll get the names. He will. I'm not strong enough."

She reached for his face, but he flinched away.

"Do you want me to kill you?"

The thought gave her pause. Perhaps in this world where she could do nothing right, that would be the better way. There was no way to undo what she had done in this life.

He pushed her from him and strode across the courtyard, his hands caught on his turban. She caught up with him, tried to touch his shoulder, and he turned around, fist clenched.

"Stay away from me." His fist trembled. His voice trembled.

The hurt betrayal and hate in his eyes made her take a step back. He had to understand. He had to know she was on his side and that what had happened between them was real—even if she had ruined herself in the doing.

"Michael, there were other names. Yaqub."

Her voice cracked. Allah, not tears. She did not want him saying she resorted to tears. She fought them, but the emotion nearly strangled her.

"You spoke of him. He was your friend. You worked together—just as you work with my father. I know that now. You—you tried to stop my brother—you...," oh Allah, the pain it brought. "You saw Yaqub die."

Michael's face paled. "I told you that?"

"When you were sick."

He jerked away as she tried to touch him again.

"Jesus."

"Don't you see?" She caught the edge of his petu. "You have to take me with you. You can't leave me for Hashemi."

He slammed her against the wall, an arm across her breast so she couldn't move, could barely breathe. His face was so close she could smell the copper scent of fever, see the burst capillaries under the skin of his face. The infection had worsened.

"You tell me why I shouldn't kill you, Khadija Siddiqui. I have loyalties to your father—and to Yaqub's memory. If either of them knew you worked for a man like Hashemi it would kill them. I'd rather kill you myself than have you sully them, understand? All those names—those are good people. Men and women who work for Afghanistan—not the Taliban, not the warlords, but for a country that deserves a right to exist on its own. Your life isn't worth anything compared to that."

"Michael, I gave you my body. You...were the first man...." She wanted to touch him, to see his gaze soften, to hear his poetry as he touched her. Instead he snorted laughter.

"You've given me nothing but your skin, Khadija. You've lied and schemed and picked my brains and most of it I've seen through, but you almost had me with your body. But you haven't given me anything of you. That's all tied up inside—in the clouds I see crossing your face."

He tapped the side of her head.

She looked away, knowing he was both right and wrong. She hadn't given him the truth, even when she took pleasure in his body. But it had been more than her skin she gave.

He hated her—would hate her more with the truth, but it had to come out. Get it done like an amputation, like a cauterized wound.

"I'm not just Hashemi's doctor."

"What a surprise." The taunting smile.

"I need your help, Michael. I need your help to get out."

"Why should I?"

"Because of my father. Because of the names. Because I—oh Allah, help me—because I love you, Michael. That's why I gave you myself to you."

The damnable tears were coming now, choking her. Couldn't he see she was begging him to save her?

"That's why I didn't want you to go into town. I knew. I knew since the river. They let me escape. Hashemi—he told me to be a tool of Islam. To do whatever I could to get the information from you or else he'd hurt my father. He told me to seduce you."

She could barely breathe.

"I was so angry at Yaqub's death, I wanted revenge. They lied…they told me that *Amrikaayi* had killed Yaqub."

She felt him go still even through her sobs. When she looked at him he was pale as death.

"My father—he did nothing to avenge Yaqub. That was wrong. I had to do what my father would not. I carried messages against the *kofr*. I carried messages in Kabul. When the opportunity came, I carried messages north to Hashemi."

She sagged between the wall and Michael's arm, suddenly not caring what he did. Kill her and get it over with. Take her with him and turn her over to the authorities in Kaabul. Her father would grieve, but he would survive, just as he had survived Yaqub's death. She was only a daughter.

She looked up at him, hoping for a change in his eyes—something to show he understood and forgave her. There was no change.

"That's all of it. I want only truth between us."

He released her and went back into Seyyed's house. Khadija dug her fingers into the mud-daub wall to hold herself upright. The wind skirled harsh music around the corners of the house and lifted dust into her eyes. When he came out, he carried only the old Lee Enfield rifle.

Seyyed and his father ran past Michael out the gate and Seyyed's wife brought them out a small bag of lentils.

The old man brought their gelding and another horse to the gate, both saddled, and Seyyed returned with five, half-meter-wide rounds of naan.

These, Michael tore into quarter pieces and, with the lentils, stuffed them into their pack. Then he turned to Khadija, who still stood by the courtyard wall.

"Mount up. The truth is, I may still kill you."

Chapter 41

Mohammed clung to Hamidah's arm as Zahra crunched beside them. The young woman was like a colt in the spring, trotting around them in the market to examine everything she saw. He wished he could see her. Somehow he thought she would remind of the Khadija of before.

The thought brought a pain to his chest and he stumbled. Hamidah quickly caught him.

"Uncle, what is it?"

"Nothing, daughter-of-my-friend. A stone, perhaps." It stuck in his throat to call her "daughter" so he'd extended the name. "Daughter" was still reserved for Khadija, just as "*Pishogay*" was.

The two young women thought he was an old man in mourning, but truly he held his daughter fiercely in his mind. If no one would speak of her disappearance, it did not stop that fact from being ever present. Now, today, he was going to begin his enquiries. He *would* find out what had happened. He might be old, but he was no doddering fool, and while he might be blind, his other senses stood him in good stead.

He patted Hamidah's arm. "You lead me well, my dear. It's been a long time since I walked the avenues of Mikrorayon. I'd heard the streets were no more than bombed-out tracks."

Through her arm, he felt Hamidah shake her head, then she caught herself. She still had not fully learned what it meant to deal with the blind.

"It's not so bad. The buildings are damaged, though. I'd not thought Kaabul was like this. There's nowhere to go that you can't see destruction."

"The warlords fought over the dregs of Kaabul when the Taliban left. Before that it was the Russians and the Taliban themselves. This is their gift."

"It's sad to see the palace and the museum."

"Sometimes—sometimes I think it better I've lost my sight. I can hold Kaabul in my mind as she was, the Light Garden of the Angel King."

"It must have been very beautiful to call it that."

Mohammed shrugged. "It was a city with all the flaws of any city, but there are stories of its early days when it was a Buddhist city. Then the pavement was of silver and onyx and the gates of gold. Rubies and freshwater pearls were used to make designs on the walls. In the garden of the largest temple, a fountain gave such water that it could make a sterile tree bear fruit." He smiled.

"That's a story for children. Kaabul is a Muslim city."

He chuckled, hearing the disapproval in her voice. "Not always. Archeologists don't even know how the city began. It might be named after Cabool—Cain, as he is known to the Christians. It might be a combination of *ka*, or straw, and *pul*, meaning bridge in ancient Persian—from a tale of a king who built a bridge across the swampy land that used to be here. But it was a Buddhist city once—before Islam came.

"But that is enough of old tales. Tell me, both of you, what does Mikrorayon look like today? Are there many people about?"

"Some," Zahra said. "Most of the women are in *burka*. I think I shock them in my scarf." He could hear the dangerous pride of her youth.

"Many of my friends lived in Mikrorayon. I wonder if they still do."

He waited to see if the girls would go to his bait. He was lucky that Hamidah's fiancée's family resided in this battered part of the city. He had planned to bring the girls here sooner, but Hamidah and Zahra protested that they needed time to shop and to buy gifts for the young man's family.

The delay had frustrated him, because it kept him from his enquiries, though his work in the clinic had brought him bits of news—yes, there were girls named Mirri living in Mikrorayon. That much was confirmed.

"Perhaps we could help you find them?" Zahra offered.

Mohammed smiled as he set the hook.

"It will not be easy. Many no longer live where they did. I think Khadija found a friend once, a girl named Mirri."

The girls fell silent. He knew they probably looked at each other, that they wondered whether they should even acknowledge this reference to his missing daughter. It had been like that before.

"That is sad, she never brought you," Hamidah said softly.

"We could find them. It would be like a treasure hunt, the three of us investigating where your friends live now!"

Zahra's youth broke through her concern. A coltish girl, certainly. He could practically hear her leap and curvet.

"I don't know," he paused. "It would be trouble for you and we have

Hamidah's marriage to be concerned about."

"Really, it would be no trouble, would it Hamidah? While you help him walk, I can ask questions of the people we meet. I can tell them that Mohammed Siddiqui is looking for an old friend named Mirri. What is her last name, Uncle?"

That was the question he feared. He knew the girl's family, but was uncertain if the Mirri she saw now went by the name her General father had given her. "Her parents were killed and she may be married now. It was Shahabuddin. She had two brothers; one's name was Mizra." Of that, at least, he was sure. His daughter had had an insistent suitor.

"At least you have a name—two names. You keep going, Hamidah. Let me see what I can do."

He heard the clatter of her new shoes over the rubble and the distant laughter of children. Let his daughter's friends know he wanted to find them.

They would come for him, he was sure, because the more he thought about it, the more he was certain that whatever had happened to Khadija, it had begun here in Kaabul.

Chapter 42

Michael glanced over his shoulder down the sandstone gorge and felt like he was being swallowed down a long red throat. The river rushed beside him. The twists of the high walls allowed only a narrow view of Skazar anymore—hopefully that meant his passage had not been marked. The westering sunlight placed a glow over the town and winked in the windows of the Mujehaddin leader's house.

The narrow road turned a corner and cliffs blocked the view. There was only himself and his faithful gelding and the betraying woman trailing behind on the fat roan Seyyed had traded for the rifle.

It had been a bad deal on Michael's part, really. The horse would probably have traded for the Enfield, but Michael had no time for spirited barter. He just needed to be away before he changed his mind and left Khadija.

Or killed her.

Too many lives depended on those names remaining secret.

He squeezed his horse and the gelding jogged on. The truth was, he couldn't have killed her. Every time he looked at her, something inside him softened and he could not hold to his anger at what she had done. He cared for her.

"Michael, how long is this journey?"

He didn't turn back to her although her question surprised him. She'd been silent, cowed, as they left Skazar, her *chador* masking her huddled form on the horse.

At least they didn't ride together. It stopped the worst temptation. Now there was only the sight of her and the jagged ache of his heart. Dammit, he had set feelings like these away years before. They were trouble: a weakness in the landscape of his life.

More feeling than he'd had for many years.

"The pass takes about a day by Jeep. By horse, who knows? Four days if we're lucky. Then there's the Panjshir Valley."

She pushed the roan so the horse's head was even with Michael's hip and then rode with him, silence falling again except for the wind in the rocks and the rushing river. Overhead, a brown falcon hung on an updraft above the gorge.

"How can I make you understand?" Her voice was soft, pleading.

"I understand perfectly. You're Hashemi's messenger." He left "whore" unsaid.

Silence, then: "I was never anyone's whore."

She didn't sound like she believed it any more than he did.

He urged the gelding into a trot to stop his string of accusations. What was it you were when you gave yourself to me? What was that show after the river? What was the way you fucked me each night?

Yes, fucked. It was no more than that. His chest pained him and he pressed his arm against the wound. The roan kept up as the road lifted out of the gorge and began to track across a mountain slope almost barren except for the occasional dry patch of close-cropped grass. Sheep still grazed there.

"There was only you, Michael. You know that. I gave myself to you because...."

"You love me. I heard. But lovers don't plot to turn each other over to enemies. Lovers don't carry messages that may get their paramour killed. Lovers don't become lovers because they're trying to pry secrets out of each other."

"Why won't you listen? You choose to be mad! You want a reason to push me away."

Her furious voice almost made him look at her, but to look at her would cut through him. *Hold to the knowledge of her shadows, her clouds.*

"You've already given me more than enough reason."

He pushed the gelding into a trot again and heard the roan clatter behind. Wind rushed in his face, almost too cold. The sky hung clear and blue, but chained by the backs of the mountains that surrounded him. The sun was already falling away from noon and he had to push them. He had been on the road too long. His time had to be running out.

Soon.

They followed the Anjoman River as the road wound upwards. Here the water flowed north, the Anjoman Pass demarking the watershed of central Asia from that of the Indian subcontinent.

It felt like he was running from all the things that had happened on this side of the Hindu Kush. He wanted to get over the pass—not just for his mission, but also so he could return to his life, forget the things that had happened here. The trouble was, he was following a fault line to do it. The earth was unstable under his feet.

By the time evening came, he had pushed them hard. The horses were sweating in the thinning air. The wind howled around them and the sky was full of heavy, tufted clouds that clung to the mountain peaks ahead. Ignoring his own fatigue and the ache in his side, he kept them riding long past the time it was safe for the horses to scramble the slopes. He finally called a halt when the gelding stumbled and almost went to its knees.

He stopped them in a spot where the river ran next to the road and a stunted group of barren mountain ash grew close to the foot of the cliff. The remains of past fires in the shelter beside the cliff spoke of this being a favored camping spot for those who had come before. The gelding he set loose to graze. The roan he tethered on a long rope amid the trees, not knowing whether to trust the animal.

When he had finished, he found Khadija had gathered tinder and fallen branches and had begun to build a fire.

He squatted beside her and took over the task. She sat back on her heels, her face exposed by the *chador* she had pushed back over her head.

"I can make a fire."

"If you want to do something, get water."

Silently she obeyed, returning to wait with the dripping pot as he finished with the flame. While the water boiled they mouthed dry lentils in strained silence.

Their fire was a single eye in the darkness and Michael pulled his *petu* around him and leaned back against the cliff face, hoping for a break from the wind. His side gnawed at him and it was difficult to get comfortable. A shiver ran through him and he knew his fever had come back. If he could just get a decent night's sleep he would be better. He opened his eyes and saw Khadija still seated by the fire.

"You should sleep. It'll be a long ride tomorrow."

She nodded and pulled the folded-back *chador* around her shoulders.

"Michael, I've been thinking—about what you told me about China. That something is about to happen. I think…I think I might know something."

He met her gaze, and saw frown lines between her lovely dark eyes. Michael looked away.

"Do you think I want this world in ruins? I see ruins all about me in Kaabul and all over my country. No one would want that for the world!"

"You did. It's a *kofr* world."

"Bloody hell, Michael, would you listen!"

She scrambled to her feet, her face ablaze with the anger of the British epithet. It surprised him she would use it.

"You're as closed minded as I was—your secular West is as bad as the fundamentalists! They're both extremes. The West condemns Islam because they don't understand—and don't want to. You condemn me even though I want to help you. People can change, Michael. People can realize they're wrong and change. Can you? Can your West?"

She went to her knees in front of him.

"Listen to me. You said you didn't know when this thing will happen. I think I do. I told you, I brought a message north for Hashemi. It was nothing—a string of numbers. I thought it was a code, but now I'm not sure. It could be a date."

He looked at her, really looked at her and saw the hope, the fear, in her gaze. She was trying—would try anything to get his trust.

"Tell me." His voice was harsh.

"The numbers were 1-4-2-3-2-7." She looked at him and waited. "The first four numbers could be the year—in the Islamic calendar."

Michael sat up. The numbers *could* be a date. The Islamic calendar. It began in 622 and was eleven days shorter than the western Julian calendar.

"And the last two numbers could be month and day, last—in metric style," he finished.

She looked up at the sky where the clouds covered the last sliver of a moon. The Islamic month began at the sighting of each new moon.

"The new moon will be in a few days. The month of Rajab."

"The second day of Rajab."

She turned back to him. "I converted it to the western calendar. It is September 9. On September 9, 2001...."

Michael scrambled to his feet, forcing Khadija aside. "On September 9 the Lion of Panjshir—General Massoud—was killed by Taliban agents disguised as foreign media. It was the signal for the attack on the World Trade Towers."

"Couldn't the attack in China be the same—a signal? A sign?"

A precursor quake, like there was often a tremor before a larger quake. A nuclear accident before a war between China and America. It would be far worse than the felling of the towers. So many more would die.

She had to be wrong. Dear God, let her be wrong. But it made too much sense. He couldn't take the chance. He went to the fire, kicked it over. Stamped on the embers to put them out and then turned back to her as the blackness closed in.

She already had the roan saddled.

They had no time for sleep on this journey. September 9 was only days away.

Chapter 43

The night closed in around them, the wind blowing harsh off the cliffs. The road sloped up and up, crossing the Anjoman River on a stone bridge with the rushing water grinding rocks under them so that it sounded like the mountains gnashed their teeth.

The wind cut through Khadija's *petu* and *jalabiyya*, raising gooseflesh, but it was nothing compared to what she deserved. He should have killed her back in Skazar—but then he wouldn't have the information he needed. She clung to that, and watched him ahead, bent low in the saddle as if the burden he bore weighed him down.

They pressed on through the night with only a few breaks to rest the horses and chew more dry lentils themselves.

Finally the sky lightened, filled with clouds, and dawn found them as the road leveled out and the land opened around them, bringing them out to a small town beside an ice-rimed lake.

Michael reined in, studying the town, then looked at her.

"Anjoman. Named after the lake."

Beyond the lake the backs of the mighty Hindu Kush rose topped with snow and swathed with cloud. The town, like Skazar and most Afghan towns, was only a ragged cluster of mud-brick houses set amid a scattering of stunted *jujube* trees and mountain ash—all bare now, at this height. Smoke threaded up from the houses to be torn away by the wind.

Khadija rode her horse beside his and leaned, exhausted, on the saddle. He looked pale and determined this morning, but unnatural color placed high points on his cheeks.

"We can rest the horses here. I think the gelding's started limping. He had a split hoof I want to check."

Was that a shiver that ran through him? She studied him more closely, but couldn't decide and hesitated to ask.

"A hot meal would be good, as well," she said, casually. At least that would let him rest.

"There's no time. Just check the horses. Maybe see if we can get a blanket, then keep going."

A single trickle of perspiration ran down his temple. He brushed it aside.

"You're sweating."

Michael shrugged and urged his horse forward. In the muddle of buildings, he dismounted in front of a *chai channa*.

When he bent to check the gelding's hooves, he staggered, and Khadija swung off her horse. She came up to him, but he ignored her and bent to the horse's hooves again. His breathing sounded harsh in the cold air.

She stepped closer, watching him check the horse's heel with his fingers. The animal winced slightly when he pressed his thumbs.

Michael's color—he was not a well man.

He released the hoof and straightened to look at the mountains.

"The terrain is only going to get rougher from here. Like Wakhan, it's rock and more rock, with only narrow roads next to cliffs." He glanced at her, eyes fever bright. "I need to trade horses."

"I need to check your dressings."

"There's no time."

"Michael, you need to rest. I'm talking as a doctor. You can't keep going like this."

"Watch me."

He left her for the *chai channa*. She followed, almost stumbling in the sudden warmth. The interior was painted white, with bright murals of peacocks and flowers and blooming trees that gleamed in the light through the single window.

The warm moisture of the tea maker filled the air. Michael spoke in swift Pashto to the proprietor, asking about someone who might trade a horse. Asking about blankets.

The little Tajik came around the counter clad in his vest, a *salwar kameez* shirt, and a pair of cast-off Western trousers. He sent one of his sons running out into the town. The man tried to usher Michael to a seat on one of the carpets around the edge of the room, but Michael refused.

A noise drew Khadija back outside.

The wind carried the whine of a diesel engine laboring up the last climb to Anjoman. It might be one of the brightly painted cargo trucks, but there was also the chance of it being a Jeep—like Hashemi's.

She ran inside to where Michael leaned on the counter.

"Michael. I heard engines coming from Skazar."

He swayed and she grabbed his arm. Heat. Blazing heat. She turned his face to the window and placed her palm on his forehead.

"You're burning up."

"Surprise." He tried a lopsided grin.

"We've got to do something or you'll die."

"And the alternative is I live while the rest of the world goes to hell? It's not much of a life, anyway."

He pulled away from her and staggered to the door, leaving her with the knowledge she was responsible for his desperate words and for keeping him alive as well.

Chapter 44

Khadija bent low over the roan's neck as the animal galloped across the last of the fallow fields before the road ducked into the next curve of the pass. This horse was difficult to manage; it wanted to turn back to Skazar and home.

Michael was mad—fever brained. He had to be, to do this.

He hoped to make it into the pass unseen. It would give them a few more moments head start before Hashemi learned they'd been here and gone on. But there was only one path over the pass and once Anjoman yielded the fact they'd passed through, Hashemi had only to follow the road to find them.

And this time Hashemi would know she'd betrayed him. If he caught them, they'd both pay the price. And so would Papa.

The roan galloped with the choppy strides of the unwilling. She kicked its sides again and peered over her shoulder. The glint of metal came from the far edge of the valley. Just a few more strides and they'd be in the shadows, they'd have the last copse of trees by the road to shield their escape.

Yes! The trees white branches whipped her face, tore at her *chador* and the roan's sides as they ducked into the shadows. Ahead, Michael reined in.

"Damn it. The gelding's getting worse."

His fevered eyes studied the road and then the switchback that led up to the pass. The air steamed with his breath. She smelled his heat.

"How much farther is it?"

"A good day's ride. We made good time last night."

He looked at her—really looked at her. Was that a softening in his gaze? Had he—perhaps—found it in his heart to forgive?

"Khadija." Her name was rough on his lips. "Thank you for the code—

the date. At least now I know what I'm up against."

He looked away from her and she felt the wind find its way under the edge of the *petu* and down the neck of the *jalabiyya*. He still held back— saw her as no more than a tool—just as Hashemi did. She deserved it.

"What *we're* up against, Michael. Islam's not a violent faith by its nature. We don't believe in doing evil."

"Well, someone does."

He barely glanced at her before turning his horse and threading through the trees towards the shadows where the road ran into a narrow canyon beside the river.

He looked loose in the saddle, as if he was almost as if he was ready to fall. She didn't like the way his skin shone ruddy in the muddied day light. She looked up at the sky. The cloud had thickened.

"The weather's changing," she said, urging her horse up beside Michael as his gelding broke into an uneven trot.

He glanced at the sky and shrugged.

"What choice have we got?" He rode in silence a moment, then: "It doesn't snow until October, usually. They're still picking grapes in the Panjshir."

But the Panjshir was on the other side of the wall of mountains before them.

She kept the roan even with the gelding, her gaze locked on Michael. She'd seen what the infection did to him before. If anything, relapse could come more quickly, even though he rode like a man possessed. He might seek to stop a war, but his body could not stop the war within. The infection would win unless he got medical care.

The earth trembled under them, sending a tumble of rock free from the cliff just behind them. Large rocks crashed onto the road, spooking the horses. Michael reined in and kept Khadija's mount behind him. He scanned the rock fall.

"Maybe Allah's looking out for us. It'll slow the vehicles some."

Khadija fought to quiet her horse. If only that stopped Hashemi. But this was Hashemi they were talking about.

Their path lifted into the mountains, the river falling away in a steep gorge on the left side of the road, the mountain wall on the right preventing any attempt at disappearing into the hills. They either had to beat the Jeeps up the mountains or stand and fight. The single rifle over Michael's shoulder gave little hope of the success of fighting.

As if reading her thoughts, Michael urged the horses faster. The gelding's limp was more pronounced, but he showed the animal no mercy. They carried on, snaking up the road as the wind cut through her *chador* and *jalabiyya*. How cold Michael must be. She urged her horse closer to his.

"Michael. Take this. I have the coat."

She unwound the *petu* from her shoulders and the wind caught it, almost tore it away from her.

"Don't be a fool. At least one of us has to stay healthy."

He spurred the gelding on, leaving her to fight with the loose shawl.

The whine of engines brought her head around. Far down the gorge a single, cream-colored Jeep swung into view. It slowed on a curve, then sped up as if they'd seen her. She kicked the roan's sides, keeping its head tightly reined, and cantered after Michael.

"They're here!"

She urged her horse as fast as she dared on the shifting gravel. Even this pace was a risk. They leaned low over the animals' necks, as the horses lunged up the steep slope out of the gorge. The horses' breath heaved at the effort in the thinning air. A few drops of rain slapped their faces and then increased until the sky was filled with the grey wall of deluge.

"Shit," Michael swore. The crest of the incline gave onto a boulder-littered plateau that lifted up in great steps towards the pass.

"What is it?" She brought the roan alongside.

"It's colder above. There'll be snow. We can only hope it slows the Jeep."

The dirt track they followed ran with water. It splashed up the horses' legs, soaked into Michael's trousers and Khadija's *jalabiyya*. The rain soaked through the *petu* and *chador*, pasting the clothes against their bodies. Wind gusts slammed into the horses, staggering them sideways.

The sound of engines drove them on. The two horses pounded up the slope. How far was the pass? How far could the horses go at this speed? The roan was soaked with more than rain. White foam formed on its neck, on its breast, and flew back from its mouth to dapple her *chador*.

Khadija looked back. How far? How far?

The horses cleared the first rise of the great steps to the pass. But even making the pass didn't mean safety—Hashemi's men could still pursue into the valley beyond.

The first flakes of snow stung her face, but ahead the mountain's terrain was lost in white. They plowed into it, the snow losing its moisture in the cold, leaving thick, dry flakes falling and rising in clouds at the horses' pounding hoofs.

The whine of the engine rang louder, but muffled. Michael suddenly veered the gelding off the road. The animal stumbled, almost fell, throwing Michael against its neck. The animal scrambled to its feet. The roan pounded after, but the animals' strides weren't fast enough. Never fast enough.

Not to compete with a Jeep.

They were going to be caught. Michael would be killed.

And she as well—as a traitor to Islam—a traitor to Hashemi at least. Fear sobbed in her throat. Her death would not be easy. She recalled Hashemi's men's laughter.

The snow swirled, filling the sky with blinding white so she wondered how the horse, how Michael could see where they went. The sky overhead was the color of Michael's rifle barrel. The roan's hoofs slipped on the rock. The animal scrambled to keep its feet.

But it did. It did, but the Jeep engine seemed to roar behind her, even through the muffling snow. The world reduced to the engine sound, her heartbeat and the horse's tearing breath.

Then suddenly Michael was beside her, grabbed her horse's reins and hauled the animal to a stop, tore her down from the saddle into the leeward side of a huge boulder. Heat radiated from him in the meager shelter. The rifle was already loose in his arms. He raised his chin towards the road.

"They can't see us here. The snow's our shield."

"Michael, you're not well."

Over the wind she heard the whine of the engine build as if it was almost on top of them—then recede upslope. He ignored her concern.

"They'll patrol the road."

The wind whipped his words away. The snow melted where it touched him. His face was flushed, running with more than the snow that crusted his turban. He looked back up slope through the gusting wall of snow.

"I figure we let the horses rest a few minutes. Then we carry on up slope away from the road. We have to stay where the snow is thickest."

"Can we make the pass this way?"

He shook his head.

"Before the final pass the road returns to the river edge. There's a cliff across the slope so we can't get up this way. We have to return to the road there. Hashemi will know it. He'll guard it."

He reeked of the hot-iron scent of fever. She saw the shivers he ignored.

"Michael, we have to get you warm—to shelter."

She put her arms around his broad chest, trying to share her body heat. His breath was in her hair, her face. His hand briefly touched her head, but then he set her away.

"We need to draw Hashemi from the road. On the far side of the pass there are old cave networks Massoud used to keep ready in case the Taliban was able to break through into the Panjshir. He used to keep men there, but I don't know what's happened since he died. If we can get there, Marshal Fahim, his replacement, might help us. We might rest a bit and then get down to the valley tomorrow. Fahim might be able to get a message through on my behalf."

His fever rode so bright in his eyes.

"How—how do you know we can get through?"

He looked back towards the road and the sound of the Jeep. The loss of his gaze was like a chill.

"Because there's no choice," he said as he handed her the roan's reins and mounted.

Chapter 45

The snow placed a grey veil across the dark figure that rode behind Michael. He had to get them through. If nothing else, he had to get her through. He owed Mohammed that much—the life of his daughter, when Michael had been unable to save the son.

He'd set that thought aside when he realized her betrayal, but the news of the date, her careful decoding of what her message meant—that and the way she touched him—had destroyed his resolve. It had changed things.

Like sending him on a mad dash through the mountains in a snow storm. He grinned to himself.

Like making him face the probability he was wrong about Khadija. Like making him admit what he felt for her. But there was no time to do anything about it, and there would only be hurt for her if she found out. Better if she didn't know his feelings. It would make what was to come easier.

He sighed and pain stabbed into him, stealing his strength away. It was worse than before, each breath difficult in the thin, icy air. Truth be told, there was little chance he would live through this journey. Strange that he regretted it.

The afternoon wore on as they traversed the slope, picking their way upward through the screen of snow, listening for the sound of the Jeep on the road. It seemed to stay even with them, but that was probably just the strange atmospherics that came with the weather. In any event, Hashemi's vehicle and his men were close—too close—and they barred the pass.

The sky turned darker grey as the day advanced and the wind grew colder. Rock cracked in the cold, sounding like rifle shots. Out of the snow rose the slick cliff he had known they would face. The stone groaned above them in the unseasonable cold and a trickle of gravel fell around them. It was dangerous here now and more dangerous still when a quake came.

The horses had done well to get here still in daylight. The gelding was limping badly, but still carried on. The roan had cut its right front fetlock on a hidden outcrop of stone. Its blood left bright drops in the snow.

He dismounted and was careful not to let Khadija see how he needed the horse to steady himself. He motioned Khadija off her horse and handed the gelding's reins to her. He took charge of the roan.

The question in her eyes demanded an answer.

"There's no way we can both make it through. You're going to have to carry the message." Confusion, then horror bloomed in her eyes.

"I'm not leaving you."

He smiled, wanted to take her in his arms, but time beat at him. Time and knowledge like the sense of an impending quake.

"Use that sharp brain of yours, Khadija. We've got to deliver that message. You know they outgun us. You know they want me. Hell, if they catch me, they might just forget about you."

The Jeep engine seemed to purr close enough Hashemi's men could be standing right beside them. His voice would carry through the snow as well. He pulled Khadija closer and told her his plan. She shook her head stubbornly.

"No. I'm not leaving you."

He saw the argument brewing in her eyes and pulled her into him, stroked her head a moment, then stopped himself.

"Over the pass it's only sixty miles or so down the Panjshir and then another forty to Kaabul. In the valley, you have to tell Fahim what's going on. Tell him you have to get a message to Simon Booker at the U.S. embassy. He'll know of Simon if he doesn't know him directly. Tell him the plotters are Uigher and Hui, but they're being supplied by Hashemi's fundamentalist group in Afghanistan. Tell him the date and tell him the evidence—probably the body of a U.S. agent—will point to a U.S. plot. I wouldn't be surprised if there was some attack on U.S. soil as well. They're hoping for a war or at least serious conflict. It'll pull resources away from the hotbed of the Middle East. It'll allow the fundamentalists to take control. That's what they want—fundamentalist Islamic states." He looked down at her. "Have you got that?"

She just looked at him as he set her away. He repeated his question and held her shoulders so hard he knew he hurt her. Finally she nodded, but her eyes were huge, injured pools.

Damnation, he didn't want to leave her, but this was only way to get the message out.

He mounted the roan and leaned down to her. "I'd take the gelding, but the roan's more likely to want to head back to Skazar. Downhill I'll release him to distract the men. In this storm they might think it's me trying to escape. You mount the gelding, but wait here. When you hear shots, follow the cliff face to the road. When you reach it, head up the pass and don't look back. Just go."

Not waiting for a reply, he turned the roan out into the snow. The wind had picked up, changing the snow from heavy flakes to prickly ice driving almost horizontal. It cut at him, at the horse. The animal snorted and laid its ears back, but its desire to go home kept it going. He was counting on it.

He guided it closer to the road. Closer still, and through the wind heard voices muttering epithets against the weather.

Reining in, he dismounted, pulling his rifle from his shoulder. Then he tied the horse's reins so the animal couldn't lower its head to eat.

The flat grey light made it difficult to see, the falling snow even more so. He stepped closer to the voices, pulling the horse after him. Let Khadija be mounted. Let her be ready. Let her obey him in this.

The roan's hoof came down on a rock that split in the cold. The crack ran through the air and Michael froze. Ahead the voices grew louder, calling to each other.

He couldn't ask for a more opportune time. He released the roan with a slap on the animal's rump. The horse crow-hopped and then leapt forward, trotting down slope towards Skazar. Its hoof beats sounded muffled in the snow, but they carried well enough.

Michael dropped to his belly and peered into the snow.

A shout. Someone ran after the horse.

Through the swirl of ice particles something moved. A man. Two. The snow and the sweat that ran into his eyes, made the figures fade in and out of existence. He raised the rifle to his shoulder and sighted along the barrel, but his shaking made the barrel waver. It couldn't be helped. There.

He squeezed the trigger and the ancient weapon bucked against his shoulder, the scent of gunpowder rich in his nose. A scream and one of the men fell. The other figure disappeared in the snow.

Damnation. He should have taken two quick shots, but his hands were too unsteady.

He scrambled to his feet and began to run upslope. There were shouts through the snow; he approached the road and saw a huddle of men through the white. He sent a bullet into their midst, heard another cry and shouting, then resumed his run.

The whine of the Jeep neared as it left its station near the pass. It was Khadija's opportunity.

If he could only disable the Jeep.

He went to one knee and peered into the snow. Finally he saw the darker bulk and caught the stench of exhaust on the wind. An eddy of air separated the snow briefly and he knew he might be seen, but the chance of the shot was too important. He tucked the Enfield into his shoulder and sighted on the Jeep's engine, pulled the trigger as the snow closed around the vehicle again.

Another shot rang and a bullet parted the air too close to his head. He plunged back through the snow, hearing the pursuit.

Men plowed after him. He ran farther across the slope, then paused to take aim through the gathering gloom. Now it didn't matter if he shot someone—except it made him feel a damn sight better. He spotted a moving shadow and pulled the trigger. A shout and the shadow fell.

Shouts all around him. If he wanted to be caught, just stay where he was.

Move man, just move! But even the adrenaline could barely shift his fatigued body. He stumbled to his feet. At least he could make them pay; at least he could lead them a merry chase and give Khadija time. Hell. Maybe he'd even make it past them and find his way to Khadija.

Wouldn't that be a laugh? Hell, it would be paradise. He would take her in his arms. He would tell her how he felt—apologize for hurting her—for so much.

He headed for the shadow he'd brought down, weaving through the snow to avoid voices. The man he'd shot groaned in the snow. Blood bloomed red around him from a huge hole in his chest. The Enfield was a cruel weapon. Michael grabbed the fallen man's rifle and then turned up hill. Khadija should be well into the narrow gorge by now. He could hold this end for her, allow her to escape.

The snow came down thicker, harder, driving into him. The cold—even with his running he could no longer feel his feet. The rifle felt like lead in his cold-clumsy hands.

Just keep moving. Just pray she gets away.

"*Allāhu akbar*—God is great," he groaned.

The great grey cliff rose out of the gathering darkness. The fall of rock was greater now, the ground littered with pieces of the stone sheered off the cliff face. The rock above his head groaned. Dangerous. He trotted along the escarpment and stopped by the road.

There was no sign of Khadija. The wind had blown away the gelding's prints. The road itself was a white track with only faint indentations to tell of the Jeep's passage. He lifted his head. The Jeep still idled somewhere down the road. Shit! He hadn't wrecked the damned engine.

Go back?

He looked over his shoulder at the route through the gorge. Khadija was that way and suddenly he wanted to find her, wanted the chance to live, to have the opportunity to hold her if she would have him. The Jeep—if it came back he would guard her escape.

He turned and began to limp along the road towards the final pass. The wind picked up the rush of the river, the growl of the cliff-face cracking, so the wind, the water, the earth, roared in his head.

It was cold, so very cold. He pulled the sodden *petu* more tightly around his neck and shoulders. Just keep going. He still might make it. He still might see Khadija again. Might feel her arms around him, her lips on his. Each thought was another step, another push-off from the cliff when he found himself collapsed against it for strength.

The darkness made it almost impossible to see the track or where it ended in the steep fall to the river. The cold made it almost impossible to move and his hands froze on the weapons. He staggered forward, caught in the haze of his pain, and longing for Khadija and warmth by a fire, the sound of doves in the leaves above them, the scent of grapes heavy on the air. Khadija would be laughing. They would be together in the Panjshir with the river droning nearby.

Droning.

Michael jerked upright from where he sagged against the cliff. How long had he been there lost in an impossible dream? His chest felt like it would explode. Allah, no—not now when they were coming.

He tried to run, but his legs almost gave out. Instead he took cover near the cliff face and faced the road behind him. Headlights swung through the darkness as the Jeep came around the last curve.

The lights caught him in their glare, blinded him as he raised Hashemi's man's rifle, the old Enfield across his shoulder as he tried to back away into the darkness before he was seen. The vehicle stopped and beyond the glare of lights he heard a door open.

"Don't move!" At least it wasn't Hashemi's voice.

But he couldn't see them. Couldn't see who held a weapon on him. Couldn't see who came for him. Shoot at the man he had seen or at the other door. That was where their shooter was likely to be.

Michael kept the rifle raised, as he backed away. The wind seemed to shift, pause, as he tightened the weapon into his shoulder. Where was Hashemi? Let him take Hashemi and the viper's head would be gone. Then he could die if he must.

Another step towards the darkness beyond the headlight-glare. Another.

Michael's frozen feet tangled. He stumbled, his finger tightening on the trigger. The weapon bucked. The shot went wild into the night and more shots slammed into the cliff face next to him.

He half-fell, scrambled back and back. The rifle—where was it? Lost in his fall, in his scramble. He fumbled for the Enfield as the earth trembled under him. His head thundered with the sound of the shots, with voice.

The form of a man caught in the headlights. The shriek of the wind—he couldn't get it out of his head. He had to get up, he had to get out of here. The roar increased and stone, snow, and mud rained down. The road shuddered. Shuddered again as if the earth took umbrage with his presence.

Then the mountain lurched, the cliff face tore loose and the avalanche slammed into the road.

Chapter 46

She shouldn't have left him.

The thought filled Khadija's head like the wind howling in the gorge. She had done so many other things wrong in her life and in her time with Michael. Her feelings for him were illicit according to *Sharī'ah* laws, but didn't the Prophet say the love between a man and a woman was an expression of the Divine? Didn't that mean that what she felt for Michael was right and good, not evil? Could she, perhaps, have done one thing right?

Allah, show me your straight path.

She shouldn't have left him.

The gelding kept its head down, its ears back as it picked its way along the gorge, but now the walls that had enclosed Khadija and her mount fell away. She was coming to the final pass—she must be, even though the snow swirled so thick and white she could barely see.

A sound behind made the gelding stop. It turned its head around, ears flicking forward as if trying to understand what it heard. Then Khadija heard it, too.

A gun shot, followed by others.

She'd heard them on the lower slope as she urged the horse to the road and upwards along the gorge as Michael had instructed. Then Michael had drawn Hashemi's men away.

Now? The shots sounded like the wind carried them along the gorge. She wouldn't be able to hear them so clearly if they were still on the lower slope. That meant Michael was in the gorge.

That meant he was trying to get free, to her.

A low rumble vibrated through the air and the earth trembled under the horse—another of the small quakes so frequent in this part of her country. The gelding raised its head and trotted a few steps from the river gorge.

Not small. The rumble became a roar that filled the air so even the snow seemed to dance on changed currents of air. The landscape lurched. Lurched again and the gelding stumbled. Khadija yanked its head up and turned the horse back the way she had come. Judging by the sound, it had caused part of the cliff to collapse.

Michael. She shouldn't have left him.

She kicked the gelding and twisted his head around to head downslope. The way lay slick under the snow and the horse slipped, had to use its tender foot for balance, but continued gamely under her guidance. The snow seemed thicker. In the darkness it blanked her vision, her breath, everything, so the world disappeared. There was only her steaming breath and that of the horse, and the roar as the wind tried to strip away her *petu* and rip away all warmth.

The walls of the gorge rose steep around her once more. Falling rock still bounced from the road. The gelding hesitated, but she urged him forward. The horse hesitated again. She squeezed with her legs.

The animal stumbled, stumbled again, and Khadija heard the clatter of rock shifting underfoot. Ahead, through the swirling snow, there was a greater darkness backlit by light beyond.

She blinked and then realized the light was probably headlights, that downslope the road was blocked by a wall of rock and snow. Through the wind and the river she heard shouting. Had Michael been trapped by the avalanche? Had Hashemi caught him?

"*Inshallah*, no," she whispered. "Don't take him from me."

Perhaps—perhaps he'd been caught in the slide of stone. She would not let herself think it. He had to have gotten free. Even if he were captured, at least he still lived and she could pray for his escape.

The horse stumbled again and something clattered with a metallic ring. The horse snorted and flicked its ears.

There shouldn't be metal up here.

Khadija slid off the horse into snow that was up over her ankles. She was momentarily glad for the silly city boots she wore. She dragged her feet forward and her toe struck something. Rock. Something rattled like metal.

She plunged her hand through snow and her fingers closed around something cold and slick. She pulled it free and knew what she held even before she could see.

The old rifle Michael had carried. After so many days, she recognized it. Michael would not discard his only weapon.

That meant...

Fear choked her breath as she recovered the rifle and swung its strap gingerly over her head, not liking the feel of something meant for killing. Through the billows of snow, she took in the mass of rock and earth. The cold stung the tears that refused to be denied.

"Allah, no. Please, no." She dropped the reins and took a step towards the rock fall. "Please. *La Elaha Ellallahu Muhammad-u-Rasoollullah*—there is no god but God, and Muhammad is his prophet. Please, Allah, not the man I love."

In the blurred light beyond the avalanche, a figure picked its way across the rock, unsteady footing suddenly sliding so the figure slipped, slid, half fell.

Michael? She took a step forward.

The horse snorted. Snorted again and pawed the snow. She glanced to where the animal blew steaming breath at something covered in white.

A hand moving! She was on her knees in a moment, digging the snow away from the face she so dearly wanted to see.

"Michael! Oh, Michael!" Her *chador* slipped off the back of her head.

His eyes were closed. A jagged cut on his forehead leaked a trail of dark blood across his temple. His hand was cold; his face was so hot the snow ran from it in rivulets. Shivers wracked his body. But he breathed. His chest rose and fell as if he ran a great race.

She ran her hands over his neck, his chest, his limbs, nothing broken that she could tell in these primitive circumstances—just his dear body eaten by the fever within.

"Michael." She glanced over her shoulder at the moving figure in the snow. "We have to go. You have to wake up."

She plucked at his hand, tried to lift him but that was impossible. He was too large a man. She went to her knees again. Patted his cheeks, slapped him. Still nothing.

The mission. Oh Allah, they had to get away. But she could not, would not, leave him again. She put her arms around him, placed her cheek against his, urging him to wake, pleading with him.

He groaned. And then his arm came around her and pulled her to him, his lips were on her hair, were on her cheek, found her lips, and it was all the delights Allah promised…

…and she could not give herself to them.

She pulled away and saw his eyes were open, the need strong in them.

"They're caught beyond the avalanche, but they come for you." She motioned to the huge pile of rock.

He tried to follow her gesture and groaned. "I told you to deliver the message."

"I couldn't leave you. Are you hurt?"

That lopsided, sardonic grin. "Only from an infected wound and a rock on the head. Otherwise I'm a hundred percent."

She got her shoulder under his arm, slipped and fell as he tried to rise. The edge of the gorge was too near. The darkness of the chasm seemed to yawn towards her. She ignored it and braced herself against the unstable cliff face as she helped Michael up.

"Damnation," he growled. "I shouldn't be so weak."

He was, though, and fear bloomed in Khadija's gut. He could barely stand, even with most of his weight resting on her. She took a step and he nearly fell. Took another and caught the gelding's reins.

If she could just get him up, they stood a chance. But the snow seemed to be lightening. They had to get out of here quickly or they'd be seen. Already she could hear the clatter of rock under the man on the debris pile. Already another figure had joined him, the rock grinding under their movements.

"Michael, you have to mount. I'll lead the gelding out of here."

He grunted his acknowledgement, but his body sagged more heavily against hers. What reserves of strength he had melted from him like the snow from his fever. She leaned him against the horse, helped his hands to the pommel of the saddle.

"Hold on." She stepped out from under him, and felt him sway, start to slip, but somehow he managed to hold onto the horse and tried to lift a leg to the stirrup.

She had to help him; got her shoulder under him to hoist him to the gelding's back.

He lost strength before he could swing a leg over and fell across the saddle. Slowly, slowly, he began to slide back towards her. She grabbed his hips and pushed until he lay across the saddle. His body was limp, unconscious again.

A shout came from a man on the debris pile and Khadija knew they'd been seen. She had to get them out of there.

She grabbed the reins and started to lead the gelding up the road, but Michael began to slide off the saddle's other side. She grabbed his legs to pull him back. A gust of wind caught her, blew her against the horse, and the animal swayed.

A shot cracked in the darkness and the horse crow-hopped forward. They couldn't move fast enough like this. She grabbed the empty stirrup and climbed up behind the saddle, grabbing hold of the cantle to stay on. She kicked the gelding and he jumped under her, nearly sending her sliding over his haunches, the rifle bouncing against her back.

Darkness closed around them as the horse trotted up the road. Another shot split the darkness and Khadija felt it part the air close by her head. She kicked the horse to a canter and the animal obliged, but almost fell on the slick footing. Michael slid forward onto the horse's withers and Khadija scrabbled into the saddle, Michael half-laying in her lap. She leaned forward to shelter him, hoping this would make them a smaller target.

Another shot. Another. Shouts behind her and more shots. Men ran behind.

And then the road curved, blocking the bullets. Their path began the final climb towards the open area she'd reached before.

It was cold, so cold it seemed to eat at her bones.

The snow swirled around her, but it was like the unseasonable storm had blown itself out. Still, the wind howled like wolves, tearing the fresh snow off the ground, tearing at her *petu* and *chador* and the collar of her *jalabiyya*. It tore Michael's turban from his head.

Billows of fresh snow were stinging needles in her face. Around her, the night was black. She pulled the *petu* higher to shield her face.

She gave the gelding its head as the ground continued upwards. The horse broke into a jarring trot as if it knew to get distance between them and Hashemi's men.

She peered over her shoulder. No sign of the pursuit—yet. Just keep going. Aim forward. Around them the snow lessened until suddenly she could see the sky.

The wind tore the clouds apart, revealing a glittering net of stars. Even in the darkest night of Kaabul she had not seen so many. Encircling her rose a crown of mountain peaks, glittering white, and in the east, the faintest of outlines of the moon—a crescent that would probably not be seen by those who told when the new month began, but surely the harbinger that Rajab would begin in only a day—two at most.

Chapter 47

The clatter of donkey carts, the cries of the hawkers, overlaid the bedlam in Kaabul's Char Chata Bazaar as Mohammed held Zahra's wrist. The rich scents of fresh produce and the spice *wallah*'s stalls filled the air. So much life after the destruction of not-so-long ago.

A testament to his people, Mohammed thought as Zahra aided him unevenly through the street. Hamidah was doing the marketing in preparation for her father and mother's arrival in Kaabul. The family would stay with Mohammed through the preparations for Hamidah's wedding over the next week.

Already his small house seemed both too large with Khadija's absence and too small with the lively presence of the two young women. It would only be worse when Ahmad and his two wives came. Those women grated against each other like stones even if his old friend seemed oblivious to the friction between them.

It would also make it more difficult for Mohammed to make his enquiries. The girls had tried to help his search for Mirri, but Zahra's youthful enthusiasm was no match for a few solid enquiries.

"Is all well, Uncle?" Zahra asked.

"Of course, daughter-of-my-friend. Why do you ask?"

"You sighed. It was a very sad sigh."

He smiled. He might not be able to see, but he knew Zahra's nature. She was a sensitive child with a flair for the dramatic and a mind almost as keen as Khadija's. Indeed, she reminded him of a much younger Khadija.

"I'm fine. Tell me. How go the plans for Hamidah's wedding?"

"The wedding?" He could almost hear her rolling her eyes. "Hamidah is like a chicken peck, peck, pecking at the things that need to be done without any real plan. For myself, I would make a list and check them off as I did each one."

"Aah. A list-maker. Much too organized for a poet. I thought you would throw your heart to the wind and let the air carry you to whatever duties you would do."

She stopped in the middle of the bazaar and people pushed around them, jostling him slightly. As she faced him, he caught the scent of Piran's tea from his *chai walla* stand at the corner.

"I'm not a fool, Uncle. Even poetry must have structure, though the structure must help the meaning of the poem. It is like the community—it helps set the meaning of Islam."

He patted her hand to hide his surprise. "Well said, and accept my pardon. I'd not meant to offend."

He'd known she was bright, but this showed a thoughtfulness he'd not realized was there. It was young women like this who would help his country regain itself. They should be treasured.

Someone else jostled him.

"The marketers will trample us if we stand here. Just get me to the clinic and then come back for some tea. I fancy old Piran's brew."

She led him through the main part of the bazaar and up the hill to the vaguely seen shadows that were the line of people at his clinic. Inside, she fussed with his equipment until he shushed her out the door. She could not do things as Khadija did. Always when either Hamidah or Zahra tried to help, he found things were out of place and difficult to find. He hadn't fully appreciated Khadija's work before—because it was not the same as Yaqub's. He recalled how he had always shifted equipment when she had set it out for him. Perhaps he had he pushed her away as well. And now these girls slowed his work. Their presence slowed him in other things as well.

In the past, when he needed to make contact with those to whom he passed information, or who fed it to him, he had sent a boy to old Hazim in the carpet bazaar. Then a certain man would join the line at the clinic and the information would be passed while Mohammed provided medical care.

The trouble with Zahra and Hamidah was they took their duties too seriously and would not allow him to pay a boy to carry such a message. Zahra would do it, they said. But if Zahra carried the message, Hazim would not respond.

His chance was now. He started for the door, but a sound from the back room and a change in the clinic's air flow told him someone was present.

"Hello? Who's there?"

Still silence, and suddenly the street noise from the open door disappeared. The lock clicked shut. Whoever it was could move with the stealth of a cat.

Uncertainty filled him even in this room he knew so well and he felt utterly blind. He stepped back. Back again, until he bumped against the table. At least he knew where he was. He held his breath, searching for any clue to the location of whoever was here.

"What do you want?"

"The question is, what do you want, Siddiqui?" The soft voice was right by his ear, the moist air of the tea-scented words on his cheek. He jerked sideways, knocking the small tray with his stethoscope and tongue depressors to the floor. The crash startled him as he stumbled sideways, then caught himself against the supply cupboard. He faced where the voice had been. It was male—not so old—late twenties or early thirties, he thought, and somehow familiar.

"If you've come to steal drugs, I've almost nothing and the people need it."

"You're not listening, old man," the voice hissed. "Why are you trying to find Mirri Shahabuddin?" The voice was beside him again. So close he knew he could touch whoever spoke.

Mohammed went still. So—Zahra's enquiries had brought a result. Just not the one he'd expected. He stood straighter and forgot his fear.

"She—is my daughter's friend. I hoped she and her brothers might have information to help me find Khadija."

There were footsteps, now. Soft, but discernable. "And why would she be able to do that?"

"My daughter—she disappeared in Feyzabad. I know she went to Mirri often. I know Mirri's brother courted my daughter. I think Khadija—I think she helped Mirri in more than friendship. I thought—I thought perhaps Mirri could tell me something about the people Khadija befriended. Perhaps that could lead me to my daughter."

Silence, then: "You ask dangerous questions. But then you have for a long time, haven't you? We realize that now. Perhaps it is time to ask you more questions, *neh, Doctor* Siddiqui?"

A hand gripped Mohammed's upper arm and pulled him from the safety of the cupboard. Mohammed tried to break away. "I'll yell. The people will help me."

"If you yell, you won't find Khadija, will you?" The man's soft voice carried more threat than any fist. It stopped Mohammed in his fight.

The speaker shoved him through the curtain to the second room, and then so he stumbled against the rear doorframe of the clinic. The door was open.

He stumbled out into the narrow lane and the man caught his arm and began to drag him uphill into the maze of narrow streets. His mind churned with questions. Who were these people? What had Khadija gotten involved in?

He heard traffic and knew they neared the Jadayi Maywand. He smelled wool and knew they passed through the carpet bazaar that stood at one edge of the old city. Then those sounds and smells were behind him and he no longer knew exactly where he was.

Except in danger.

Chapter 48

A pulse of fear and the glimmer of light in the eastern sky startled Khadija fully awake as she rode the gelding downhill. Something had woken her. Michael still lay across the pommel, his heat radiating into her legs.

He hadn't regained consciousness last night, though she had tried to rouse him. By the heat of him she wondered at the fact he still lived at all.

That they both did.

Hashemi's men had given her and the gelding no rest. The horse almost hobbled on three legs now as she looked behind. The animal's head was down, his sides drenched with sweat, but the noble little animal still went on through the snow, even as his riders were so near collapse. Khadija's hands shook on the reins. She could see nothing downslope, but she knew they were coming.

"Damn Hashemi. Damn them all."

All night just as she had thought she was safe and might rest, might take the time to care for Michael, voices had driven her on. She placed her hand on Michael's back and felt his chest move.

He needed a hospital. But in the snow there was not even shelter—only the need to keep going and the trial of climbing down from the horse to chip away the ice balls that formed in the bottoms of its hoofs. Each dismount had been an agony, but she'd had to do it: the ice balls left the gelding slipping and sliding, almost unseating her and Michael.

"How much farther?" she asked the dawn. "Please not much more."

All she knew was that Michael spoke of the Panjshir Valley as safety—that and the stories of heroic Massoud. Perhaps his men would be waiting to help her.

Or Hashemi's men. With the night and her wandering they could have passed her. That could be why there had been no clear voices for the last hour.

It could be because you slept as well.

Michael groaned, and she ran her hand over his damp hair. Allah, he was so hot—as if he burned from within.

"Stay with me. Medical help is close. We'll get there," she lied to herself.

The snow covered the open slope and the rough crags surrounding them, so she felt lost in a bowl of a world where white peaks went on forever. The wind had dropped in the night, but the snow had still fallen once they had left the pass. Here, there was only a thin layer that would melt with the rising sun. If only Hashemi and his men were left behind. She glanced over her shoulder again.

From what she had seen of the Arab, his men would have spent the night clearing the road while others followed. They would come. They would kill her and Michael. Stopping the message would be their only priority now, just as it was her priority to beat them.

The responsibility tightened her stomach—not like the cheap excitement she'd felt when she carried the message to Hashemi. That had been a stupid young woman's adventure. This was like preparing for trauma cases in the E.R. Life and death.

The faint eastern light became a crown of streamers piercing the heavens and the mountains were crowned in a glory of gold.

"Life," she whispered, her hand resting on Michael's damp curls. "I want life."

The sky became watercolor blue. Ahead, the road, discernable under the snow by the ruts worn by past traffic, disappeared between two crags of stone. They passed them and she reined in, feeling as if she'd stepped into some magic canvas of spring—some Xanadu.

The land fell away in front of her in great, grey-blue folds ringed in by the seemingly endless, white-capped mountains. Far away, to the south west, a haze of green trailed southwestward, speaking of fields in the valley bottom. The green seemed to wend its way towards them, up along a glittering string that fell away from their position.

The Parian River, the lifeblood of the Panjshir Valley followed the fold of the mountains. It must rise in the mountains northwest of where she sat.

She urged the gelding down through the snow. The warming air brought the sound of running water and snow collapsing off boulders and crags. A low rumble and a spume of snow brought Khadija's gaze up to a neighboring mountainside. The heat had loosed an avalanche of snow and stone and earth down the far slope. She supposed it had been loosened in the quake last night and hoped the places they were to travel were still stable.

The gelding slipped. Slipped again and went to his knees. Khadija struggled to hold Michael but his limp weight was too much. He slid forward onto the horse's neck and then tumbled to the ground as the gelding righted himself.

Khadija was out of the saddle and to Michael's side before the horse could stop. It stood, head down, lame hoof raised in the air.

"Michael! Michael!" He lay unmoving. She checked his breathing, his pulse. Still just the fever. *Just.* It devoured him. She had to get his temperature down, but there was no place here to do it safely.

The horse snorted and sidled away, his ears flicking at her, at Michael, at the slope, as if trotting away would be a good idea. She could not afford to lose the horse and their few supplies. She went after him.

"Come on," she gentled. "You've more ice balls, I think. I wish we could get down out of this snow. Don't you wish it, too?"

She stepped forward, hand out. The animal had been faithful for so long. Don't let it fail them now.

"It's not far now. There will be trees soon, and grass—beautiful rich green grass along the river. I'll bring you oats and you'll live in my garden and grow into a fat old gelding." Her desperation made her sound like a fool.

She lunged, caught the reins with shaking hands, and stroked the warm brown neck. She needed to be calm, but the adrenaline high she'd been working on was starting to wear off, leaving exhaustion in its wake. She led the horse to Michael. He still hadn't moved, but the rise and fall of his chest said he still lived. His lips moved under the fever-flush of his cheeks.

Get the horse ready to go, then get Michael up. She would find a way. She fished in her pocket. The rusted scalpel had been her only tool to dig the ice from the horse's hooves. She picked up the horse's lame fetlock. Ice glittered blue in the cup of the animal's hoof. She chipped at it, balancing the horse's hoof on her lap, until suddenly the whole lump came loose. She released the animal's leg and was repeating the action when she heard voices.

There was no cover on the slope, no place to hide. The sunlight suddenly was too bright and betraying, the crags she'd passed through too far upslope. And there was Michael, whom she would not leave. The horse's ears twitched at the slope below them, where the road ran around another rock crag.

Male voices.

She repocketed the scalpel and unslung the rifle, but her cold hands didn't work, and she couldn't steady the long barrel of the gun.

"They couldn't have gotten in front. They couldn't."

But the tears in her eyes said it was so. She was lost. Michael was lost. The world—life had lost. *Please not that. Please.* She dragged the gelding closer to Michael. If she could get him up they might escape. To where, she didn't know, but she'd try. She'd promised.

She pulled his arm up over her shoulder, but his limp body resisted. It slid down when she lifted, folded when she needed him to straighten.

The voices came closer.

"Michael! Michael, wake up!"

Nothing. Sweat beaded his face. There was no way she could get him up.

The voices—she could almost make out words. A laugh.

They would hurt him. Hurt her. She grabbed the rifle again. She had never shot one before, but she'd seen enough of them. If young boys could use them, how hard could it be?

She stood over Michael, the horse's reins in her hands, and fumbled with the bolt action to see if a shell was chambered. From around the crag came two figures.

Male. Kalashnikov rifles glittered darkly in the new sun.

"Stay where you are!" she ordered.

Khadija raised the rifle to her shoulder and prayed she did it correctly, that they wouldn't see how her hands shook, wouldn't hear how her voice shook.

The men stopped dead, surprise on their faces. They looked at each other and took another step forward, their weapons steady in their hands. How could she even think she could stand against them? She lowered her head as if taking aim.

"I said stop."

The two men were dressed in *salwar kameez* with worn weapons vests over top. They wore the traditional Afghan flat cap and their beards were cut close to their chins, symbols of pride for those who resisted the Taliban.

"You'll be dead before you can shoot us both."

"Who are you? Who do you work for?" she demanded.

The two men grinned.

"An uncovered woman questions a man? What world is this? Who are you, who walks our land?"

"Are you—are you Fahim's men?" Her rifle wavered as she spoke. She hoped she got the name right. If they were Hashemi's men, they already knew her weakness. The men looked at each other.

"Who asks?" asked the taller one, weapon lifting to ready. He had a great burn mark across his left cheek that left a bare patch in his beard.

One shot and she was dead. Two and Michael would be dead as well and their message would not get sent, the world would end in war. She had to take a chance. She lowered the rifle.

"I don't matter, but this man needs medical help. He has an urgent message for Marshal Fahim and the *Amrikaayi*."

"*Amrikaayi*? Who is he?" The man with the scar lifted his chin, suspicion clear on his face. Had she erred again?

"Help him. He's trying to stop a war!"

"A war? We have a war—have lived a war for my whole life. Will it end?" He wagged his head in equivocation—

—until a bullet slammed into him and sent him crashing backwards. The air rang with the weapon's report and with a yell from upslope and the distant sound of a Jeep engine.

Chapter 49

Khadija swung her rifle around and slipped in the snow. The weapon went off.

"Hashemi!" she screamed.

The gelding snorted and trotted two steps away. The unwounded man was on his belly, Kalashnikov rattling, fanning upslope just past her position. Khadija threw herself over Michael to shield him. The wounded man groaned in the dirt. They had to get away, they had to get free.

The uninjured man slid to his friend, who clutched his side. The injured man motioned to her.

"Get them out of here. If this is a trap, make them pay. If she's telling the truth, I'll hold them as long as I can."

The uninjured man was across the distance so fast it left her breathless. He had her, had twisted the rifle from her and her arm behind her back, before she could protest. Then he caught the horse and hefted Michael over the saddle.

"Try anything and I'll kill you both."

A shower of bullets slammed into the gravel around them as he led her at a run straight down the slope. To get out of range, she supposed. She'd seen Michael do it before. He had the scars to prove it. Above them the injured warrior let loose with a barrage of bullets, showering the double crag Khadija had ridden between. Had they been so close all night? If she had known, she would have died for fear.

The uninjured warrior cut across the slope, keeping the gelding and Michael between the gunfire and himself. Bullets spit gravel from the ground so the horse almost ran them over in its panic.

"No! Michael's the one who has to live." She grabbed the reins and tried to shift the horse to safety. The Panjshiri backhanded her and she tasted blood as he dragged her on. And then they were around the next crag and the bullets were behind them.

"If Amidullah dies it's on your head." Her captor was not a tall man and his scrubby beard spoke of not much age, but he was strong as she had seen and felt, and his gaze was brown as earth and solid.

"I don't want his death, either, *Inshallah.*"

The young man's gaze showed he almost believed her, even though she was a woman breaking oh-so-many cultural taboos just by speaking to him. "Who are you?"

"No one. A messenger. Our pursuers have chased us from Feyzabad. My—friend was a prisoner. He was tortured for what he knows. We have to get free."

Past the outcroppings, the snow disappeared as a narrow vale opened. Through it ran a glittering strand of river. The water was white with rocks and melt from the snow, but the grass was green and the trees, though bare, rustled in a breeze that still carried a hint of summer. A thin streamer of smoke ran up into the air and then was tattered on the wind. Beyond the trees an open military Jeep acted as a road block.

"I am Safit of the Panjshir," he said, his scrubby young man's beard bobbing on his chin. "I am from Dasht-i-Rewat. My father had a gun such as this." He motioned to Michael's rifle, draped across his back. "It is very old. Not modern like this." He patted the Kalashnikov in his arms like a proud parent. The stock of the gun had been carved and decorated with paintings, flowers, and the names of Allah.

They reached the grove of trees and another man came off the mountain slope just as a shout came from up hill. Amidullah came leaping down the slope, his hand bloody over his side, his breath wheezing in his lungs.

"I counted six," he said as he fell against the Jeep, a wild smile on his lips. "There are three less now, but they have a Jeep and more men—who knows how many. Time to leave, I think."

The three men herded her into the Jeep; they draped Michael into the back and Amidullah climbed in beside him, his face pale. Khadija crouched beside them.

"You have medical supplies?"

Safit said nothing, but Amidullah nodded.

"Drive," Amidullah, obviously their leader, ordered. Safit needed no urging. He cranked the ignition and the third Panjshiri leapt aboard as Safit slewed the Jeep around and they left the copse of trees in a hail of stone that startled the gelding towards the river.

"*As-salaam 'alaykum,*" she called after it, knowing she was a fool because her eyes were filled with tears. The animal had carried them so far.

She turned back to Amidullah.

"The medical supplies? I'm a doctor."

Sweat stood out on his brow. The blood ran through his fingers as he nodded at an old munitions box in the bed of the Jeep. Khadija scrambled to it as the Jeep bounced over the washboard road. She yanked open the metal clamp and dug through the contents. Amidullah looked back and shouted as a closed-top Jeep came over the crest of the ridge behind.

Khadija's vehicle careened around a bend in the road, throwing her over Michael as medical supplies scattered in the rear of the open Jeep. She grappled with the mess of dressings, syringes, tourniquet, and vials of drugs. They rattled as the Jeep leapt from pothole to pothole. Her fingers couldn't seem to hold anything. She could barely keep from being thrown from the vehicle.

The Panjshiri man in the front seat was on his knees, facing backwards, Kalashnikov at his waist. Khadija looked behind. The other Jeep careened around the curve behind them in a cascade of gravel. The Panjshiri yelled and Khadija ducked as he let loose with a barrage at the following vehicle.

Michael! Make sure he was all right!

But Michael wasn't bleeding. She knew his status. Triage.

She pushed Amidullah back and ripped open his vest. The felted fabric was sodden and the grey *salwar kameez* was awash with red.

She pulled the fabric out of the way, revealing a bubbling crater in the man's lower chest. She looked up at his face. Skin paling even as she looked. Blood on his lips. Blood flowing down his chin. The lung, then. The man was formidable just to have made it back to the camp.

A hail of bullets slammed into the Jeep and the Panjshiri gunman screamed, toppled, and fell from the vehicle, his weapon with him. Amidullah yanked Khadija down over him.

Safit slammed the gas peddle and the Jeep fishtailed on the road. Poplar trees flashed past on either side. The road curved. Curved again, denying their pursuers a clear shot. She pushed herself up from Amidullah. Her *jalabiyya* was sodden with his blood. His breath came in short gasps, but still his fingers held her upper arm.

"I have to get something on this or you'll bleed to death."

His black eyes were on her, his facial scar livid on the pallor of his skin. He nodded, but still did not release her. The vehicle crossed a narrow bridge and the road followed the river's edge. The vehicle bounced so hard there was no way she could do anything other than try to stop the worst of the bleeding. She fumbled for dressings. Slapped one on his side.

Blood overwhelmed it. Another and she grabbed Amidullah's arm, forced it down over the dressing.

"Hold it." He was losing blood too fast. He needed fluids. She dug in the medical pack.

There had to be fluid packs. There had to be. She pulled equipment out of the case until she reached the bottom. Nothing. She turned back to him. His black eyes were on her, his breath ragged. The trickle from his lips had increased, rouging his lips like a child who had eaten too much pomegranate.

"You need blood. Where we're going—is there a clinic? A doctor?"

Amidullah shook his head and his eyes fluttered closed. His fingers relaxed on her arm as he drew in a breath. It frothed in his mouth as he exhaled, as his head slumped to the side and his mouth went slack.

Khadija checked his pulse. Nothing. She went to her knees and began compressions, but bullets stopped her. She threw herself down as the projectiles slammed into the rear of the Jeep.

Michael. If she couldn't save Amidullah, she had to save him. The glint of a familiar-looking vial sent her scrambling for it. She grabbed it, rolled it over in her hand.

Chloramphenicol. For once what she needed was to hand. She fished in the litter of medical supplies for a syringe.

Allah, let this help. Let him live.

Syringe filled, she stabbed it into Michael's left arm. Let the bacteria that was eating him not have developed immunity.

The Jeep flew down the road, Safit sitting low in his seat against the bullets that came at them. Amidullah's weapon lay against her thigh. She had to do something. She wrestled the weapon from the dead man and held it to her shoulder. Use it?

With no returning gunfire, Hashemi's men were gaining on them—were now no more than a hundred feet away—and with each yard their aim was improving. If Safit was hit, then they'd all be dead. She fought for balance and pulled the weapon tight into her shoulder, bracing herself against the seatback. The weight felt strange in her arms, the black metal, slick. Evil.

She trained the muzzle on the Jeep, found the trigger, and pulled. Nothing. There was something that stopped these things from firing. Otherwise just bouncing in such a vehicle could set them off. There. A small switch by the magazine.

She pulled the weapon back to her shoulder as someone loosed a barrage of bullets at her. Her Jeep careened wildly, but stayed on the road. Safit—had he been hit?

She fought for balance, aimed for the engine—she did not want to kill—and pulled the trigger. The recoil beat into her shoulder, bounced in her hands, tore at her fingers, and she almost let go. She jerked her finger off the trigger, but she had already done her damage.

The windscreen exploded—her shot had gone high. The vehicle shot sideways—towards the cliff face away from the river. It slammed into the rock fall. The engine hood accordioned, but the vehicle's speed didn't allow it to stop. The driver's side drove up onto the rocks, drove along the cliff, and then caught, twisted. The vehicle hung in the air, then slammed down on its side, skidding to a stop broadside across the road.

Safit kept the Jeep going as Khadija looked at the weapon in her bloody hands. She had killed. She gazed at Amidullah still sprawled across the back, his blood spreading in the bottom of the Jeep. Another bullet had caught his right shoulder, so his right arm hung only by a shred of skin. She had caused something like that.

Numb, she collapsed back into the rear of the Jeep. She set the safety and dropped the machine gun, then looked at Michael. He lay in a widening pool of blood and she feared the bullets had caught him, too. She checked him.

ABCs. His airway was clear. His chest still rose and fell and his pulse still ran strong. She ran her hands along his body, his arms and legs, checking for wounds. There was only Amidullah's blood—nothing she could do about that, except get rid of the body.

She slumped back against the seat back as the Jeep slowed, came to a stop, and the engine died. Safit didn't move. She swung around to him, then clambered forward over the seat.

Safit lay over the steering wheel, a bloody hole as large as Khadija's fist in his upper back.

"Safit?" She climbed into the passenger seat.

He turned his head and smiled at her, a sweet smile of youth.

"They kill me."

Then his eyes closed and his breath wheezed in his chest. Khadija scrambled to grab the medical supplies from the back, but he grabbed her wrist.

"You live. You remember us, yes?" Then his eyes closed and his body relaxed against the wheel and there was only the silence of the wind and distance.

Chapter 50

A bird of prey's rasp brought Khadija to her senses. She wondered how long she'd been like this, Safit's words echoing in her head. She still crouched on the passenger seat, amid the blood of the Panjshiri man whose name she didn't even know. Above her, the blue bowl of the sky was edged with snowy peaks and the black wings of the eagle circling far above.

Closer in, the constant rush of water and wind over rock filled the air. No, there was something else. Movement and she didn't know if she could move again, fight again.

Sparrows twittering in the trees. Something small, rushing over the stony ground on the slope above the road. Life. Something closer. Adrenaline sent another shock of alarm through her limbs.

She scrambled for the rifle, pushed herself up from where she'd sagged against the passenger seat. If someone had survived the crash of Hashemi's Jeep she couldn't afford to be helpless. She looked at Safit—brave young Safit.

"I will honor you." But now she needed to get away. She needed to get Michael to a doctor and his message to someone who would listen. Another sound. So close. She had to get them away. Safit was dead. But she wasn't and neither was Michael—yet.

"I'm sorry. I'm sorry. I'm so sorry," she said as she pushed Safit's body sideways.

He tumbled out the open side of the Jeep, landing like a small boy collapsed in exhaustion—except for the exit wound in his chest.

Look away. You can do nothing for him. Triage. If you cry, your tears will blind you. She scrambled into the driver's seat. She needed to see. She needed to get them out of here. She needed to remember the things Dr.

James Hartness had taught her about driving a car.

The driver's side floor was red with Safit's blood. There was no help for it—she had to do this. Her city boots rested in the sticky mess as she pressed down the clutch and the gas. She found the ignition key and turned. The engine turned over—once—twice—three times. Start damn you!

It caught and roared: the sweetest sound she had heard in a long time—just as a hand grabbed her shoulder.

She screamed. The Jeep jerked, stalled, and she pulled out of the grasp. Safit's gun…

It lay on the far side of the passenger wheel well—beyond her easy reach. They couldn't catch her now—not so close to freedom and help. She scrambled out of the seat and half-fell over Safit's body. Then she turned to see her attacker.

No one.

No one at all.

She was going crazy—had gone mad as the crazies she'd seen brought into the London Emerg. She'd end up locked in a ward somewhere. But the noise came again. Close. Very close. She peered into the Jeep's back and Michael stared up at her, his eyes pale as light on snow. His mouth twisted in that grin she had come to know so well. It no longer taunted her.

"I didn't…mean to scare you." His voice was faint. His breath wheezed in his lungs as he leaned against Amidullah's body. So the infection had traveled.

But he was awake. He was alive. He had strength enough to pull himself to her. She caught him in her arms. "*Allāhu akbar*—God is great," she murmured into his neck.

His arms came around her. His hand found her hair, her back. Tender, so tender, but then he pulled away.

"We have to get to Kaabul. Can you drive this thing? I don't think I can."

All she wanted was his arms around her, his breath in her hair, his kisses, and that look of need fulfilled she had seen in his eyes just once.

But he did not want that. He had held her away in the snow as well. He had a mission and that was most important to him. It would always be most important. In that he was like Yaqub—always driven by his need to win and his work.

She tried to close off her heart and nodded through the pain. Stay the detached professional. Treat this as you treated all things in medicine. Wasn't that what the Inglisi had taught her—stay uninvolved even in matters of the heart?

She had learned that well—too well. She inhaled a ragged breath.

"Just rest. I found chloramphenicol in the Jeep's supplies. I gave you some, but you need broad spectrum antibiotics, rehydration—something you can only get in Kaabul."

"We should get rid of the body."

She did as she was told, pulling Amidullah out of the Jeep and fighting to drag him and Safit to the side of the road. She hated to leave them like that, hated more having to defile their bodies for any money they might have, but it was the best she could do.

She returned to the Jeep and prayed she hadn't flooded the engine. It roared to life and she slowly, slowly, released the clutch. The vehicle jerked. Jerked again as the clutch caught and she drove forward. Gradually she increased the speed, growing more confident as she maneuvered down the narrow road towards the long green valley she had seen from high up the mountains. Driving this was much different than sedately driving a quiet country road in England. She pressed down on the accelerator.

The wind blasted through her hair, tugged at her clothing as the Jeep careened along the road. She wasn't a good driver, nor an experienced one, but desperation drove her to the limits of her skill and beyond. Down the mountains slope. Down to the green and life. That was what she wanted most of all.

She blasted through a small town along the river, scattering sheep and old men with a blast of her horn. No one tried to stop her. It took all morning, and the sun had fallen towards the western mountains when she reached the valley floor. The road was so flat and easy she could barely believe it.

She slammed the throttle down and the Jeep fishtailed until its wheels caught. She could almost yell for joy. They were free of the mountains, free of Hashemi, and the road lay clear before her to Kaabul. Sixty miles, Michael had said, and she had cleared the worst of them. Then another forty of the best highway remaining in Afghanistan. She could do this.

The wind whipped past as the afternoon stretched on. It carried the scent of mulberry and grapes like an intoxicating wine. It would be between the two harvests of the fruit. The fields were still green here. There were still leaves on the trees and the villages were teeming with people and animals. Cattle in the fields. Horses. Along the road sulked the carcasses of tanks. In some places the busy farmers had enlarged their fields and built the tanks into their fence lines. Khadija smiled at the way the Panjshiri thumbed their noses at the might of Russia.

The towns—she counted them—coming to Dasht-i-Rewat—Safit's town—as the sun lowered close to the mountains. It would be evening soon and she felt fatigue like a blanket. She kept finding her eyes had closed. She couldn't remember the last time she'd truly slept. Before the pass, certainly. Before Skazar? She remembered warm arms around her.

The slide of the Jeep jerked her awake. The vehicle was sliding off the road.

"Allah, no!" She cranked the wheel. The vehicle wobbled, its wheels seeking traction in the road's soft shoulder. The Jeep fishtailed. The right front wheel caught the road.

The Jeep slid, spun. 90 degrees. 180. Was backwards on the road, sliding sideways. Another field waited. One of the hulking tanks. She slammed her feet on the clutch and brake. Braced herself for the impact, the pain, the fall as she tumbled from the Jeep.

Gravel sprayed behind them. The Jeep's engine roared, stalled, and suddenly they were stopped. Her side of the Jeep rested in the soft soil on the opposite side of the road. The engine ticked over.

When she managed to release the steering wheel, her hands shook. The tremors ran up her arms, sending deep shudders through her that kept her in her seat. She needed to check on Michael. She needed to make sure he was all right.

She managed to climb out of the Jeep, but her legs gave and she clung to the vehicle. When she could stand, she pulled herself to the rear.

Michael lay with his arms wrapped around the medical box. He grinned up at her.

"One hell of a ride."

Her legs gave again and she sank down beside the Jeep, her knees to her chest. She had to rest. She had to sleep or there was no way she could keep going.

"I'm going to find a place to pull over and sleep for a few hours. Otherwise I'll kill us both."

He grunted agreement.

Just get back in the Jeep and turn it around. Just find a place the road is wider and pull over. That's all you have to do. It was like talking to a child, coaxing herself to crawl to the front seat, to climb in to where the blood had dried on the floor. The heels of her boots were stained, too.

She started to giggle. She'd tried so hard to keep the darn things clean and shining in Kaabul—had scrubbed Omar's handprints from them.

She breathed deep as she tried the ignition. The Jeep sputtered, then rumbled under her, the vibrations setting off her shaking again.

She didn't know if she could drive, but she had no choice. She eased her foot off the clutch and managed to turn the Jeep around. Then she drove slowly until she found a copse of trees along the road. She pulled in beside them and turned the ignition off.

There was the ticking of the cooling engine, the wind in the leaves, and the gradually deepening blue of the sky. The sun fell past the mountains, sending a crown of rays into the heavens. Just follow them home.

Home and Kaabul and her father and safety.

Then she was asleep.

Chapter 51

The floor of Mohammed's room was hard under his knees. He had never noticed it before. He faced Mecca, performing his first prayer of the day. Relating to Allah was the one thing he could do that gave normalcy to his life.

"The All-Powerful. The Majestic. The All-Merciful. The Forgiver. The Gentle." He murmured the names of Allah, while in his house the voices of invaders performed their own version of the morning prayer. He wondered how it had come to this—Kabulaay against Kabulaay—the warlords' fighting that had torn this country apart now brought down to the level of friend against friend, daughter against father. In a country of devout, it made no sense that Islam could not bring them together. He supposed that was what the Taliban had tried to do.

When he was finished with his prayer, Hamidah helped him back to the corner he had taken as his own. Zahra waited there. She crowded into his right side just as Hamidah pressed into his left. The two girls were terrified—had been since strange voices dragged them home and pushed them into Mohammed's room. They had been together ever since. And tomorrow Ahmad Mali Khan and his two wives would walk right into this.

His home as a prison since the voice took him from his clinic and walked him through darkness until he was dragged into the main room of the house and forced to his knees while questions barraged him.

Why they brought him here, he still could not fathom: perhaps because it gave them room. Perhaps because no one would question the isolation of a man who had just lost his daughter. He wished for his marigolds, for the days he had his garden, for even amongst the debris, if given water the good earth of Afghanistan could bring forth riches.

He caught the girls around the shoulders and pulled them to him.

"I'm sorry you've been brought into this. I should never have used you to ask questions. I should never have agreed to have you come."

"Hush, Uncle. How could you know these men would do this? Besides, my wedding is coming. I had to come." Hamidah's soft voice.

"And you could not live by yourself. Besides, I wanted to see the world. Feyzabad is nowhere as grand as Kaabul."

Zahra's sense of adventure seemed to give her a facsimile of strength, even as her slim fingers dug into Mohammed's arm.

He patted her hand. "You're both very brave, but you see, it's not just that I tried to find Khadija." He lowered his voice. "I've played a part in this war. That is why these men are here. They want—something—from me."

Information. That was what they wanted and he could not—would not—give it. Too many people would die. Michael Bellis's face crossed his mind. Yes, Michael would be threatened too, and that man had given far too much over the years, even risking demotion and punishment when he did what *he* thought best for Afghanistan—rather than following orders in keeping with American foreign policy. Michael, who had disappeared once more to investigate information he feared boded ill for everyone.

So far, Mohammed knew, he and his wards had been spared the worst that their captors could give. He'd treated enough victims of the Taliban to know their kinds of maiming. He could only think it was because they were not sure if *he* was The Doctor that rumors said aided those who fought the Taliban. Their spies had sought that man all the long years of their occupation. Hiding in plain sight was the only thing that saved him.

He closed his eyes. The Doctor. It was a name that had been borne by two men who had worked so closely together they could have been one— Yaqub and himself—the body and the head, he supposed. But now the body was dead and for once he had no idea what to do.

It was like everything inside him had unraveled since Khadija's disappearance. All the strength that had preserved him through the years of hardship, that had kept him fighting when Yaqub had died, had dissolved. Knowing Michael still lived had helped Mohammed deal with Yaqub's loss. The younger man was, in some ways, almost a second son. But Michael wasn't here now.

In the center of the house, the voices came closer.

"We should act now. Get the information before he comes. It will gain his favor, *neh*?" The soft voice. It sent a shiver up Mohammed's back. "We have the girls. They will help convince him."

"And he hath said we wait. Do you want to get us killed, brother? Are you such a fool? Hathemi said to hold them until he arrives; he knows the way to free a man's tongue."

Mohammed stiffened at the name.

"Uncle? What's wrong?" from his left.

"Nothing. Nothing at all." But everything was wrong. His daughter gone. These two girls prisoners because of his actions.

Surely he had given enough to this cause. His sight had been given to preserve secrets. His son to helping others. Khadija—he supposed he'd given her up to keep her and himself safe.

He'd wanted the closeness they had enjoyed when she was young, but somehow he had pushed her away by not sharing his beliefs, who he was, what he stood for. He had feared she would reject him and so he had never tried.

Islam said you could fight to preserve yourself and your faith. He had not wanted to see his faith, his country, defiled by the warped Islam the Arabs brought to Afghanistan. He did not want to see the young men tortured and killed—hung in the square for all to see—or the women and children slaughtered just because they embraced a different face of Islam.

That was what his beliefs had said. Yaqub had believed that, too. But Mohammed had never trusted that Khadija would want to fight, too. She was, after all, a woman. That saddened him when he needed that strength of belief to sustain him now.

Someone pounded on the front door and he heard the woman go to the door. She had been a silent figure in the background as they questioned him, but he recognized her. Mirri. Khadija's friend. That meant the soft voice had been Mizra. Mizra who had sought Khadija's hand. The thought that he had liked the boy, had even considered giving his permission, sent a chill down his back.

A murmur and then the door swung wide and a gust of cool wind entered the room, carrying with it the scent of snow and the brown dust of Kohi Asamayi. Somewhere, nearby, a woman cooked a meal of goat and onions, as all his senses strained to learn who came.

Hushed voices came from the main room and then a movement of air. Zahra and Hamidah cowered closer. Mohammed raised his blind eyes towards the shadow that fell across his face.

"What do you want in my home? You have no business here." His voice sounded thin, old—the words of a querulous old man.

Cloth rustled and then a hard, narrow hand caught his, removed it from Zahra's, and hauled him to his feet. He smelled mint tea and sweat and dust and an old fear swept over him. His old man's bladder almost let go.

"We meet again, Siddiqui—or should I say, 'Doctor'? I suppose you've realized by now that there are worse things than blindness." The hand dragged him away from the girls, to the other room. "Bind him."

Other hands caught him, tied his hands behind him, and then forced him to the floor. The rope bindings cut his skin as old memories sliced through him—winter and being naked and hosed with cold water and left. That voice—it was cold as the wind over the mountains, its accent a strange combination of Arab sparseness and *Inglisi* hauteur. He shivered as the scent of mint came again—so close he almost gagged. So memorable he almost cried.

"You do not look so fierce, Doctor. You will tell me what I need to know, just as your son did. I wonder—will you squeal like he did, before you die?"

Chapter 52

Michael opened his eyes to blackness. The sound of a rushing river and wind, the scent of fading leaves and damp earth, reminded him he was alive. That and the cramped feeling of his back and neck from how he had slept. Overhead the stars were brittle in the sky and the ghost of a moon floated over the eastern mountains.

He pushed himself to sitting and pain rammed into his side. The moon wasn't quite a crescent. Surely it wasn't. The Imams wouldn't yet recognize the faint moon as marking the new month. They couldn't. He needed another day. Just another day!

"*La Elaha Ellallahu Muhammad-u-Rasoollullah.*" There is no god but God, and Muhammad is his prophet. "Please Allah, give me another day."

They had to get moving. He shifted to the side of the Jeep, seeking Khadija. Yesterday was a blur of pain. The jolting of the Jeep, the throb in his side, had all conspired to keep his mind numb, unable to determine what to do, too weak to do whatever he decided.

Not in the driver seat. A thread of fear ran through him and he clamped his jaw against his concern. He could not feel anything more for this woman than he did for any other agent he worked with. He peered over the side of the Jeep.

She lay curled in the dust, her knees drawn up to her chin, so she looked like a small child, not like the woman he had known so intimately on this journey. A swell of tenderness almost choked him. He wanted to stroke her hair and feel the rise and fall of her breathing under his hand.

It was too late for that and the time too desperate.

"Khadija."

No movement.

"Khadija!" His voice was harsh as she stirred and rubbed a hand across her eyes. "Get up. The moon is almost here."

She sat up and pushed her hair back from her face in a dark wave. She stood and swayed, grabbing the side of the Jeep to steady herself, but her gaze was all for him. "How are you? How do you feel?"

"I'll live."

Her clinical "doctor" expression dropped over her face. Then she shook her head.

"The chloramphenicol is helping, but you're still not well. We need to change dressings and drain the wound." Her voice was crisp as she leaned over the Jeep for the medical supplies.

"There's no time. Just get in the Jeep and drive."

She flipped open the lid of the medical pack and dug through, then looked back at him.

"You've got no choice. I'm not letting you die."

She pushed him back and climbed into the Jeep, then stripped up his shirt. He was so damned weak he wanted to scream. Her methodical cleansing of the wound, the draining of the infection left him breathless, in pain, and fuming. She strapped a new dressing in place, injected him with more antibiotic, and sat back.

"You can stay here in the back, or I can help you to the passenger seat."

If he was going to prove that he was well enough to make the rules, then the front seat was his place. He tried, but hadn't the strength to shift his body. Exasperated, he had to accept her help.

He was panting at the pain as Khadija climbed in the driver seat. She glanced at him, then cranked the ignition. The engine roared, masking the river sounds.

"How much farther is it? We passed through Dasht-i-Rewat yesterday."

"From Khenj to Charikar it's about forty miles. Another thirty miles from there to Kaabul. Depending on the roads, we should be there by noon." He braced himself against the seat as Khadija dumped the Jeep into gear and they turned out onto the road.

The ghost moon set as they followed the Jeep's headlights through the darkness. Another of the small towns came into view and Khadija slowed to avoid the chickens and goats that roamed the street. Their eyes glowed green in the headlights.

The shape of the mountains against the sky, the valley that ran opposite the town told him they were at Khenj. The valley held some of the best emerald mines in Afghanistan. Once he had visited this place and marveled at the beauty of the orchards, the fields. There had been a woman here that he enjoyed.

He closed his eyes and let the Jeep rumble under him and the night-bound countryside flow by. He needed to conserve his strength.

In truth, Khadija's ministrations had eased the pain, but he knew the fever lurked in him and ate his strength, now when he could least afford to be weak.

The next town would be Marz, where Marshal Fahim had his home. Stop there and try to tell their story? Radio to the embassy for help? It would be dependent upon Fahim being there and not out in the field with his men. If he was away, it was unlikely Michael would get access to the radio and more likely he and Khadija would be taken prisoner for arriving in a bloody Panjshiri Jeep with no Panjshiri men.

Keep going was the better choice. Hell, he didn't even know if Fahim would recognize him. It had been years since they last met.

The Jeep bounced from pothole to pothole, careened around a bull feeding at the edge of the road. Southwestward. Always southwestward.

When Michael opened his eyes again, the mountains to the east were rimed with dawn. They hadn't reached Rokha yet, but the steep mountainsides and the orchards heavy with the last of the fruit and the stubble-filled cornfields told him they were near Jangalak—Massoud's village.

The Jeep rounded a curve and the dusty town revealed itself. He'd spent time with Massoud once; the man had been a magnetic personality, but thoughtful—an engineer who had been called to leadership in the fight against the Russians and who carried on against the Taliban. A green flag waved from the top of the highest hill above the village. Michael bowed his head at the grave of the Lion of Panjshir, than he caught Khadija's arm.

"We need to change positions."

Khadija barely glanced at him, her gaze held by the road. Her pale knuckles on the wheel said she was not a certain driver, but she had got them this far.

"I thought you were passed out."

"Resting my eyes." He grinned and saw a spark of a smile cross her face before the road needed her attention again. "We're nearing Rokha. There's a checkpoint there. I should be driving."

The vehicle slowed as Khadija looked at him. Her studied gaze was that of the doctor again. She finally shook her head and looked back at the road.

"You're not strong enough. You'll drive us off the road."

"Dammit, Khadija, they'll stop us. They'll arrest us for the Jeep. We can't afford that."

"So what were you going to do? Ram through?"

He closed his eyes. "Something like that. Now stop the Jeep."

She glanced at him again and a smile caught on her lips as she stomped the gas peddle down. The Jeep bucked forward.

"Like hell," she said in English. "Watch me."

Chapter 53

The wind blasted Khadija's face, tore her hair back. She knew she should cover her head, but for this moment—just this moment—she didn't care. She was wild. She was alive. Too alive. All she could think of was to laugh, but it caught in her chest.

Instead she focused on the road. She would get them through. She would get them through. It became a song set to the wild Hindi music of Kaabul.

The road eased around a curve of hill and there sat the mud-daub buildings of Rokha. Its fields were golden with corn not yet harvested. The streets of the village were littered with dogs and children and old men smoking outside a *chai channa.*

Beyond the town she could see the little shed of a police check. Her fist blatted the horn into the clear morning air. Heads turned. People dove for the side of the road. Chickens scattered in a flurry of feathers. Goats stepped away, bored, as the Jeep plunged through the town.

Faces swept past. Gazes of surprise. A woman driver. A woman with wind in her hair. She eased up on the gas pedal as the checkpoint came into view. A lone, cantilevered pole blocked the road. She blatted the horn once more.

Police fumbled out of the shed and saw her.

Let them lift the barricade. Instead they lifted their guns. Stop or go? The laughter burbled in her lungs. She needed to get it out. She needed to keep going. She tromped on the gas pedal and the Jeep fishtailed in the loose gravel. She fought the wheel and aimed for the pole.

"Brace yourself!"

Michael already was, a hand against the dash and his legs against the floorboards as she flashed a grin in his direction. A police officer stepped into the road to sight his weapon, but she held the Jeep straight, ducked low in her seat and slammed the vehicle on. The officer got a single shot off. It rammed into the Jeep's hood before he leapt out of the way to avoid certain death. The pole barricade exploded over them.

They were through and the laughter broke free of her chest. The wildness filled her—one she'd never felt before. The vehicle raced southwest, but she grabbed Michael's hand, brought it to her lips, kissed it. She would kiss him all over if she could only stop now. She would tell him how she felt.

Alive. Finally alive.

But not now. Afterward. After this vibrant, living world was safe. After she and Michael were safe in each other's arms. When she had to deal with her father and confess the truth. It brought a chill to her. What would he say? What would the world think and do if they knew? It was bad enough that she did. Somehow she would deal with it.

The road widened after Jebal Seraj and turned southward in the pitted remains of the main highway north from Kaabul. Finally Charikar came into view, its more Western-style buildings ruined from the fighting that had raged through so much of the country. But still there was life, there was color in the brightly colored trucks, in the low caps of some of the men— even in the blue of the *burka*.

Music streamed from a loudspeaker along the road and she wanted to stop, wanted to leap out of the Jeep and dance one of the old Tajik dances her mother had taught her. Instead she fought the Jeep through traffic and aimed south. Kaabul waited.

She felt Michael's gaze on her and glanced in his direction. His eyes were bright, but it was not just fever. Heat ran through her body and she felt herself color. She wanted to touch him again, wanted to feel him inside her again. Wanted to learn his body wholly and wanted him to learn hers, but knew she didn't dare. He was a warrior first, had no place in his heart for her.

She turned back to the road and drove between the dry hills she had thought so dead. Now she saw the lone falcon in the updraft, the folds of green mountain ash and willow, the sparrows bathing in the dust and the golden cat that darted after them.

They passed Istalif where her family had picnicked in the places once graced by Emperor Babur and his entourages, and then followed the river through fields south to Kaabul.

The city spread wide across the plain between the brown mountains. Once this area was filled with marshes that had filled the air with waterfowl. Now there were kites along the mountainsides and dust after the long droughts. Still signs of life, even amid the devastations of war.

Her father helped the Afghani people. She would help the people as well. They would rebuild Afghanistan and Kaabul would again be the Light Garden of the Angel King—only this time the king would be Allah.

The Saraki Kabul Wa Parwan Road ran straight into the centre of Kaabul. To the south lay Kohi Asamayi, the T.V. tower poking into the sky like a defiant spear. She wanted her father, wanted to go to him and show him she was alive, beg him for forgiveness for scaring him so, but there was Michael and the mission. The embassy of the *Amrikaayi* sat northward along Bibi Mahro. Her father would have to wait.

She twisted through traffic, narrowly avoiding pedestrians, donkey carts, the behemoths of brightly colored trucks. How could she have missed that there was so much life here? The men spoke together, played games of chance. Old women sold rags in the street. Others floated past in their *burka* and *chador*, but here and there a young face was bare.

She caught the amazed looks on people's faces as she passed, caught them staring at her and realized her head was still uncovered. No way to keep herself anonymous, her past secret. She yanked at her *petu* and Michael gently eased it up from her shoulders and over her head.

His gaze seemed locked on the people they passed. The crowd grew thicker as she maneuvered towards the crossroads by the Mausoleum of Abdut Rahman. The square was a madhouse. People marketing and children playing overflowed the tattered remains of Zarnegar Park. The air stank of diesel and dust and mutton grilling. Vehicles were wedged together in the traffic to allow the passage of a foreign military convoy. She glanced at Michael.

"I should have taken Chicken Street and avoided this. We'd have made it to the embassy quicker."

He shook his head. "I think…." He looked at her and shook his head again. "Something doesn't feel right. Something in my gut. I see— watchers, I think. People where there shouldn't be. People I don't trust."

She maneuvered around a donkey and glanced at him. What he said made no sense. "How can you know all the people in Kaabul?"

He shrugged. "I don't. But something isn't right. When you've done this as long as I have, you know. I want to get you home and then I'll drive to the embassy."

She was about to protest, but he stopped her with a look.

"About this I won't budge. I'm strong enough. You've seen to that. But if my gut's right, the embassy'll be watched. They'll try to stop me." He caught her hand, and those pale eyes cut through her. "The last thing I want is you in danger. Understand? Your father needs you."

It shouldn't hurt her; what he said was true. But she wanted him to need her, too. She wanted him to say it but after all that had happened, he still would not. She knew it was her failure. If only she could convince him she would never fail him again.

If only she could convince herself.

She turned towards Kohi Asamayi and uncertainty built in her. What would she say to her father and friends? How could she keep what she had done a secret? Mirri would no longer be her friend, of that she was certain. Their beliefs no longer ran the same path.

"Slow down," Michael ordered.

She did and his gaze ran over the people at the sides of the road. He nodded to himself as they neared Darulaman Road, which arrowed towards the battered remains of the king's palace and the foreign military encampment. Even there—even among the ruins, she saw her people moving, children playing. Life amid the war zone that was her country—and the war still waged with all of them as soldiers and hostages.

"Look at them all." She felt Michael's glance. "The people. I've been thinking of Kaabul as half-dead. But it's not. It's fighting hard for life."

He nodded, but his gaze was back on the street and she saw him stiffen.

"Shit. Farid." He motioned with his chin at a man at the side of the road, even as he slid down in his seat. But a Jeep with a woman driving was a magnet for the eyes. The pox of bullet holes in its rear didn't help.

"Get us to your father's—now!"

"Why?"

"Because Farid betrayed me once before. Your father is in danger."

His lips were thin over his teeth. There was fear in his eyes, and not for himself. Khadija gunned the motor between a man herding two donkeys and a pile of debris from a blown-out building. A cat scampered across her path and she braked, the rear end of the vehicle sliding as she cranked the wheel up the narrow street that led uphill to her father's house.

A cold wind seemed to fill the street, her ears, as the Jeep filled the narrow way. It forced women and men against the battered daub walls. The fender scraped as she tried to turn a corner. Getting the Jeep out of here would be a challenge. They came to the narrow lane that joined two of the hillside roads.

"Stop. I'll walk from here."

She obeyed and he leapt out of the vehicle and almost fell. Khadija was around the Jeep to him, but he pushed her away.

"I want you to take the Jeep and go to the embassy. Ask for Simon Booker. You'll be safe there and you can give him the message. Without me the watchers won't suspect. There's a good chance you'll get through."

"No."

"You can't help me, Khadija. You don't know this business."

He grabbed Safit's fallen Kalashnikov from the floorboards and covered it with a drape of his *petu*.

"He's my father."

He grabbed her arm.

"Do you have any idea who these people are? They have no mercy. They're the ones who slaughtered millions of Hazzara because they weren't Sunni. They're the ones who turned in doctors to the Taliban. They're the ones who blinded your father."

Her body wouldn't move. It couldn't be the truth. She had helped those same people, or ones like them.

"My father? He...it was cataracts that blinded my father."

"No. It wasn't. He may have had the start of cataracts, but it was the Taliban who burned out his vision. It happened after you left for England. He'd been a leader against the Russians for years, working with men like Massoud. Then he worked against the Taliban. They suspected and took him in for questioning. We bribed the guards to let him go, but he was lucky they left him alive. Luckier still they didn't realize they had the man they were looking for all along. Since then we saw little of each other—until Yaqub's death. Then I came by once to arrange people to help him."

Her father. She hadn't known he was a leader in the resistance. How could she not have known while she was growing up?

Because he was her papa and she did not think of him like that. Because he did not share those secrets with her, in an effort to protect her. She was the one who had been blind—for far too long. So many secrets and now she had her own. The question was whether she should keep them as well. Or wanted to. She looked up at Michael.

"He's still my father. Besides—look at you—you're still too weak."

There was no way she was being left behind. He must have seen it in her face, because finally he turned and started towards her house.

The narrow way left no avenue of approach that could not be watched. Michael scanned the rooftops, the hillside of Kohi Asamayi. The late afternoon light turned the hillside golden and a lone red kite rode the updraft.

Khadija pointed. "There's a man."

Michael grabbed her arm and pulled her to him.

"You never let them know they're seen. Now just keep walking. Whatever waits, we have the advantage of knowing they're there."

The pocked door soon came into view and Michael pushed her behind him. Let her father be all right. Let everything Michael suspected be the result of his fevered imagination.

Before they reached the door it swung open and her father stood there, his blind eyes searching.

"*Pishogay?*" His voice cracked with pain. "Run!"

"Papa!" She tried to pass Michael but he caught her arm. Her papa struggled for freedom, but someone dragged him back into the darkness of the house and a black-turbaned man replaced him, armed with a gun.

Khadija thought she just might be sick from all her betrayals. She should have listened to Michael. She should have carried the message. Now there was no one to do so.

"Hashemi," was all Michael said.

Chapter 54

"You'll come in, of course." In the darkened doorway Hashemi stood aside and motioned them from the dusty street with the Kalashnikov.

Michael didn't move, but allowed his senses free rein as he hefted his rifle underneath his *petu*. Yes, there were the rooftop shadows he'd felt. On the hillside, movement showed where a man in grey-brown clothing moved closer; he had blended into the stone before. His lone Kalashnikov would be no match in these circumstances.

He released Khadija and it was like releasing sunlight, but he had to get her free. She could still carry the warning.

"Let her go. She knows nothing."

"But she has her uses, does she not? You have a taste for the daughters of Islam, I think. This one in particular."

Hashemi turned his gaze on Khadija and there was such venom there, Michael wanted to protect her. He would not answer the innuendo in the man's voice. What had happened between he and Khadija should not have, but it was not evil.

"Your comment dishonors this woman."

"Come, come, Michael. I know your secret. I know you care." He lifted his chin at Khadija. "She told me herself. Now come in before I grow impatient. I have The Doctor. He can tell me as much as you—more perhaps, before he dies."

Michael swallowed, trying to find the strength to attack. He had expected this, hadn't he—once he saw the watchers in the streets? He'd come anyway, because he knew his old friend was in danger. Hashemi must have sent his men to Skazar while he flanked Michael and returned to Kaabul by an easier route.

He sighed and stepped forward. It least this would get him inside.

Perhaps his rifle could be used then, when his enemy didn't have him in their sights. He shrugged the *petu* lower to shield the weapon further.

At the door he stopped. Close quarters beyond and he excelled at that.

"I'd wondered where you went. When your men died in the mountains, you weren't with them."

Hashemi's face darkened. Another figure—young, strong, male—stepped out of the darkness and yanked Michael inside.

"Mizra?" Khadija's voice, disbelieving. She followed Michael inside. "What are you doing?"

A stir of motion across the room and she turned.

"Papa!" She pushed past across the room to where her father stood, guarded by a hair-lipped man. Her arms rounded his chest, her cheek pressed into his chest; Mohammed's arms came around her.

"*Pishogay.* My *Pishogay.* They told me you threw off your *chador* and ran away with a man. Was it Michael?" There was wonder in his voice.

"I'm sorry, Papa. So sorry for how I've acted."

He ran his hands over her head, held her close. The tears in the old man's blind eyes were painful to watch. Michael rounded on Hashemi. Beyond him, in Mohammed's room, two young women cowered. Not a threat and Mohammed would know what to do.

"Bind him," Hashemi ordered.

Michael whirled and brought the weapon up—slammed the barrel into the gut of the young man at the door and pulled the trigger. Rapid fire exploded. The man staggered back and back and back, his stomach gone. He hit the wall and slid, leaving a long smear of blood down the wall.

A scream from across the room as he turned. A knife flashed, slashed his forearm. Hashemi lunged—too close for Michael to bring the weapon to bear.

Another scream. So many screams and Khadija's voice: "No! Stop." Her voice cut short.

"Drop the weapon or she dies."

A woman's voice. A short, plump, *burka*-clad figure held Khadija by an arm twisted behind her back, a knife at her throat. The tremor of the kitchen curtain told him where the woman had come from. Dammit, he was losing it. Should have seen, have known.

The woman yanked Khadija's head back. The knife-edge had brought blood to the surface. It ran down to the edge of her *jalabiyya*. Pain and fear flooded Khadija's face, but she shook her head.

"Save them," she said, but the woman's knife cut off Khadija's words.

"I'll kill her right now, for what you did."

"Mirri, that's enough. Michael knows what he must do." Hashemi held out his hand for the Kalashnikov, a gloating smile on his face. "Your brother's death is unfortunate, but Paradise awaits all warriors of the faith. Besides, look at this one's face. He'll do what we say for her life, just as her father will."

Fear gripped Michael as his gaze locked on Khadija. If she came to harm, he would kill the Hashemi's woman. To hell with what it might cost him.

Might cost the world.

To hell with the world! It was Khadija that mattered.

God, what was happening to him? What was it Khadija evoked in him? He wanted to live. He wanted a chance to be with her, to protect her forever.

He lowered the gun barrel.

"Michael, no!"

He allowed Hashemi to take the gun. Don't show how you feel. But he knew it was too late. Far too late, for everything.

The hair-lipped man limped across the room and grabbed his arms, twisting them behind him, binding them, then lifting them until Michael was forced down to his knees. The floor was hard. The pain in his shoulders was overwhelmed only by the sense of skin tearing across his wounds.

"You have a choice, *Amrikaayi*. Give us the names. If you do, we might let the women live. If you don't, we'll turn our questions on the old man. Who knows how long he'll live."

Michael kept his gaze down. His lank hair shadowed his eyes. He shook his head. The yank up on his arms brought a groan to his lips.

"You'll have to do better than that."

Hashemi's taunt brought another yank that sent red streaks across Michael's vision. His body was too weak for this, and he knew it. Well, if they killed him, it would only be what he deserved. He closed his eyes.

"Who works for you in Kaabul?"

"The entire American Embassy." It earned him a kick in the ribs from Hashemi that would have toppled him if not for the hair-lipped man's hold.

"Who in Kaabul?"

"Fuck you."

The toe of Hashemi's boot caught him in his wound. He screamed. Worse than the knife blow. Worse than the bullet. It cut through to his heart—seemed to grab it and squeeze. The hair-lip released him, let him fall on his face on the floor. Hashemi's boots found him them.

Again. Again. Again. The room filled with screaming. Khadija. Other female voices. His own groans. Until the Arab ordered him on his knees again. He swayed, where he knelt, only upright because of the other man's hold.

"Tell me." Hashemi bent over him. "Tell me or we'll start on Siddiqui."

His pain will be your responsibility."

Michael shook his head. The blood on his lips joined sweat to taste of salt and copper.

"Let the others go. Siddiqui's old—harmless. I'll give names then."

He'd lie. Tell them names of men already dead. Just get the others away.

Hashemi's laughter cut through Michael. It was a sound from his nightmares. A sound that haunted him awake or asleep. The Siddiqui house disappeared and he was back in a crumbling mud-daub ruin and the night ran thick with screams. Too many victims. Too little time, and he and Yaqub weren't prepared.

Screaming all around, faces of Hazzara women lit by the fires destroying their homes. Red off the cliffs. Gun fire and explosions.

Stop the screaming! Stop the laughter! He shook his head but it caught in his ears like a smell catches in the nose. He toppled, his arms twisting almost out of their sockets until he was released.

Then everything went dark.

Screams in the dark. Screaming that lifted to the sky to dissipate like smoke. No one listened to the screaming—except Michael and all he wanted was to cover his ears as Yaqub's voice joined with the others.

"*Allāhu akbar*!" Yaqub screamed. God is great. It echoed off the red cliffs. It caught in the wind across the leaves.

There was a shot. Two-three-four-more. Who could say how many and Yaqub was screaming now. Screaming and there was laughter in the night as shot after shot rang out and the screaming just wouldn't die.

Michael came to with Khadija's hands on his face. He lay on the floor in Mohammed's room, sweat stinging his eyes. The two stranger women cowered against the wall, Mohammed between them. The air stank of fear and urine. Someone had soiled themselves. He tried to move but the attempt sent pain spearing through him.

"Don't," Khadija whispered. "If they know you're awake, they'll come for you again."

"We can't stay like this."

"They'll kill you."

"And I hope to die—after you're free."

"Michael, no."

He grinned up at her, trying to find some fierceness for his gaze. He knew how it rankled her when he looked at her like that. He'd seen it in her gaze too many times.

"You got a better idea?" He asked it in English, using a mawkish Southern drawl.

She looked at her father and the other two women, then back at him. "How?"

"If I can get loose, they won't be expecting an attack. It'll give you a chance to get the others out. Can you do that?"

Her gaze held all the gravity of the world as she shook her head.

"Why cling to a life until it is soiled and ragged?"

He saw her blink at the Sufi poetry, saw her expression harden. Good. Let her get angry. Let her think she would be better off without him.

"I have this." From her pocket she produced the old scalpel, hidden in her palm.

"*Allāhu akbar*! Now cut me loose."

She did as she was told, each sawing motion tearing at his battered body. Who was he kidding? Did he really think he could free them? He had to try.

When she was done he demanded the scalpel and hid his hands under his *petu*. "Where are they?"

"Hashemi and Mirri are in the garden. They bury Mizra. Ratbil—the man who bound your arms—he guards us. He's seated in the other room."

Slowly he pushed himself to sitting. The movement was agony, and his hands were numb. He nearly fell over. Just get this done. Just get them free.

"Go to the embassy. Take your father. They know him. Do I still have the Jeep keys in my pocket?"

She felt under his *petu* and blushed as she pulled them from his clothing. He glanced at Mohammed and was glad the old man did not see. When she had them, he tried to stand.

Once he would have been on his feet in one graceful movement, but Wakhan had changed all that. He didn't know if he'd ever be the man he was before. Probably it was a good thing.

Slowly he stood, Khadija at his side, but he refused her aid. This he had to do himself.

When he was upright, he took deep breaths to set the pain aside. *A stone I died. This time I will die a man and who knows what I will become.*

He grasped her hand briefly, then padded to the door. Ratbil sat reading the Quran, his head bobbing as his lips moved. His forehead bore the kiss of the faithful—the red mark that came from all the bows in prayer.

Michael was on him before he could move. The scalpel slashed. *Metal on meat.* It cut through Ratbil's forearm and he screamed.

"Go!" Michael shouted.

Khadija had the others were at the door. Please, Allah, let their way be open. Let the gunmen be gone. He slashed again and caught his foe on the face, splitting his lips into dangling flesh.

Pounding footsteps came from the rear of the house. He looked up in time to see a cast iron kettle coming towards his head.

Chapter 55

Khadija hauled Hamidah through the door. The woman was almost immobilized by what had happened. Her *salwar kameez* stank of urine and fear.

"Khadija, come!"

Her father's voice. He clung to Zahra's arm, leading the young girl down slope towards Asamayi Road. Khadija checked the rooftops but could see nothing. There had been men there earlier.

"Stay close to the walls," her Papa said.

They hurried down to the Jeep. Zahra helped her father in. Hamidah looked shocked as Khadija climbed behind the wheel. She fumbled the keys into the ignition and the engine started with a growl.

Just get them out of here and to the embassy. There would be safety there. There would be help there. She had to save Michael somehow. Perhaps the embassy men would know how.

She eased the Jeep around the first corner, but the fender caught in a jut of wall when she tried to turn downhill. She tried backing up, but there was not enough room. Tried gunning the motor and slamming the Jeep into gear. All it did was make the Jeep more firmly plug the road.

A shout came from uphill.

"They're coming! We have to run for it!"

She stumbled out of the Jeep and grabbed her father's arm, helping him clamber out of the vehicle.

"Just go!" she screamed as Hamidah hesitated. Zahra caught her sister's arm and dragged her downhill.

Khadija came behind with her father. With no Jeep there was no way she could make it to the embassy on time.

"Allah, no. Don't let Michael die."

"If anyone can get free, it's him."

Her father's voice. She hadn't realized she spoke aloud. Down Kohi Asamayi, running through the people who stopped to visit, past the rubble of fallen houses, the children playing in the dirt. She let the slope lead them. Just get as far as possible. Save her father. Save herself.

They reached Saraki Kabul Wa Khandahar—the road to Kandahar city. Across the broad avenue was Darulaman Road and the long straight route to the remains of the royal palace and the camp of the *kofr* military.

She stopped and turned back up the hill. Michael had risked his life for her. He had brought her safely from Feyzabad. She would not leave him behind.

From down the road came the rumble of an approaching military convoy. She dashed into the street, placed herself in front of them and knew she was risking her life. Too many foreigners had been hurt by suicide bombers. They were apt to just shoot her.

"Help!" she yelled in English as the first Humvee neared. Armed soldiers stood lookout on the roofs of the armored vehicles. The convoy didn't slow.

"Help us!"

She waved her arms. They weren't stopping. They weren't listening. Oh Allah, please. She had sinned so many times but this time it was for the good of her country, for the good of the world, and for the good of the man she loved. Michael did not deserve to die in her service. He deserved a chance at life.

"Help, please!" She went to her knees. "An American is injured. He's being held prisoner!"

She didn't know if her words were heard or if it was something else. All she knew was that the convoy slowed and two soldiers leapt out of a truck, guns ready.

"Get out of the road," the first soldier said in badly accented Pashto.

"You don't understand." Her Oxford English gave him pause. She explained Michael's need, saw his incredulous look, the way he looked at his partner. He shook his head.

She had to do something.

"You have to believe me. My father is Mohammed Siddiqui, the doctor. The man who is held is Michael Bellis, an American agent. The man who holds him is Abdullah Hashemi—the Arab terrorist. It was he who led the destruction of Bamiyan. He leads Taliban forces now. He plans this war against all that is not Islam."

Make them believe. Just make them believe, when she saw by their eyes they did not. Michael could be dead by now.

There was only one thing she had left—her truth. The same truth that had made her pull an old man from the front of these very same trucks. She held out her hands, the fear in her throat bringing tears to her eyes, even as her anger faded.

"Please. Michael Bellis is a good man. I give myself to your custody for his life. I know these things because I worked for Hashemi. I helped him in his plans. I help him no longer."

Suddenly she was a prisoner, and as suddenly she knew her life had changed. Her fear and anger were gone.

Chapter 56

Michael rolled to the side, the kettle slamming into his shoulder. Numbness and pain he could not afford to feel. He pushed it away, readied his stance.

Hashemi raised a weapon and Michael was on him. Finish this man and his kind, and there was a chance for Afghanistan.

Kill him. Just kill him. He slashed at Hashemi's belly, but the man ducked back, trying to gain enough distance to use the gun. Don't let him. Stay on the attack. Where was the woman?

His body was slow. Too slow. Stay on Hashemi. Take off the head of the snake. He followed Hashemi back, back, slashing with the scalpel. He sliced through the kitchen curtain, when Hashemi tried to entangle him. He followed through the rear door to the garden. The light glowed on the red-husked pomegranates and the newly dug grave.

He didn't want to die. He didn't want to kill in Mohammed's garden. Hashemi slammed the gun barrel at him. It caught Michael in the stomach and he doubled over. Somewhere nearby a gun discharged.

Michael stumbled, righted himself. Don't let Hashemi get the distance or he was dead. Pain. Pain through his body. The world narrowed to a tunnel with Hashemi at the end.

The Arab's face was twisted in hate. Michael slashed again and caught Hashemi's white robes. Crimson flowed like one half of an X-marks-the-spot. He lunged and the whole world shuddered.

Gun fire behind him. *I'm dead. Finally, dead.* He waited for the slam, the numbing pain. Slashed again and felt his blade cut. Metal on meat. Michael grinned at his opponent.

With nothing to lose, he lunged and felt the blade bite deep.

Hashemi froze. He looked down at his chest and Michael followed his gaze. A huge bloom of blood covered Hashemi's abdomen. He looked back at Michael and sagged into his arms, his weight carrying the scalpel blade upward into his chest.

Pulsing blood ran down Michael's arm and he found he could barely stand. A stranger—soldier—caught him. The man wore NATO and Canadian insignia on his uniform. Another took Hashemi from his grasp.

"Bellis?"

Michael nodded. He could barely stand, barely focus.

"Shit, man, you're shot."

Michael looked down at his leg and saw the blood pulsing through his trousers. Funny, that. He didn't feel anything.

Then his legs gave and everything went black.

Chapter 57

Khadija sat beside her father in the garden amid the debris of yesterday's wedding. Hamidah's day had been delayed two weeks, but it had been worth it—glorious, with her dressed in the traditional Tajik wedding costume, silver jewelry bedecking her arms and high-crowned headdress, and bright crimson for her dress.

The other women had taken advantage as well, dressed in the finery they had hidden through the long wars, and the groom had been funny and sad in his earnest tenderness towards the stranger who would be his wife.

The garden on Kohi Asamayi had been filled with lantern light and fire and laughter and the music of *tabla* and *rubab* and the wailing *sorna*—so long banned under the Taliban.

The garden was not so glorious now. Charred torches remained on the walls. Bits of food and bright cloth littered the earth. The marigolds, though, they were a brilliant circle of color at the back of the garden. Somehow the revelers had respected their blooms. And the pomegranate tree was heavy with fruit.

It brought Anaargórrey to mind, and a pantheon of memories amid a larger loss. She sighed.

"What is it, *Pishogay*?"

She looked at her father who sat in the last rays of fall sunlight. She had spent the day cleaning the inside of the house of the debris from her houseguests. Tomorrow she would tidy the garden, but Papa had asked her to sit with him awhile. She took the time for those things, now.

Her father was even more precious for all he had given for her and his people. It was his vouchsafe that had freed her from the Afghani prison after five days she did not want to remember. It was his word that had kept her safe while there.

"Why do you ask?"

"I hear the sigh in your breath." He reached and caught her hand, somehow knowing where it was. "*Pishogay.*" His voice was soft. "Michael is a good man, but he has many duties. He is a man broken—a man driven—by pain and guilt and longing for what he has not learned—peace."

"Michael has nothing to do with it."

Her papa was silent, but his blind eyes seemed to see so much. She had not told him of her intimacy with Michael, nor of her failings in England. Could he love her through that as he had for her time with the *jihad*? It was time to know. She would not hold secrets from him.

"Papa, I need to tell you something."

"I'm here."

His blind gaze seemed to see inside her. His body stilled in that way that had disturbed her before, but now seemed to show his ability to sense all that went on around him.

"Papa, I know this wedding puts you in mind of a marriage for me. I felt it in the grasp of your fingers and heard it in your discussions. You seek a good man for me, but you need to know the truth. No one will want me."

He chuckled. "That is the fear of all maidens and their mothers, but don't you worry. I'll act the mother and make you a match."

"Papa, you're not understanding. The young men you seek won't want me. I don't want them. I'm—I'm ruined, Papa."

The word was so quaint and yet in her culture it was the truth. She rushed on against the sickness she felt.

"It happened in London. I was seduced by the freedom and so I was seduced. I've sinned, Father. Since I returned to Kaabul I tried to rededicate myself to Islam and find my honor, but I only became more confused. I couldn't undo what I had done, or what I had become." She swallowed. Saying this was the hardest. "And so I fell again. With Michael. Papa, I loved him, but he's gone."

Her voice had softened so her papa had to lean forward to hear. She saw the tears fill his eyes and trail down the lines of his cheek. Felt her tears follow similar tracks. She had failed him so. Had failed everything he believed in.

"Oh, my daughter." He came across the carpet she had spread and caught her in his arms. "My heart. My Khadija. My *Pishogay*. You fill yourself with pain when the Sufis say that lovers tear away the veils of intellect and shame and modesty to find the love that is the true love of Allah. Don't feel shame. Feel joy you have tasted this thing. Hold on to the love of Allah. It's his gift."

His *petu* smelled of spices and torch fire and antiseptic—the scents of her father, the scents of her childhood. He rocked her against his chest,

stroking her hair to comfort her, and she could not believe he had found a
way to forgive her.

"I wish you'd told me," he said quietly, stroking her hair. "You came
home from London so distant and I thought I had forced you away. You
harbored so much anger—I heard it in your voice, felt it in your actions—
but I didn't know why. The *Inglisi* stole something precious from you, but
that can never mean you're less precious to me or to those who love you."

He tightened his arms around her and all the emotions, all the secrets
and lies flooded through her. She buried her sobs in his *petu*. When she was
done she dried her eyes.

"Papa, I'm so sorry for everything I've done. I thought you would hate
me and I didn't want to hurt you. I've wanted to tell you a thousand times
since the thing with Hashemi and the *Kaanaada* soldiers took Michael
away, but there never seemed to be the right moment."

"Hush. We are together, and any man who would not want you is a
fool. Even Michael."

"You never named me fool before, old friend. But perhaps you were
too polite."

"Michael!"

Khadija scrambled to her feet, was across the garden to the kitchen
door, but remembered herself a foot from him and stopped. She did not
know how he felt.

He stood straight, the lines of pain no longer etching his features, his
pale gaze on her face. He leaned on a cane. His hair was brushed back from
his face and he wore Western trousers and a crisp buttoned shirt that he kept
shifting on his shoulders, as if it made him uncomfortable.

She waited as he studied her. He had expressed his disdain for her in
Skazar and though he had been kind to her while they worked together and
had helped her family to freedom, he'd not expressed any commitment to
her.

She had been through enough rejection in England. She would not set
herself up again. She averted her gaze and nodded her greeting.

He looked to her papa.

"I apologize for entering unbidden. I knocked, but no one answered.
Your neighbors said you were home."

She could see the tension in his body, could hear it tightening his
voice. He still carried his disdain, then. The realization made her heart ache.
She would have to make the best of it.

"Michael, my son," her papa said. He rose to his feet.

"You're well?" She forced a smile at him. "Your side? Your leg?"

"Both well, though the cure sometimes seemed worse than the
wound." He limped forward and touched his side with a grimace.

"Debriding's not something I'd recommend to anyone."

"Come. Sit. I'll make more tea."

She tried to fall back on polite hospitality, though her heart was pounding so hard she was sure he would hear. His pale gaze felt like it burned her skin.

"Pardon the mess. Hamidah's wedding was last night."

She ducked past him through the curtain and stood shaking in the dimness. Michael had come! She turned back to the door. It was surely just that he had business with her father. But he looked so different in the Western clothing. So foreign.

She dipped water into the kettle and set it to boil, then found herself standing close to the curtain. What were they saying? How would her father deal with Michael now that he knew of their intimacy?

She felt like a child as she pressed her face against the door frame, parting the curtain to peek through to the sunlit garden. Michael had caught her father's arm and led him away from the house. At least they were not fighting.

They stopped under the pomegranate tree and Michael examined one of the fruit. They weren't quite ready. He shook his head and spoke quietly with her father, so Khadija could not hear.

More business. Always it would be missions and messages and spying. That was what Michael was all about—all he wanted in his life. He'd been clear, so she should quit twisting her insides wishing for something else.

She shook her head in futile denial. She had her father and her work— as well as helping her father, she had begun a new medical residency at the Kaabul Hospital. At least she had that. Suddenly her father began to sag. He seemed to fold in on himself, begin to fall until Michael caught him.

She rushed through the curtain.

"What is it? Papa?" She glared at Michael. "What have you done to him?"

She caught her papa's arm from him. She would not let anyone harm her family again. Inside the house, the kettle whistled. It could wait. She faced Michael, her father at her side.

"What did you do? Haven't you torn this family apart enough?"

His blue eyes were grave and he sighed.

"I came to ask a question and to apologize—to you—to your father before I leave. I came to tell him how Yaqub really died—that I was responsible, and to try to make amends. They've asked me to take a desk job in the States and I've accepted—unless certain things can be—dealt with."

She froze, her mind locked on the fact he was leaving, and looked at the face she had come to know so well. The part of her that had felt hope when she saw him, died anew.

A hollow ache inside. She would carry it always. She studied Michael's face, intent on burning it in her memory.

Those blue eyes. That hard smile. The shock of coppered hair. Resolve filled his gaze, and guilt and grief that didn't quite make sense to her.

"Can you bring the tea, Khadija?"

She nodded obediently. Perhaps saying goodbye would be easier for him over tea. Perhaps it would make grief easier for her.

She hurried to the kitchen, her mother's china clattering in unsteady hands. Perhaps she should be slow—keep him here as long as she could.

Stop this. You never had him, so why grieve for what you never had?

Then why did she feel like she was dying, when she did not want to die? The earth was opening under her feet again, when for a short time it had felt firm.

She managed to bring the tea and settle herself on the carpet she had spread for her and her father. Neither Michael or Papa had seated themselves. Instead Papa stood still as stone and Michael studied the garden.

"They removed the body," he said. "It was a good wedding?"

Khadija couldn't bring herself to answer. It hurt enough to breathe.

"A fine match. A great celebration," Papa said.

"Good. Life should go on."

He was so calm. So cool and uninvolved as if life no longer involved him. Terrified, she couldn't stop herself.

"The soldiers—they would not let me see you, but they said you were shot in the leg." She kept her gaze averted. "They took you away to their hospital and would not let me visit after my release. They treated you well? Did they stop the rebels in China?"

Michael's gaze barely touched on her and it broke her heart. As if he could not bear to see her. He nodded to Papa.

"After I got the message to Simon Booker at the embassy, the lines must have burned up between Washington and Beijing, but they stopped the bomb at the nuclear plant and found the American agent's body. As for me, I'm fine. The leg will heal. It's Yaqub I must speak of."

"Yaqub?" Papa's question.

"*Khpel amal da lari mal,*" Michael said. What you do, will come back to you.

It came out like flood of self hatred she could barely stand to hear.

How it was his fault Yaqub had been caught by Hashemi, because he allowed Yaqub to take the group of women alone. How Hashemi had tortured Yaqub while Michael sought a way to rescue him, and what he had found when Hashemi was done.

"He was too far gone to carry out. He was the doctor—so there was no one to give medical care. I tried. Allah knows I tried, but he cried when I touched him, there was so little left. He begged for mercy and compassion and there was only one mercy I could give."

The horror was too much. Papa staggered back. Khadija was too numb to move. Michael had carried this wound all this time?

"I begged Allah for healing but he was deaf to my plea. I swore vengeance as I set my gun to his head. As I pulled the trigger. As I held Yaqub's body in my arms."

Khadija couldn't stop her cry.

"No. No. It can't be!" Papa shook his head. "Hashemi said he killed him."

"He lied. Now do what you will to me." He faced them, bared his chest.

Papa's face was grey. Khadija was immobilized by the wish for death on Michael's face.

Her brother. Her beloved brother dead by this man. Allah, where was the reason for this? By Afghani tradition they were enemies to the death.

"I should have told you sooner, but how could I expect your compassion when even I can't stand myself?"

It was so hard to think. So hard to know. There had been so much death. Far too much. She had no energy for hatred anymore. There was only pain at the loss, and sorrow at what Michael had gone through. She met his gaze and realized she was crying.

For Yaqub. For Michael. For all of Afghanistan.

"You're a greater friend than you know." Her trembling words seemed to shock him, but she rejected his disbelief. "Yaqub was with someone he loved—who loved him—when he died. Not caught in evil. That, at least, is a comfort."

It was, though the sorrow cut deep and the wind held the chill of Hindu Kush snow.

"My daughter speaks well. She's listened more than I thought, all these years. Allah has given each of us life and he will give us another and another and another, just as the sun uses a hundred lives each moment."

Sufi poetry again. That was her papa. But Michael could not seem to bear their compassion.

He crossed the garden, looking up to the slopes of Kohi Asamayi where the kites were flying free in the afternoon wind. She went to him there, praying he would listen.

"Michael?"

She placed a hand on his arm in the golden light of the afternoon. Those shattered pale eyes cut straight to her heart. He still didn't believe, had lost the drive to live. It was testament to him he'd come here at all, and oh Allah, she didn't want him to leave.

"Michael, I…." Dared she tell him how she felt? She would if she could only know he'd believe. She realized she was no longer chasing after Yaqub. He was at peace. It was Michael she had to heal, to love.

In one motion of surrender she stepped up to him and his arms took her in. She pressed into him, became one with him, as her arms encircled his neck.

"Michael." It was all she managed to say before his lips were on hers.

"Praise Allah, Khadija." He kissed her face again, again, again. "When you're with me the window of my soul opens and you heal me. Give me a reason to stay in Afghanistan. Will you be my wife?" He murmured it into her hair, her neck, her heart.

She nodded and all the broken pieces of her honor, her life, her past were mended. Her body filled with a great light.

She knew, across the garden, the sun would find her papa smiling.

About the Author

Karen L. McKee is a well-traveled writer who has explored the cultures and countries that border Afghanistan. She is the author of literary, erotic and fantasy fiction. She lives on the west coast of Canada with two Bengal cats that aren't quite as well traveled as she is.

If you'd like to learn more about her, visit her alter-ego at www. karenabrahamson.com.

Proof

Made in the USA
Charleston, SC
01 November 2010

CreateSpace
100 Enterprise Way, Suite A200
Scotts Valley, CA 95066

IN THIS SHIPMENT

Billing Address:
Karen Abrahamson
Twisted Root Publishing
86-9012 Walnut Grove Drive
Langley V1M 2K3 CA

Shipping Address:
Karen Abrahamson
Twisted Root Publishing
86-9012 Walnut Grove Drive
Langley V1M 2K3 CA

Your Order of 11/01/2010 09:40:54 AM (Order ID 12674919)

Qty   Item